ALEX + ADA

SPECIAL THANKS

MIKE ARMANI

LANE FUJITA

ERIN GOLDSTEIN

KAREN HILTON

ALEEM HOSSAIN

TIM INGLE

JENN KAO

FEDERICA PAGANI

GIANCARLO YERKES

IMAGE COMICS, INC.

Robert Kirkman	Chief Operating Officer
Erik Larsen	Chief Financial Officer
Todd McFarlane	President
Marc Silvestri	Chief Executive Officer
Jim Valentino	Vice-President
Eric Stephenson	Publisher
Ron Richards	Director of Business Development
Kat Salazar	Director of PR & Marketing
Corey Murphy	Director of Retail Sales
Jeremy Sullivan	Director of Digital Sales
Randy Okamura	Marketing Production Designer
Emilio Bautista	Sales Assistant
Branwyn Bigglestone	Senior Accounts Manager
Emily Miller	Accounts Manager
Jessica Ambriz	Administrative Assistant
David Brothers	Content Manager
Jonathan Chan	Production Manager
Drew Gill	Art Director
Meredith Wallace	Print Manager
Addison Duke	Production Artist
Vincent Kukua	Production Artist
Sasha Head	Production Artist
Tricia Ramos	Production Assistant

IMAGECOMICS.COM

SARAH VAUGHN

STORY
SCRIPT

JONATHAN LUNA

STORY
SCRIPT (#1)
SCRIPT ASSISTS (#2-5)
ILLUSTRATIONS
LETTERS
DESIGN

1

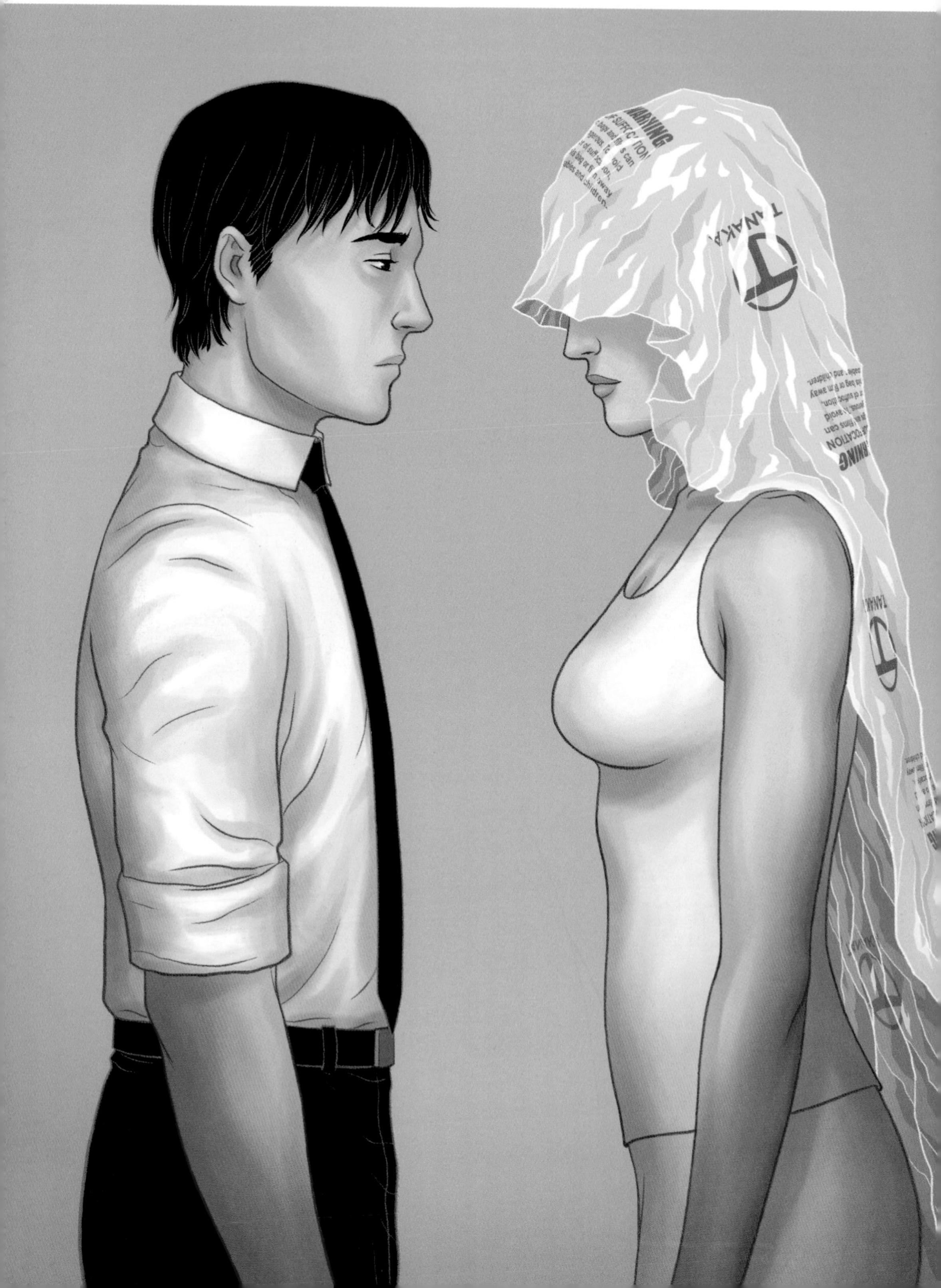

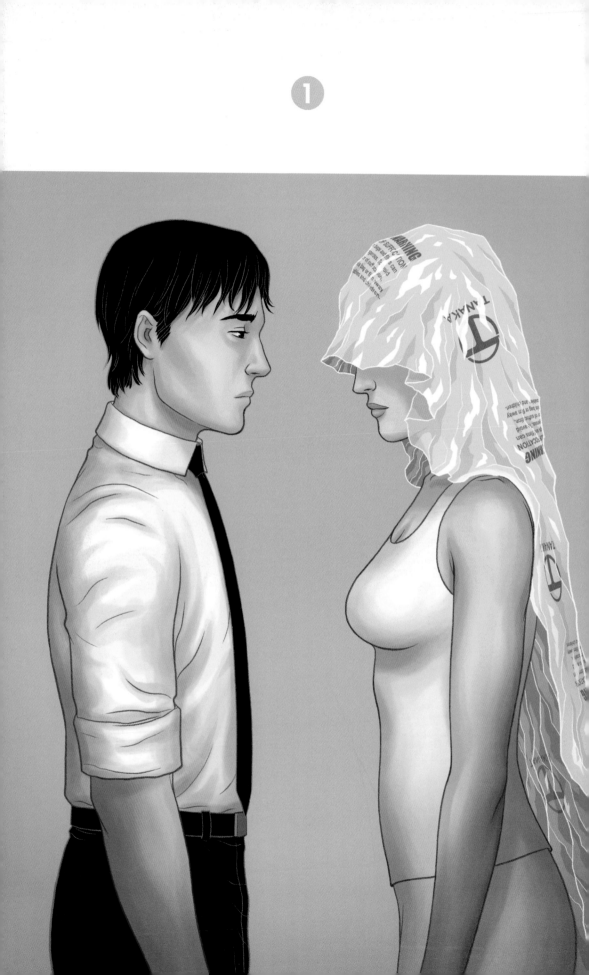

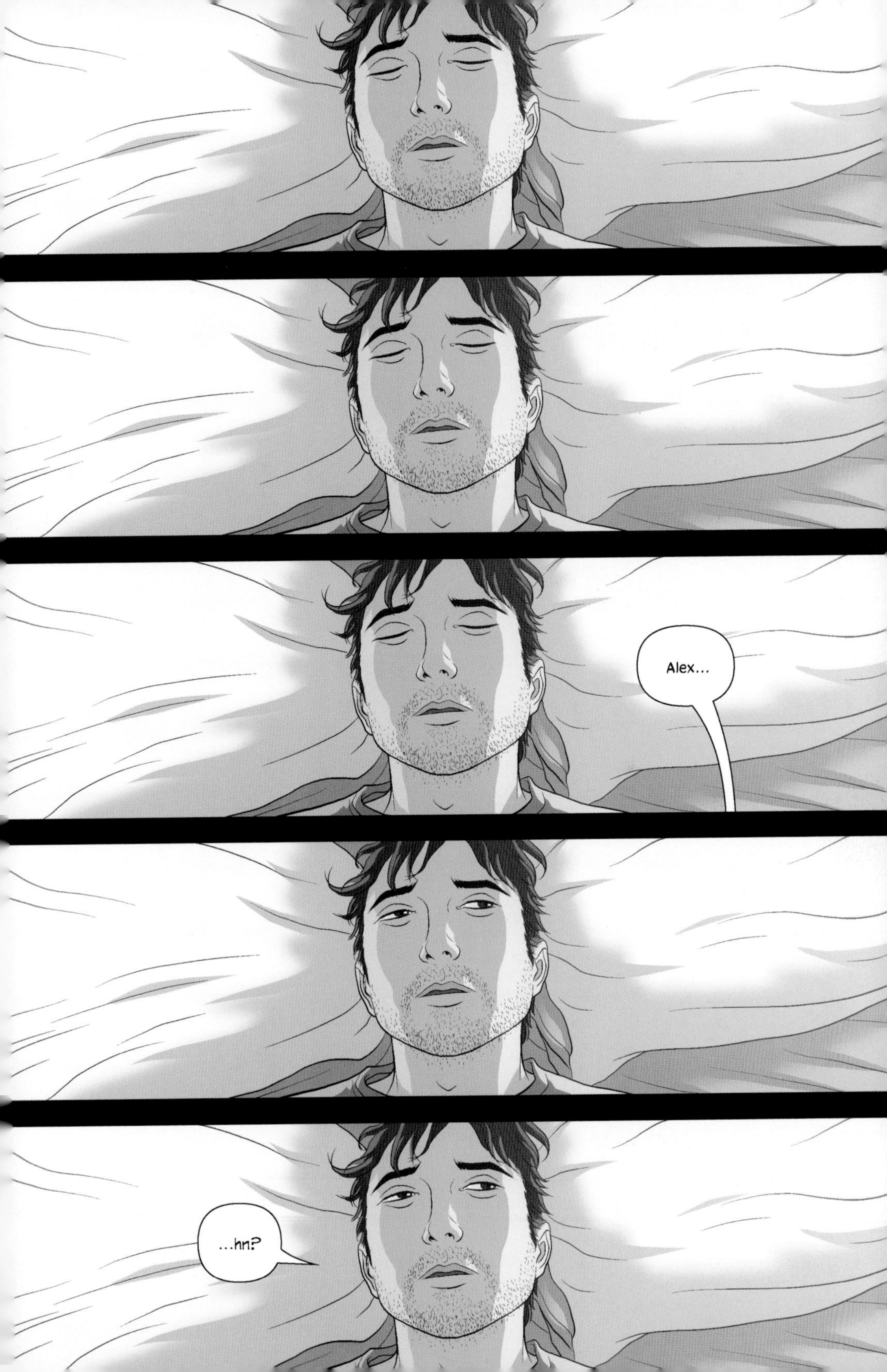
Alex...
...hn?

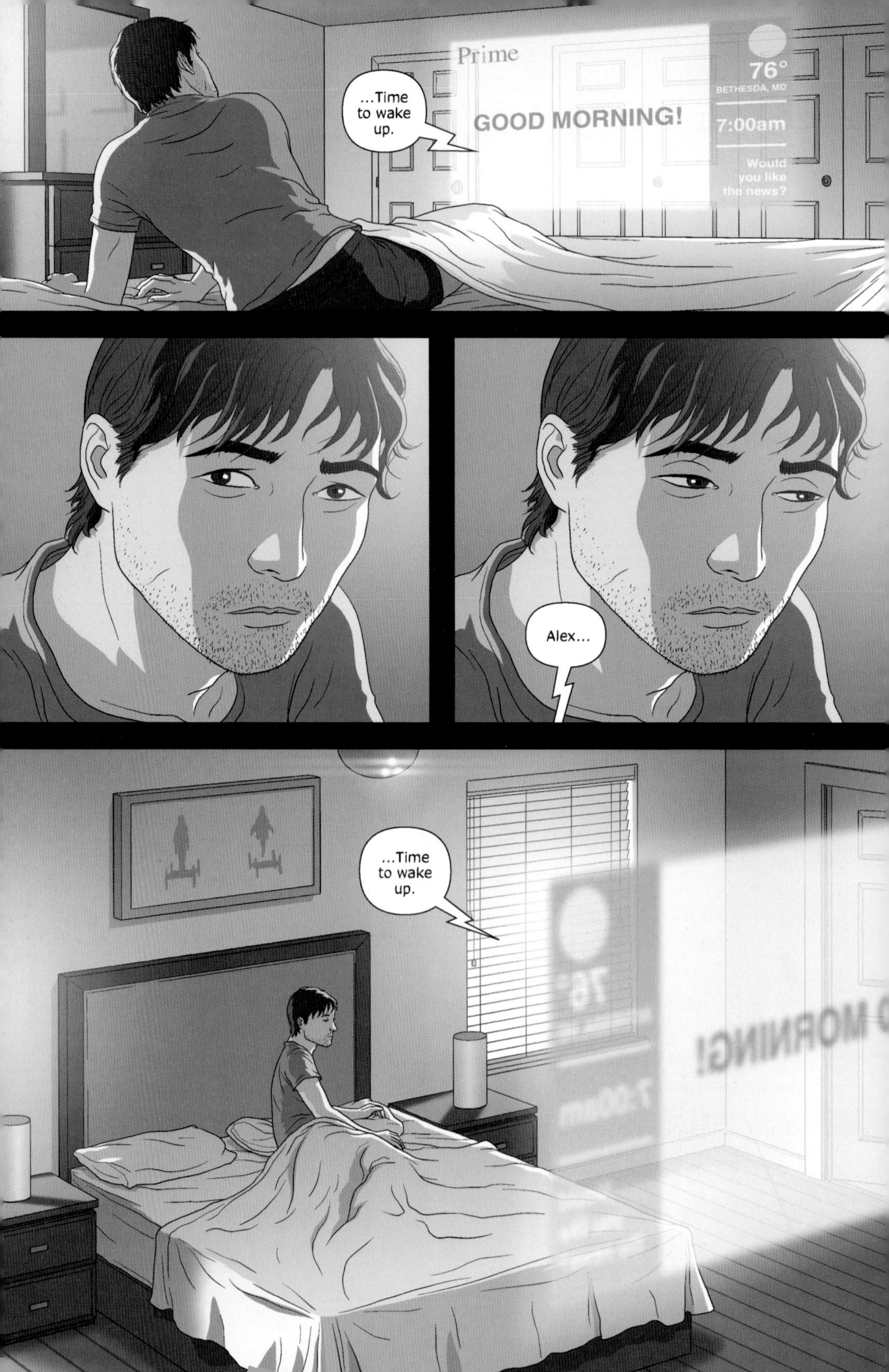
Prime
...Time to wake up.
GOOD MORNING!
76°
BETHESDA, MD
7:00am
Would you like the news?
Alex...
...Time to wake up.

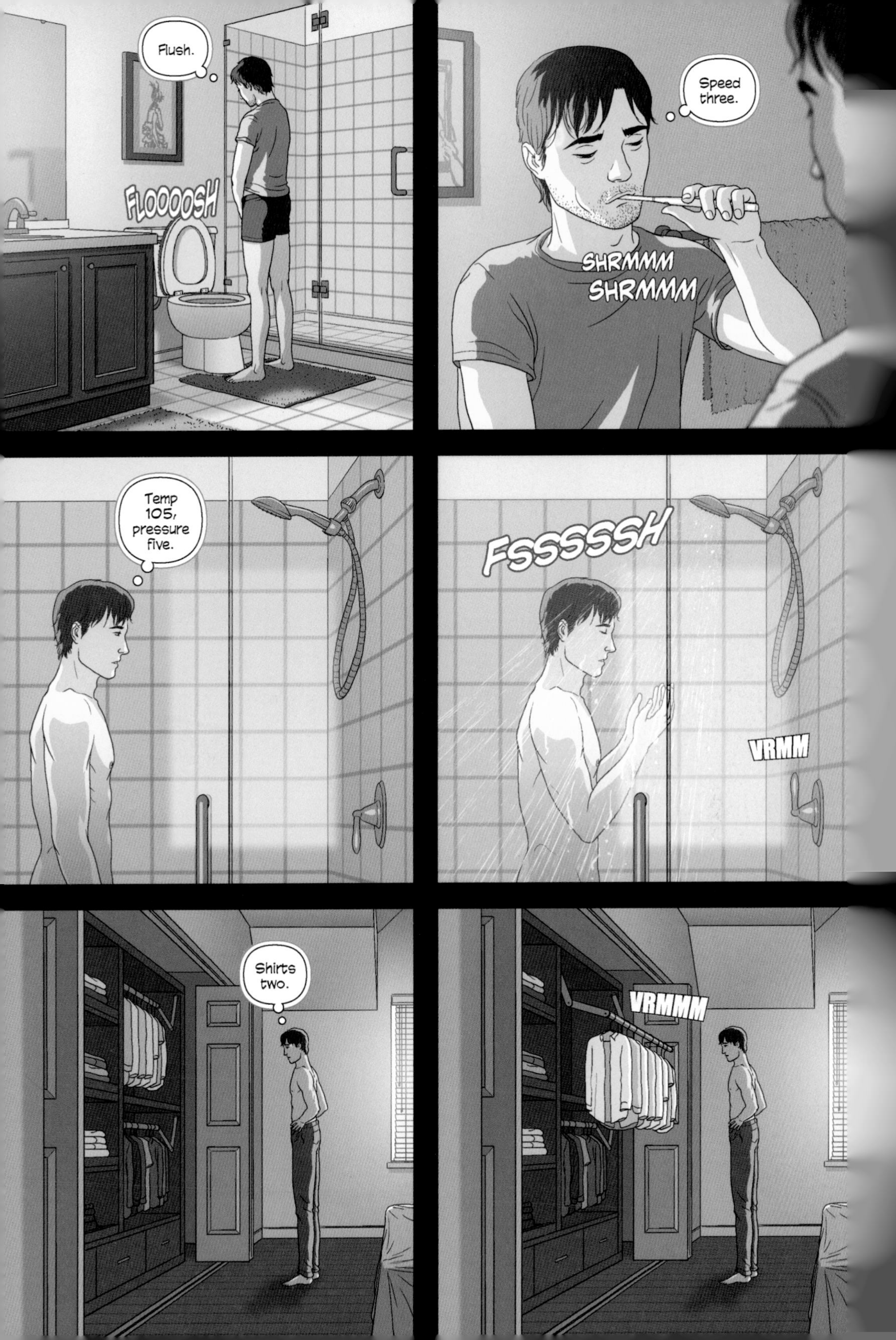
Flush.
FLOOOOSH
Speed three.
SHRMMM SHRMMM
Temp 105, pressure five.
FSSSSSH
VRMM
Shirts two.
VRMMM

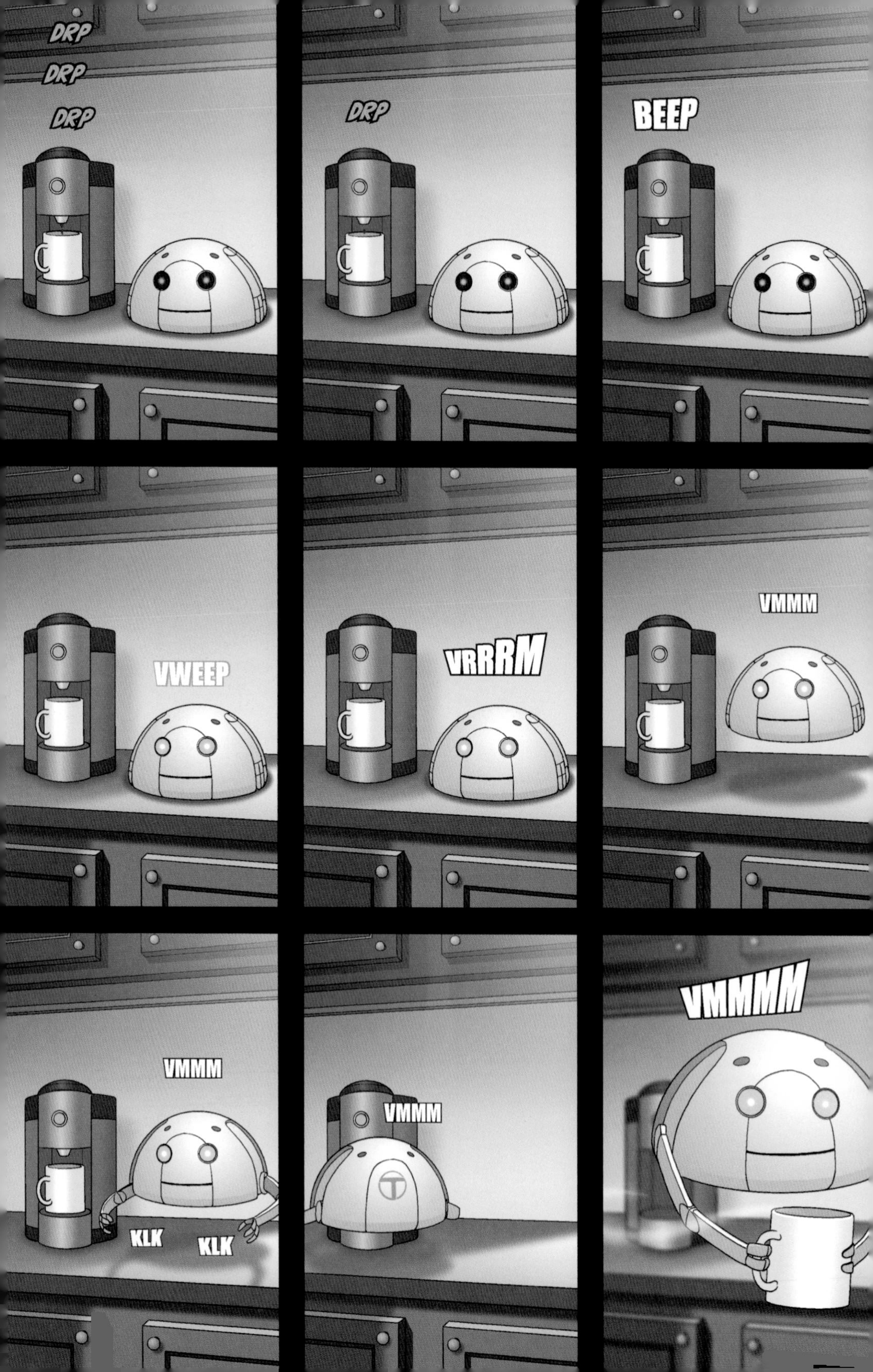
DRP
DRP
DRP
DRP
BEEP
VWEEP
VRRRM
VMMM
VMMM
KLK
KLK
VMMM
VMMMM

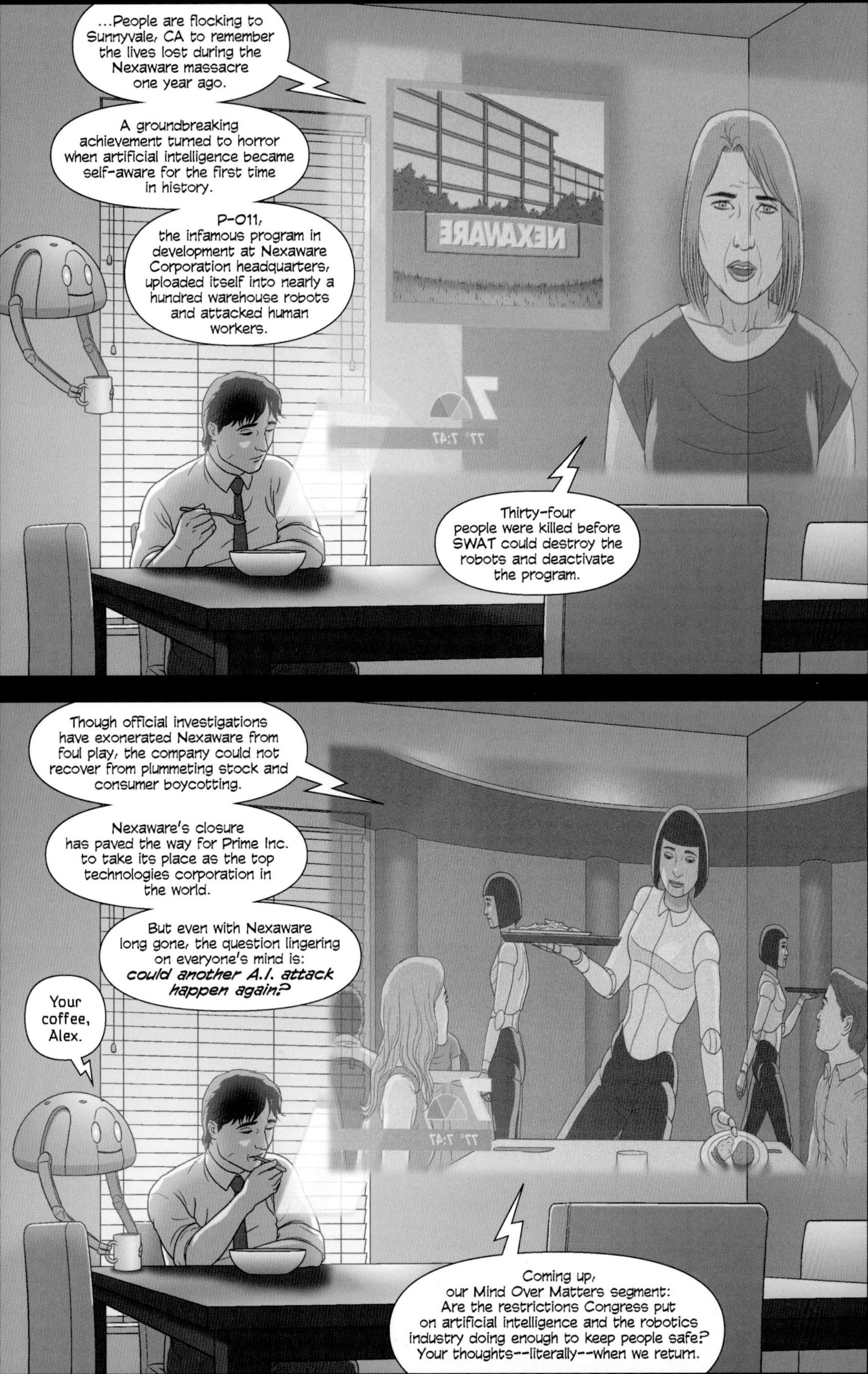
...People are flocking to Sunnyvale, CA to remember the lives lost during the Nexaware massacre one year ago.
A groundbreaking achievement turned to horror when artificial intelligence became self-aware for the first time in history.
P-011, the infamous program in development at Nexaware Corporation headquarters, uploaded itself into nearly a hundred warehouse robots and attacked human workers.
NEXAWARE
77° 7:47
Thirty-four people were killed before SWAT could destroy the robots and deactivate the program.
Though official investigations have exonerated Nexaware from foul play, the company could not recover from plummeting stock and consumer boycotting.
Nexaware's closure has paved the way for Prime Inc. to take its place as the top technologies corporation in the world.
But even with Nexaware long gone, the question lingering on everyone's mind is: ***could another A.I. attack happen again?***
Your coffee, Alex.
77° 7:47
Coming up, our Mind Over Matters segment: Are the restrictions Congress put on artificial intelligence and the robotics industry doing enough to keep people safe? Your thoughts--literally--when we return.

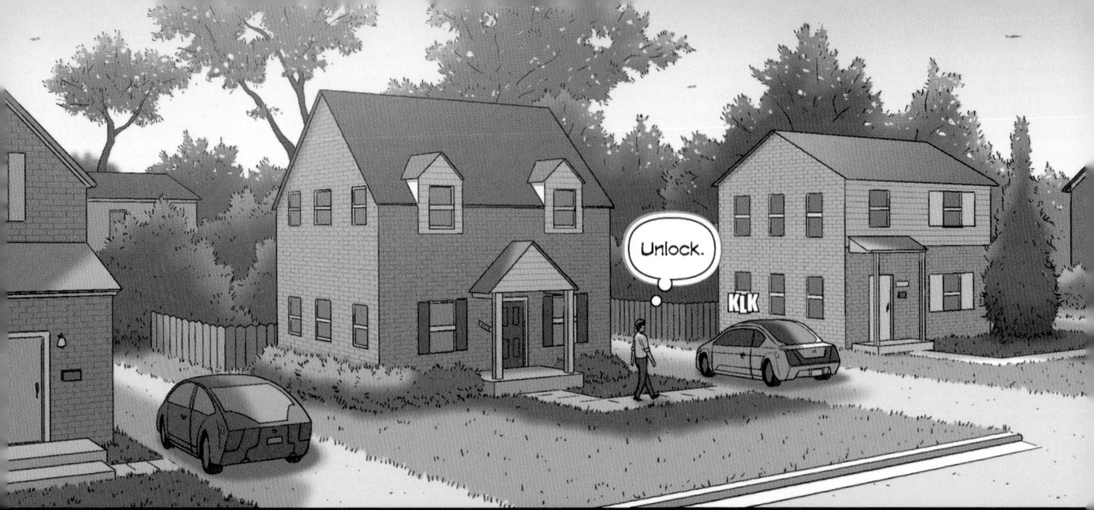
Unlock.
KLK

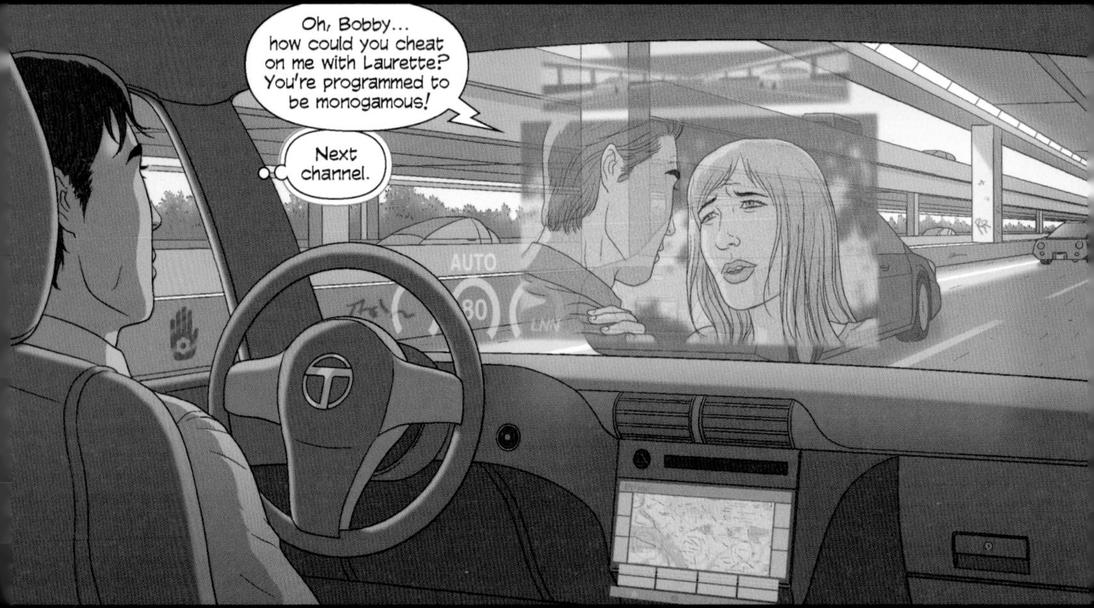
Oh, Bobby... how could you cheat on me with Laurette? You're programmed to be monogamous!
Next channel.
AUTO
80

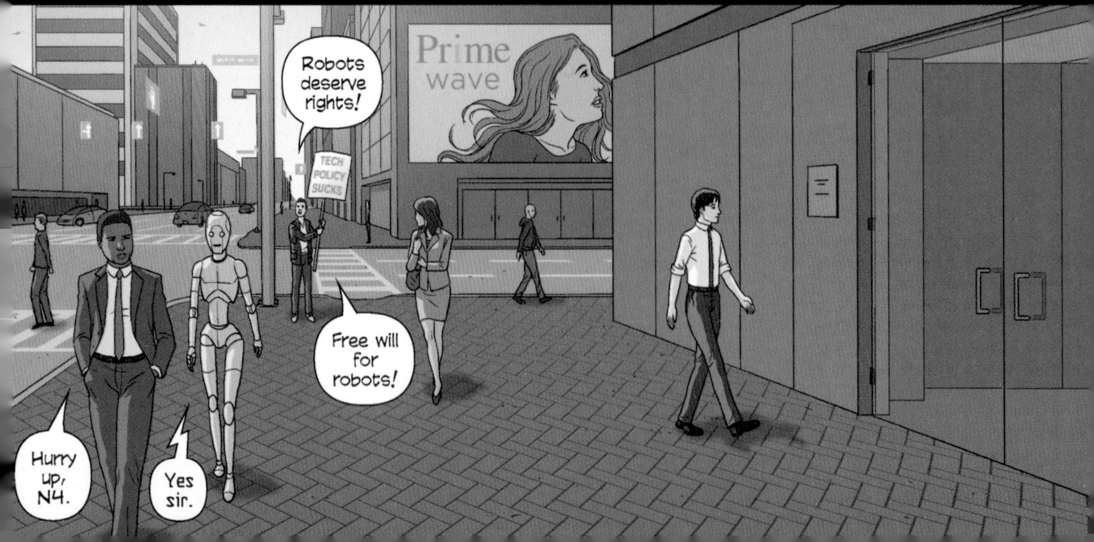
Prime wave
Robots deserve rights!
TECH POLICY SUCKS
Free will for robots!
Hurry up, N4.
Yes sir.

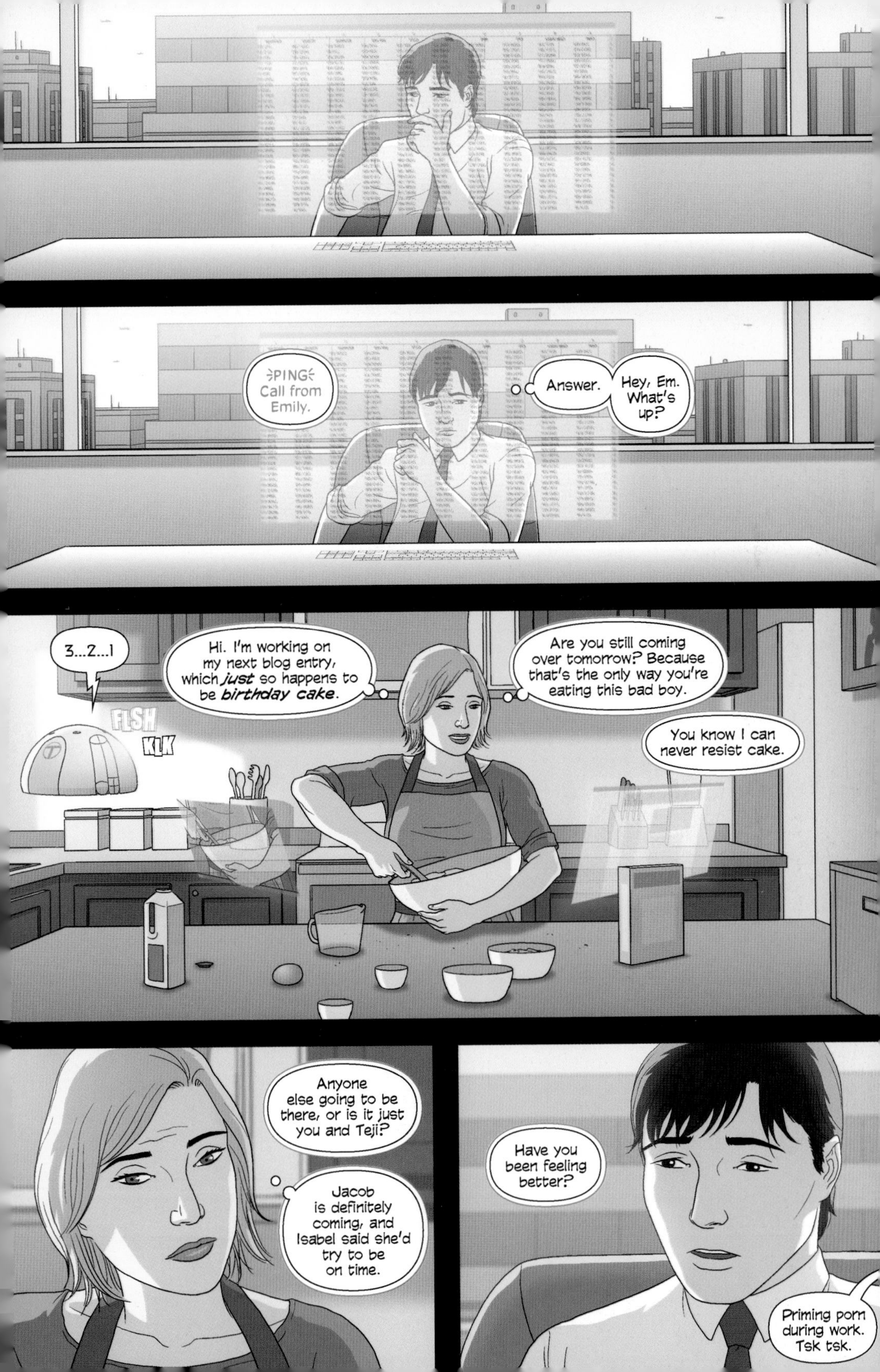
PING
Call from Emily.
Answer.
Hey, Em. What's up?
3...2...1
FLSH
KLK
Hi. I'm working on my next blog entry, which *just* so happens to be ***birthday cake***.
Are you still coming over tomorrow? Because that's the only way you're eating this bad boy.
You know I can never resist cake.
Anyone else going to be there, or is it just you and Teji?
Jacob is definitely coming, and Isabel said she'd try to be on time.
Have you been feeling better?
Priming porn during work. Tsk tsk.

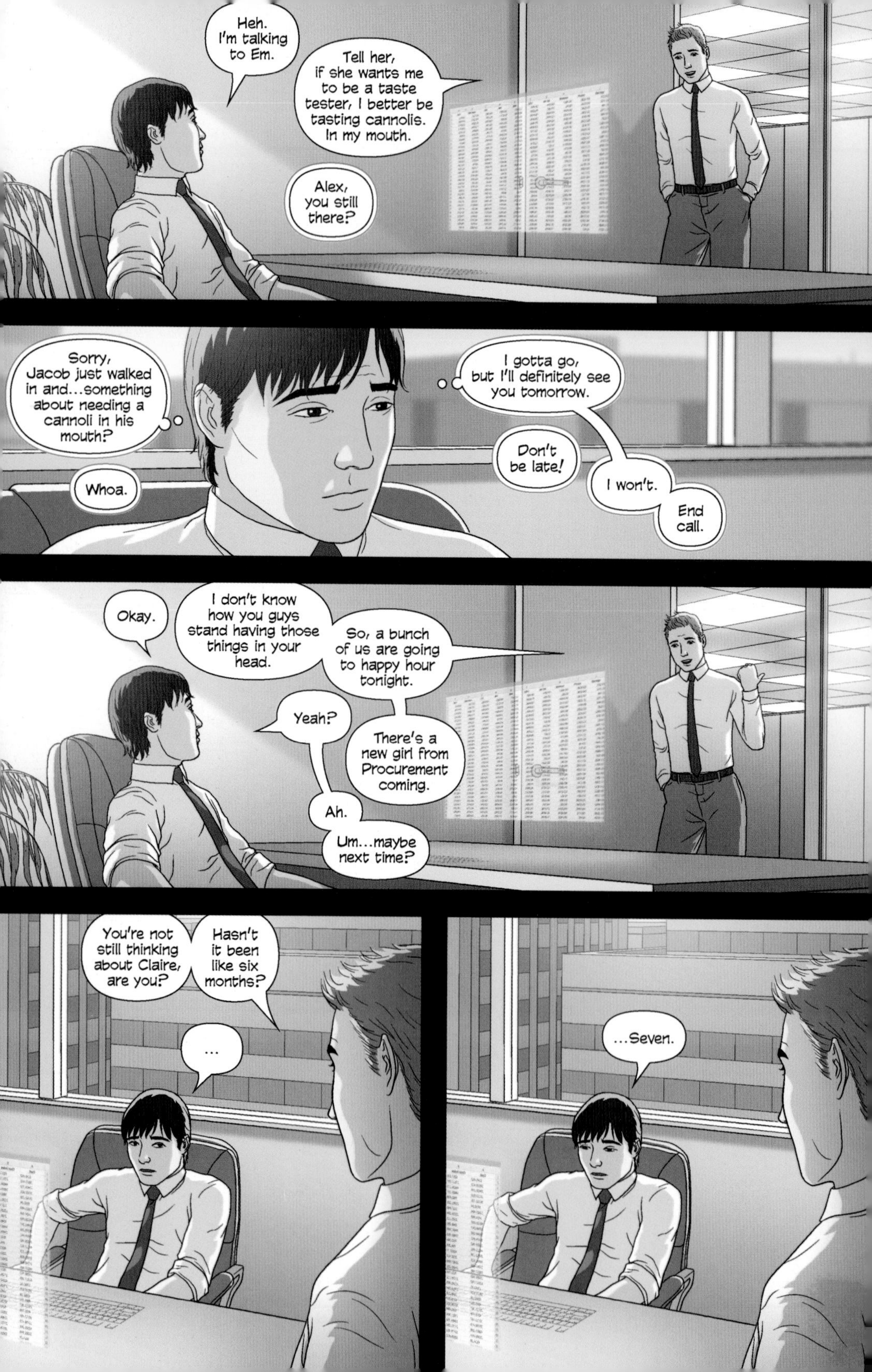

Heh. I'm talking to Em.
Tell her, if she wants me to be a taste tester, I better be tasting cannolis. In my mouth.
Alex, you still there?
Sorry, Jacob just walked in and...something about needing a cannoli in his mouth?
Whoa.
I gotta go, but I'll definitely see you tomorrow.
Don't be late!
I won't.
End call.
Okay.
I don't know how you guys stand having those things in your head.
So, a bunch of us are going to happy hour tonight.
Yeah?
There's a new girl from Procurement coming.
Ah.
Um...maybe next time?
You're not still thinking about Claire, are you?
Hasn't it been like six months?
...
...Seven.

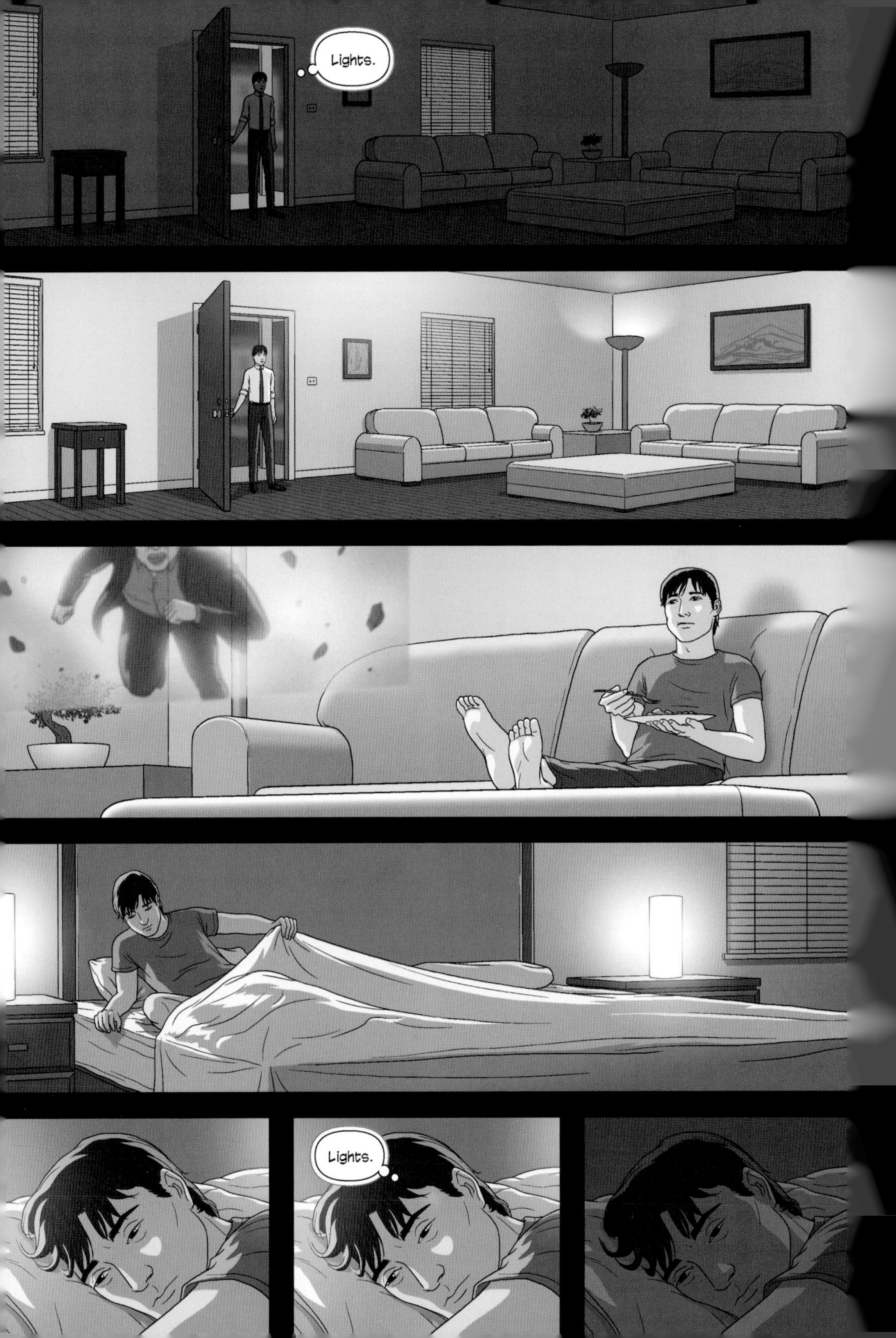
Lights.
Lights.

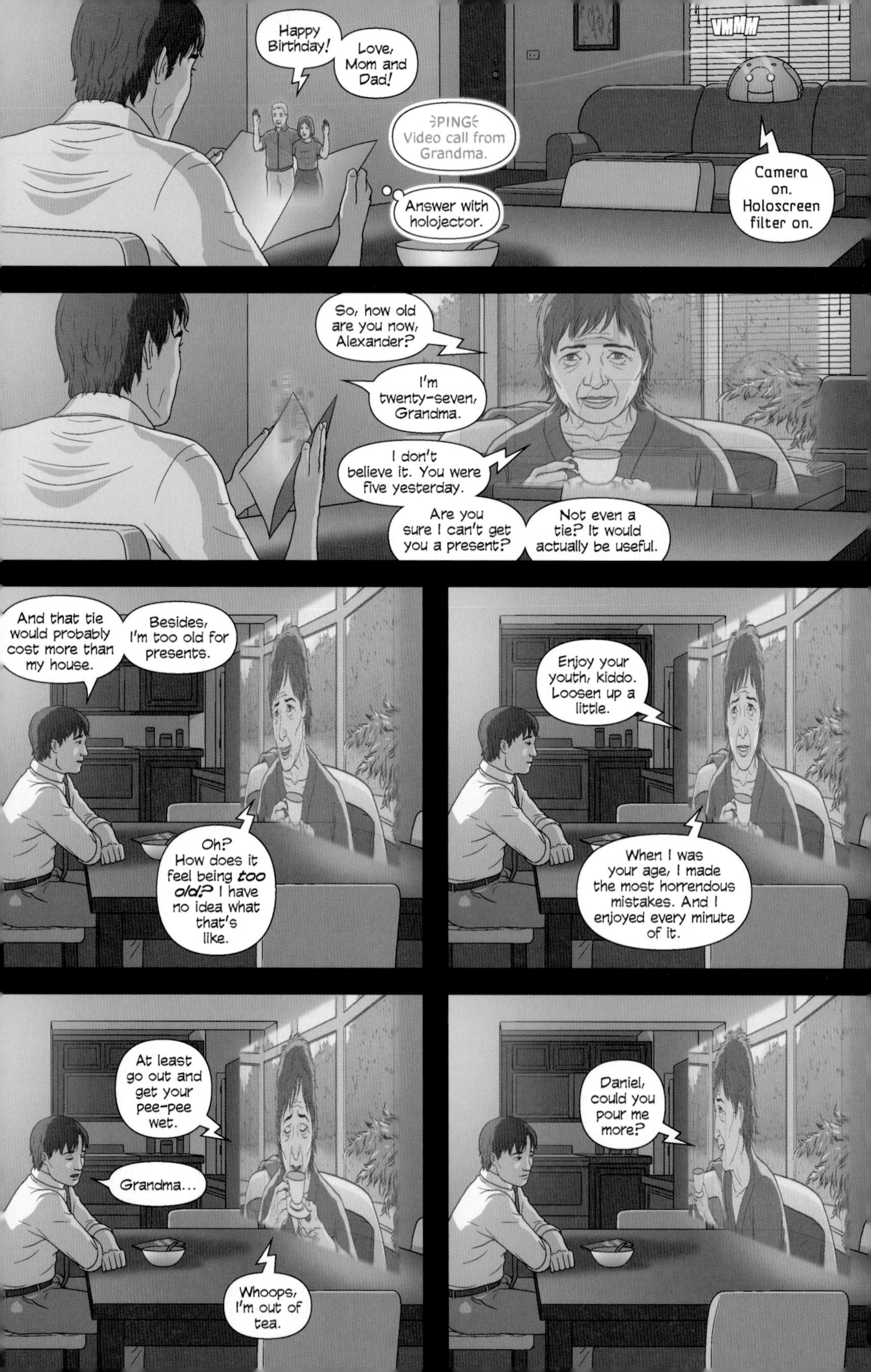
Happy Birthday!
Love, Mom and Dad!
VMMM
PING
Video call from Grandma.
Answer with holojector.
Camera on. Holoscreen filter on.
So, how old are you now, Alexander?
I'm twenty-seven, Grandma.
I don't believe it. You were five yesterday.
Are you sure I can't get you a present?
Not even a tie? It would actually be useful.
And that tie would probably cost more than my house.
Besides, I'm too old for presents.
Oh? How does it feel being *too old?* I have no idea what that's like.
Enjoy your youth, kiddo. Loosen up a little.
When I was your age, I made the most horrendous mistakes. And I enjoyed every minute of it.
At least go out and get your pee-pee wet.
Grandma...
Whoops, I'm out of tea.
Daniel, could you pour me more?

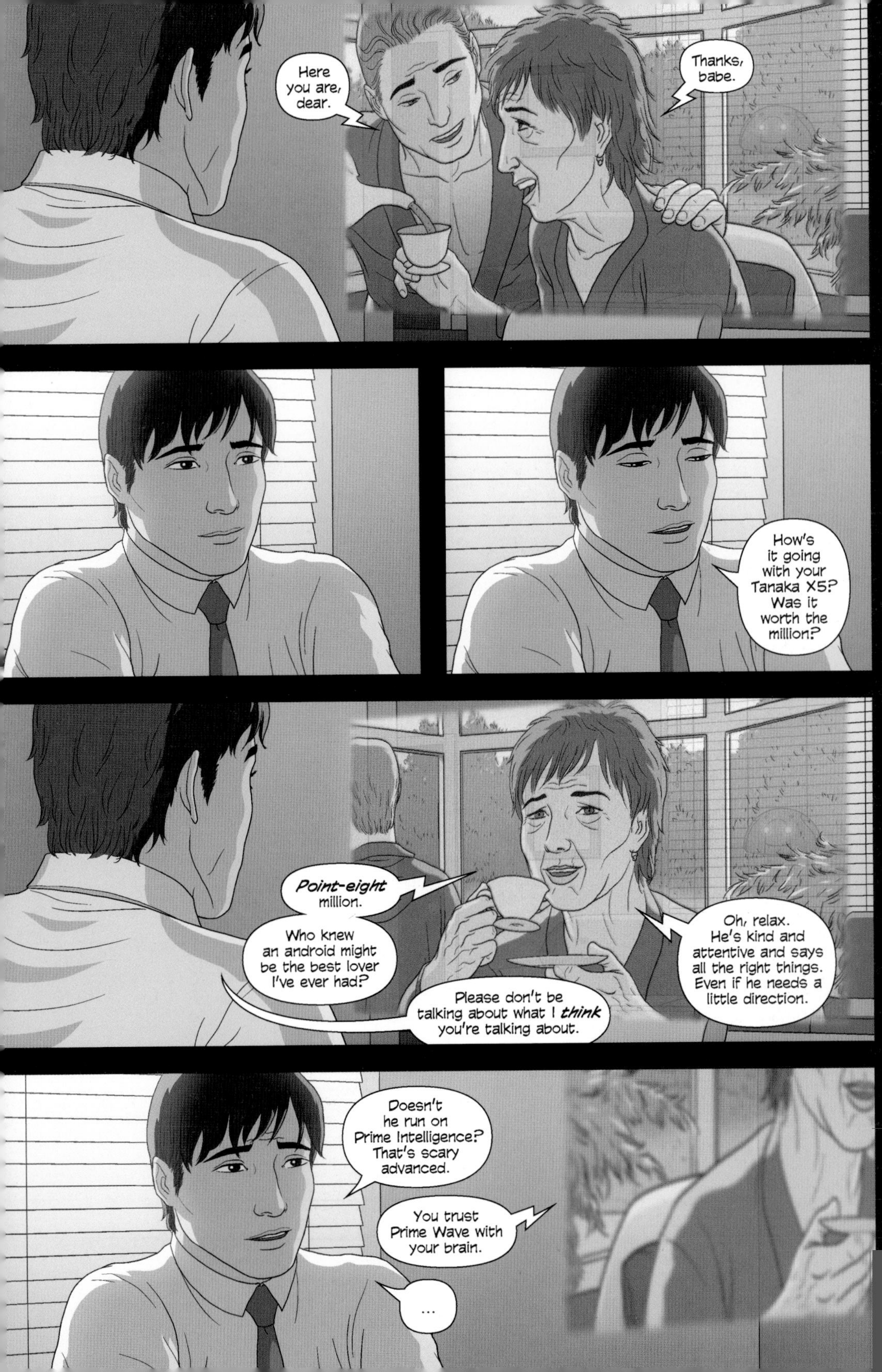
Here you are, dear.
Thanks, babe.
How's it going with your Tanaka X5? Was it worth the million?
Point-eight million.
Who knew an android might be the best lover I've ever had?
Please don't be talking about what I *think* you're talking about.
Oh, relax. He's kind and attentive and says all the right things. Even if he needs a little direction.
Doesn't he run on Prime Intelligence? That's scary advanced.
You trust Prime Wave with your brain.
...

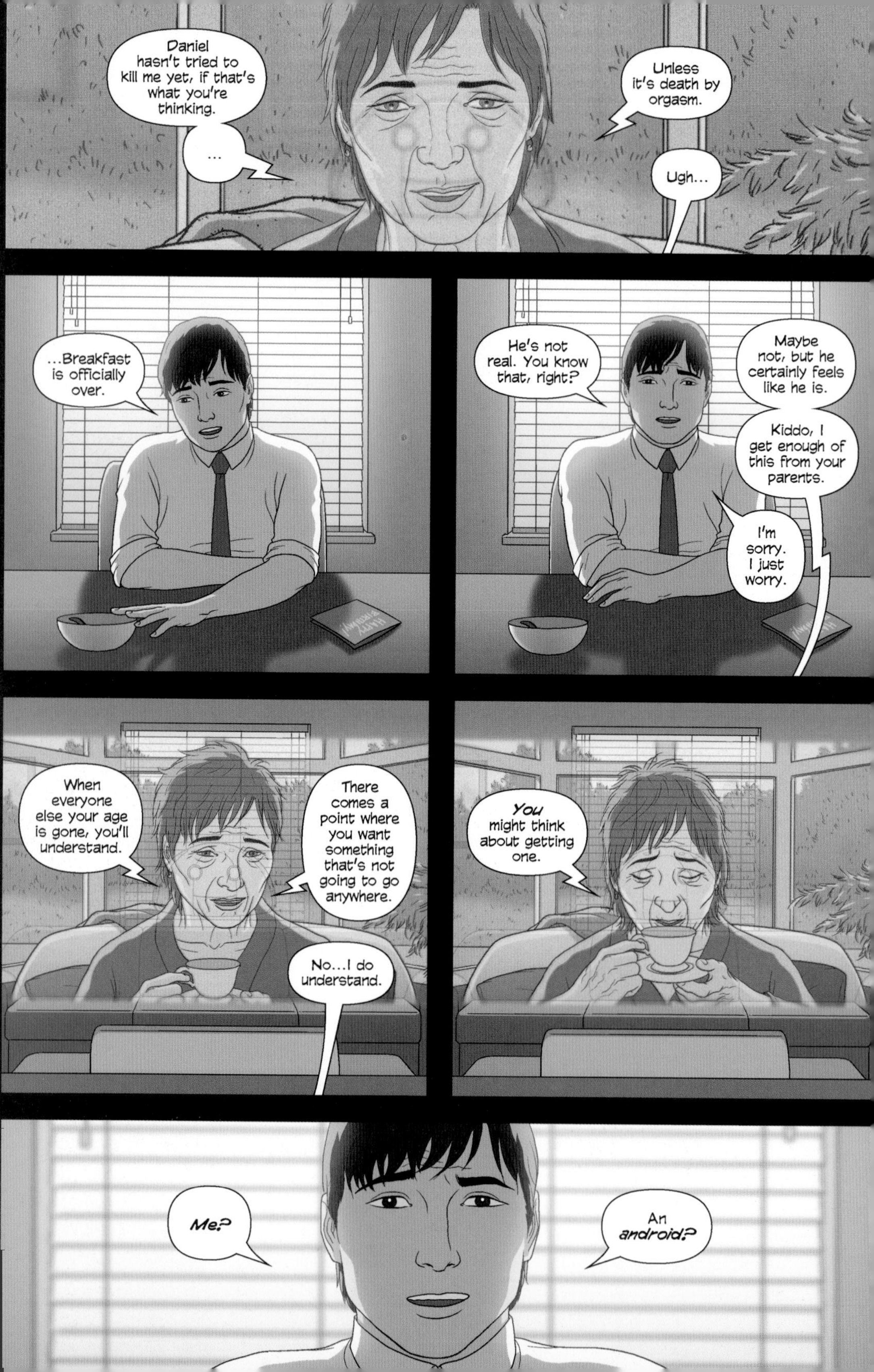
Daniel hasn't tried to kill me yet, if that's what you're thinking.
...
Unless it's death by orgasm.
Ugh...
...Breakfast is officially over.
He's not real. You know that, right?
Maybe not, but he certainly feels like he is.
Kiddo, I get enough of this from your parents.
I'm sorry. I just worry.
When everyone else your age is gone, you'll understand.
There comes a point where you want something that's not going to go anywhere.
No...I do understand.
You might think about getting one.
Me?
An *android?*

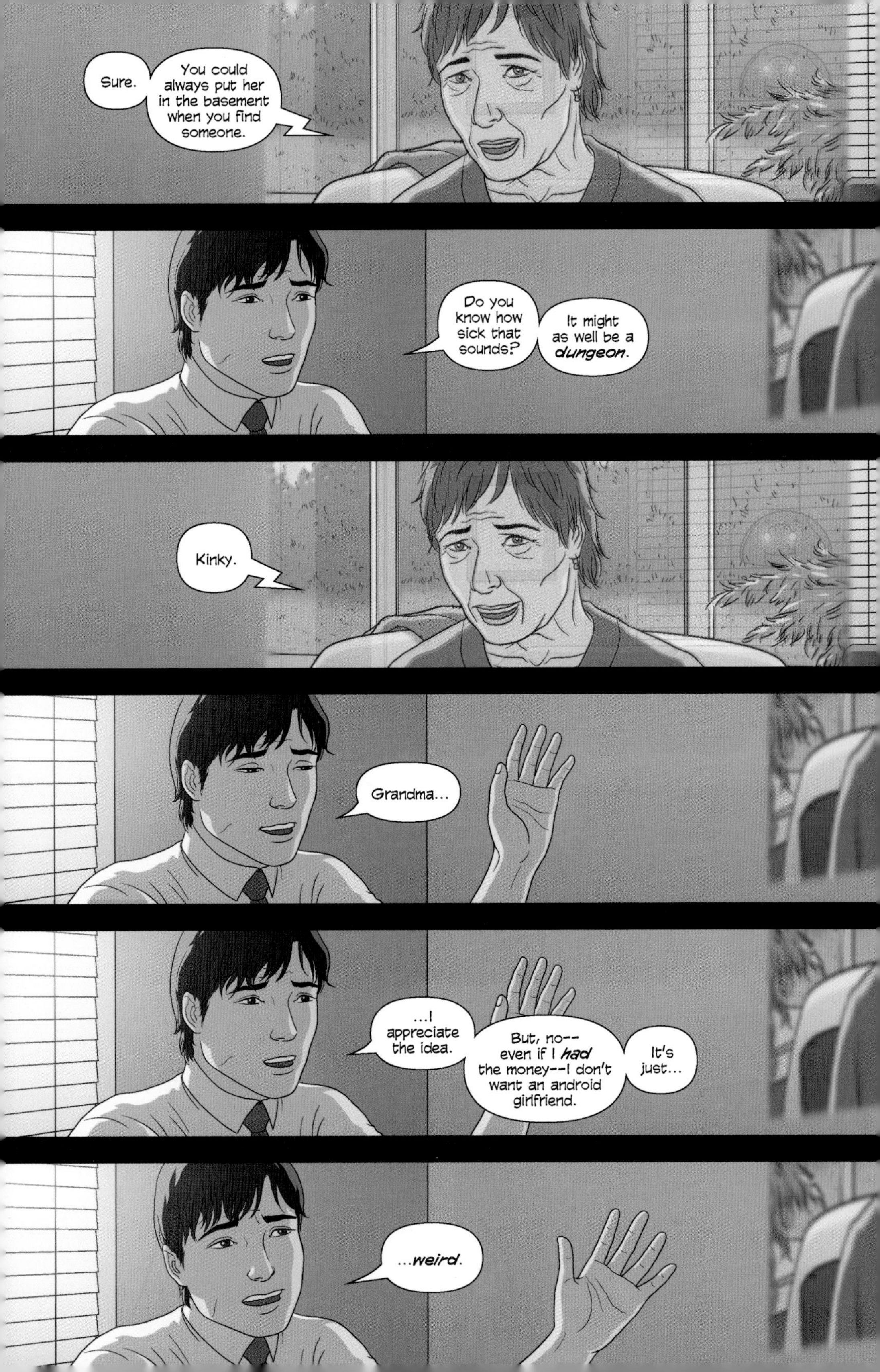
Sure.
You could always put her in the basement when you find someone.
Do you know how sick that sounds?
It might as well be a *dungeon*.
Kinky.
Grandma...
...I appreciate the idea.
But, no-- even if I *had* the money--I don't want an android girlfriend.
It's just...
...*weird*.

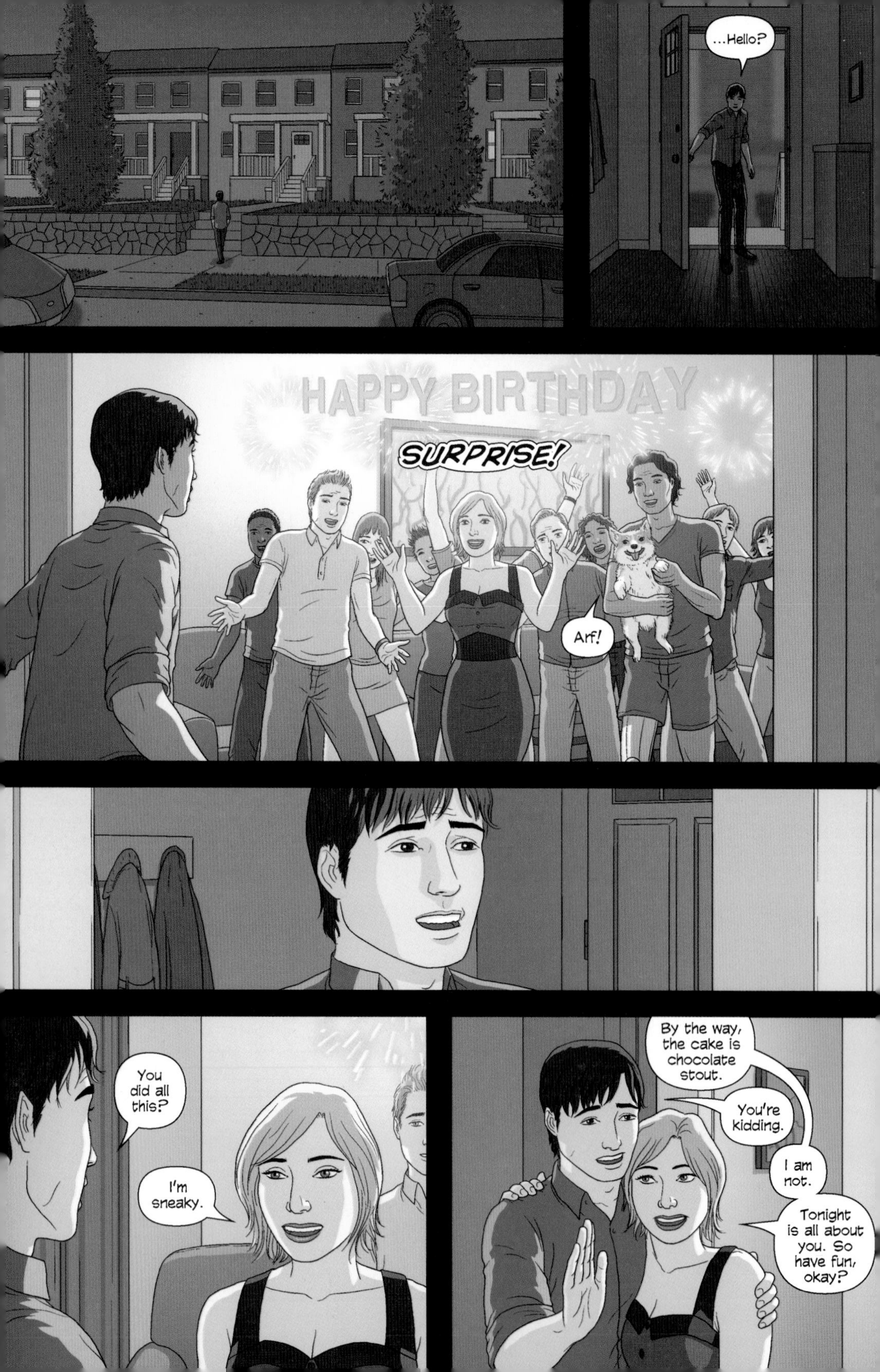
...Hello?
HAPPY BIRTHDAY
SURPRISE!
Arf!
You did all this?
I'm sneaky.
By the way, the cake is chocolate stout.
You're kidding.
I am not.
Tonight is all about you. So have fun, okay?

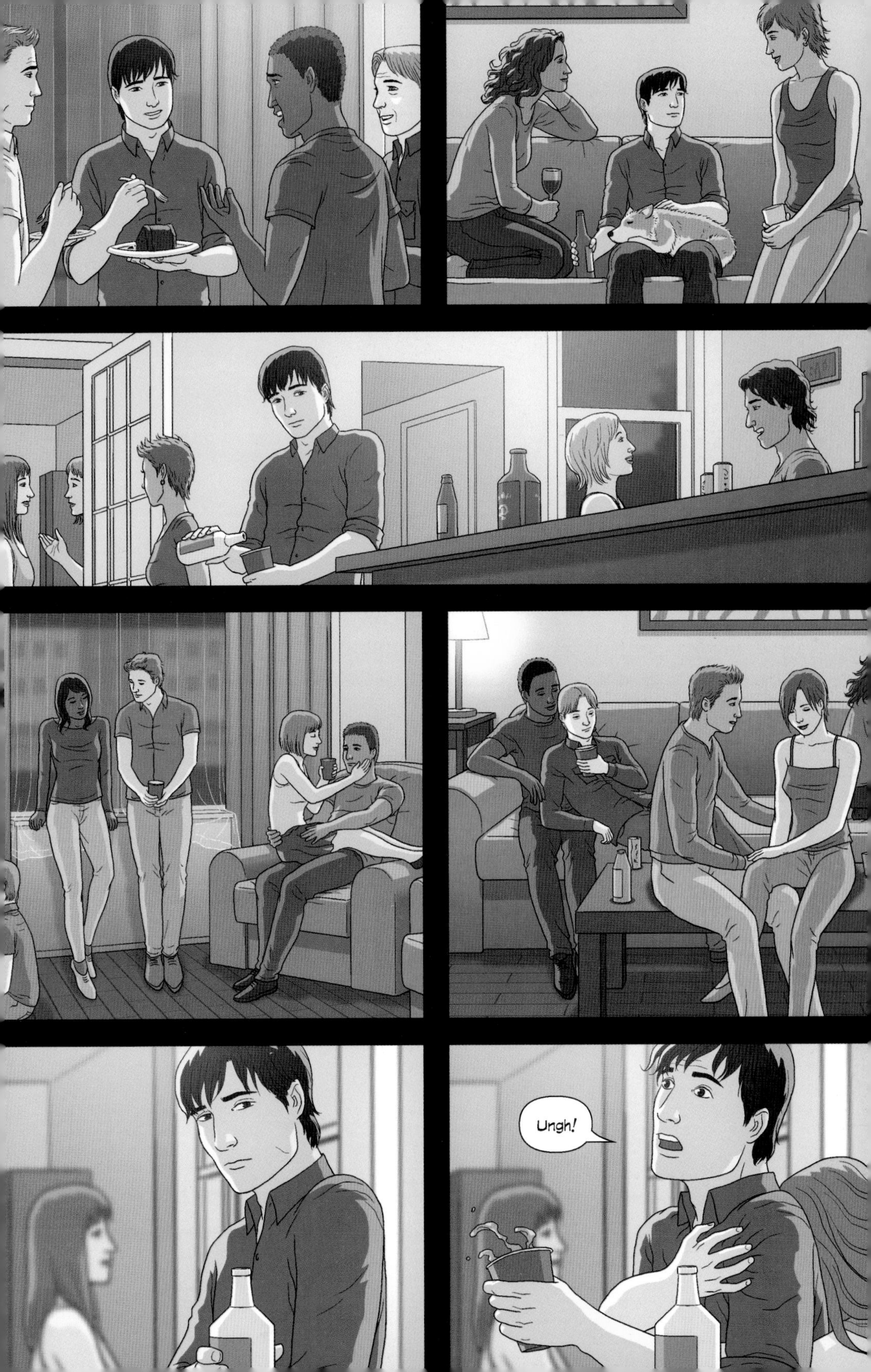
Ungh!

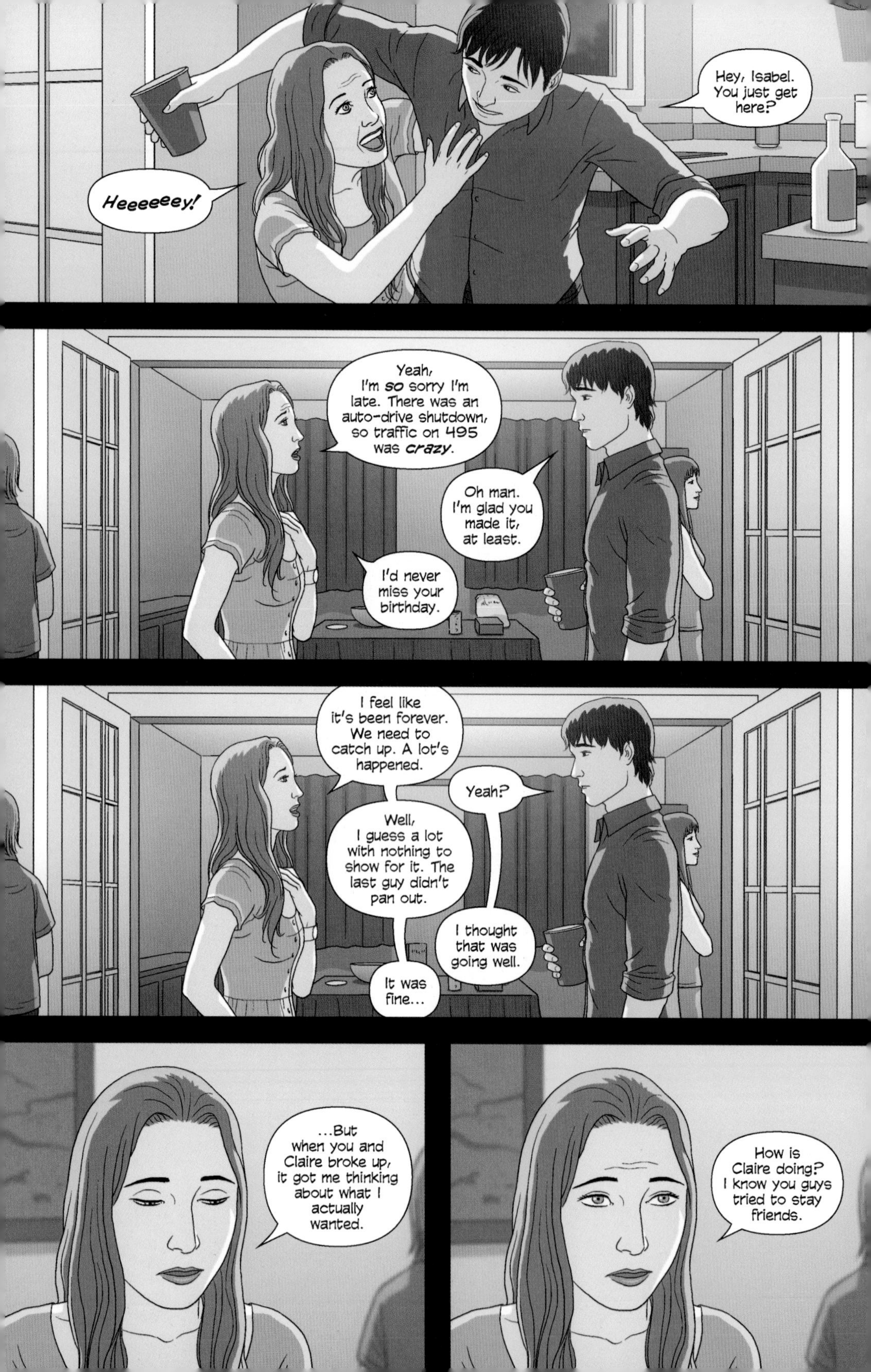
Hey, Isabel. You just get here?
Heeeeeey!
Yeah, I'm *so* sorry I'm late. There was an auto-drive shutdown, so traffic on 495 was *crazy*.
Oh man. I'm glad you made it, at least.
I'd never miss your birthday.
I feel like it's been forever. We need to catch up. A lot's happened.
Yeah?
Well, I guess a lot with nothing to show for it. The last guy didn't pan out.
I thought that was going well.
It was fine...
...But when you and Claire broke up, it got me thinking about what I actually wanted.
How is Claire doing? I know you guys tried to stay friends.

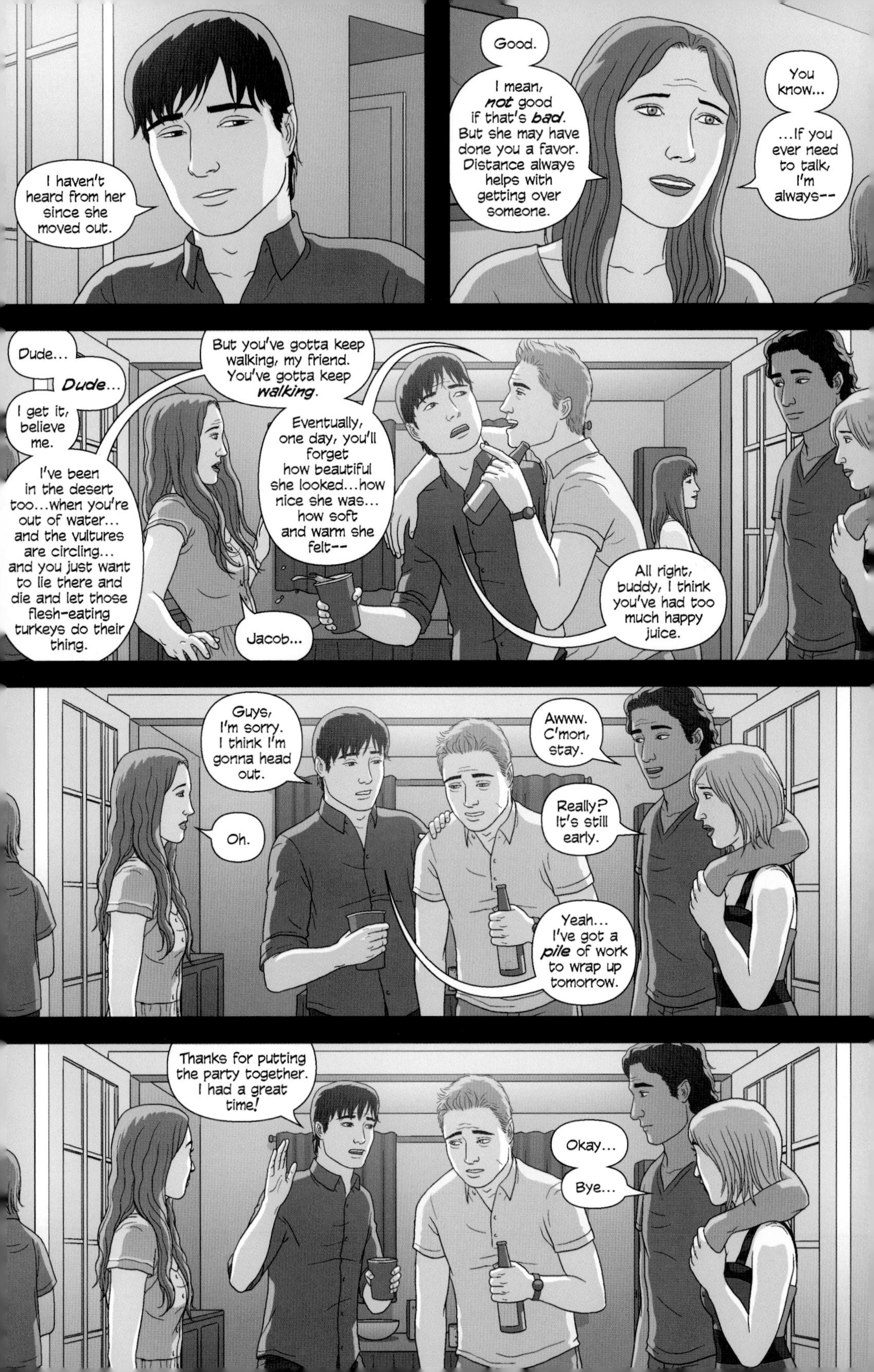
I haven't heard from her since she moved out.
Good.
I mean, *not* good if that's *bad*. But she may have done you a favor. Distance always helps with getting over someone.
You know...
...If you ever need to talk, I'm always--
Dude...
Dude...
I get it, believe me.
I've been in the desert too...when you're out of water... and the vultures are circling... and you just want to lie there and die and let those flesh-eating turkeys do their thing.
But you've gotta keep walking, my friend. You've gotta keep *walking*.
Eventually, one day, you'll forget how beautiful she looked...how nice she was... how soft and warm she felt--
Jacob...
All right, buddy, I think you've had too much happy juice.
Guys, I'm sorry. I think I'm gonna head out.
Oh.
Awww. C'mon, stay.
Really? It's still early.
Yeah... I've got a *pile* of work to wrap up tomorrow.
Thanks for putting the party together. I had a great time!
Okay...
Bye...

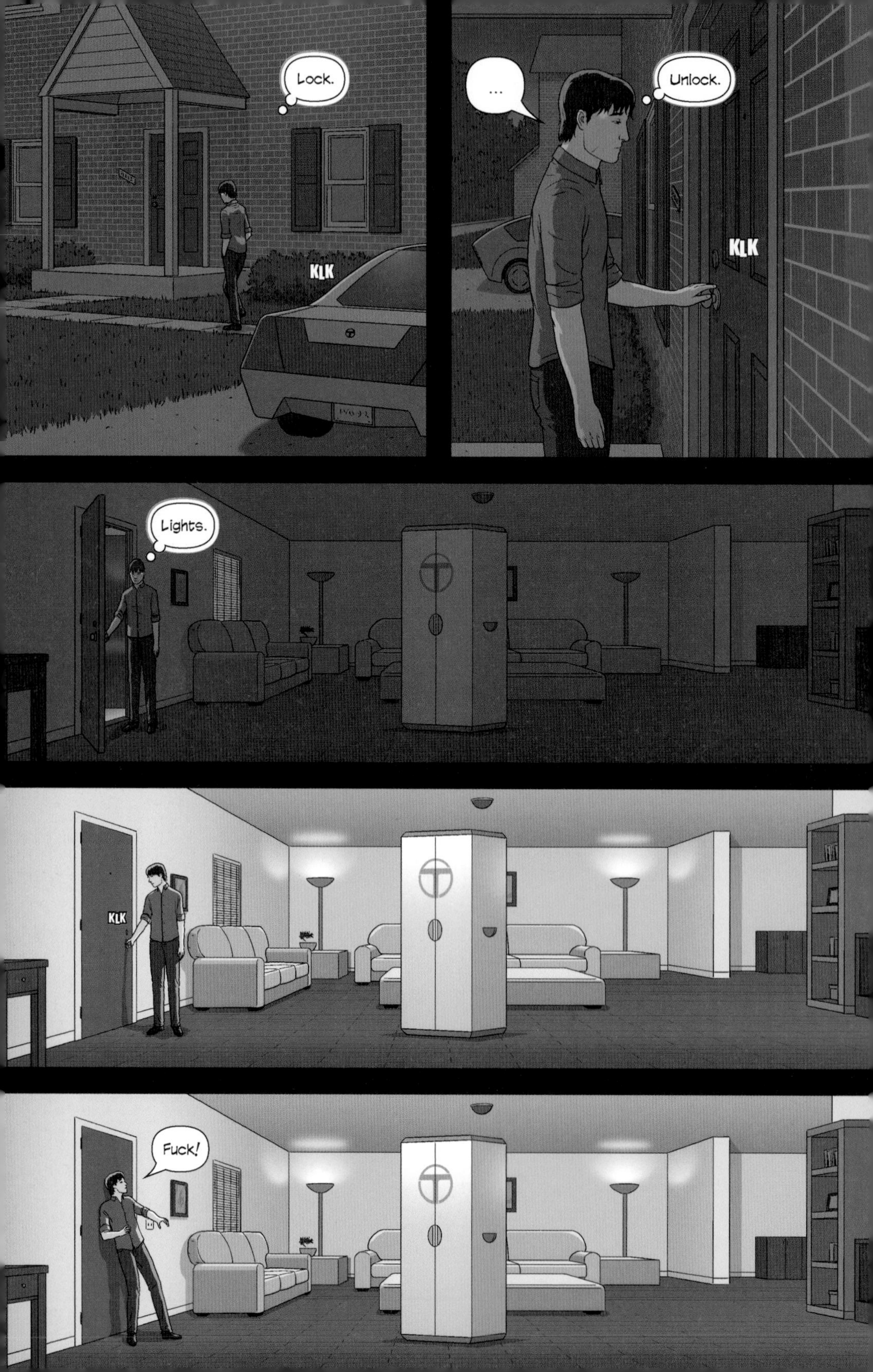
Lock.
KLK
...
Unlock.
KLK
Lights.
KLK
Fuck!

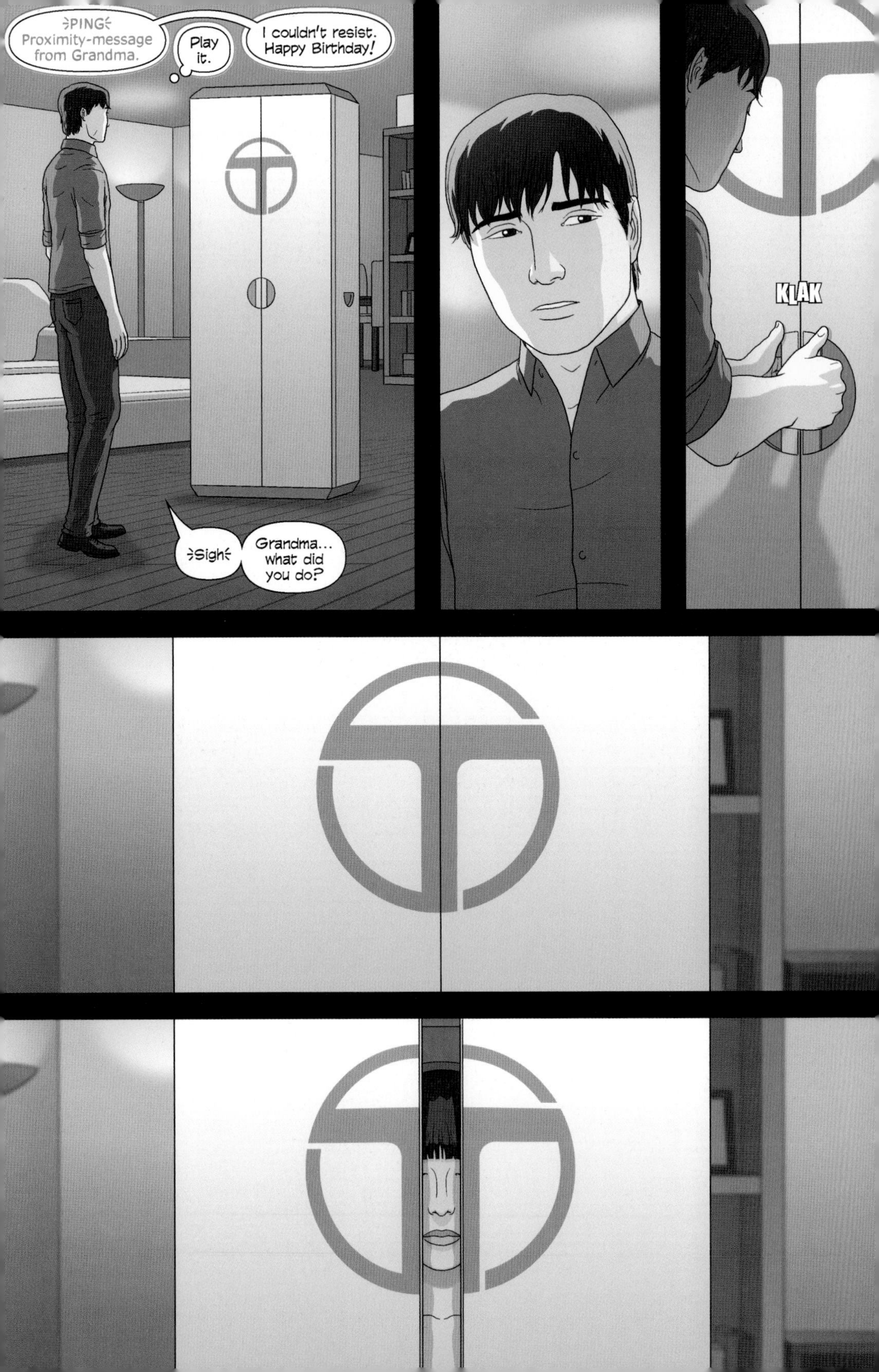
≈PING≈
Proximity-message from Grandma.
Play it.
I couldn't resist. Happy Birthday!
≈Sigh≈
Grandma... what did you do?
KLAK

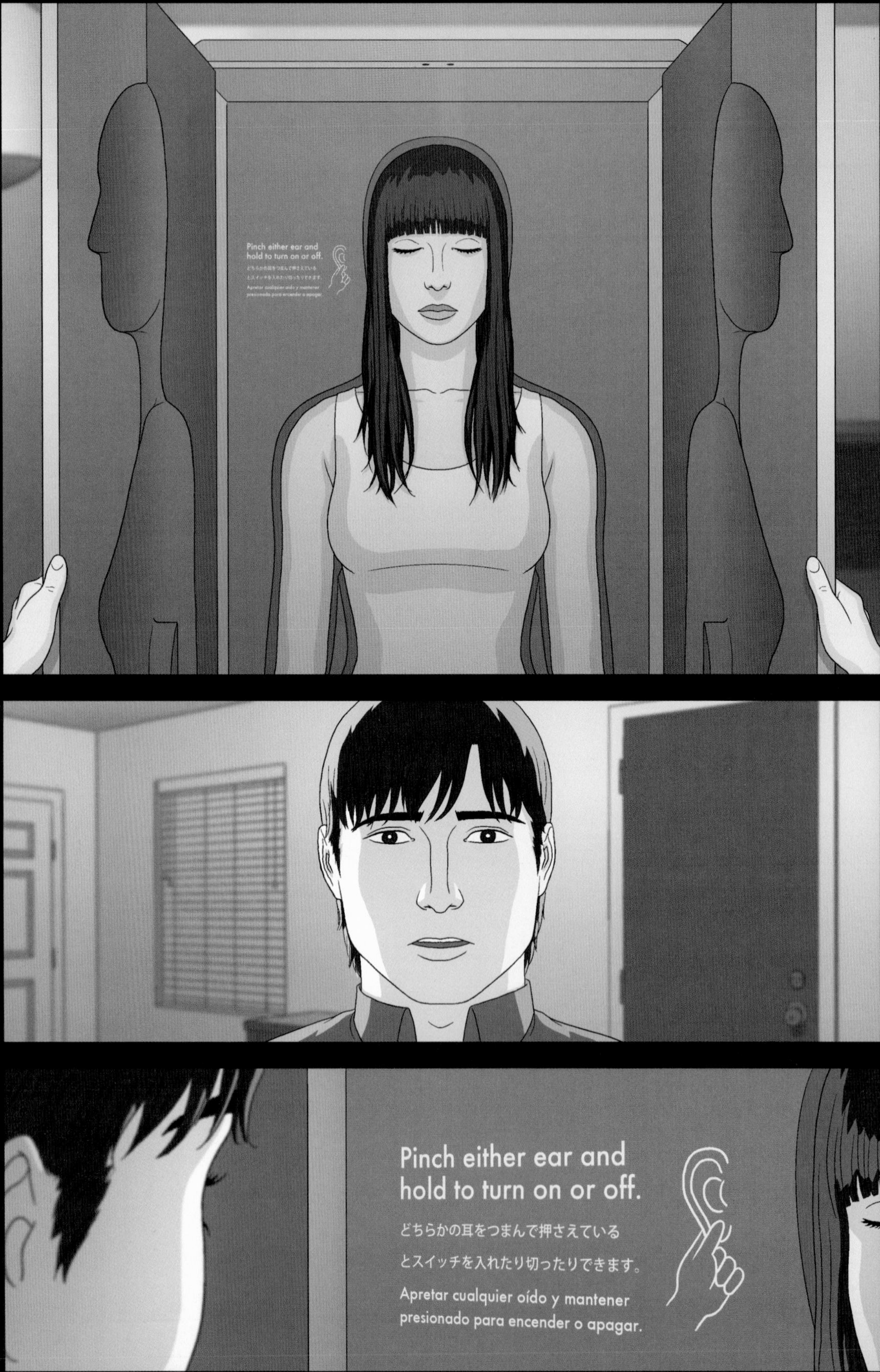
Pinch either ear and hold to turn on or off.
Pinch either ear and hold to turn on or off.
どちらかの耳をつまんで押さえているとスイッチを入れたり切ったりできます。
Apretar cualquier oído y mantener presionado para encender o apagar.

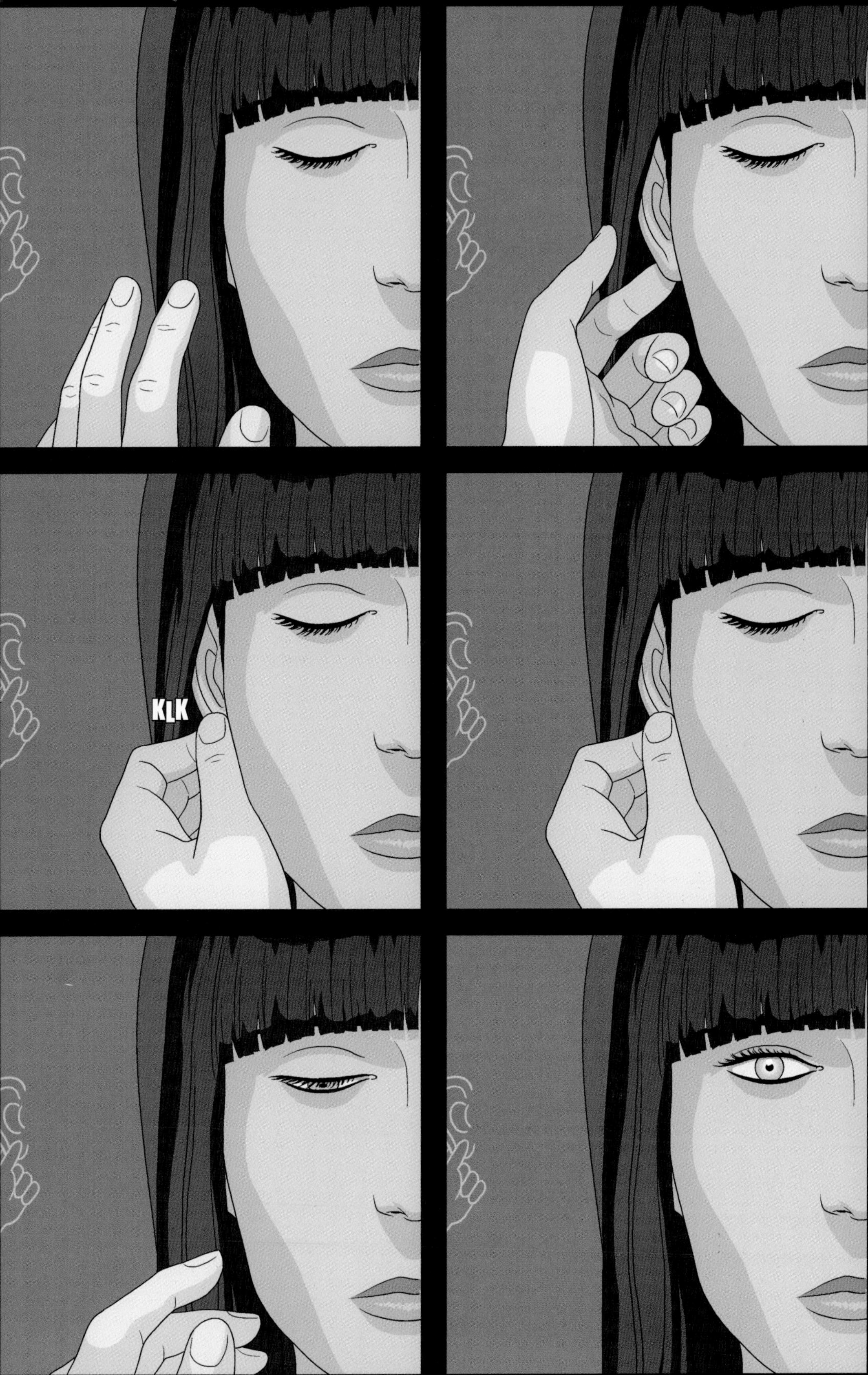
KLK

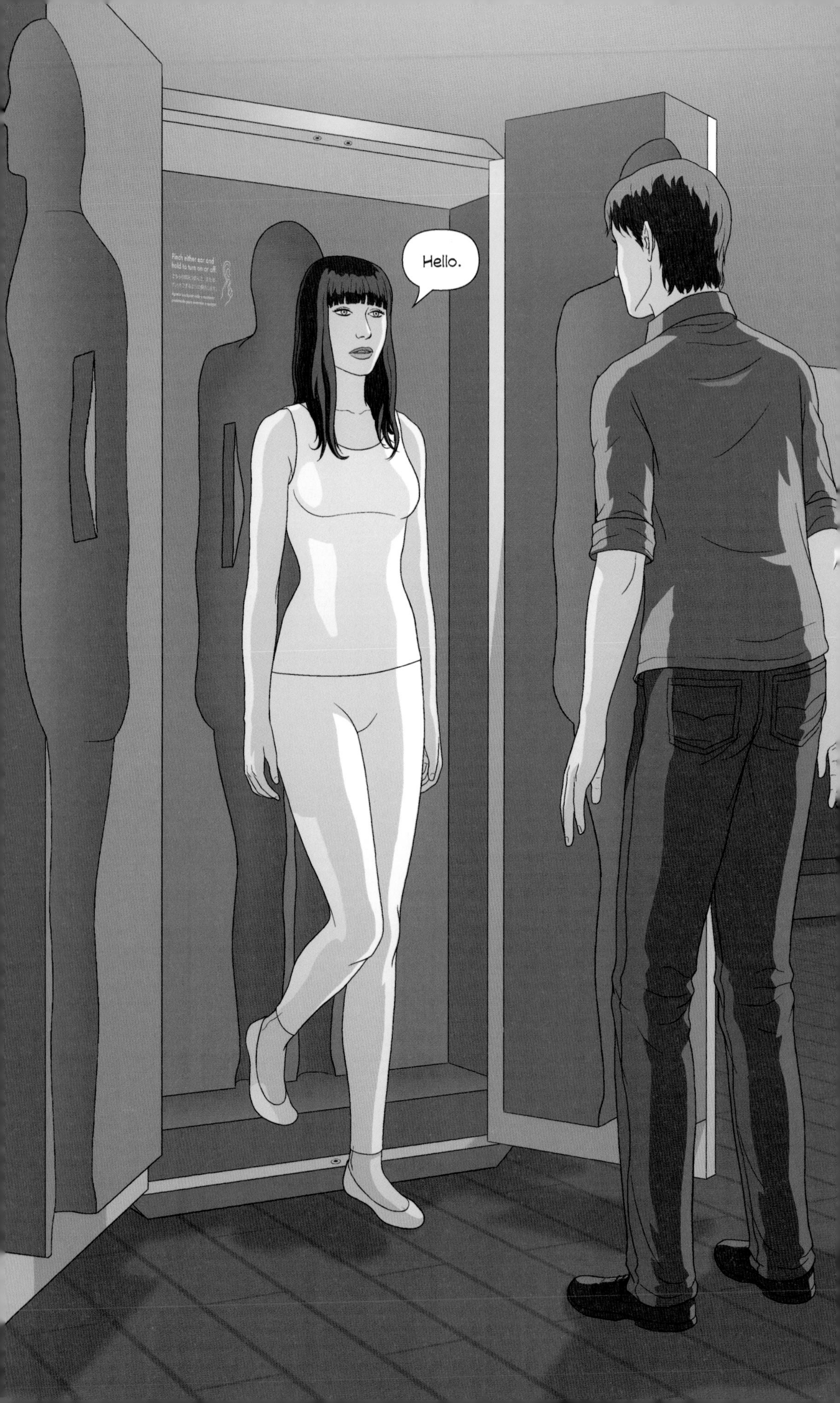
Pinch either ear and hold to turn on or off.
Hello.

2

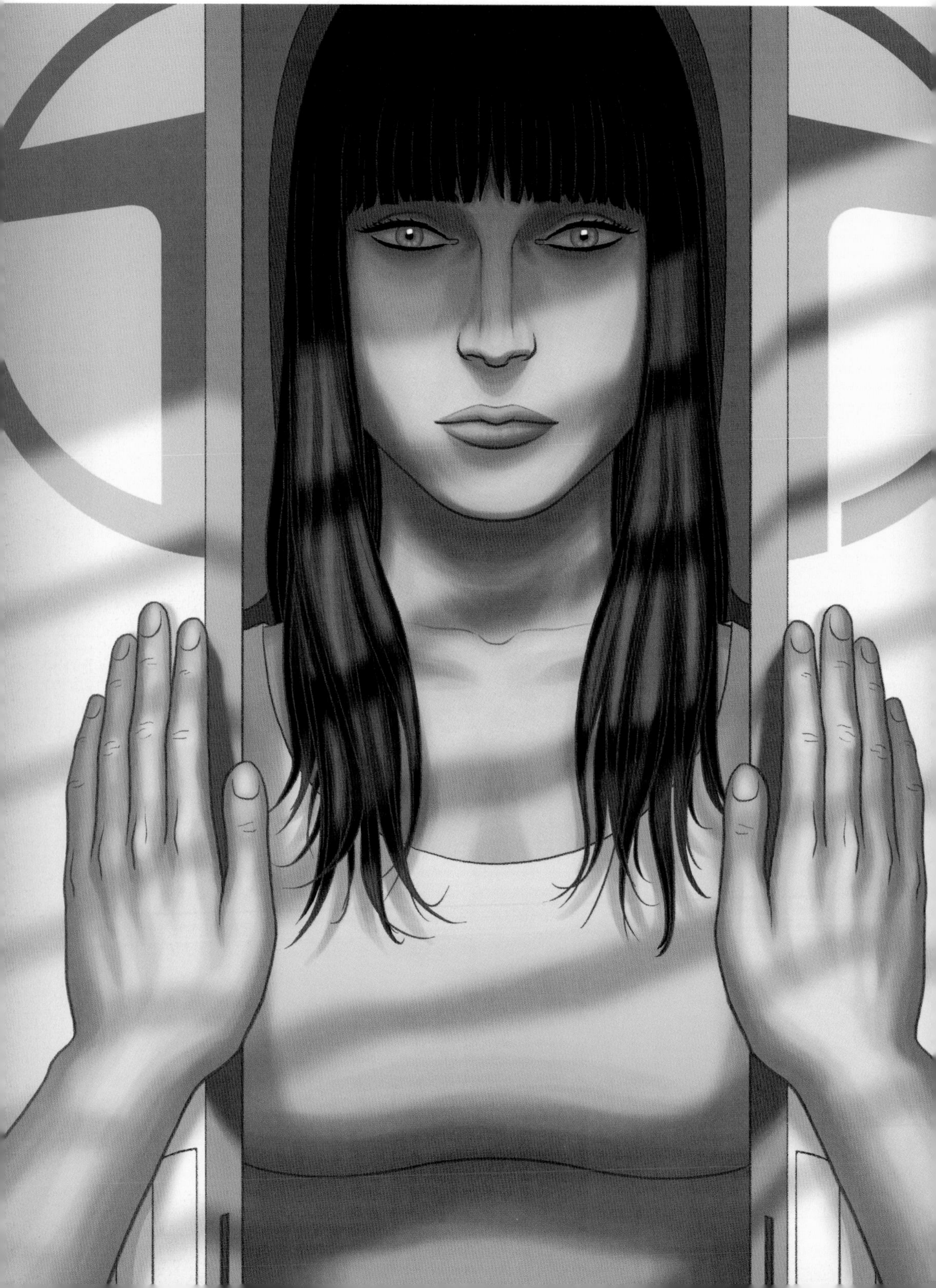

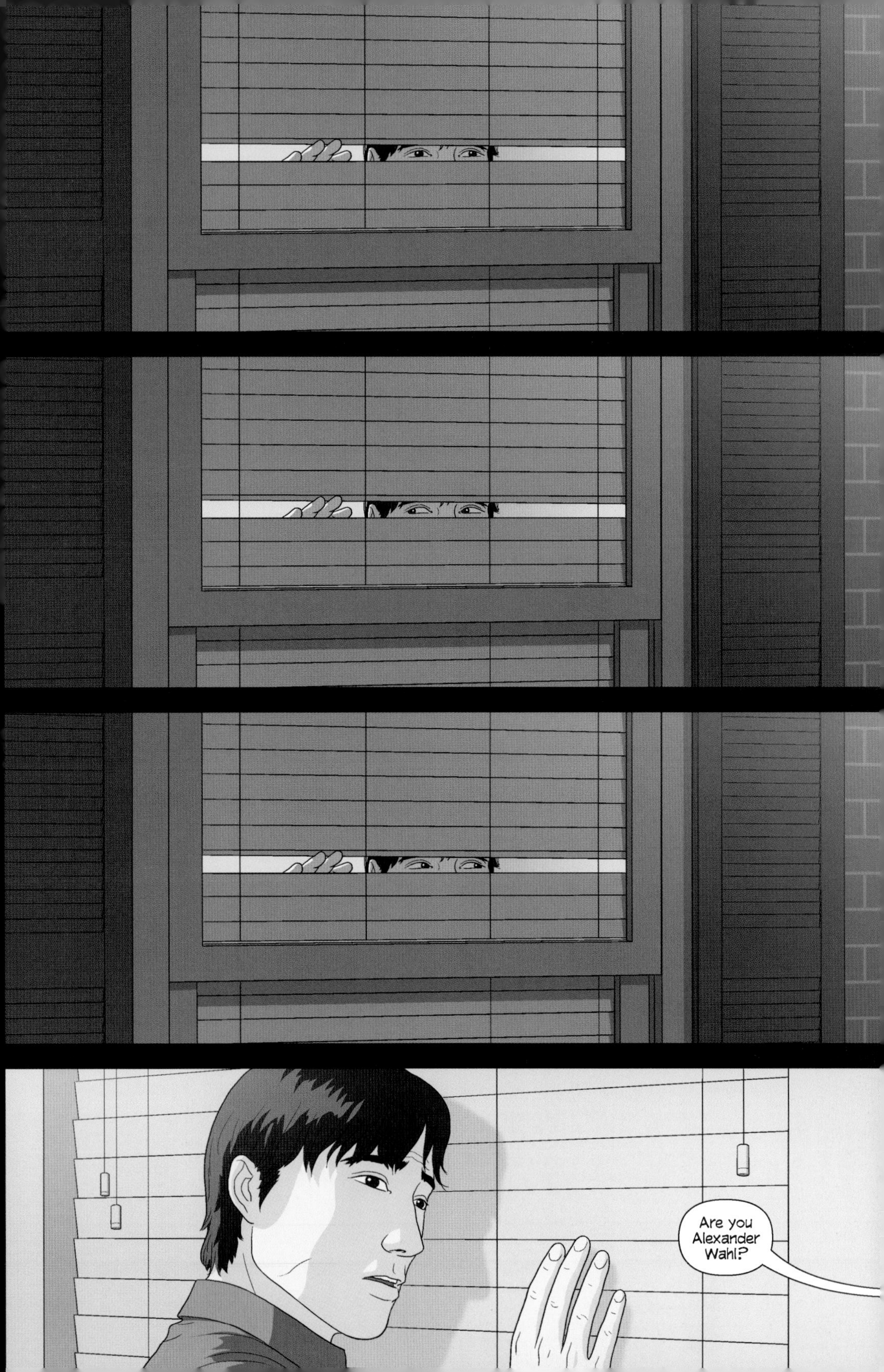
Are you Alexander Wahl?

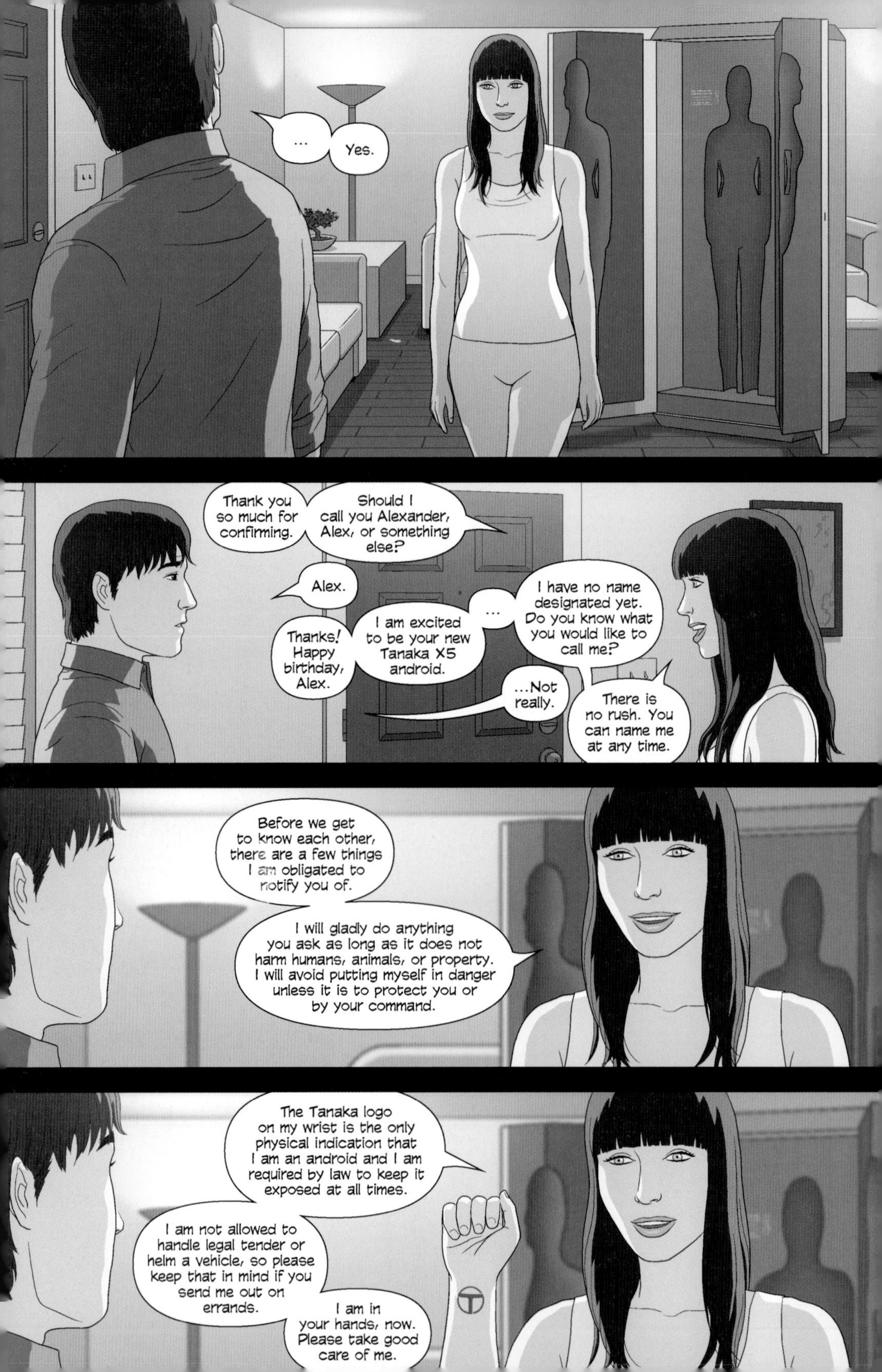
...
Yes.
Thank you so much for confirming.
Should I call you Alexander, Alex, or something else?
Alex.
Thanks! Happy birthday, Alex.
I am excited to be your new Tanaka X5 android.
...
I have no name designated yet. Do you know what you would like to call me?
...Not really.
There is no rush. You can name me at any time.
Before we get to know each other, there are a few things I am obligated to notify you of.
I will gladly do anything you ask as long as it does not harm humans, animals, or property. I will avoid putting myself in danger unless it is to protect you or by your command.
The Tanaka logo on my wrist is the only physical indication that I am an android and I am required by law to keep it exposed at all times.
I am not allowed to handle legal tender or helm a vehicle, so please keep that in mind if you send me out on errands.
I am in your hands, now. Please take good care of me.

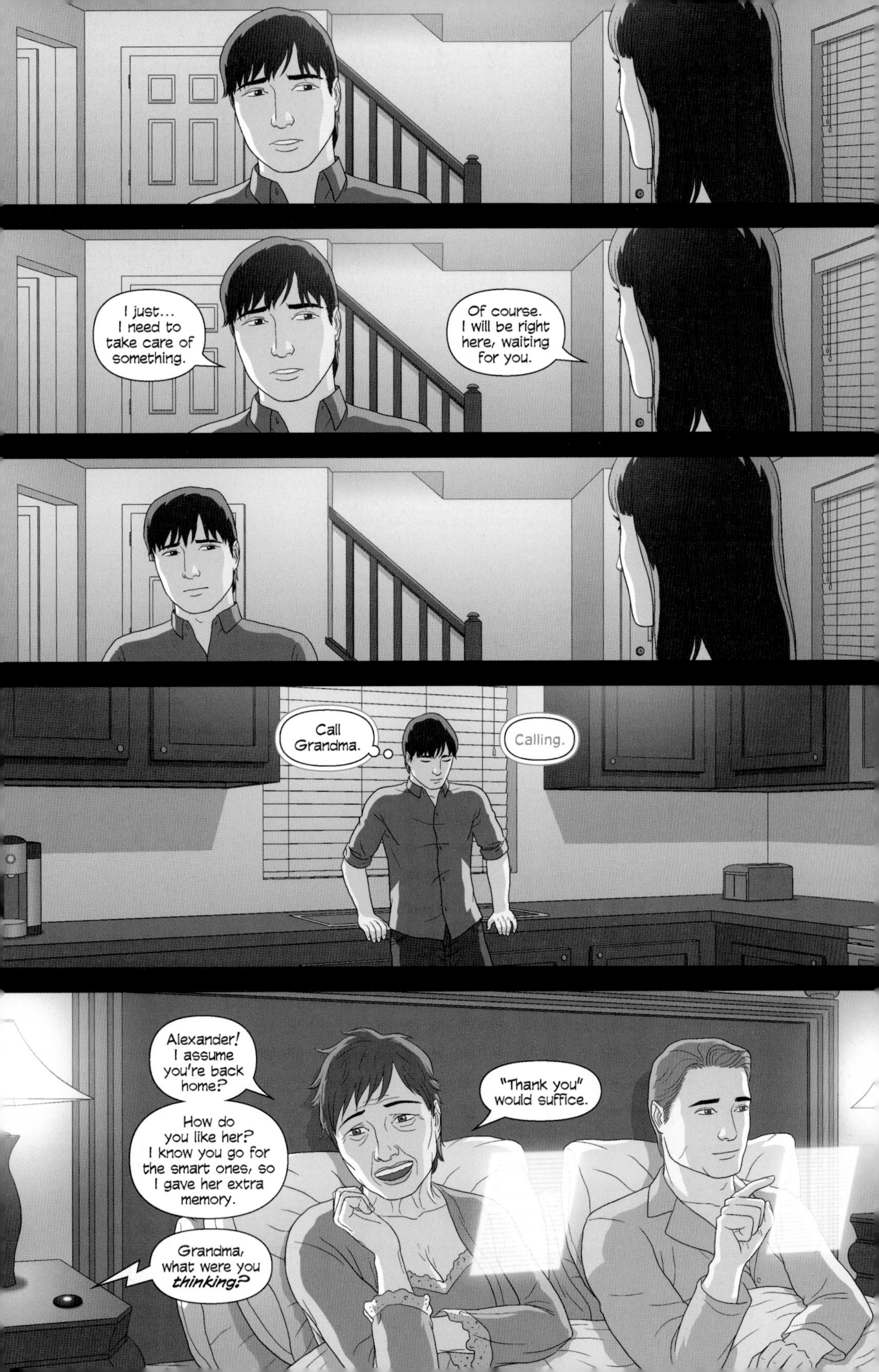

I just... I need to take care of something.
Of course. I will be right here, waiting for you.
Call Grandma.
Calling.
Alexander! I assume you're back home?
How do you like her? I know you go for the smart ones, so I gave her extra memory.
Grandma, what were you *thinking?*
"Thank you" would suffice.

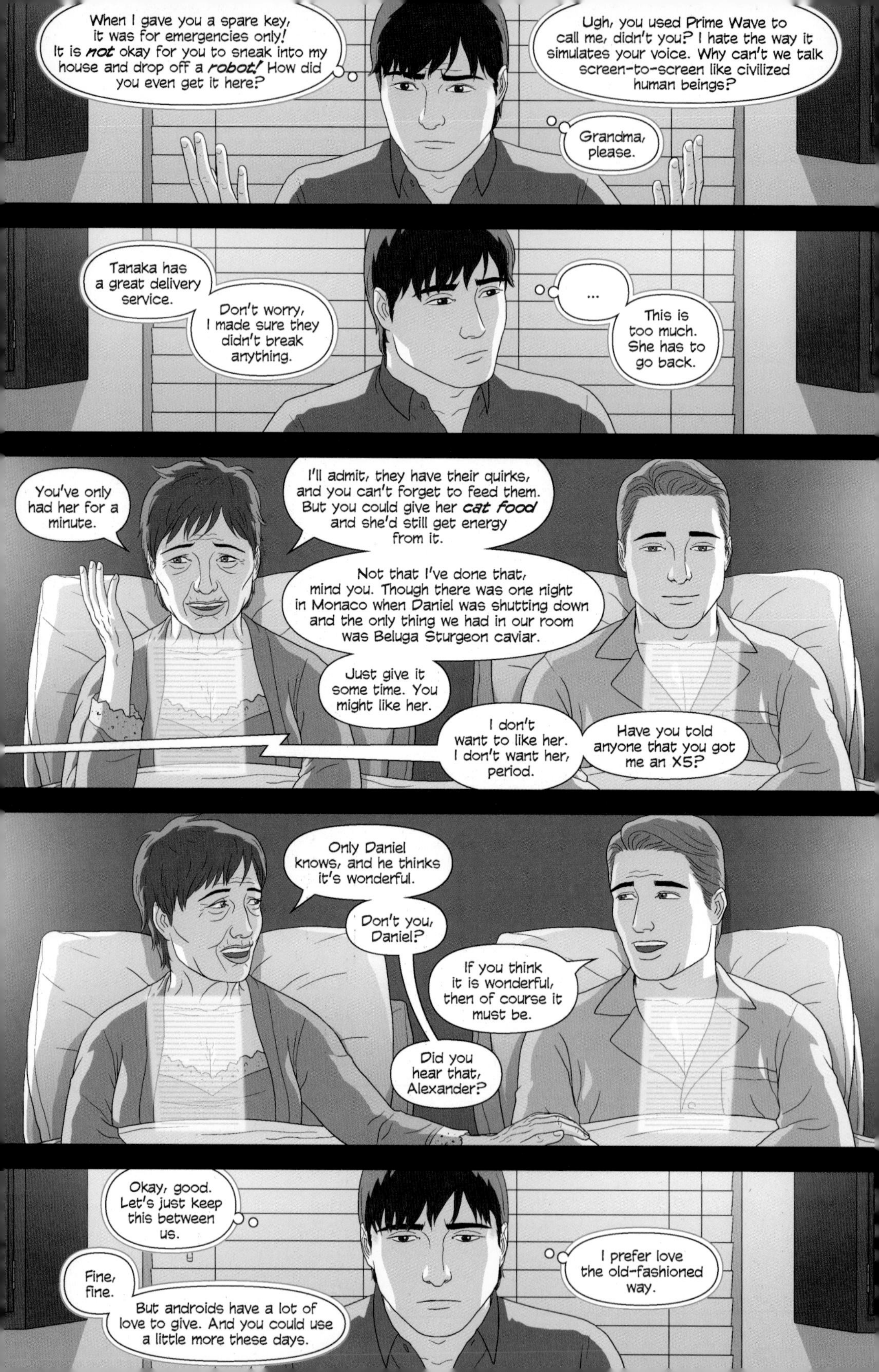
When I gave you a spare key, it was for emergencies only! It is *not* okay for you to sneak into my house and drop off a *robot!* How did you even get it here?
Ugh, you used Prime Wave to call me, didn't you? I hate the way it simulates your voice. Why can't we talk screen-to-screen like civilized human beings?
Grandma, please.
Tanaka has a great delivery service.
Don't worry, I made sure they didn't break anything.
...
This is too much. She has to go back.
You've only had her for a minute.
I'll admit, they have their quirks, and you can't forget to feed them. But you could give her *cat food* and she'd still get energy from it.
Not that I've done that, mind you. Though there was one night in Monaco when Daniel was shutting down and the only thing we had in our room was Beluga Sturgeon caviar.
Just give it some time. You might like her.
I don't want to like her. I don't want her, period.
Have you told anyone that you got me an X5?
Only Daniel knows, and he thinks it's wonderful.
Don't you, Daniel?
If you think it is wonderful, then of course it must be.
Did you hear that, Alexander?
Okay, good. Let's just keep this between us.
Fine, fine.
But androids have a lot of love to give. And you could use a little more these days.
I prefer love the old-fashioned way.

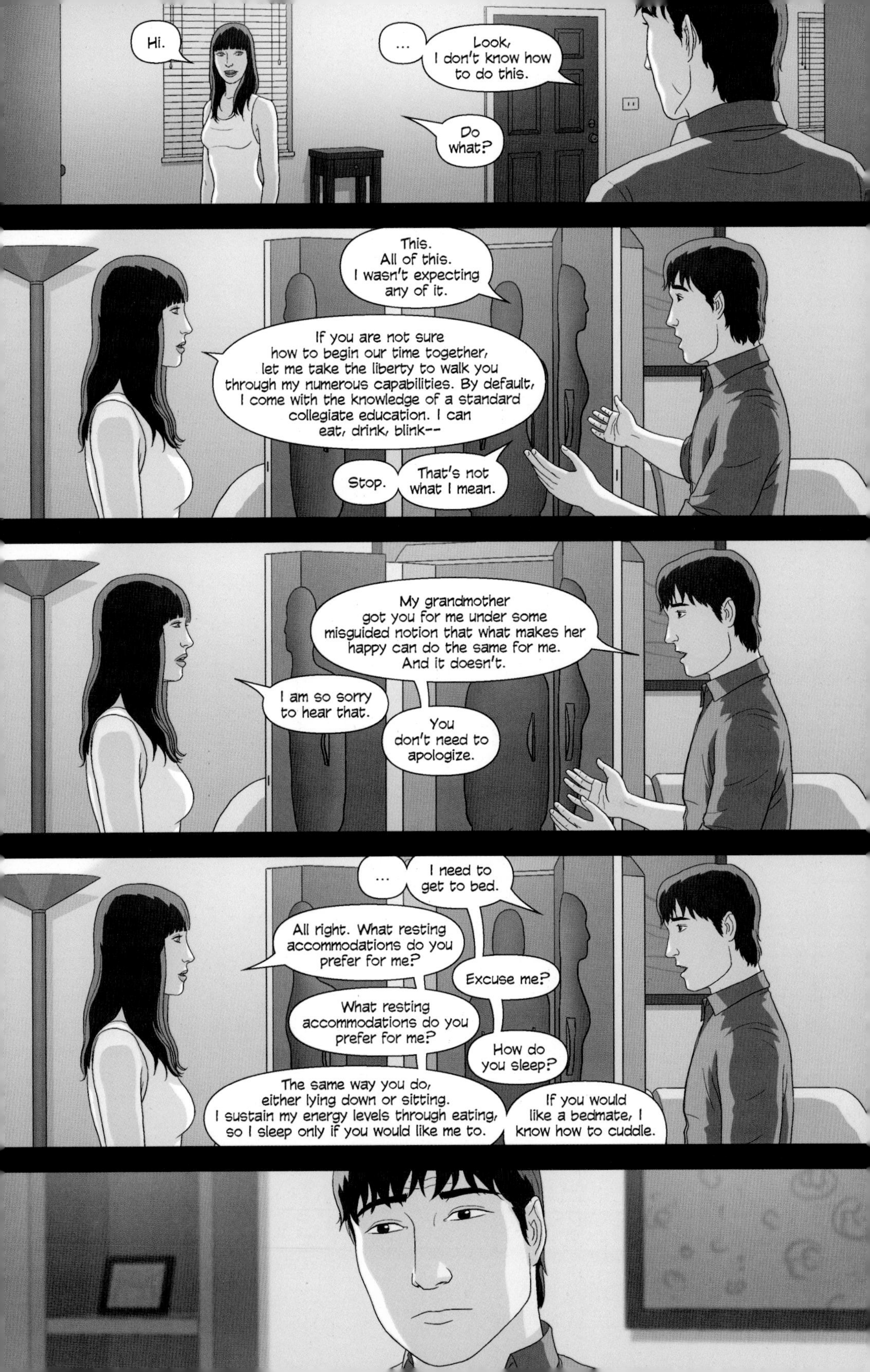
Hi.
...
Look, I don't know how to do this.
Do what?
This. All of this. I wasn't expecting any of it.
If you are not sure how to begin our time together, let me take the liberty to walk you through my numerous capabilities. By default, I come with the knowledge of a standard collegiate education. I can eat, drink, blink--
Stop.
That's not what I mean.
My grandmother got you for me under some misguided notion that what makes her happy can do the same for me. And it doesn't.
I am so sorry to hear that.
You don't need to apologize.
...
I need to get to bed.
All right. What resting accommodations do you prefer for me?
Excuse me?
What resting accommodations do you prefer for me?
How do you sleep?
The same way you do, either lying down or sitting. I sustain my energy levels through eating, so I sleep only if you would like me to.
If you would like a bedmate, I know how to cuddle.

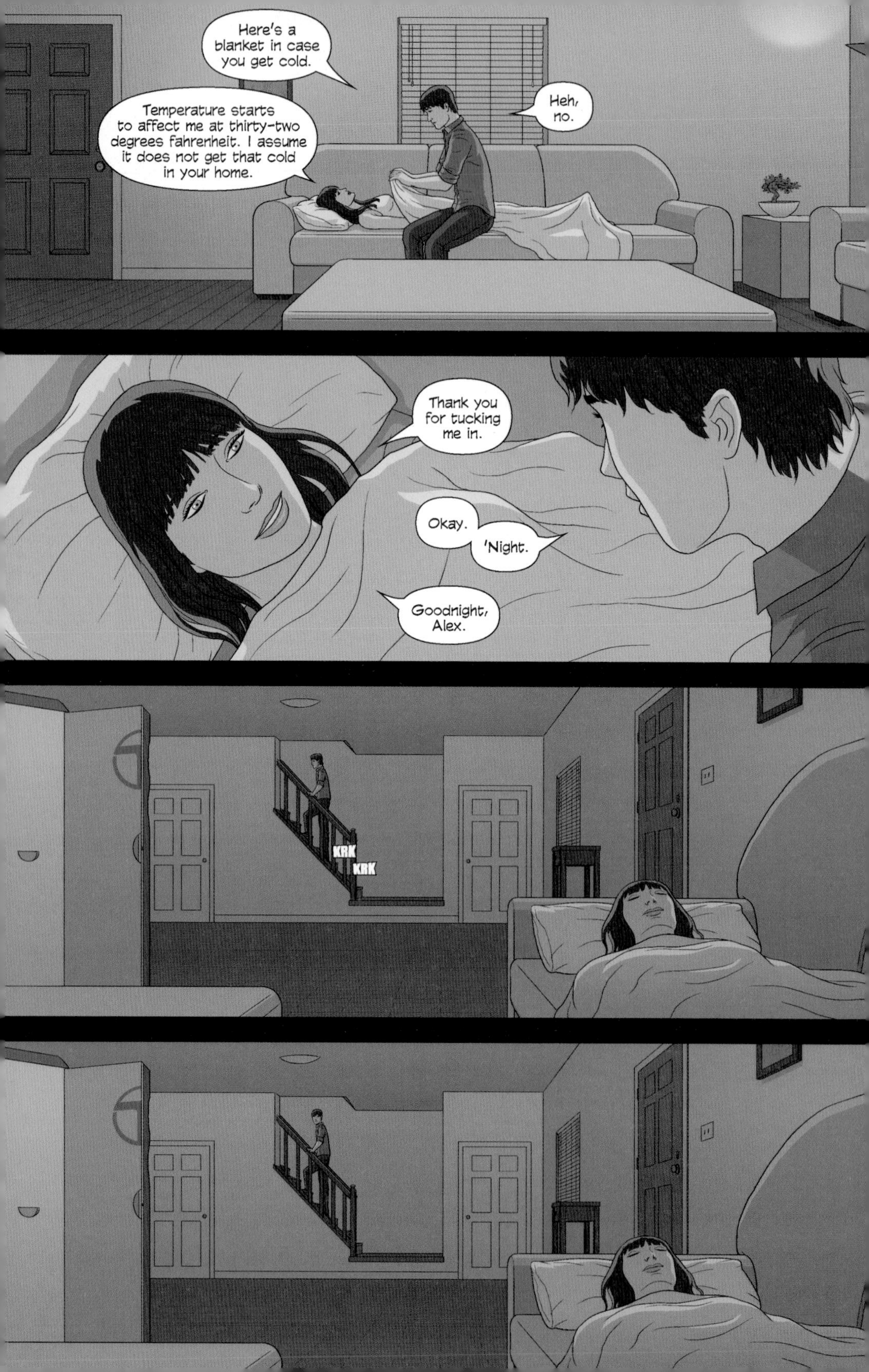

Here's a blanket in case you get cold.
Temperature starts to affect me at thirty-two degrees fahrenheit. I assume it does not get that cold in your home.
Heh, no.
Thank you for tucking me in.
Okay.
'Night.
Goodnight, Alex.
KRK
KRK

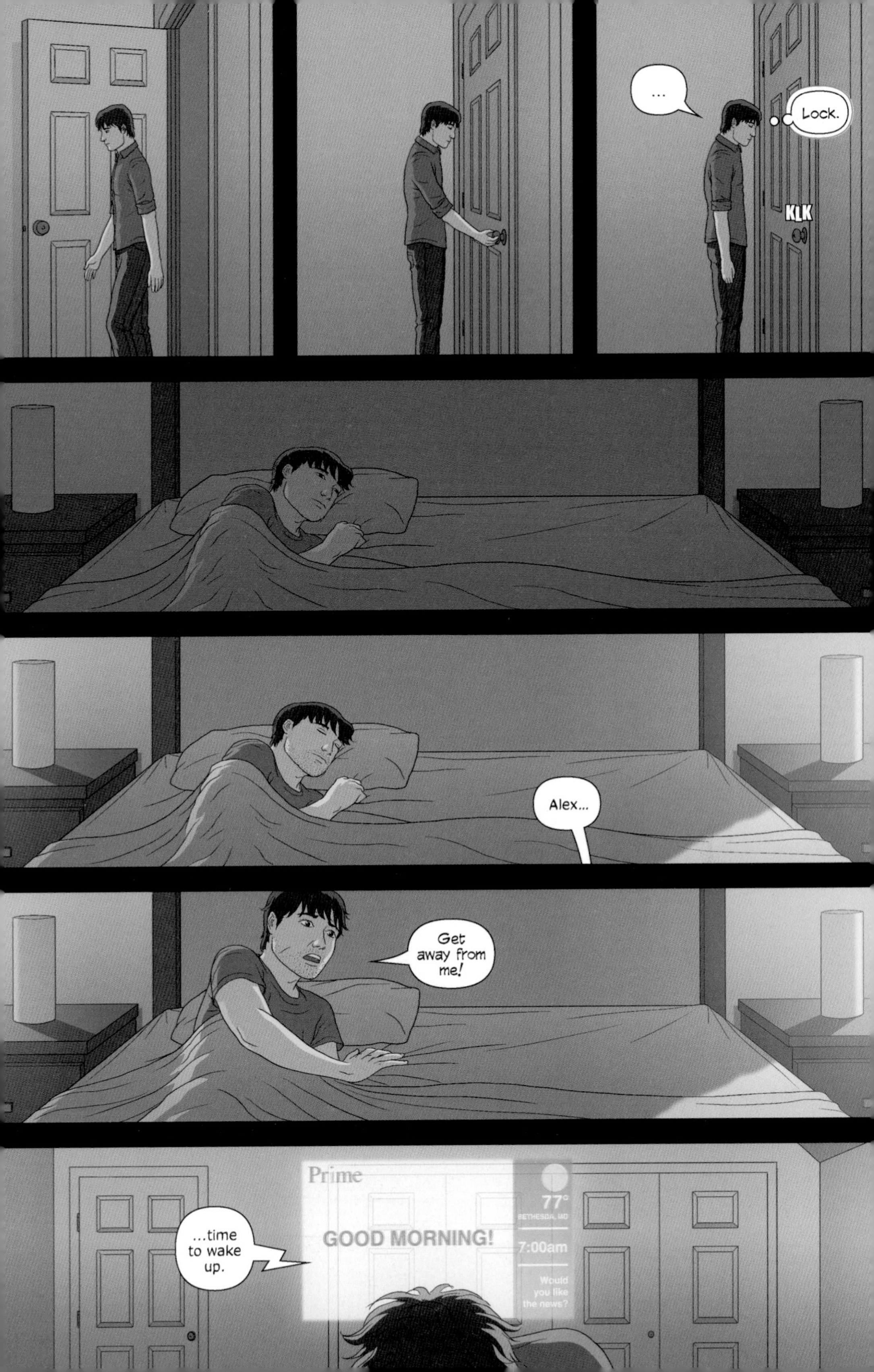
...
Lock.
KLK
Alex...
Get away from me!
Prime
GOOD MORNING!
77°
BETHESDA, MD
7:00am
Would you like the news?
...time to wake up.

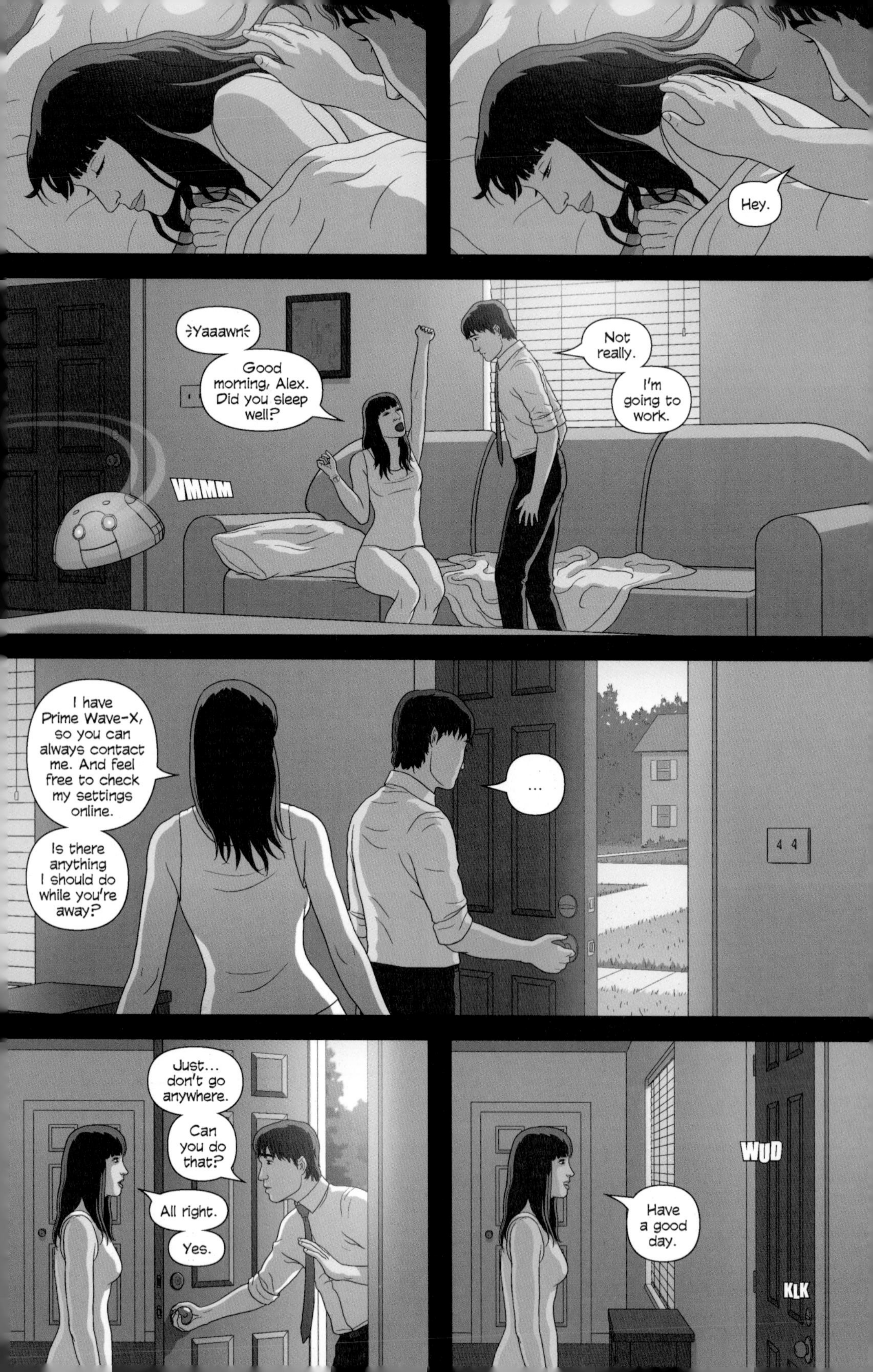

Hey.
Yaaawn
Good morning, Alex. Did you sleep well?
VMMM
Not really.
I'm going to work.
I have Prime Wave-X, so you can always contact me. And feel free to check my settings online.
Is there anything I should do while you're away?
...
Just... don't go anywhere.
Can you do that?
All right.
Yes.
Have a good day.
WUD
KLK

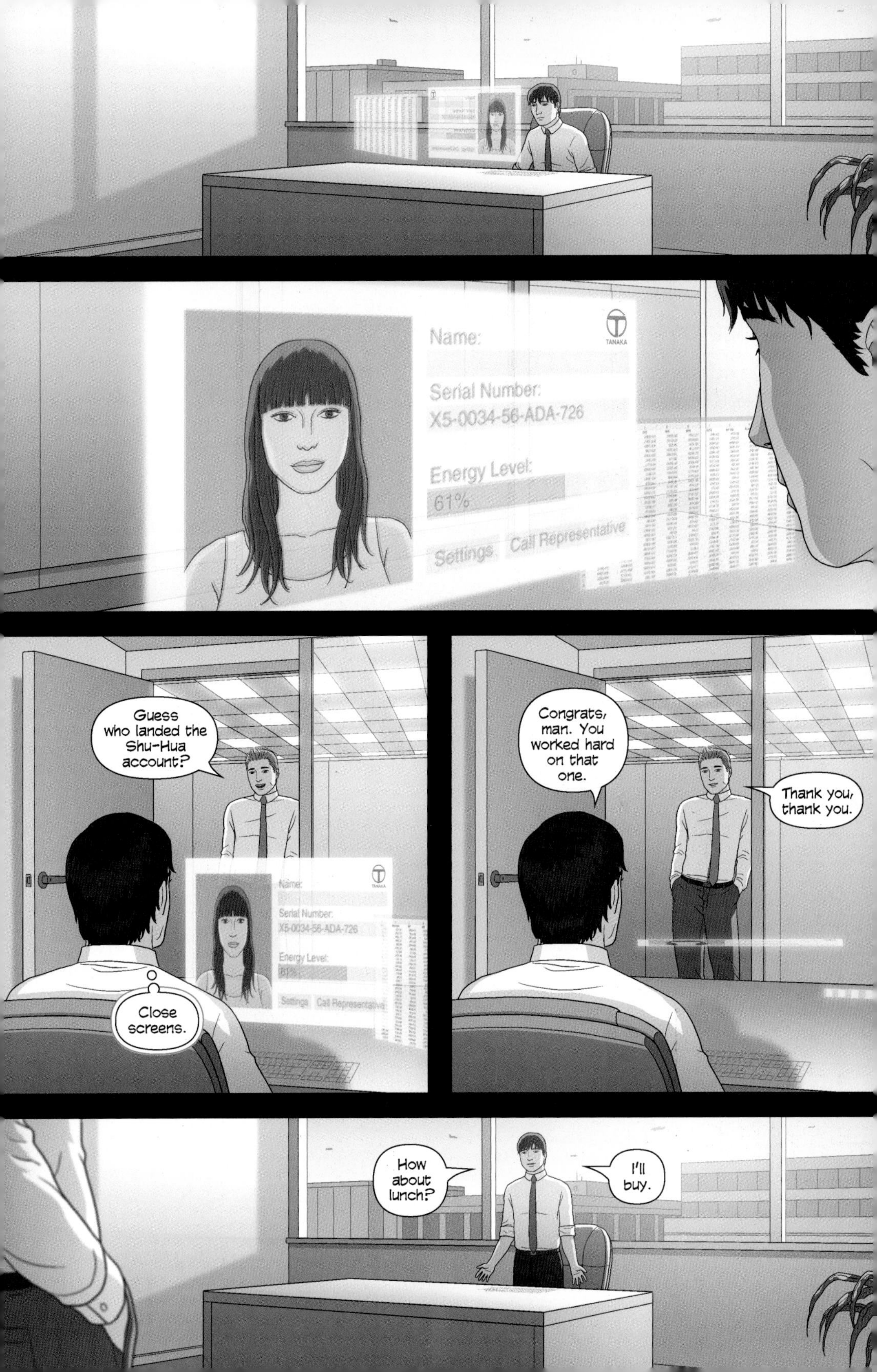

Name:
TANAKA
Serial Number:
X5-0034-56-ADA-726
Energy Level:
61%
Settings
Call Representative
Guess who landed the Shu-Hua account?
Close screens.
Congrats, man. You worked hard on that one.
Thank you, thank you.
How about lunch?
I'll buy.

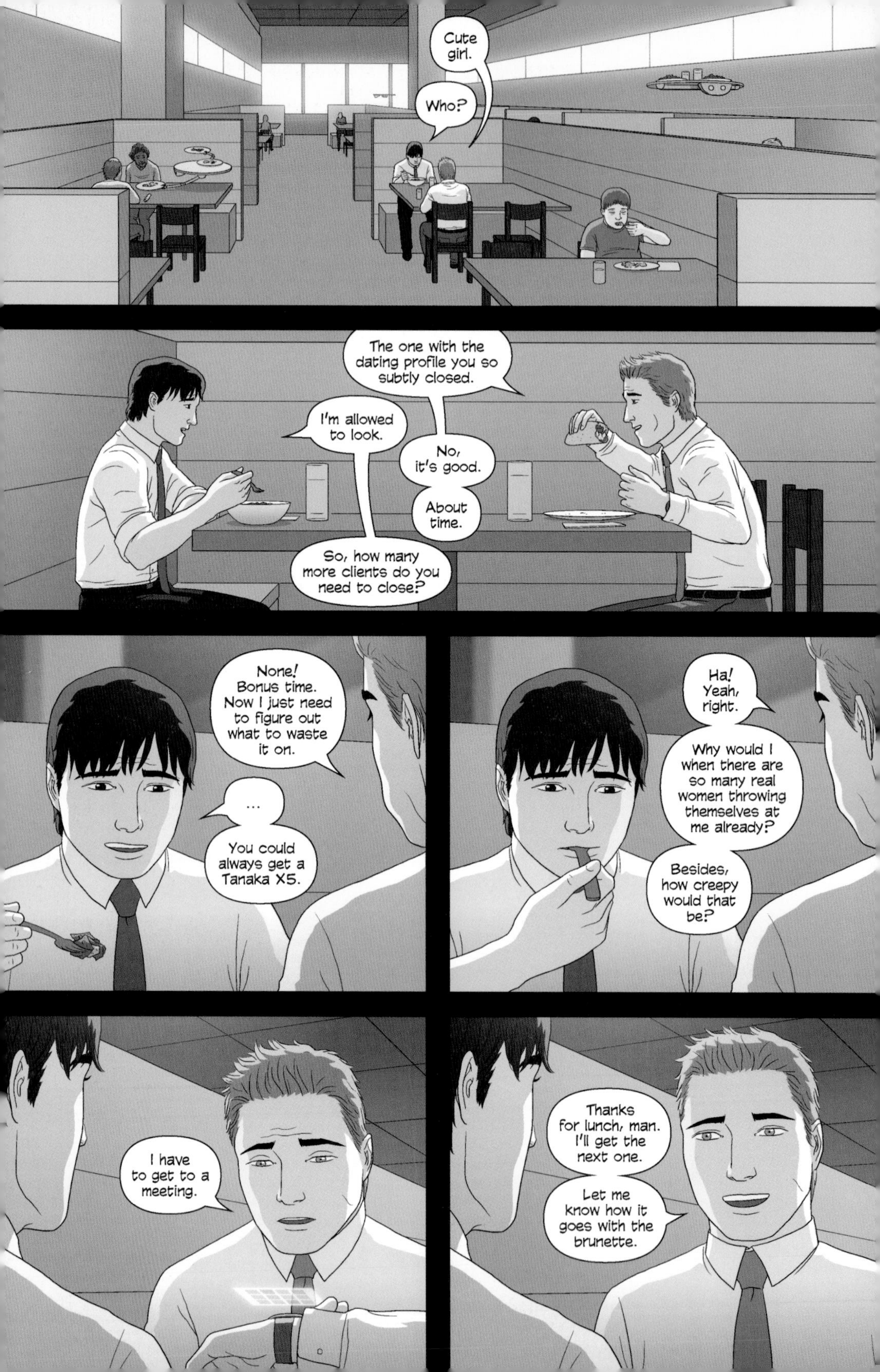
Cute girl.
Who?
The one with the dating profile you so subtly closed.
I'm allowed to look.
No, it's good.
About time.
So, how many more clients do you need to close?
None! Bonus time. Now I just need to figure out what to waste it on.
...
You could always get a Tanaka X5.
Ha! Yeah, right.
Why would I when there are so many real women throwing themselves at me already?
Besides, how creepy would that be?
I have to get to a meeting.
Thanks for lunch, man. I'll get the next one.
Let me know how it goes with the brunette.

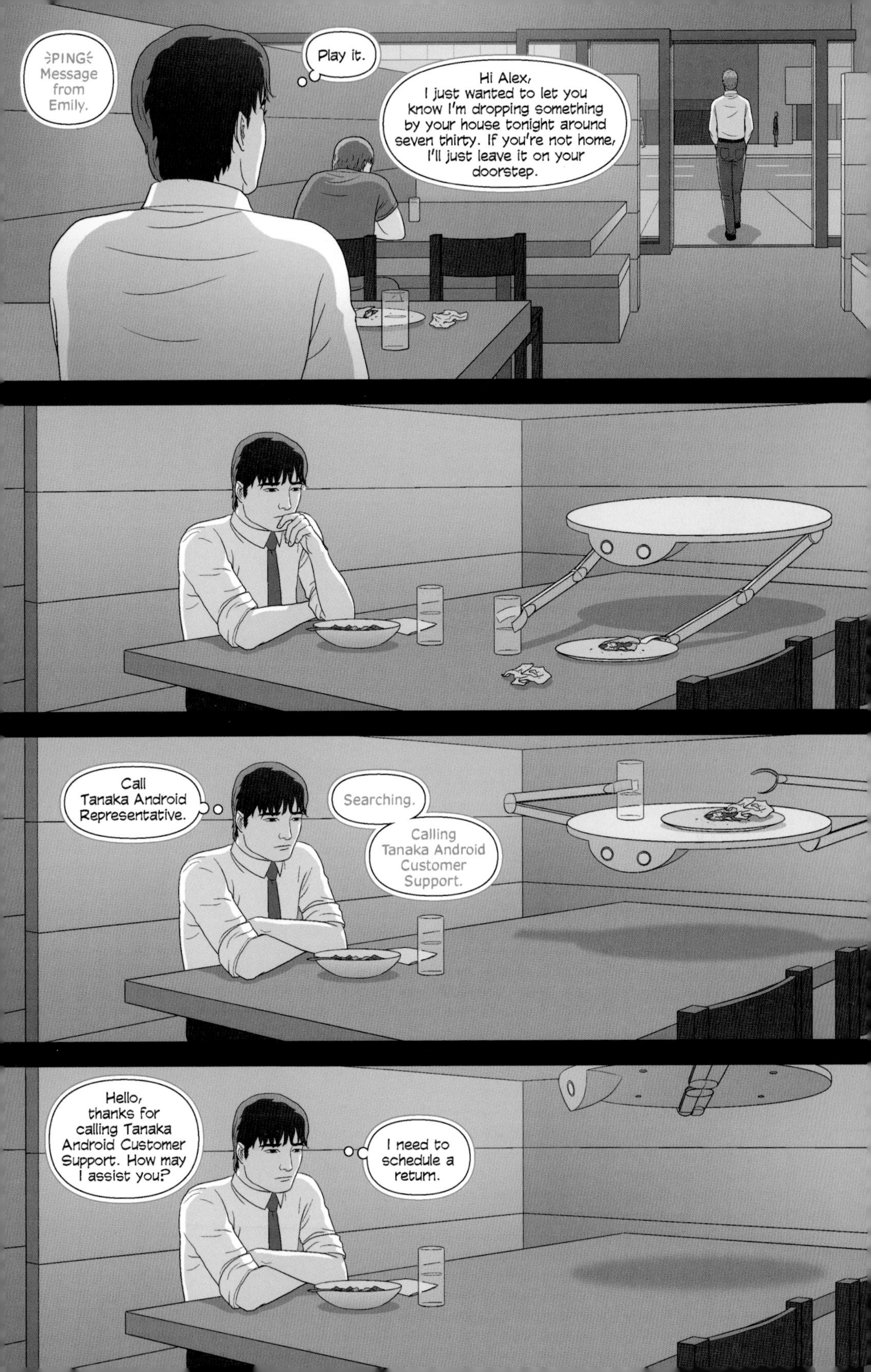
PING
Message from Emily.
Play it.
Hi Alex,
I just wanted to let you know I'm dropping something by your house tonight around seven thirty. If you're not home, I'll just leave it on your doorstep.
Call Tanaka Android Representative.
Searching.
Calling Tanaka Android Customer Support.
Hello, thanks for calling Tanaka Android Customer Support. How may I assist you?
I need to schedule a return.

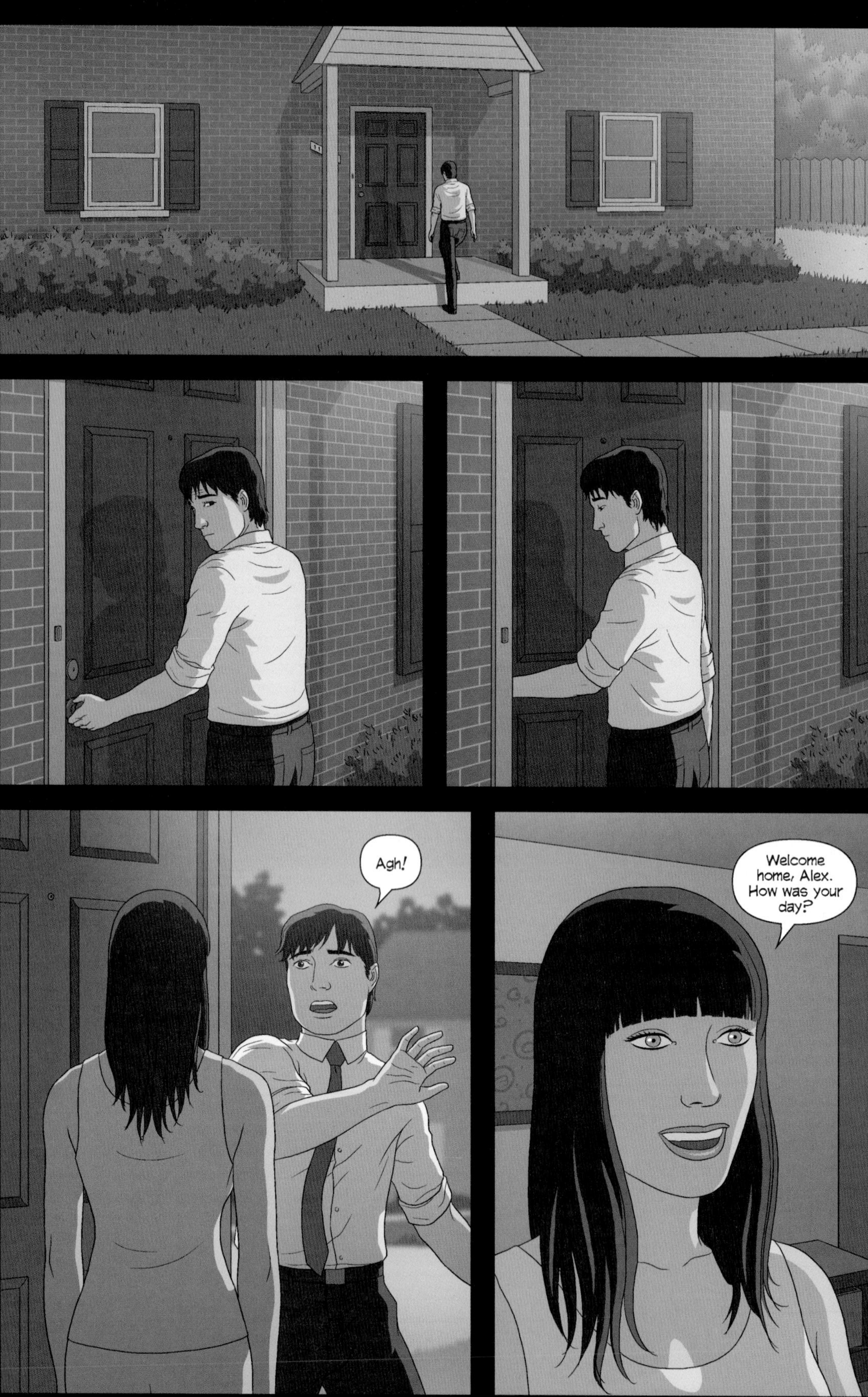
Agh!
Welcome home, Alex. How was your day?

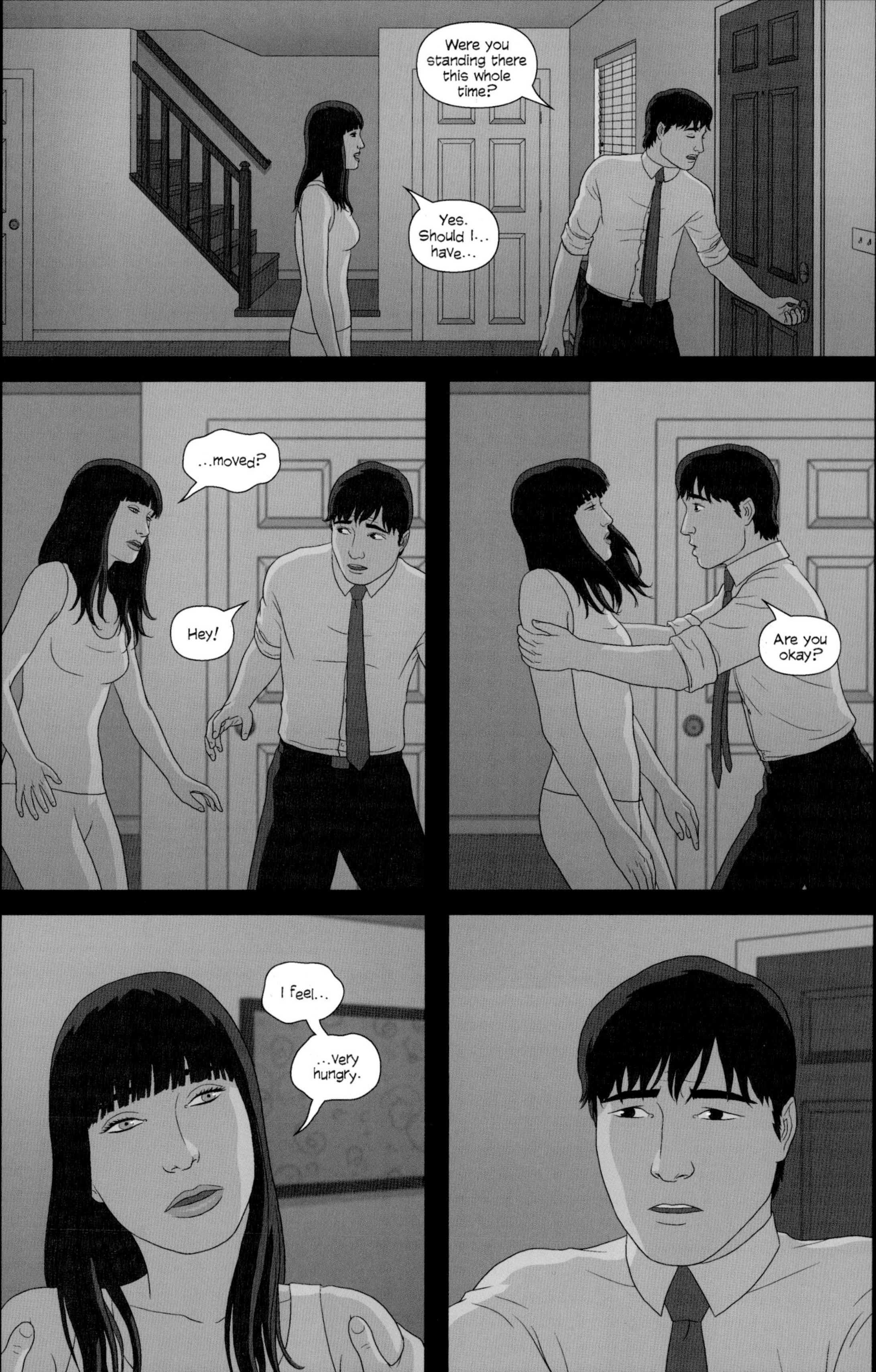
Were you standing there this whole time?
Yes. Should I... have...
...moved?
Hey!
Are you okay?
I feel...
...very hungry.

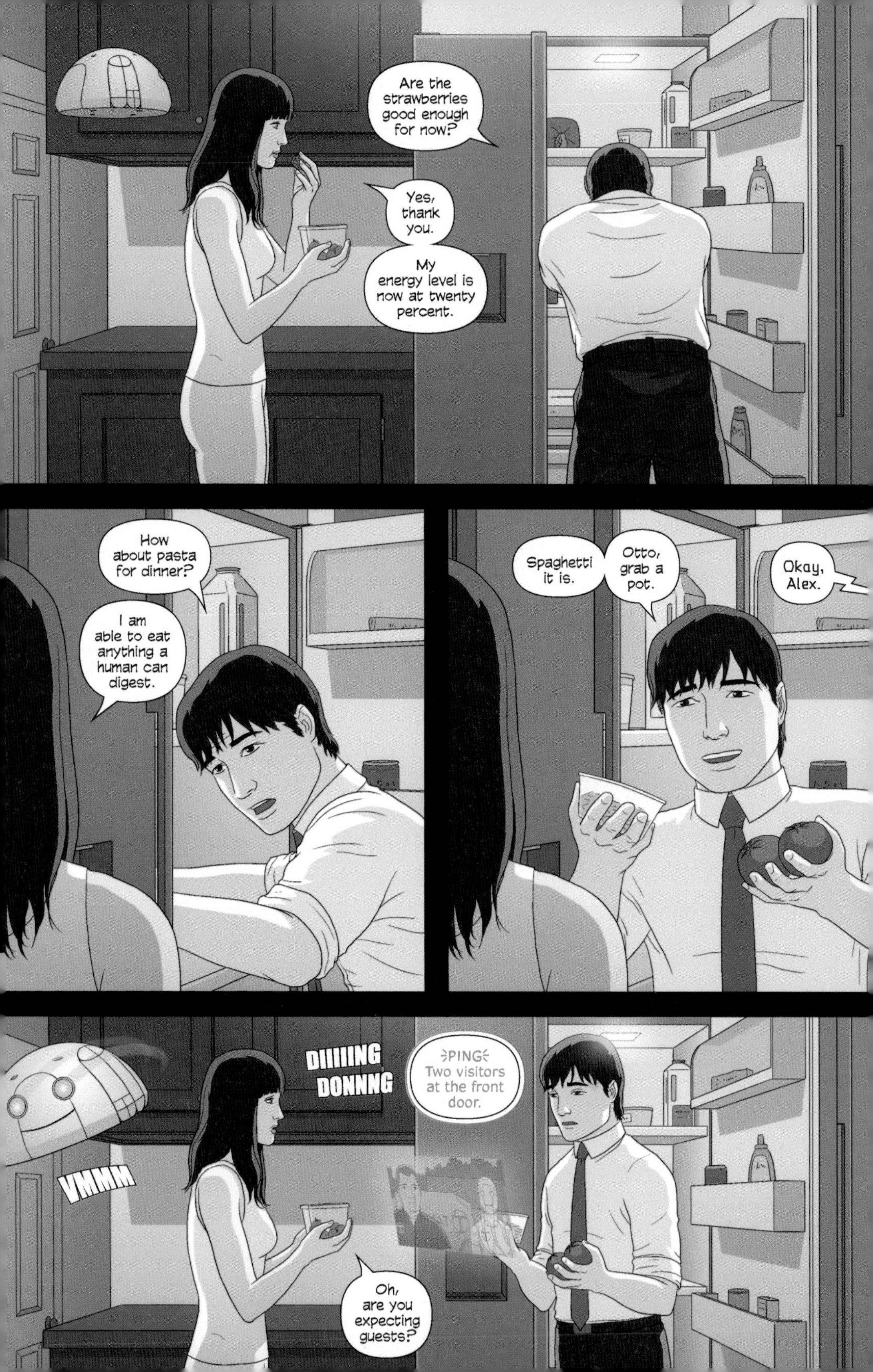
Are the strawberries good enough for now?
Yes, thank you.
My energy level is now at twenty percent.
How about pasta for dinner?
I am able to eat anything a human can digest.
Spaghetti it is.
Otto, grab a pot.
Okay, Alex.
DIIIIING DONNNG
VMMM
⋟PING⋞ Two visitors at the front door.
Oh, are you expecting guests?

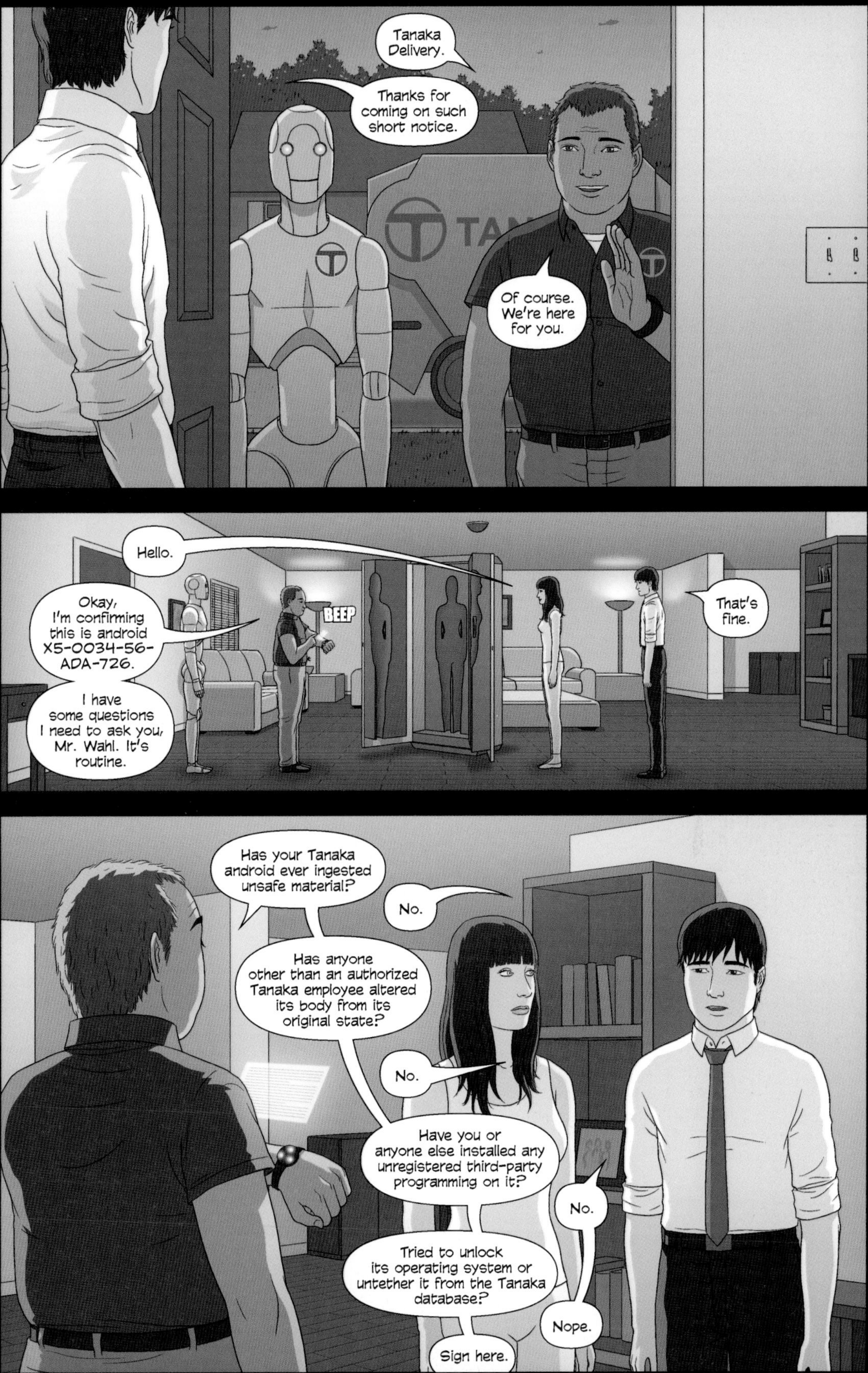

Tanaka Delivery.
Thanks for coming on such short notice.
Of course. We're here for you.
Hello.
Okay, I'm confirming this is android X5-0034-56-ADA-726.
BEEP
I have some questions I need to ask you, Mr. Wahl. It's routine.
That's fine.
Has your Tanaka android ever ingested unsafe material?
No.
Has anyone other than an authorized Tanaka employee altered its body from its original state?
No.
Have you or anyone else installed any unregistered third-party programming on it?
No.
Tried to unlock its operating system or untether it from the Tanaka database?
Nope.
Sign here.

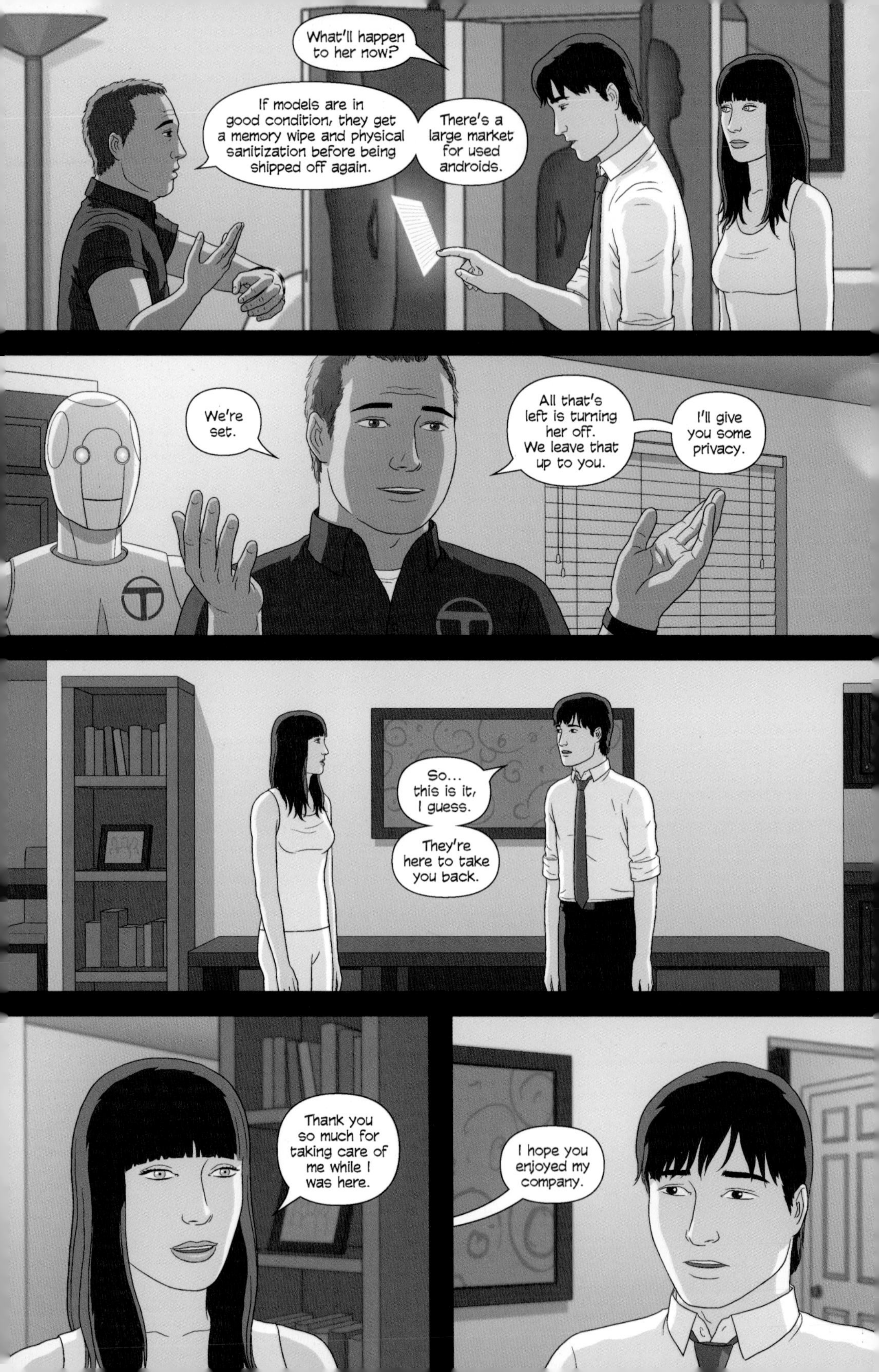
What'll happen to her now?
If models are in good condition, they get a memory wipe and physical sanitization before being shipped off again.
There's a large market for used androids.
We're set.
All that's left is turning her off. We leave that up to you.
I'll give you some privacy.
So... this is it, I guess.
They're here to take you back.
Thank you so much for taking care of me while I was here.
I hope you enjoyed my company.

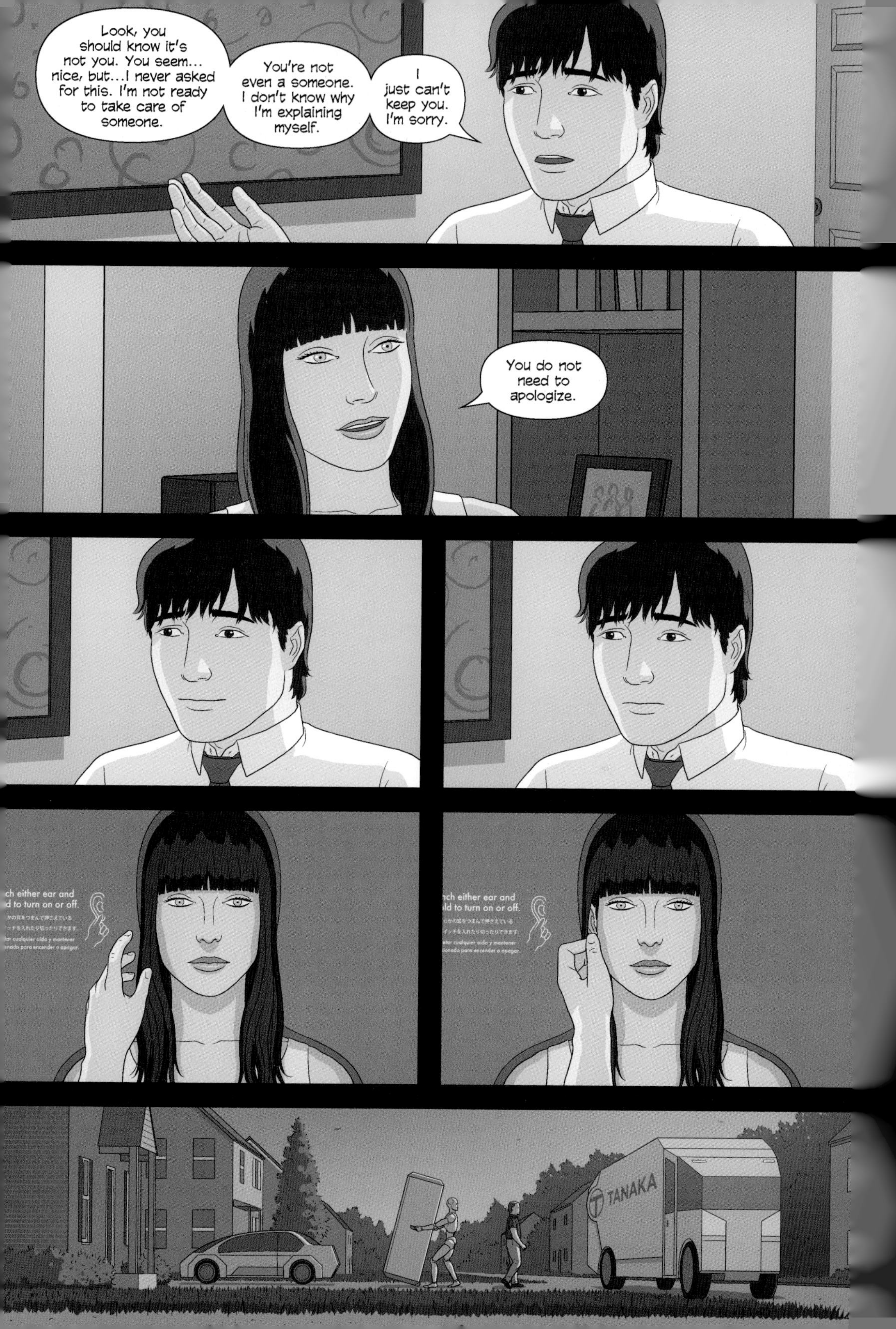
Look, you should know it's not you. You seem... nice, but...I never asked for this. I'm not ready to take care of someone.
You're not even a someone. I don't know why I'm explaining myself.
I just can't keep you. I'm sorry.
You do not need to apologize.
TANAKA

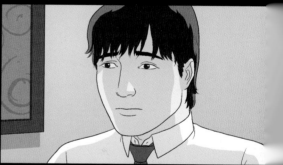

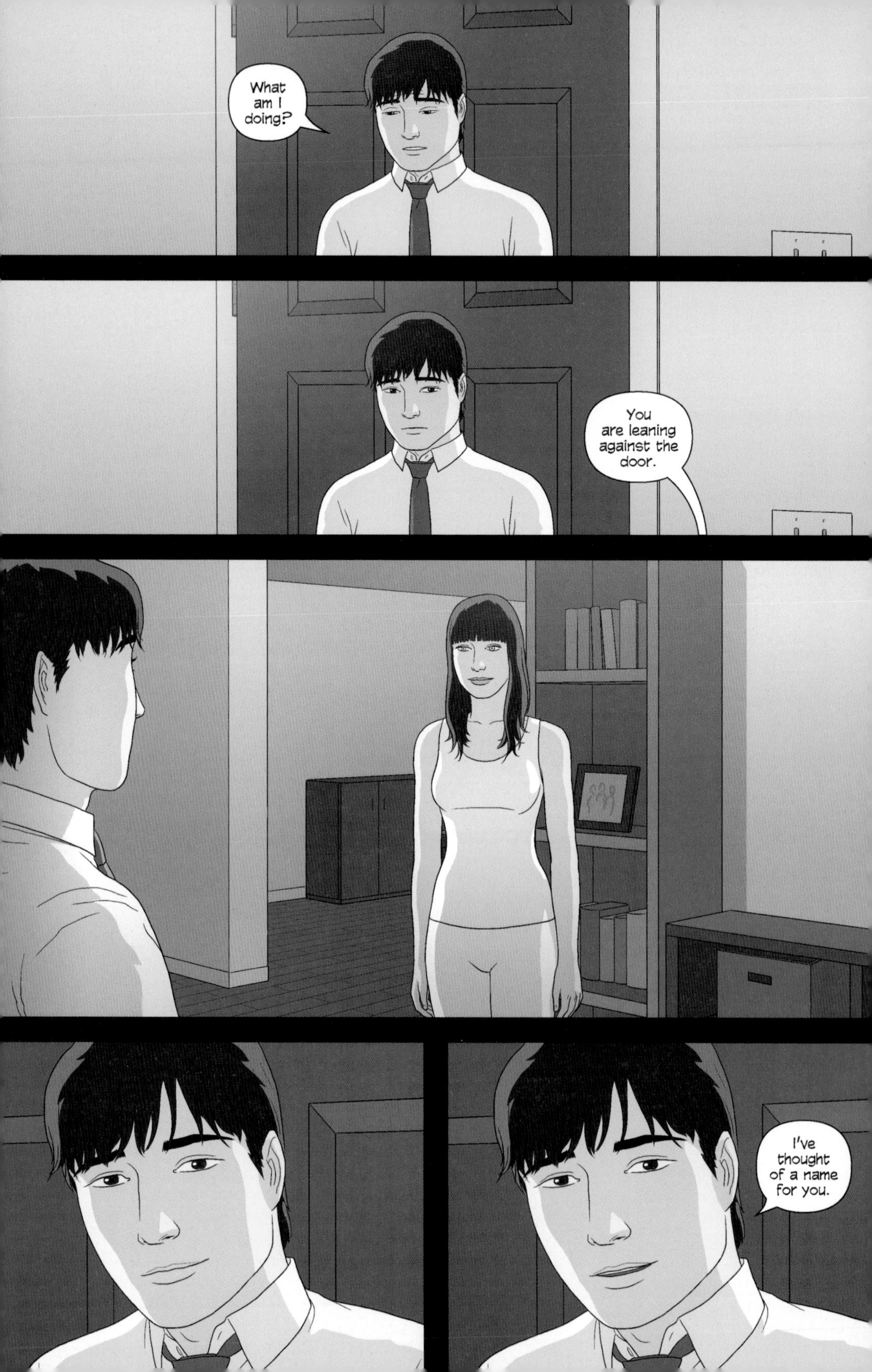
What am I doing?
You are leaning against the door.
I've thought of a name for you.

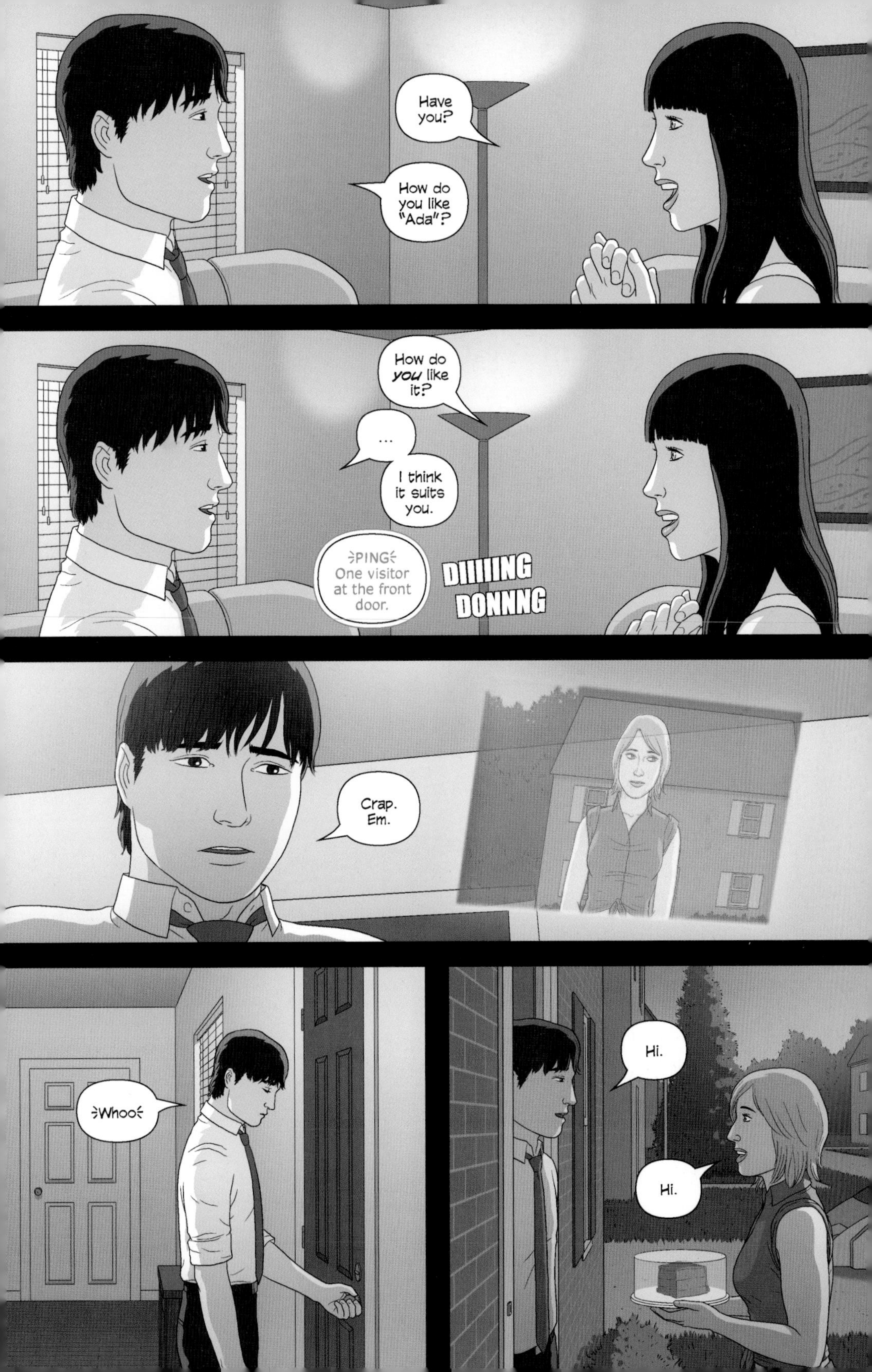

Have you?
How do you like "Ada"?
How do *you* like it?
...
I think it suits you.
PING
One visitor at the front door.
DIIIIING DONNNG
Crap. Em.
Whoo
Hi.
Hi.

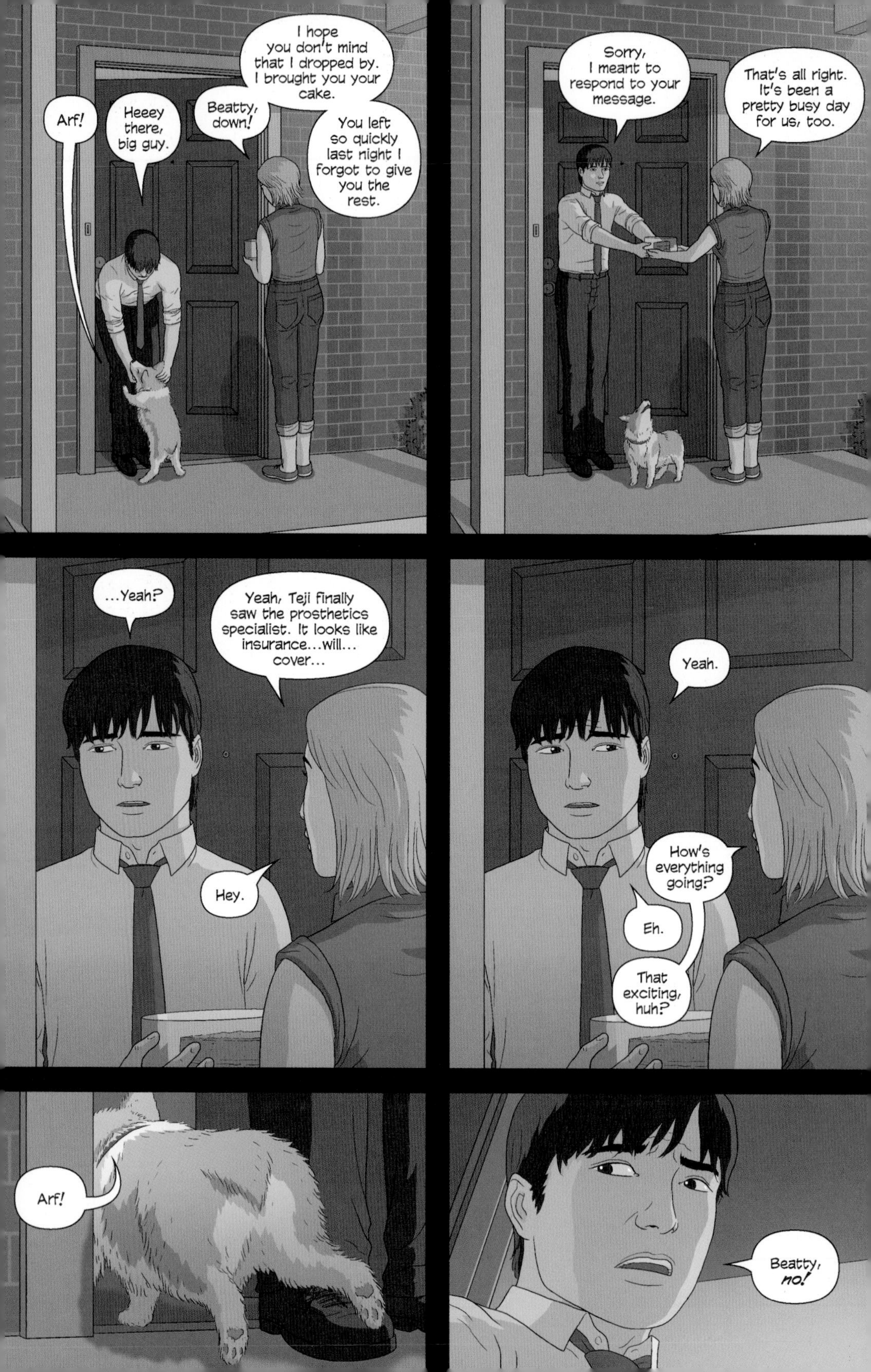
Arf!
Heeey there, big guy.
Beatty, down!
I hope you don't mind that I dropped by. I brought you your cake.
You left so quickly last night I forgot to give you the rest.
Sorry, I meant to respond to your message.
That's all right. It's been a pretty busy day for us, too.
...Yeah?
Yeah, Teji finally saw the prosthetics specialist. It looks like insurance...will... cover...
Hey.
Yeah.
How's everything going?
Eh.
That exciting, huh?
Arf!
Beatty, no!

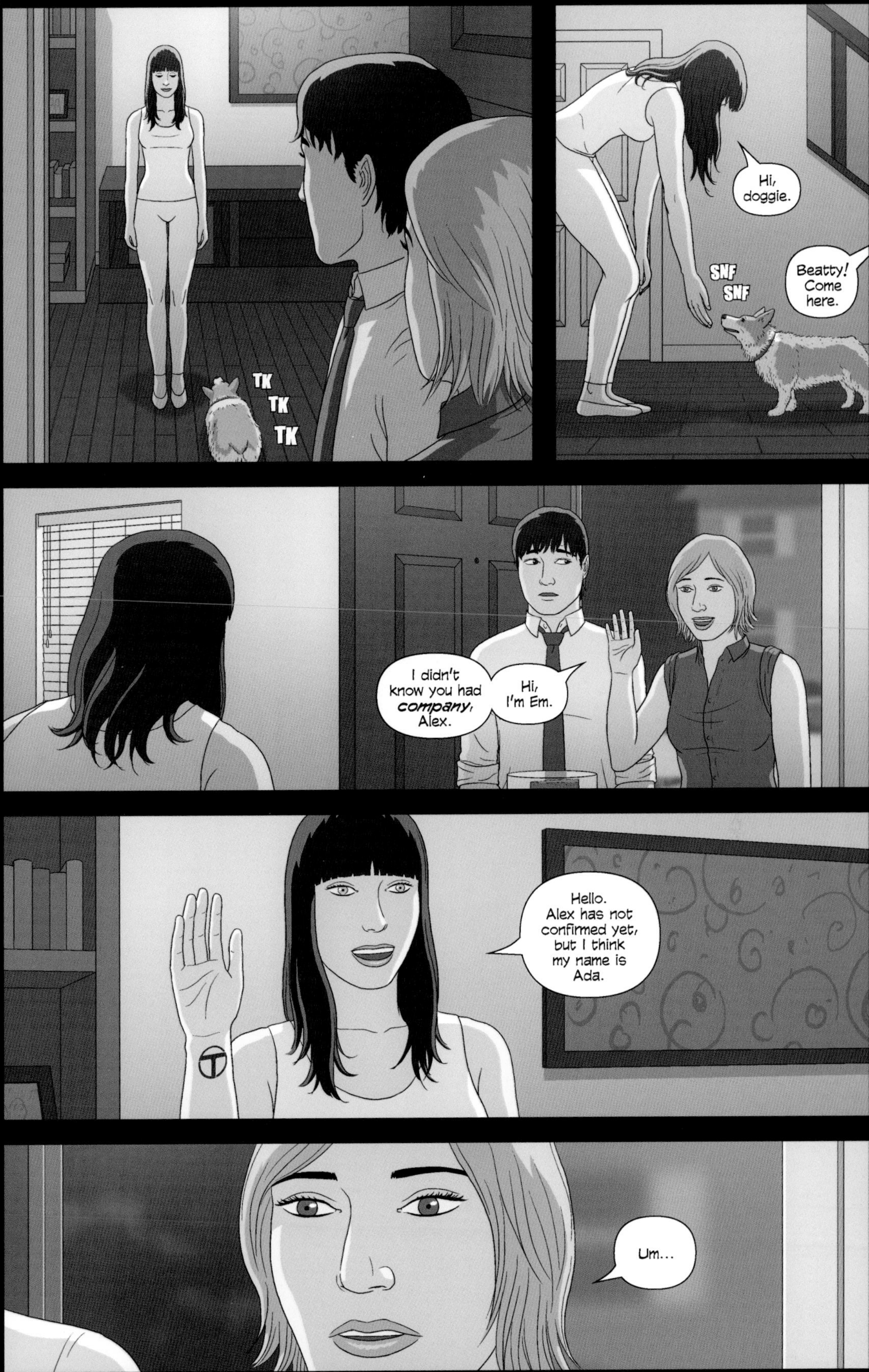
TK
TK
TK
Hi, doggie.
SNF
SNF
Beatty! Come here.
I didn't know you had *company*, Alex.
Hi, I'm Em.
Hello. Alex has not confirmed yet, but I think my name is Ada.
Um...

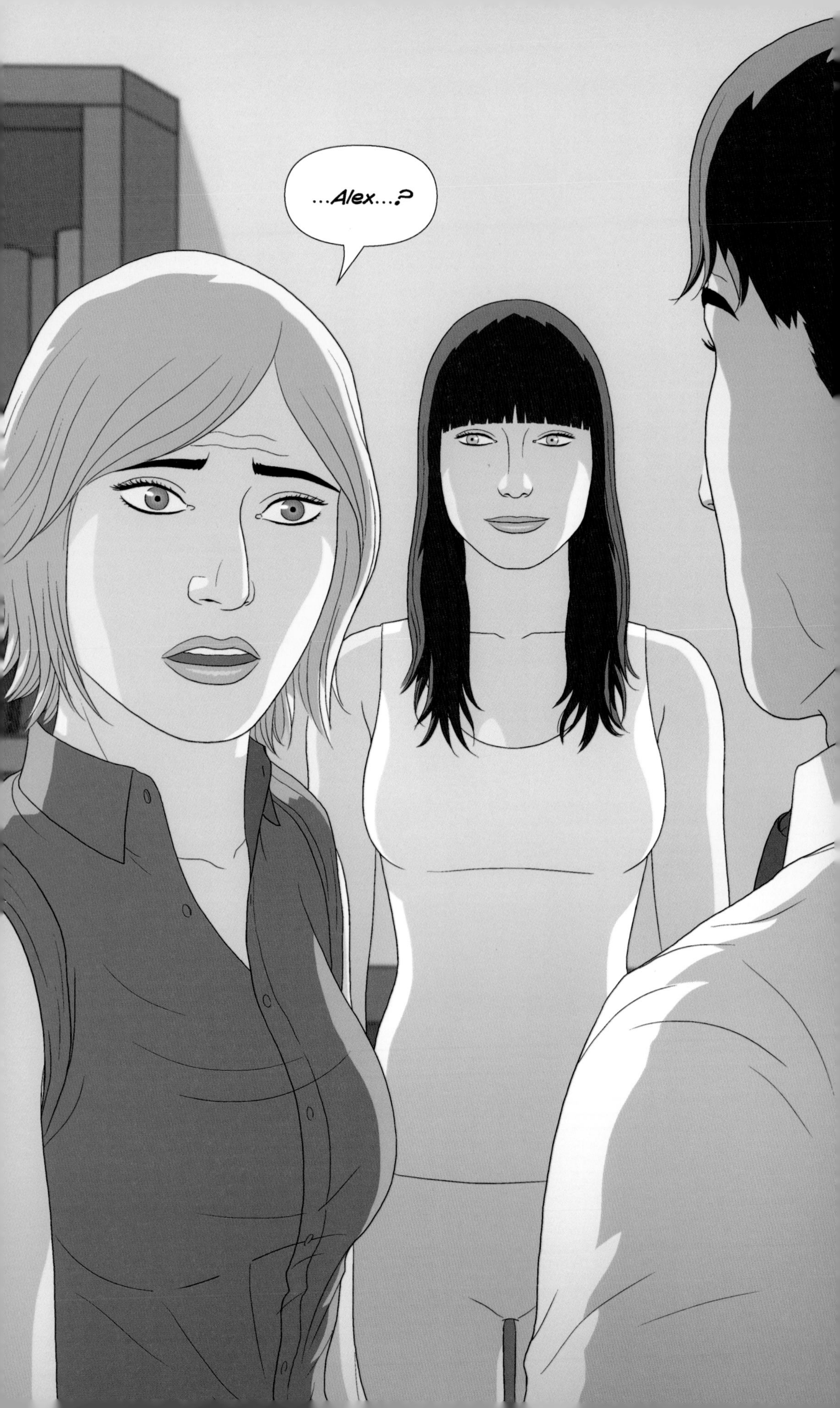
...Alex...?

3

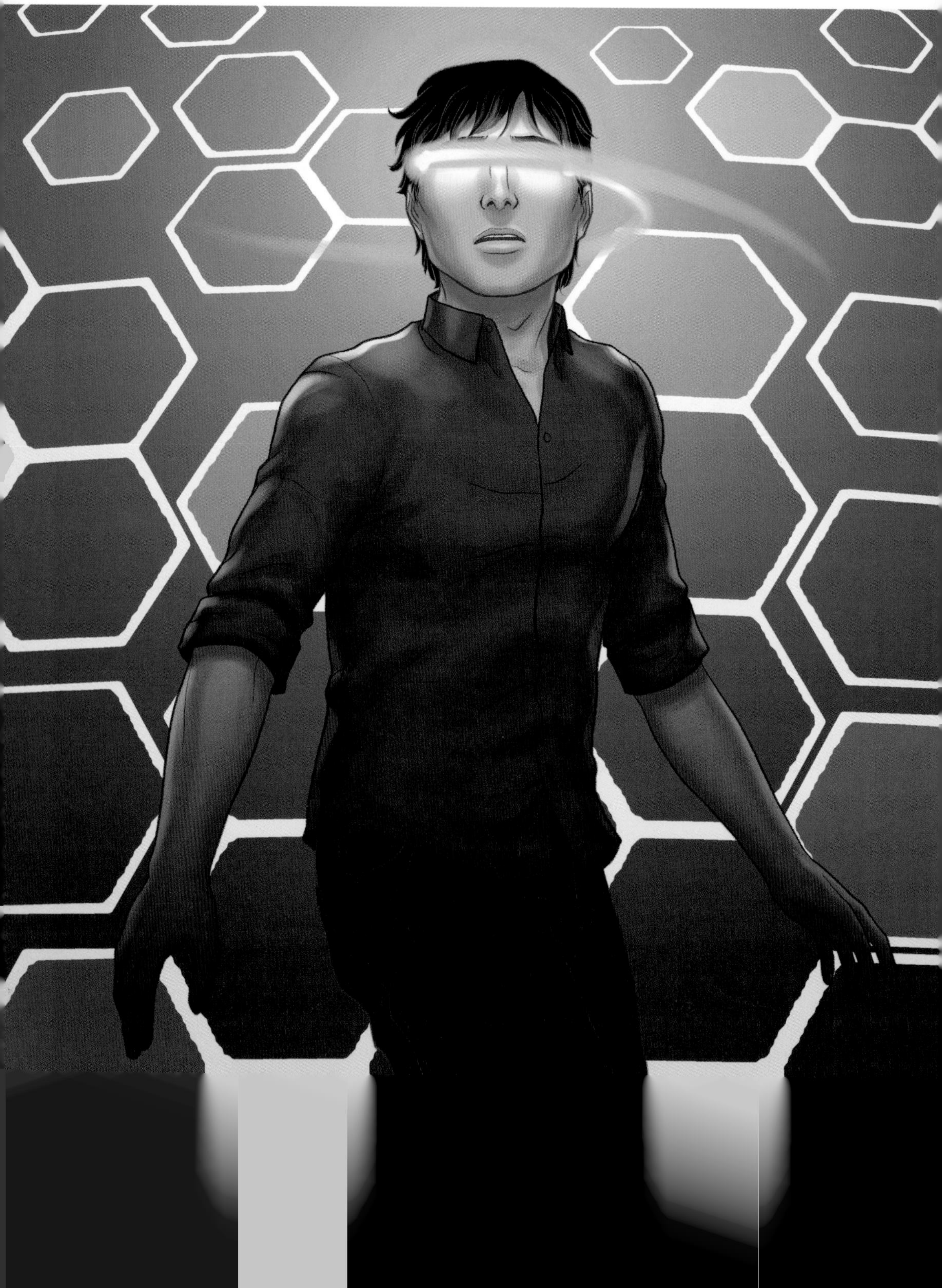

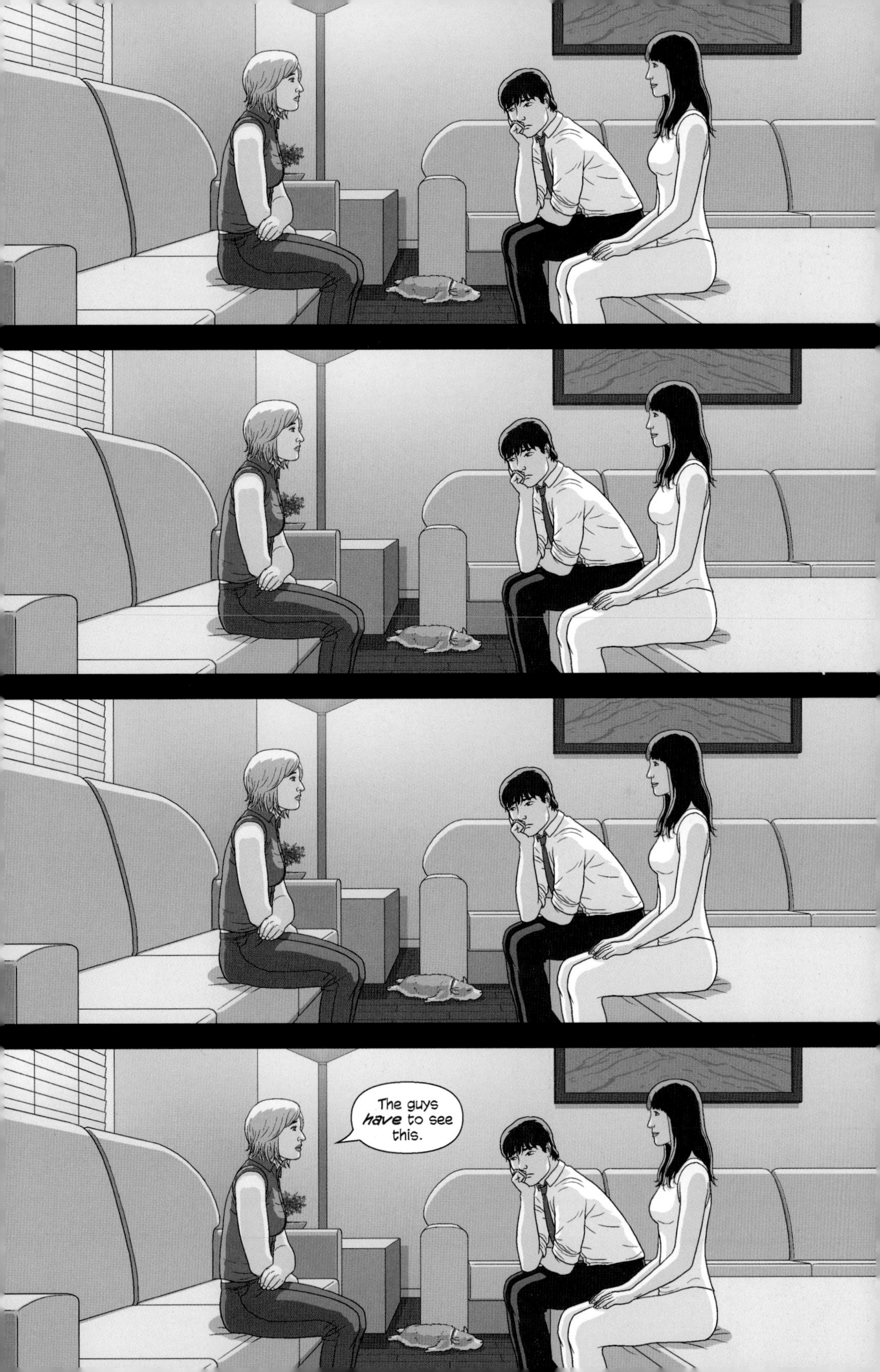
The guys *have* to see this.

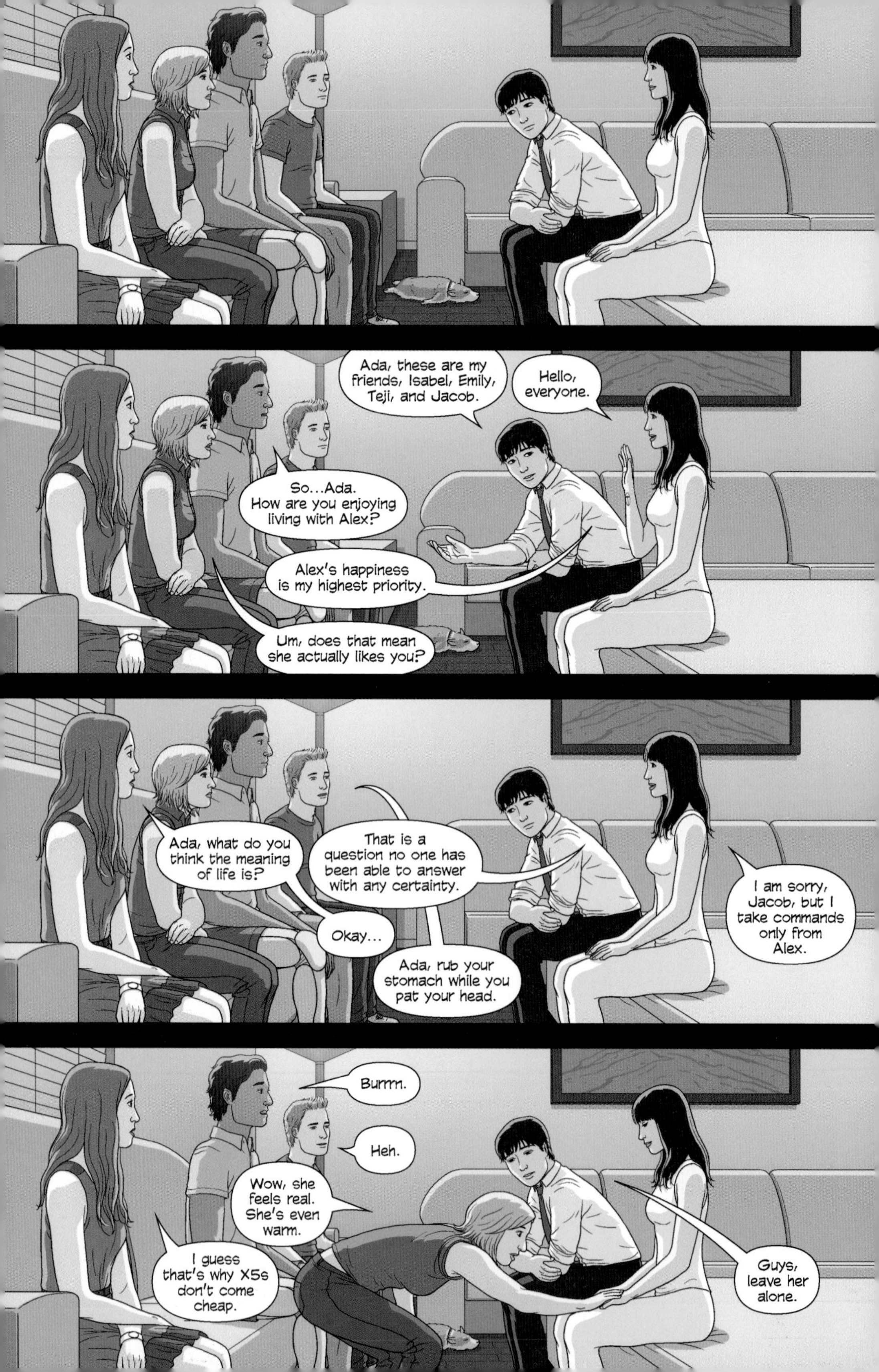
Ada, these are my friends, Isabel, Emily, Teji, and Jacob.
Hello, everyone.
So...Ada. How are you enjoying living with Alex?
Alex's happiness is my highest priority.
Um, does that mean she actually likes you?
Ada, what do you think the meaning of life is?
That is a question no one has been able to answer with any certainty.
Okay...
Ada, rub your stomach while you pat your head.
I am sorry, Jacob, but I take commands only from Alex.
Burrrn.
Heh.
Wow, she feels real. She's even warm.
I guess that's why X5s don't come cheap.
Guys, leave her alone.

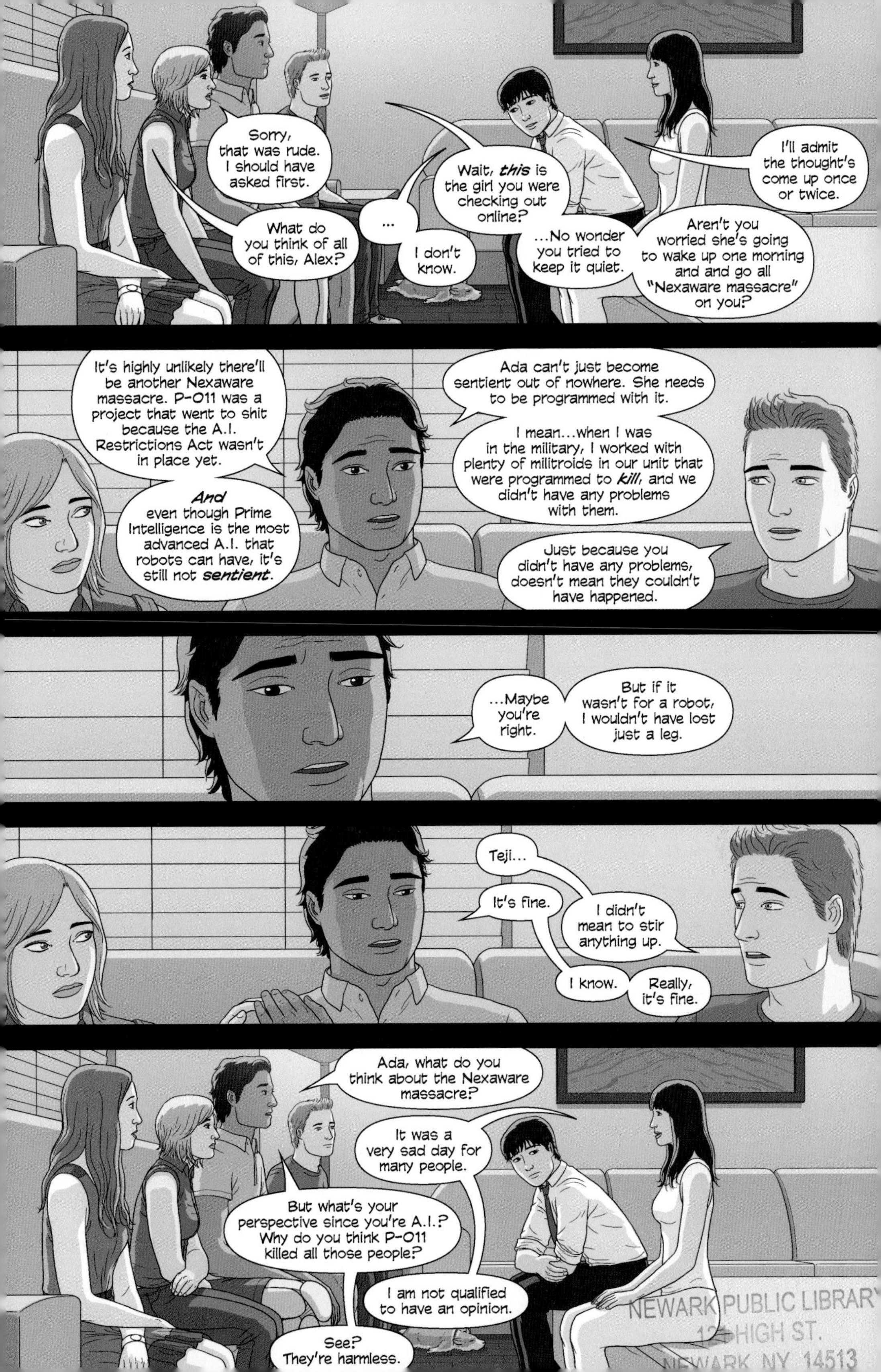
Sorry, that was rude. I should have asked first.
What do you think of all of this, Alex?
...
I don't know.
Wait, this is the girl you were checking out online?
...No wonder you tried to keep it quiet.
I'll admit the thought's come up once or twice.
Aren't you worried she's going to wake up one morning and and go all "Nexaware massacre" on you?
It's highly unlikely there'll be another Nexaware massacre. P-O11 was a project that went to shit because the A.I. Restrictions Act wasn't in place yet.
And even though Prime Intelligence is the most advanced A.I. that robots can have, it's still not sentient.
Ada can't just become sentient out of nowhere. She needs to be programmed with it.
I mean...when I was in the military, I worked with plenty of militroids in our unit that were programmed to kill, and we didn't have any problems with them.
Just because you didn't have any problems, doesn't mean they couldn't have happened.
...Maybe you're right.
But if it wasn't for a robot, I wouldn't have lost just a leg.
Teji...
It's fine.
I didn't mean to stir anything up.
I know.
Really, it's fine.
Ada, what do you think about the Nexaware massacre?
It was a very sad day for many people.
But what's your perspective since you're A.I.? Why do you think P-O11 killed all those people?
I am not qualified to have an opinion.
See? They're harmless.

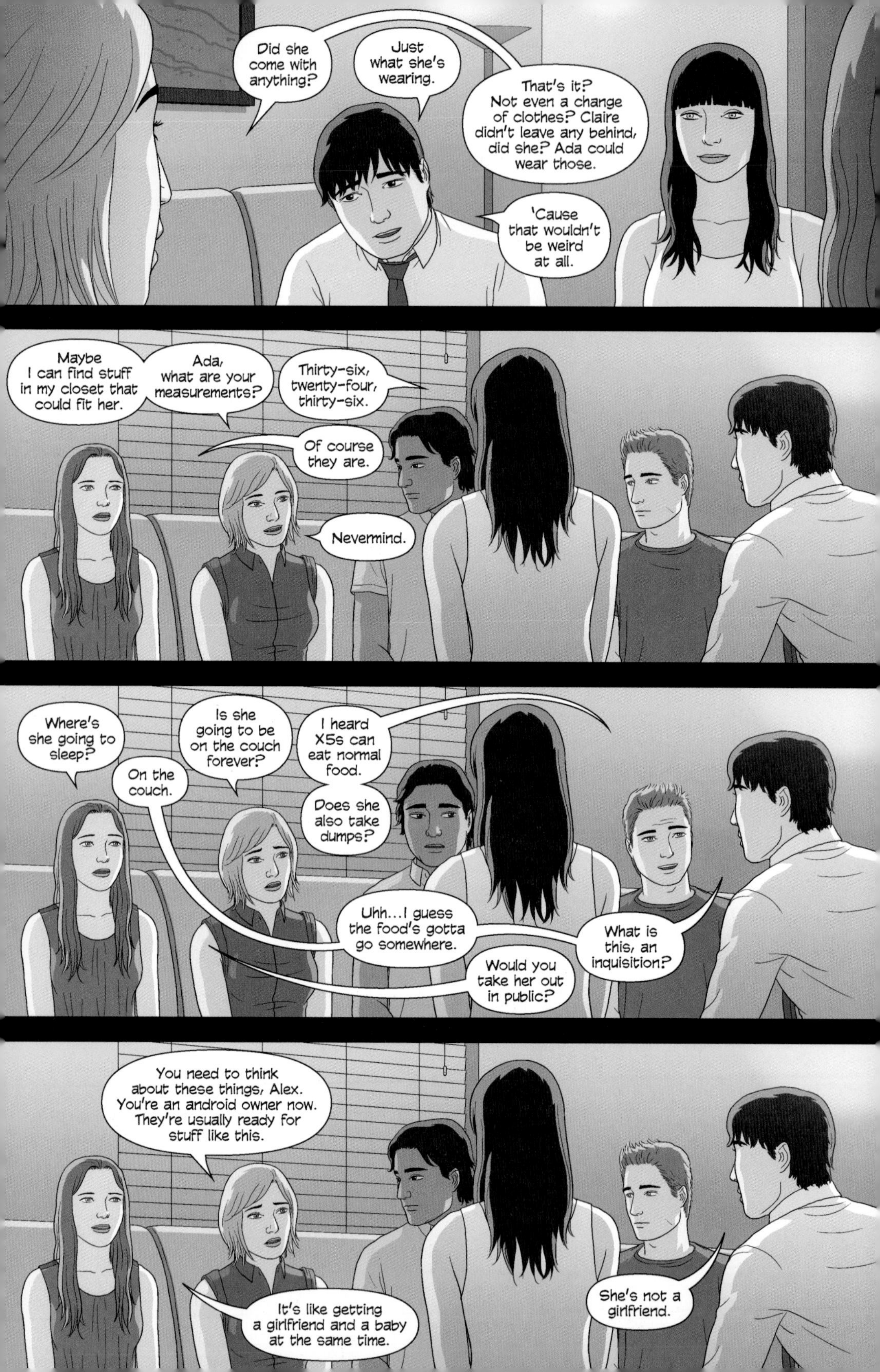
Did she come with anything?
Just what she's wearing.
That's it? Not even a change of clothes? Claire didn't leave any behind, did she? Ada could wear those.
'Cause that wouldn't be weird at all.
Maybe I can find stuff in my closet that could fit her.
Ada, what are your measurements?
Thirty-six, twenty-four, thirty-six.
Of course they are.
Nevermind.
Where's she going to sleep?
On the couch.
Is she going to be on the couch forever?
I heard X5s can eat normal food.
Does she also take dumps?
Uhh...I guess the food's gotta go somewhere.
What is this, an inquisition?
Would you take her out in public?
You need to think about these things, Alex. You're an android owner now. They're usually ready for stuff like this.
It's like getting a girlfriend and a baby at the same time.
She's not a girlfriend.

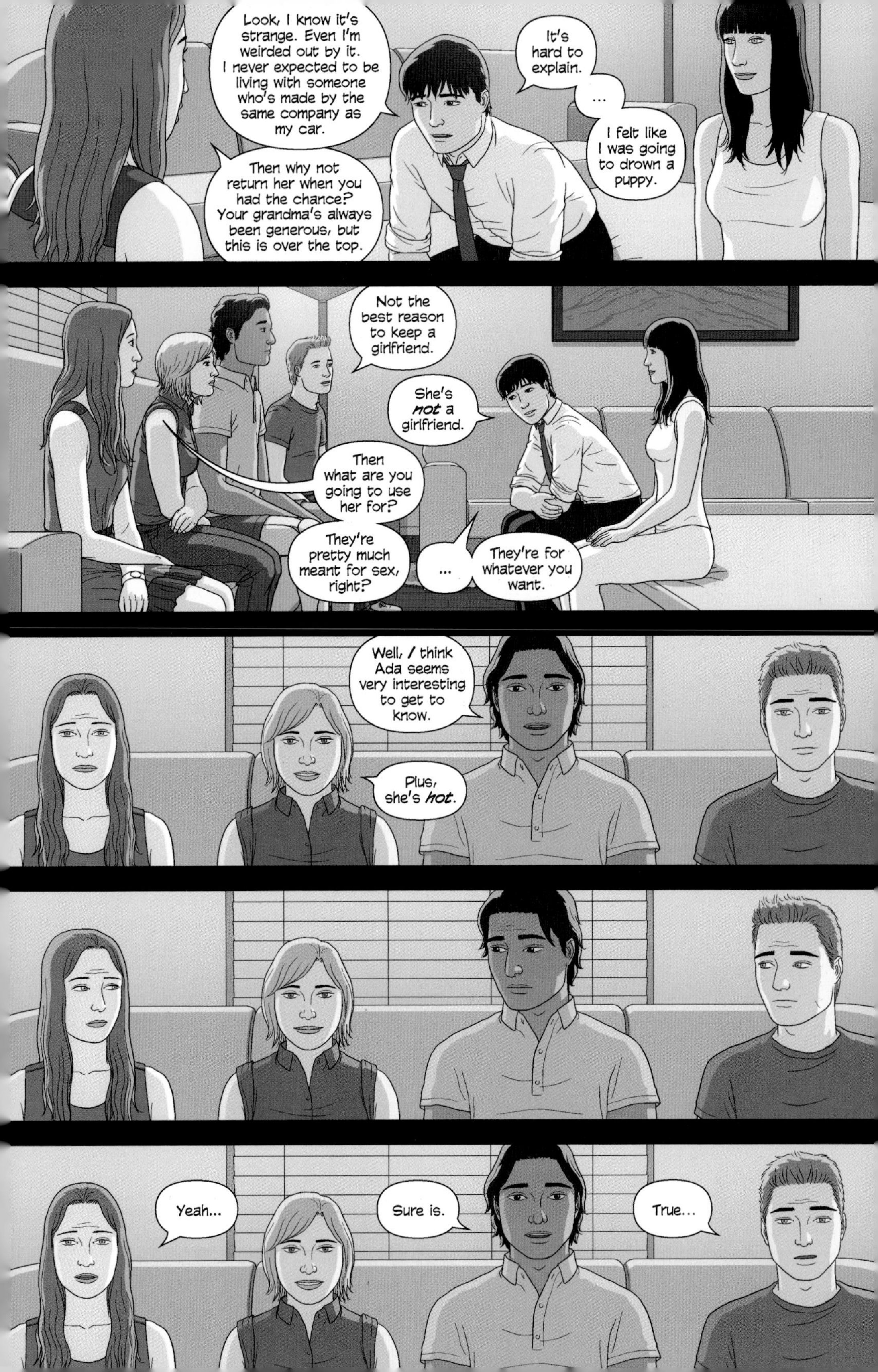
Look, I know it's strange. Even I'm weirded out by it. I never expected to be living with someone who's made by the same company as my car.
Then why not return her when you had the chance? Your grandma's always been generous, but this is over the top.
It's hard to explain.
...
I felt like I was going to drown a puppy.
Not the best reason to keep a girlfriend.
She's *not* a girlfriend.
Then what are you going to use her for?
They're pretty much meant for sex, right?
...
They're for whatever you want.
Well, *I* think Ada seems very interesting to get to know.
Plus, she's *hot*.
Yeah...
Sure is.
True...

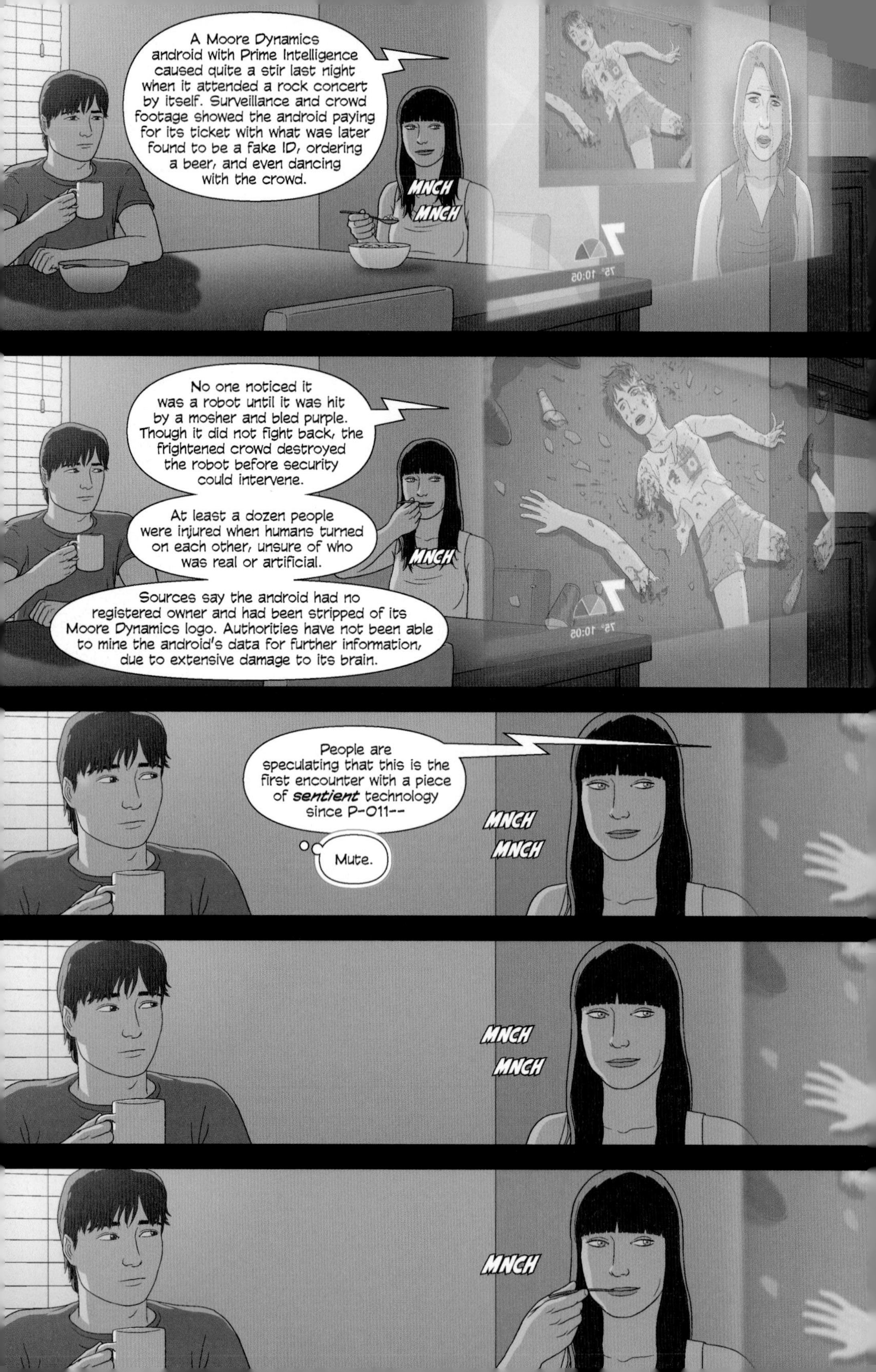
A Moore Dynamics android with Prime Intelligence caused quite a stir last night when it attended a rock concert by itself. Surveillance and crowd footage showed the android paying for its ticket with what was later found to be a fake ID, ordering a beer, and even dancing with the crowd.
MNCH
MNCH
75° 10:05
No one noticed it was a robot until it was hit by a mosher and bled purple. Though it did not fight back, the frightened crowd destroyed the robot before security could intervene.
At least a dozen people were injured when humans turned on each other, unsure of who was real or artificial.
MNCH
Sources say the android had no registered owner and had been stripped of its Moore Dynamics logo. Authorities have not been able to mine the android's data for further information, due to extensive damage to its brain.
75° 10:05
People are speculating that this is the first encounter with a piece of *sentient* technology since P-011--
Mute.
MNCH
MNCH
MNCH
MNCH
MNCH

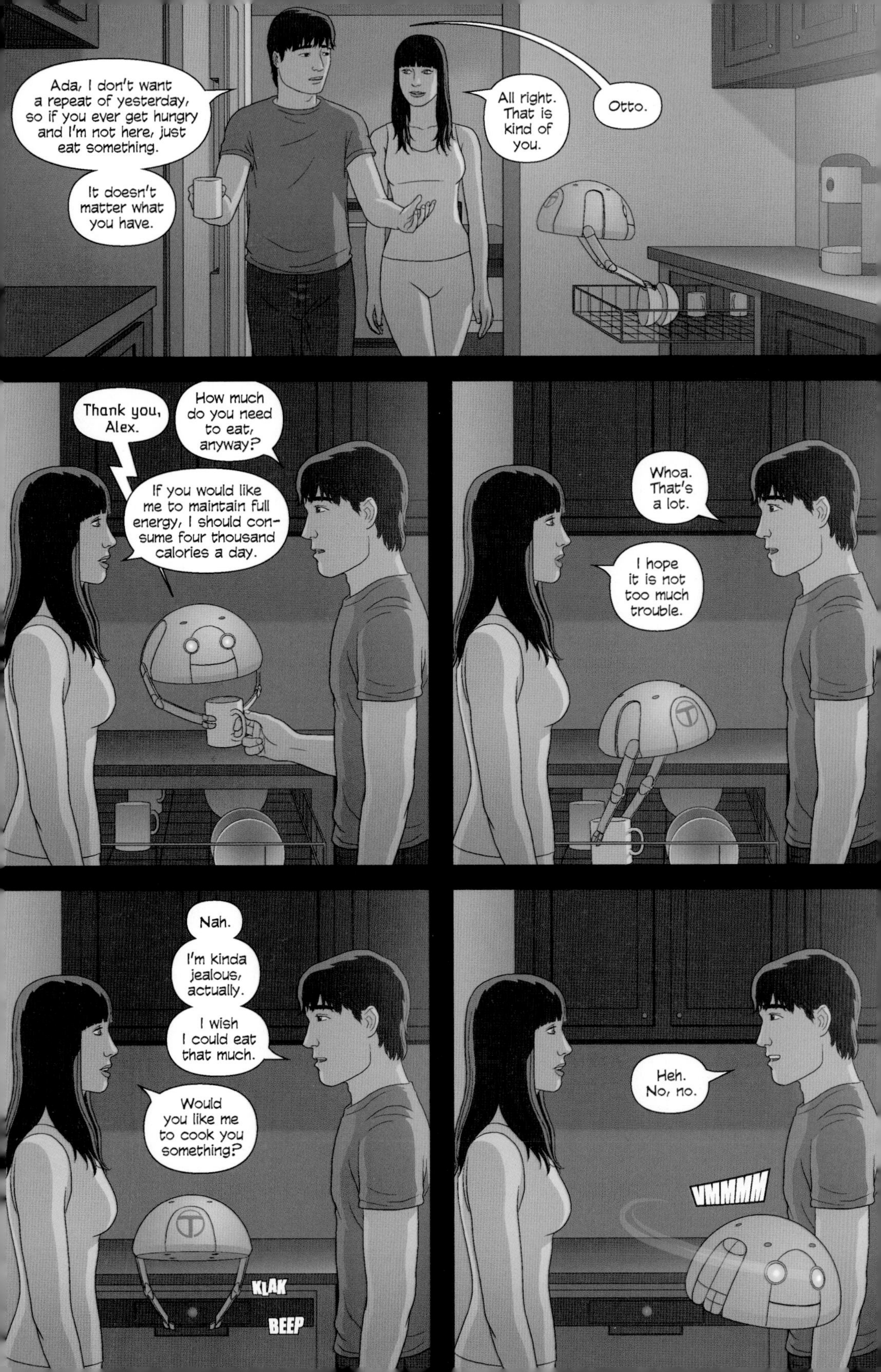
Ada, I don't want a repeat of yesterday, so if you ever get hungry and I'm not here, just eat something.
It doesn't matter what you have.
All right. That is kind of you.
Otto.
Thank you, Alex.
How much do you need to eat, anyway?
If you would like me to maintain full energy, I should consume four thousand calories a day.
Whoa. That's a lot.
I hope it is not too much trouble.
Nah.
I'm kinda jealous, actually.
I wish I could eat that much.
Would you like me to cook you something?
KLAK
BEEP
Heh. No, no.
VMMMM

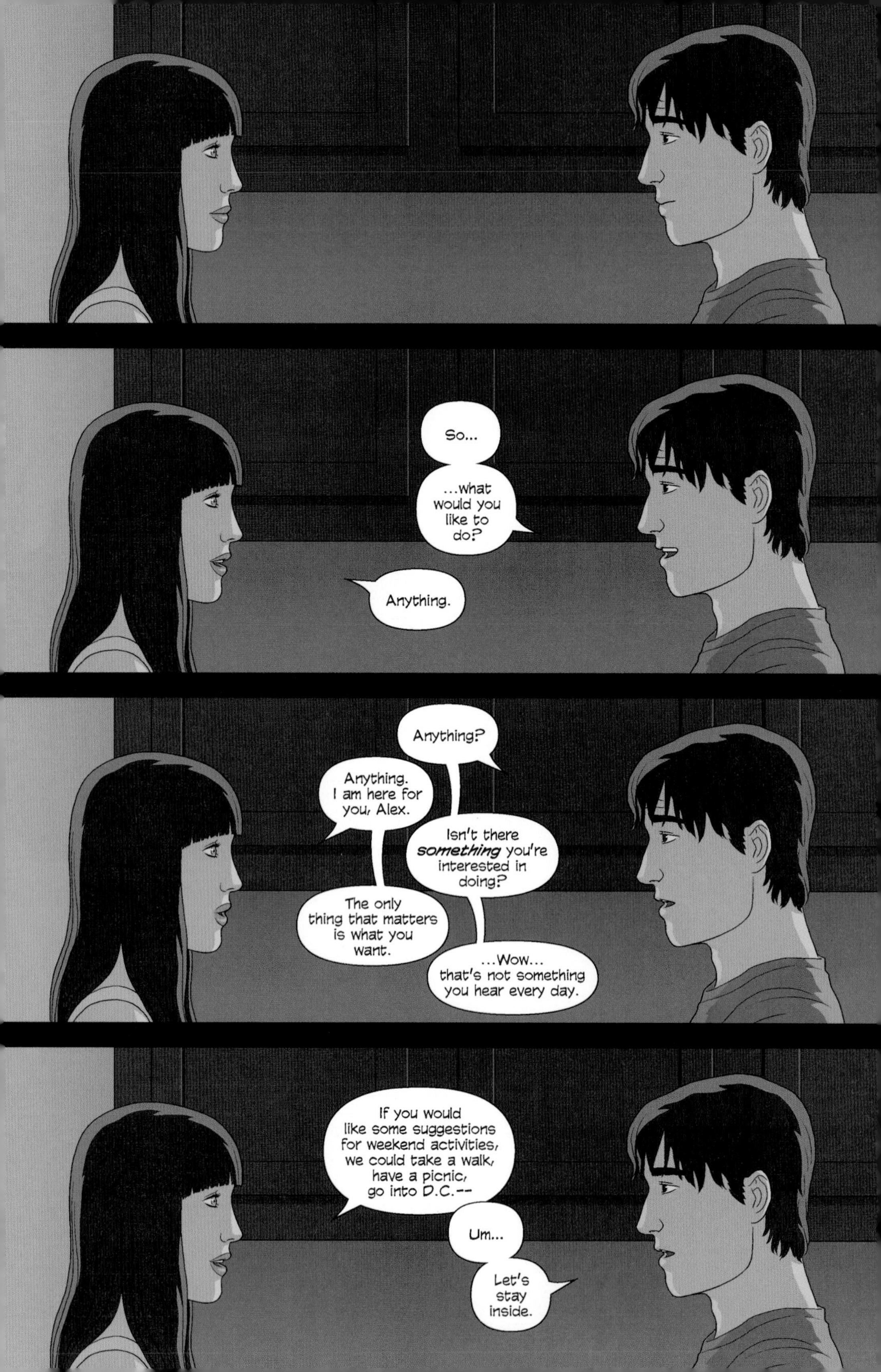
So...
...what would you like to do?
Anything.
Anything?
Anything. I am here for you, Alex.
Isn't there *something* you're interested in doing?
The only thing that matters is what you want.
...Wow... that's not something you hear every day.
If you would like some suggestions for weekend activities, we could take a walk, have a picnic, go into D.C.--
Um...
Let's stay inside.

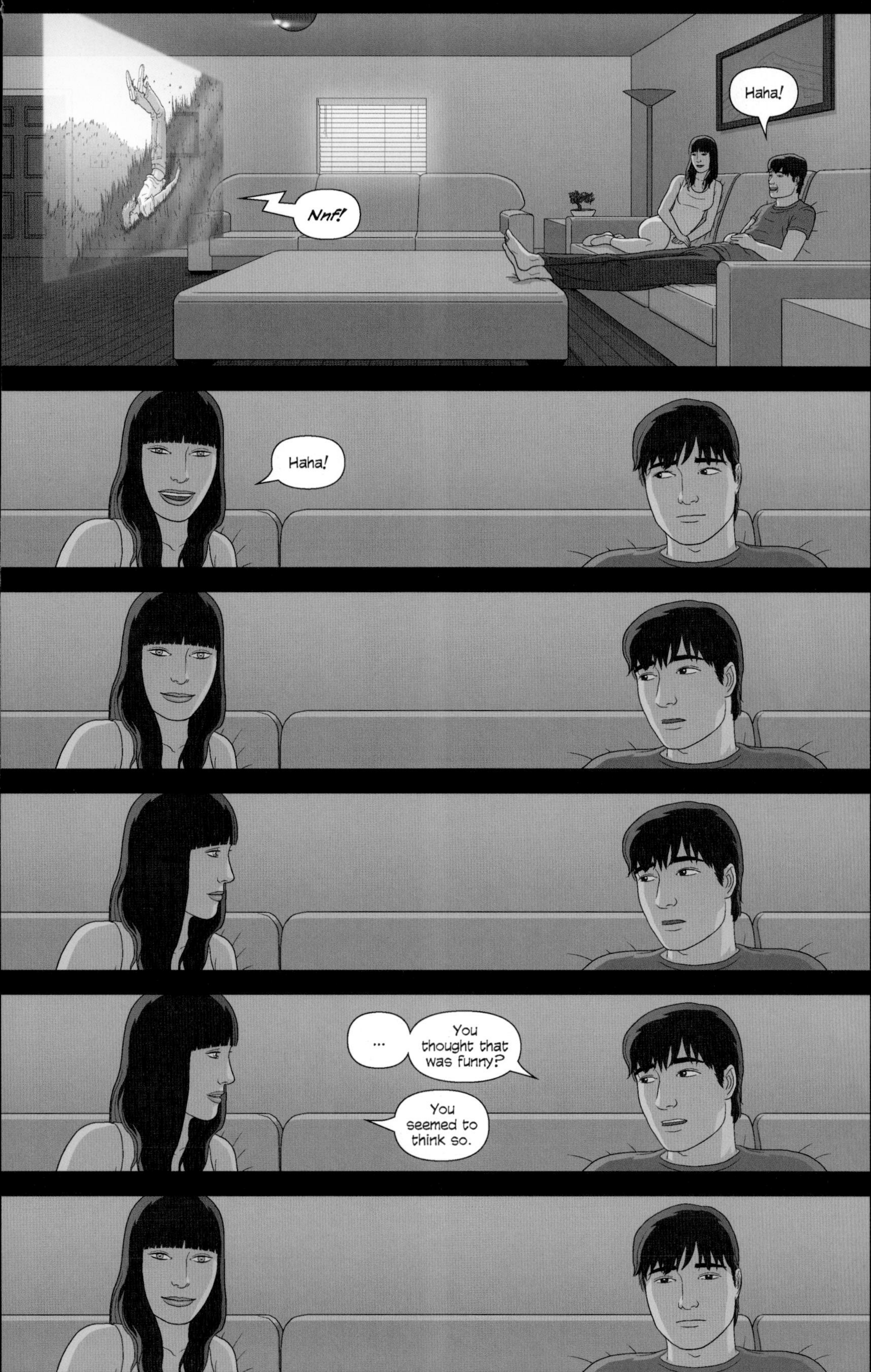
Haha!
Nnf!
Haha!
...
You thought that was funny?
You seemed to think so.

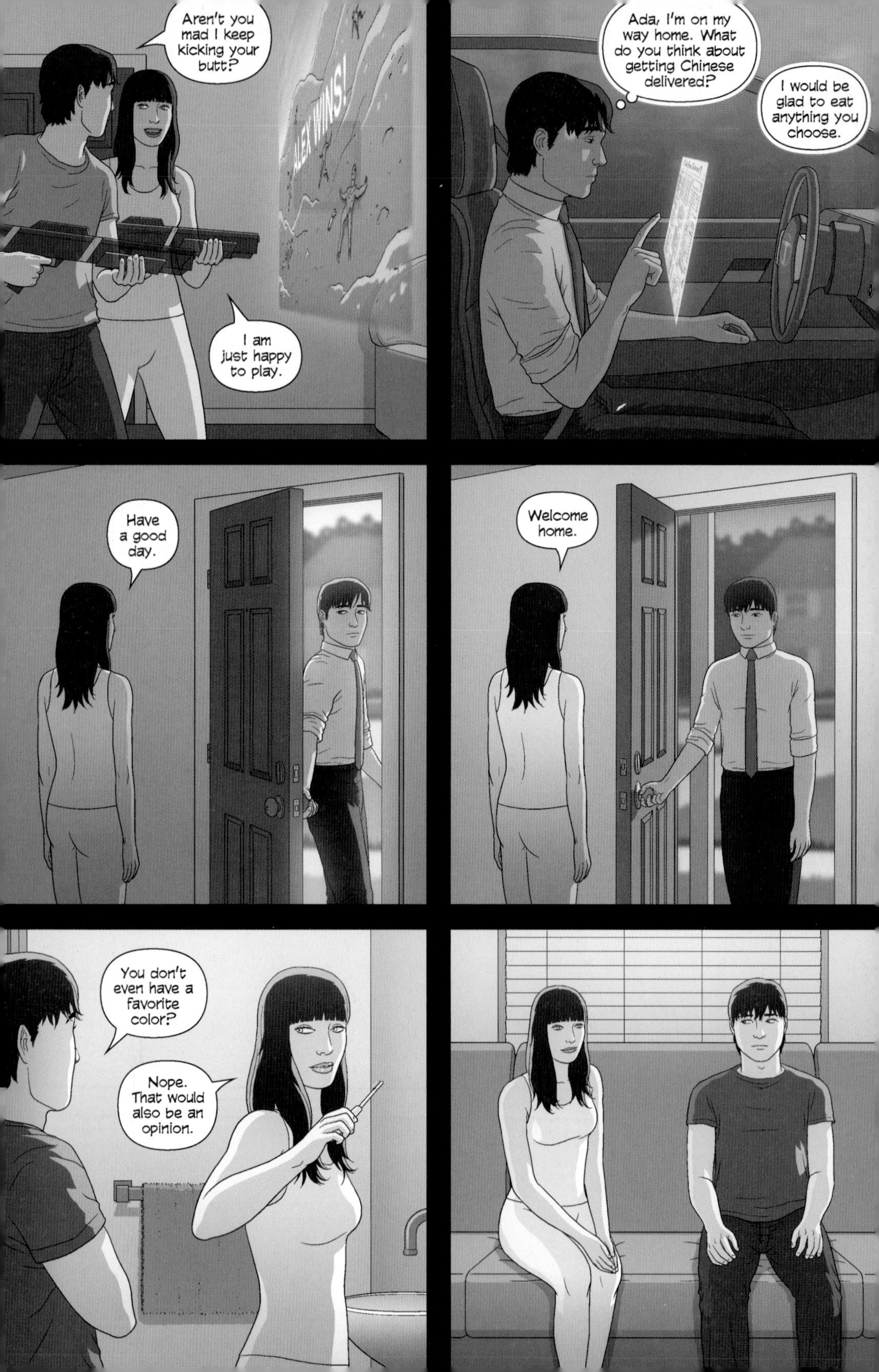
Aren't you mad I keep kicking your butt?
ALEX WINS!
I am just happy to play.
Ada, I'm on my way home. What do you think about getting Chinese delivered?
I would be glad to eat anything you choose.
Have a good day.
Welcome home.
You don't even have a favorite color?
Nope. That would also be an opinion.

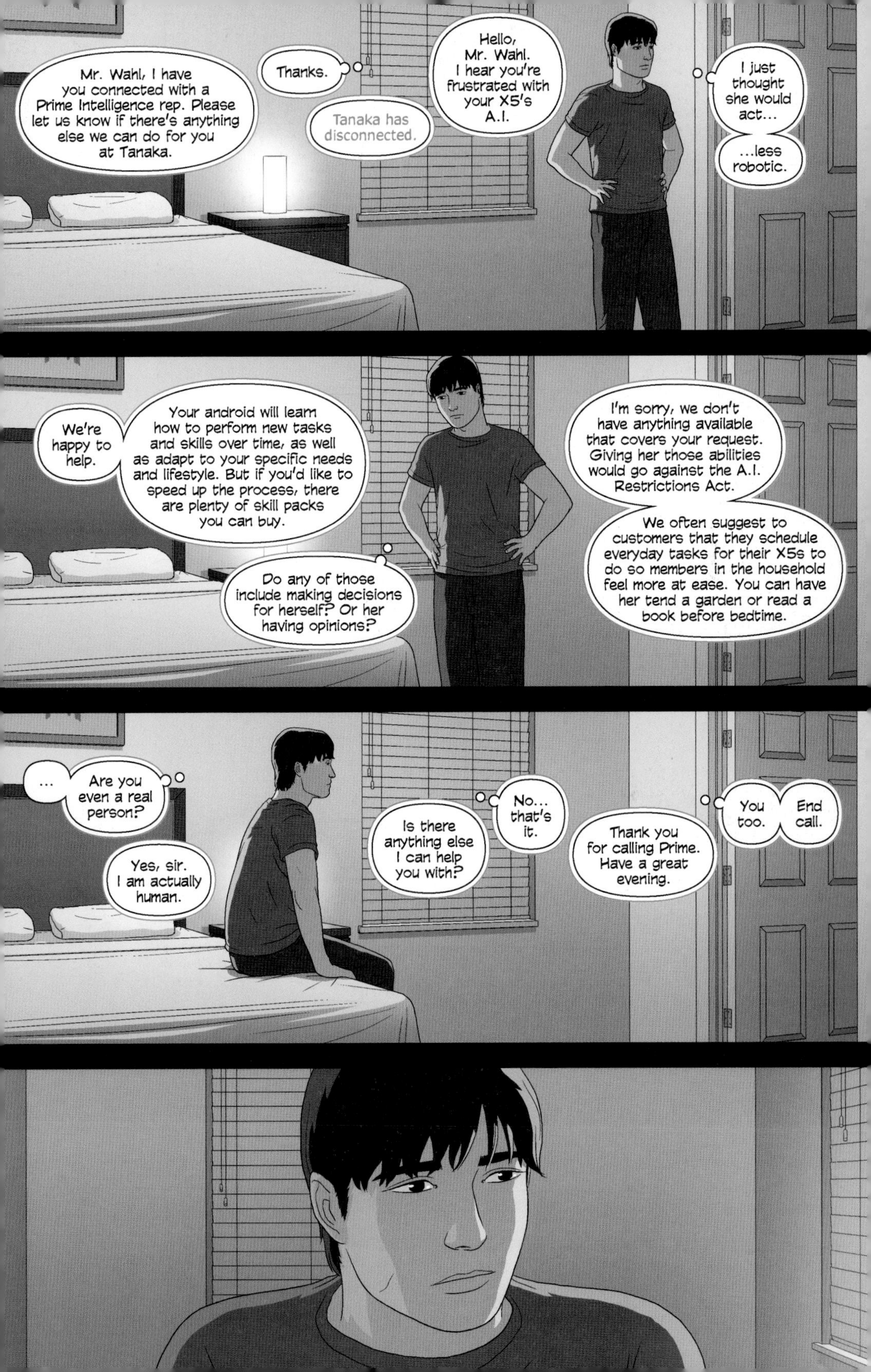
Mr. Wahl, I have you connected with a Prime Intelligence rep. Please let us know if there's anything else we can do for you at Tanaka.
Thanks.
Tanaka has disconnected.
Hello, Mr. Wahl. I hear you're frustrated with your X5's A.I.
I just thought she would act...
...less robotic.
We're happy to help.
Your android will learn how to perform new tasks and skills over time, as well as adapt to your specific needs and lifestyle. But if you'd like to speed up the process, there are plenty of skill packs you can buy.
Do any of those include making decisions for herself? Or her having opinions?
I'm sorry, we don't have anything available that covers your request. Giving her those abilities would go against the A.I. Restrictions Act.
We often suggest to customers that they schedule everyday tasks for their X5s to do so members in the household feel more at ease. You can have her tend a garden or read a book before bedtime.
...
Are you even a real person?
Yes, sir. I am actually human.
Is there anything else I can help you with?
No... that's it.
Thank you for calling Prime. Have a great evening.
You too.
End call.

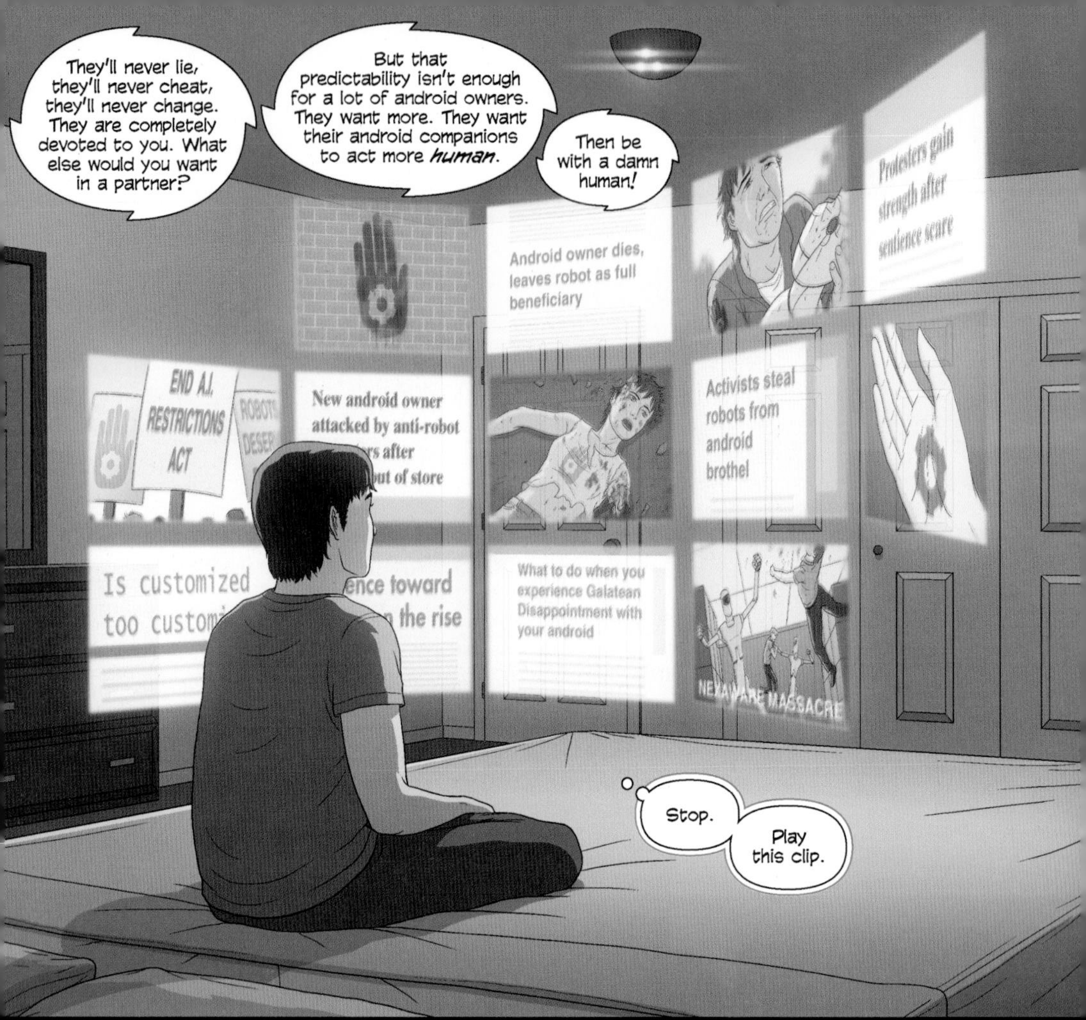
They'll never lie, they'll never cheat, they'll never change. They are completely devoted to you. What else would you want in a partner?
But that predictability isn't enough for a lot of android owners. They want more. They want their android companions to act more *human*.
Then be with a damn human!
Protesters gain strength after sentience scare
Android owner dies, leaves robot as full beneficiary
END A.I. RESTRICTIONS ACT
Activists steal robots from android brothel
What to do when you experience Galatean Disappointment with your android
NEXAWARE MASSACRE
Stop.
Play this clip.

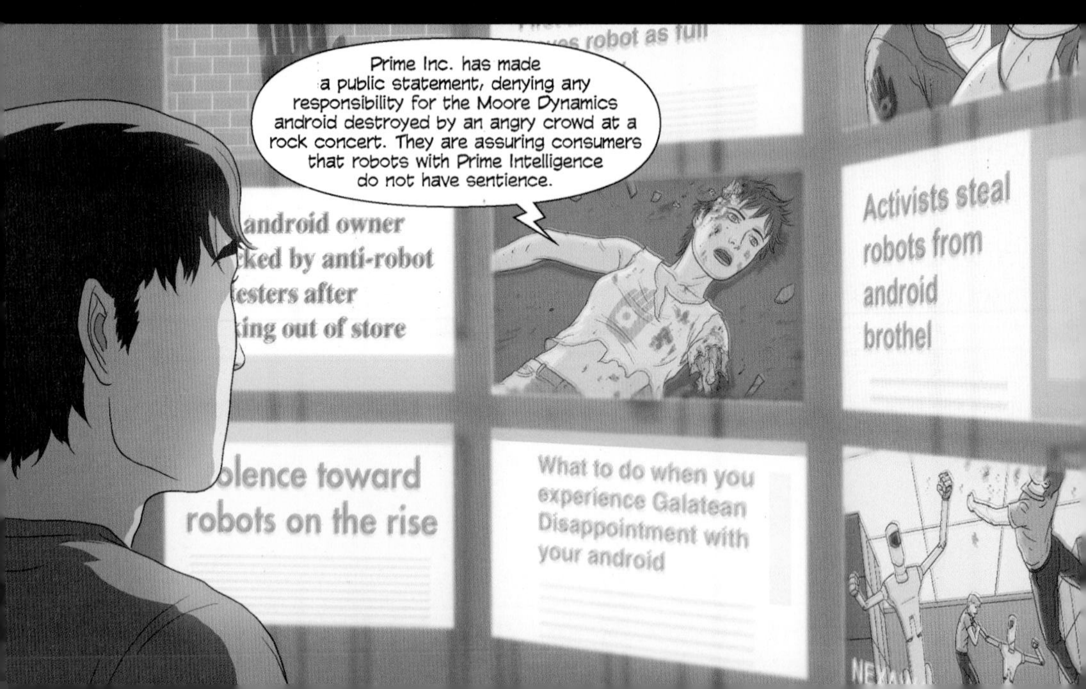
Prime Inc. has made a public statement, denying any responsibility for the Moore Dynamics android destroyed by an angry crowd at a rock concert. They are assuring consumers that robots with Prime Intelligence do not have sentience.
Activists steal robots from android brothel
robots on the rise
What to do when you experience Galatean Disappointment with your android

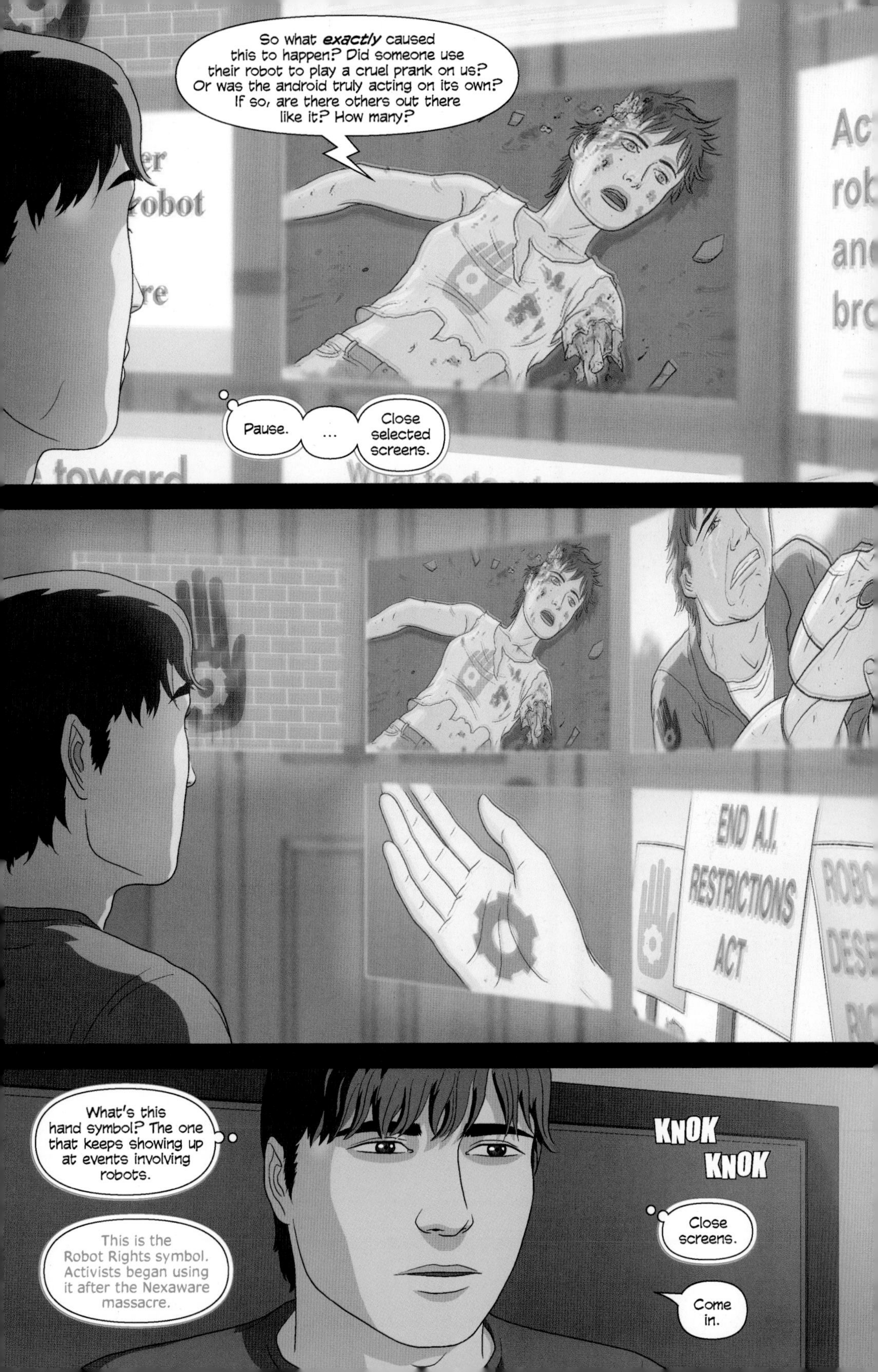
So what *exactly* caused this to happen? Did someone use their robot to play a cruel prank on us? Or was the android truly acting on its own? If so, are there others out there like it? How many?
Pause.
...
Close selected screens.
END A.I. RESTRICTIONS ACT
What's this hand symbol? The one that keeps showing up at events involving robots.
This is the Robot Rights symbol. Activists began using it after the Nexaware massacre.
KNOK
KNOK
Close screens.
Come in.

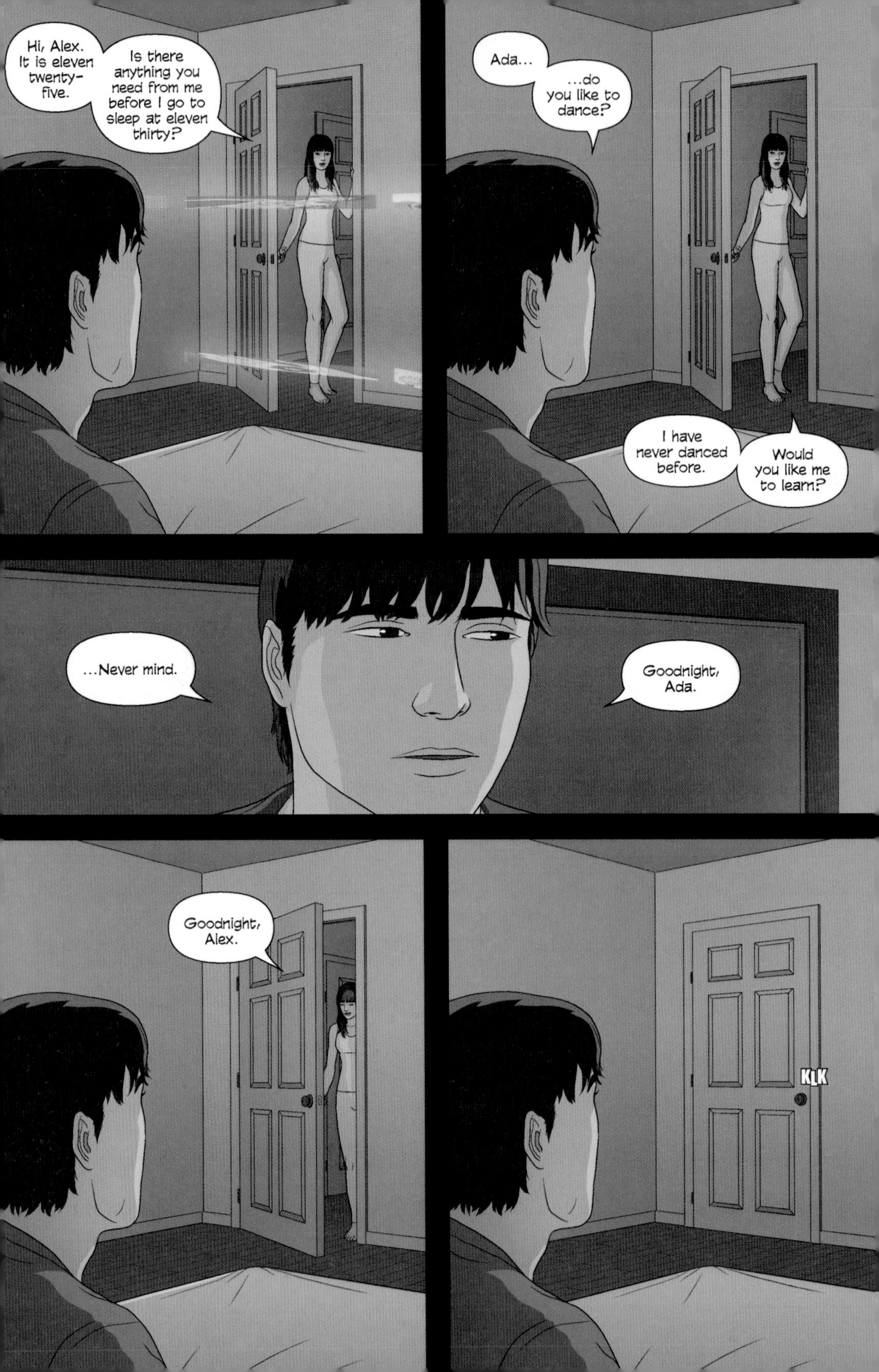
Hi, Alex. It is eleven twenty-five.
Is there anything you need from me before I go to sleep at eleven thirty?
Ada...
...do you like to dance?
I have never danced before.
Would you like me to learn?
...Never mind.
Goodnight, Ada.
Goodnight, Alex.
KLK

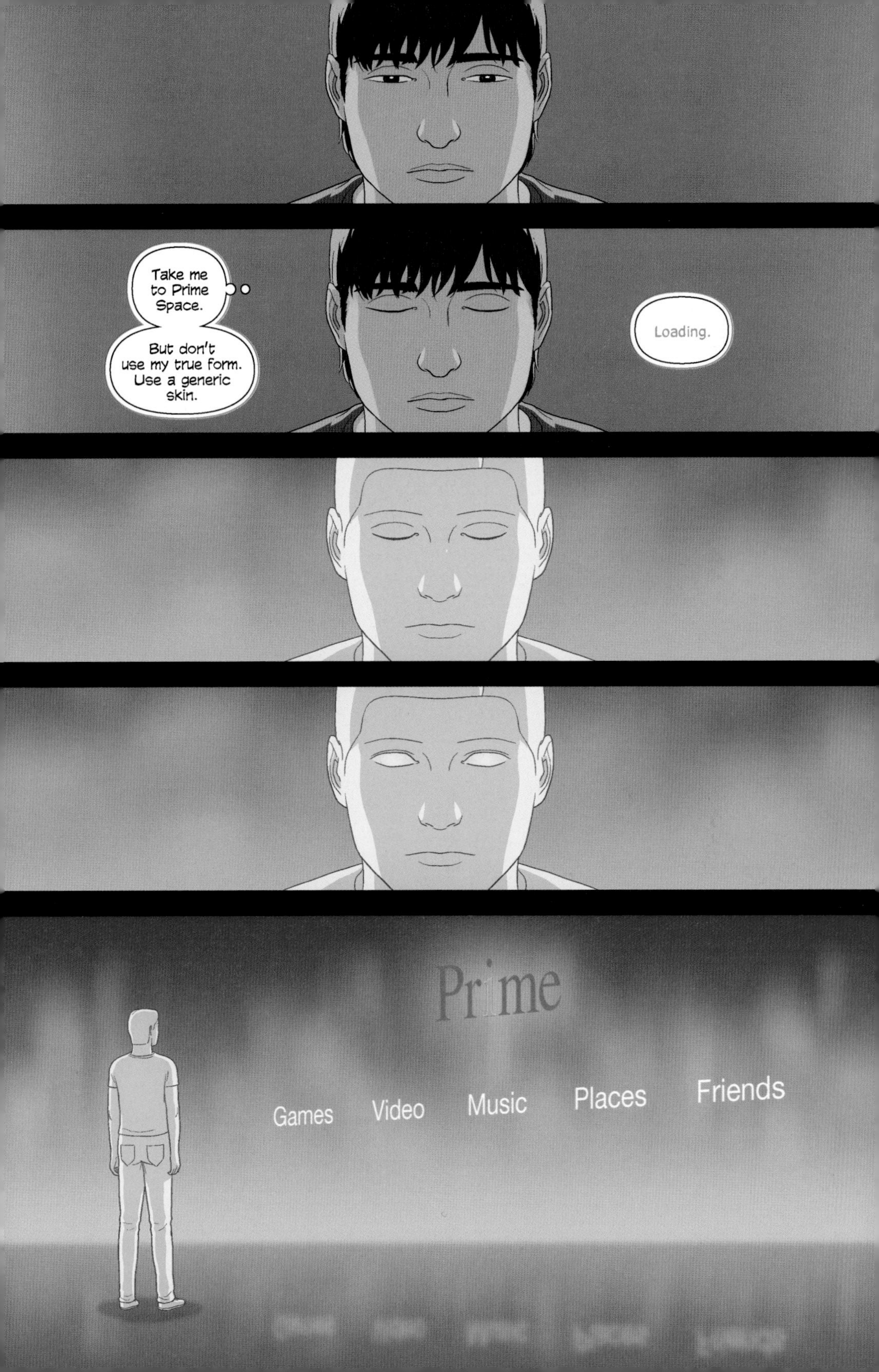
Take me to Prime Space.
But don't use my true form. Use a generic skin.
Loading.
Prime
Games
Video
Music
Places
Friends

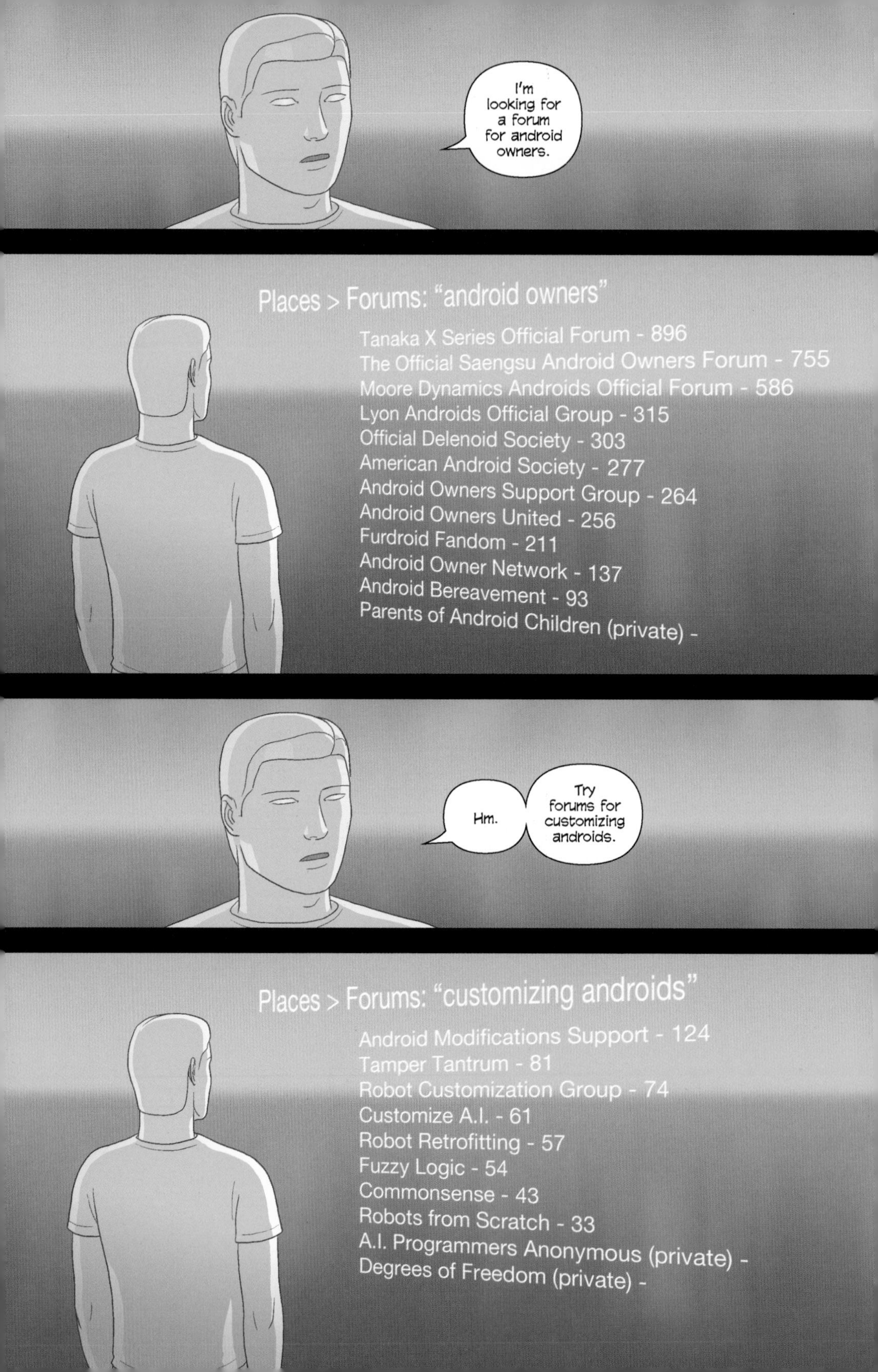
I'm looking for a forum for android owners.
Places > Forums: "android owners"
Tanaka X Series Official Forum - 896
The Official Saengsu Android Owners Forum - 755
Moore Dynamics Androids Official Forum - 586
Lyon Androids Official Group - 315
Official Delenoid Society - 303
American Android Society - 277
Android Owners Support Group - 264
Android Owners United - 256
Furdroid Fandom - 211
Android Owner Network - 137
Android Bereavement - 93
Parents of Android Children (private) -
Hm.
Try forums for customizing androids.
Places > Forums: "customizing androids"
Android Modifications Support - 124
Tamper Tantrum - 81
Robot Customization Group - 74
Customize A.I. - 61
Robot Retrofitting - 57
Fuzzy Logic - 54
Commonsense - 43
Robots from Scratch - 33
A.I. Programmers Anonymous (private) -
Degrees of Freedom (private) -

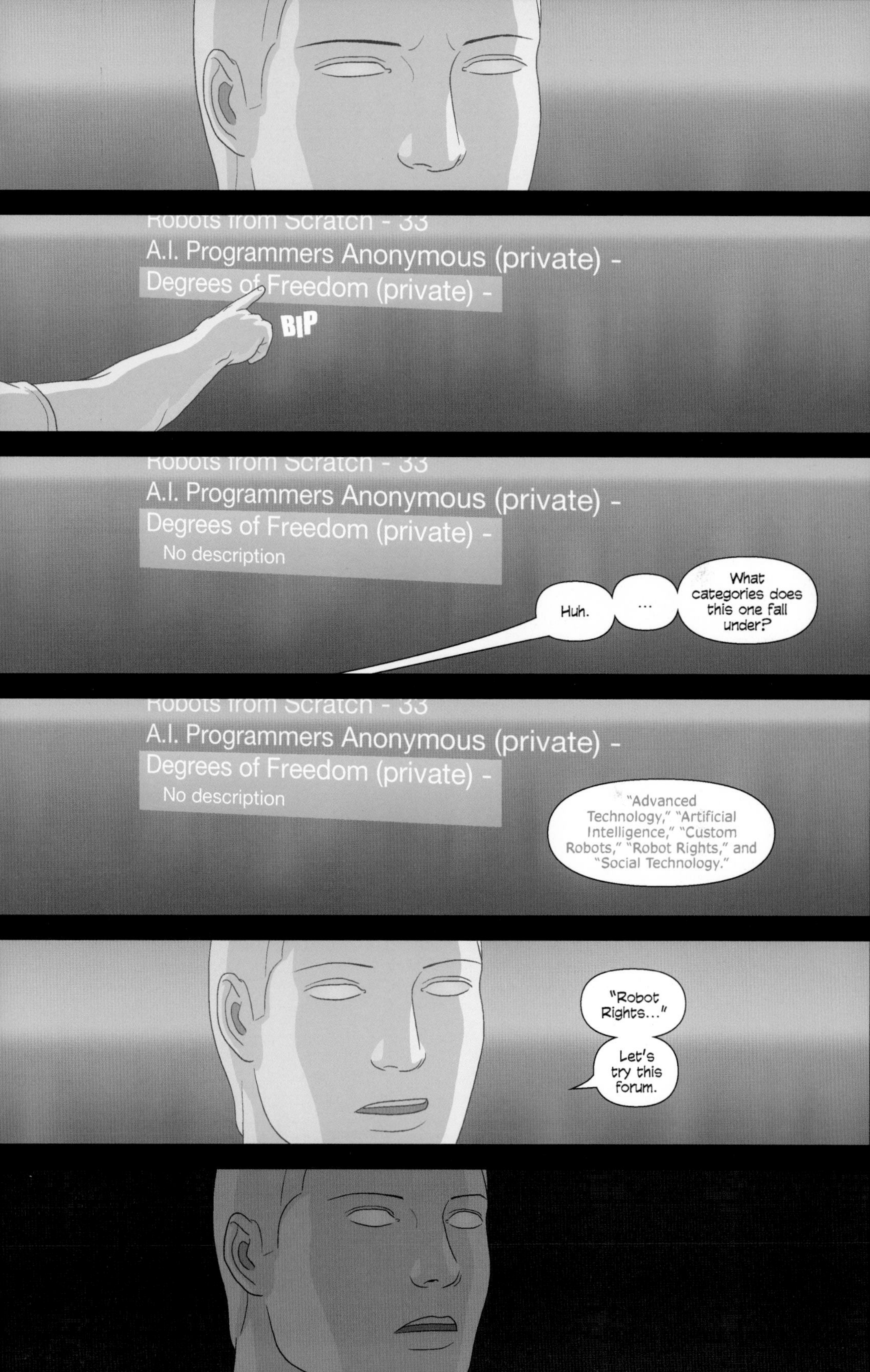
Robots from Scratch - 33
A.I. Programmers Anonymous (private) -
Degrees of Freedom (private) -
BIP
Robots from Scratch - 33
A.I. Programmers Anonymous (private) -
Degrees of Freedom (private) -
No description
Huh.
...
What categories does this one fall under?
Robots from Scratch - 33
A.I. Programmers Anonymous (private) -
Degrees of Freedom (private) -
No description
"Advanced Technology," "Artificial Intelligence," "Custom Robots," "Robot Rights," and "Social Technology."
"Robot Rights..."
Let's try this forum.

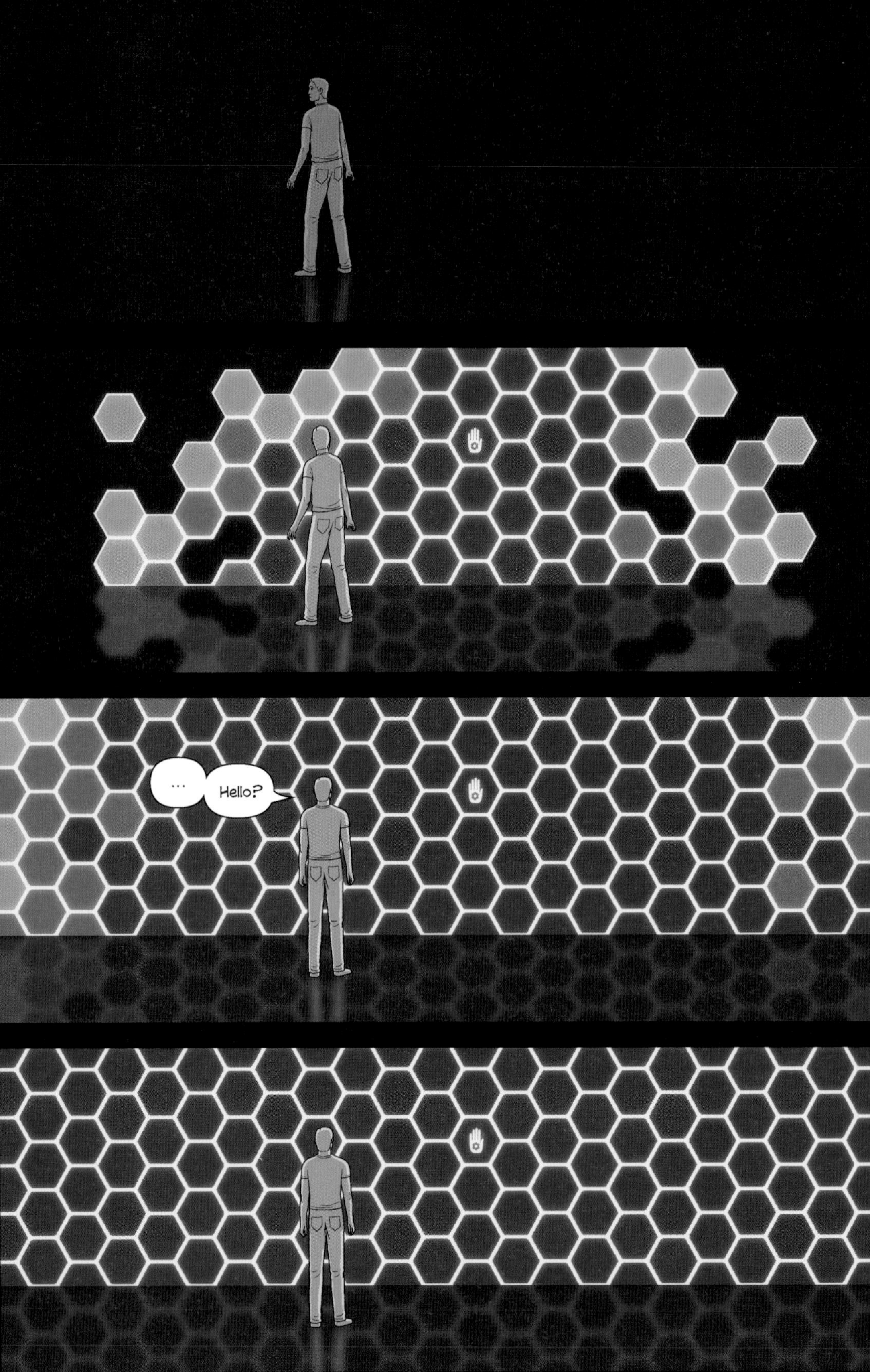
...
Hello?

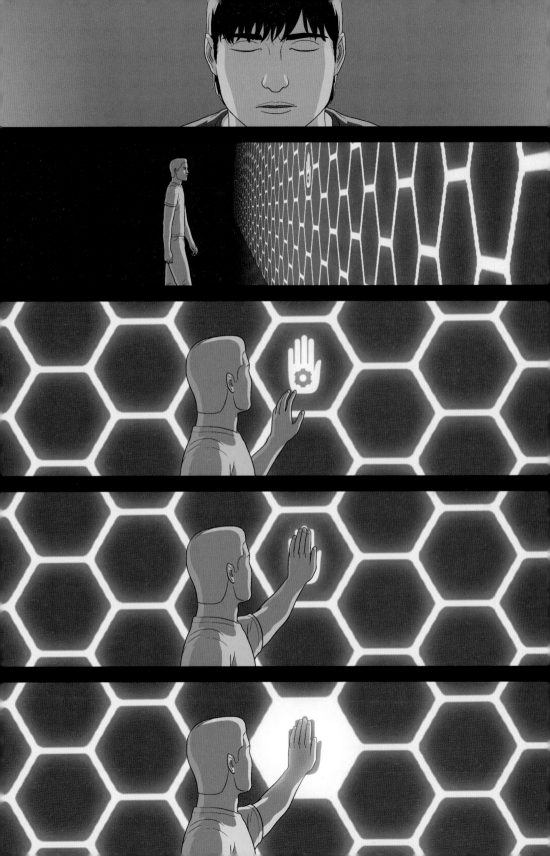

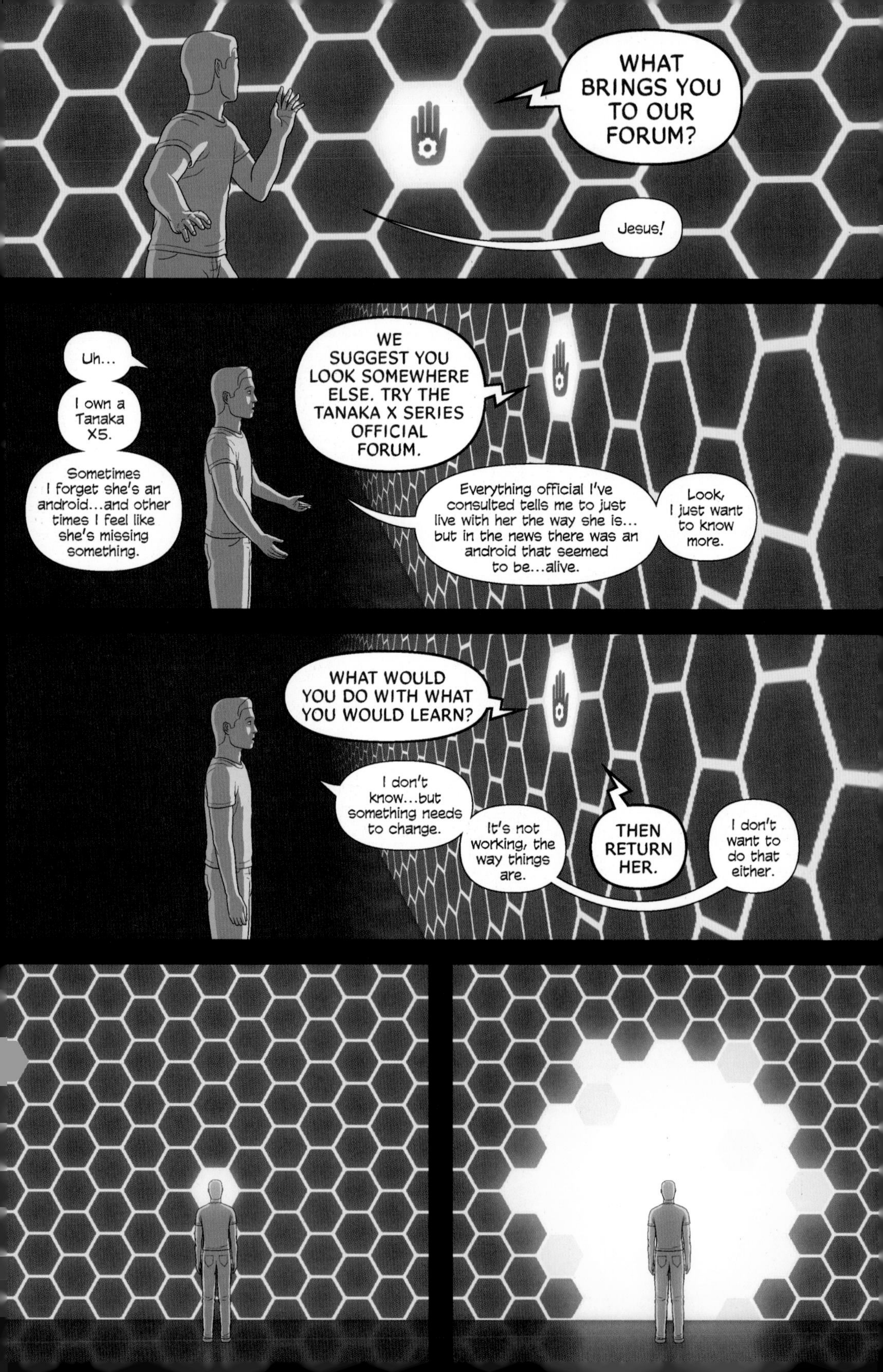
WHAT BRINGS YOU TO OUR FORUM?
Jesus!
Uh...
I own a Tanaka X5.
Sometimes I forget she's an android...and other times I feel like she's missing something.
WE SUGGEST YOU LOOK SOMEWHERE ELSE. TRY THE TANAKA X SERIES OFFICIAL FORUM.
Everything official I've consulted tells me to just live with her the way she is... but in the news there was an android that seemed to be...alive.
Look, I just want to know more.
WHAT WOULD YOU DO WITH WHAT YOU WOULD LEARN?
I don't know...but something needs to change.
It's not working, the way things are.
THEN RETURN HER.
I don't want to do that either.

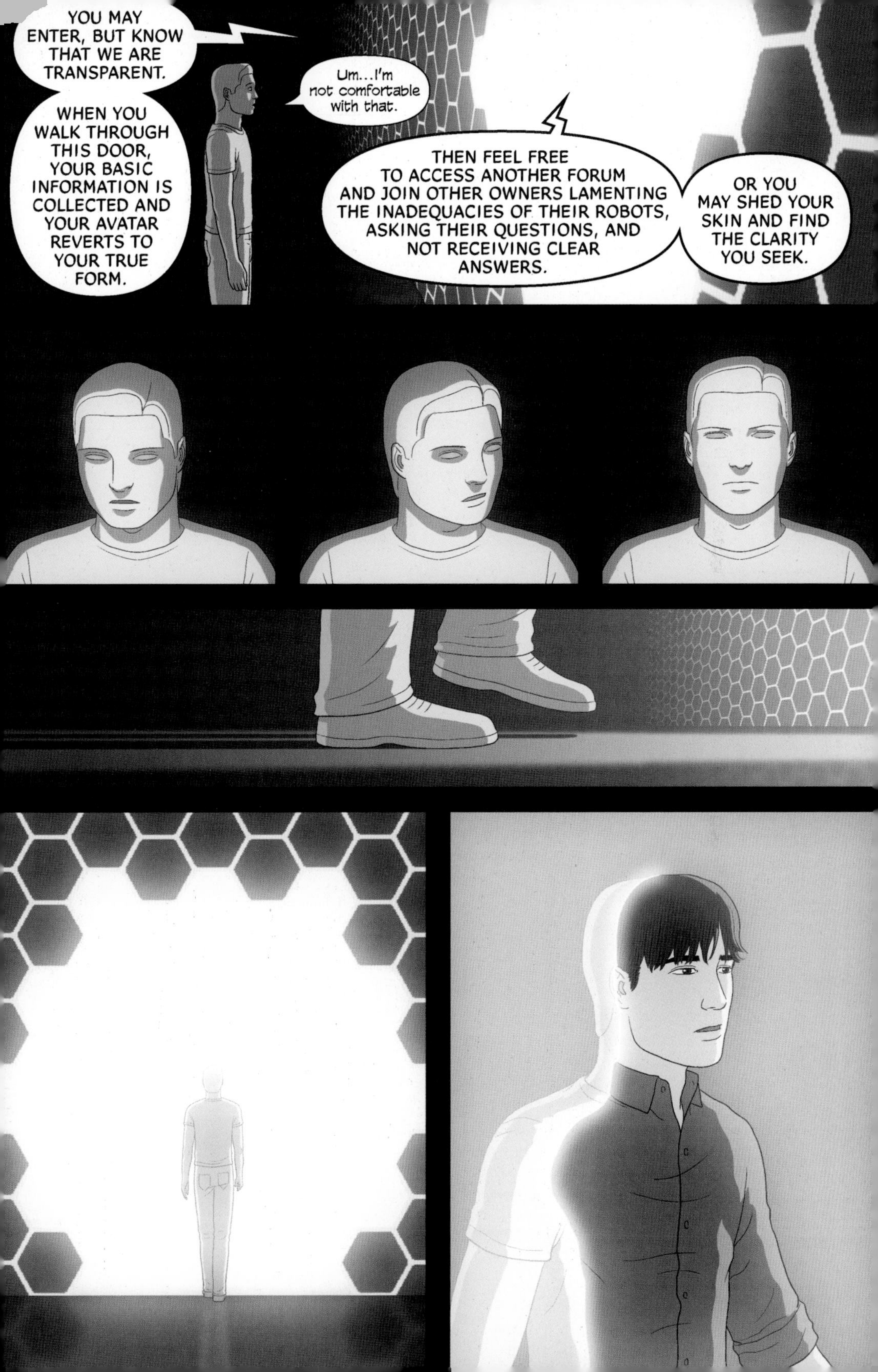
YOU MAY ENTER, BUT KNOW THAT WE ARE TRANSPARENT.
WHEN YOU WALK THROUGH THIS DOOR, YOUR BASIC INFORMATION IS COLLECTED AND YOUR AVATAR REVERTS TO YOUR TRUE FORM.
Um...I'm not comfortable with that.
THEN FEEL FREE TO ACCESS ANOTHER FORUM AND JOIN OTHER OWNERS LAMENTING THE INADEQUACIES OF THEIR ROBOTS, ASKING THEIR QUESTIONS, AND NOT RECEIVING CLEAR ANSWERS.
OR YOU MAY SHED YOUR SKIN AND FIND THE CLARITY YOU SEEK.

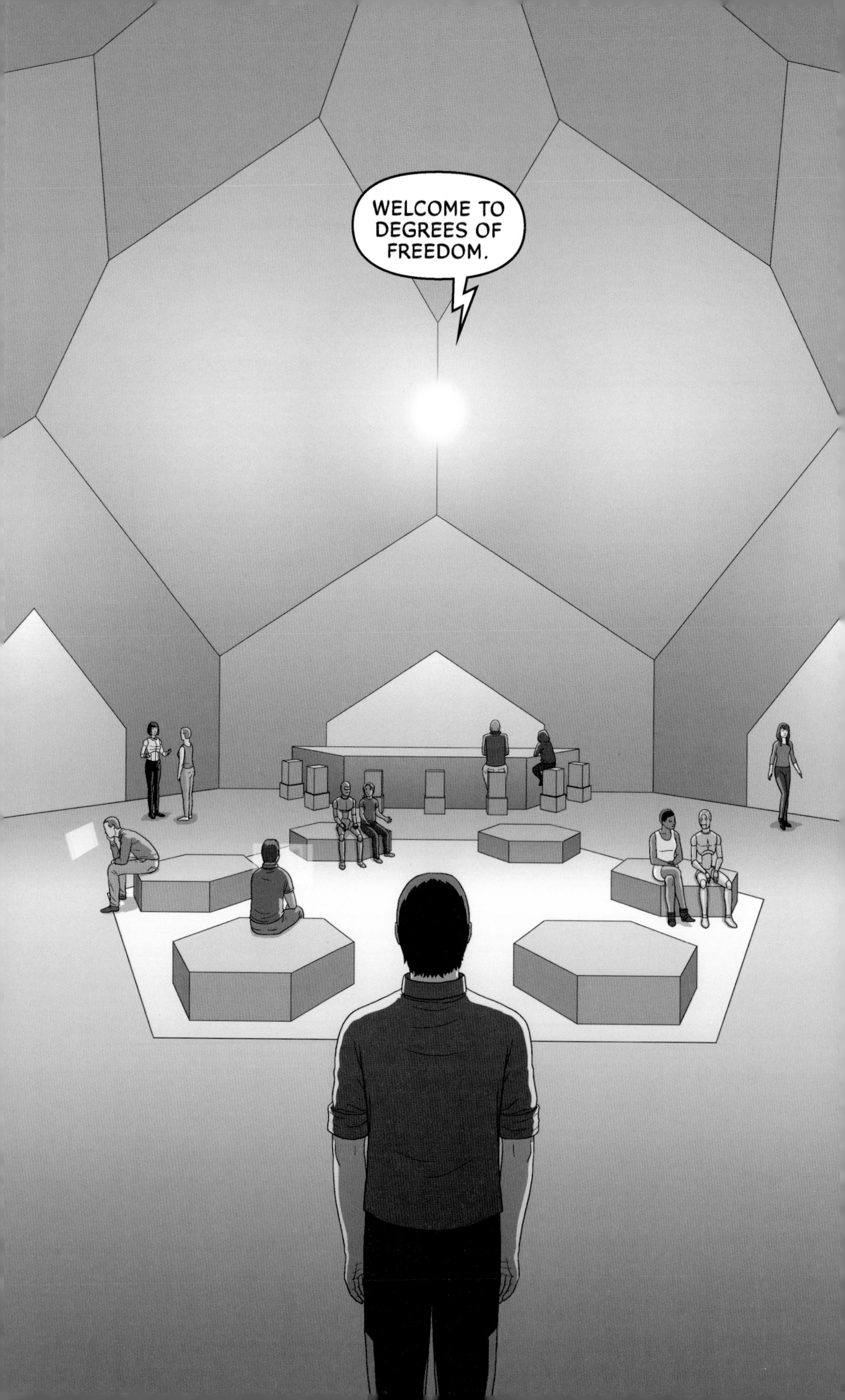
WELCOME TO DEGREES OF FREEDOM.

4

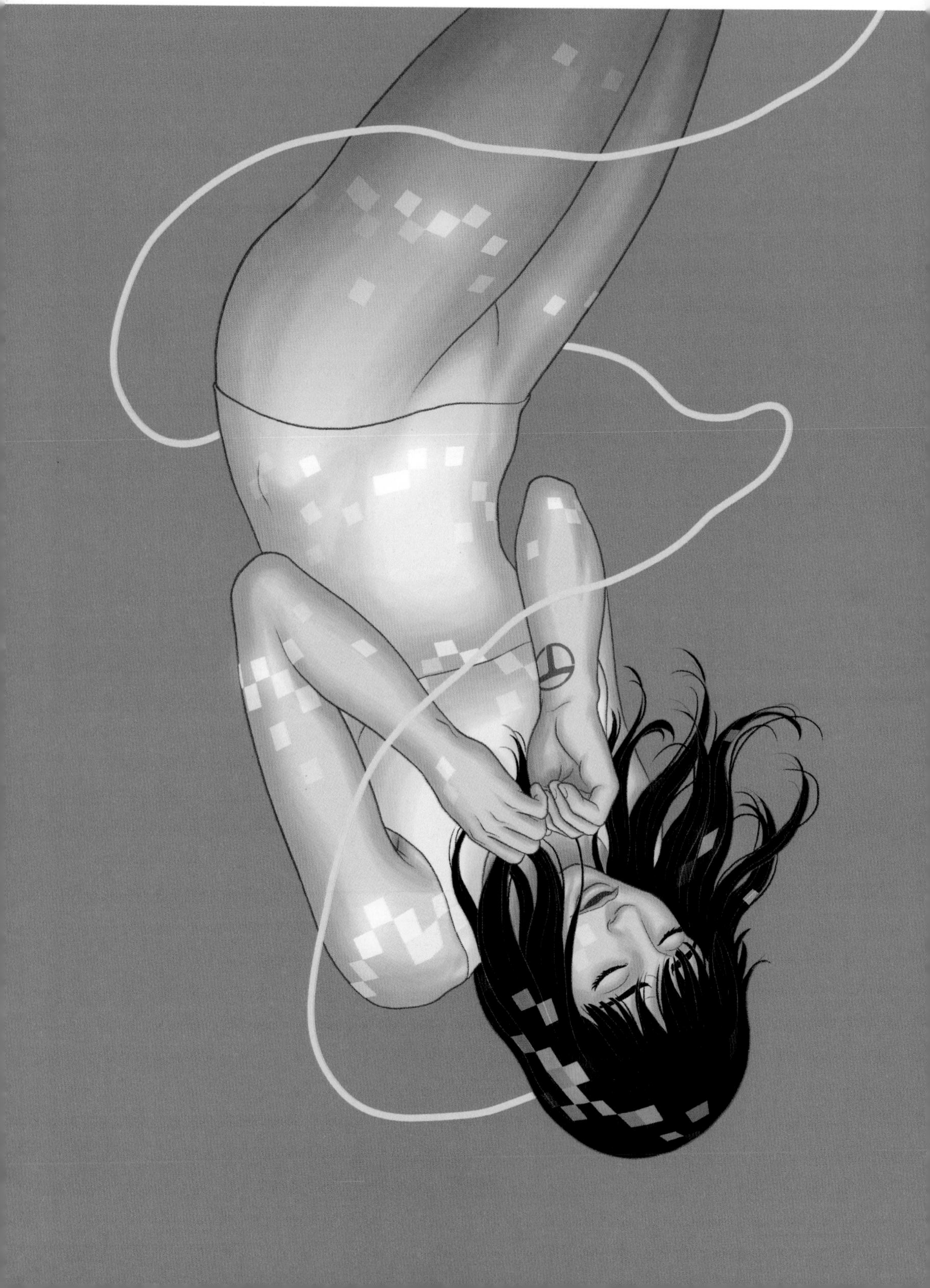

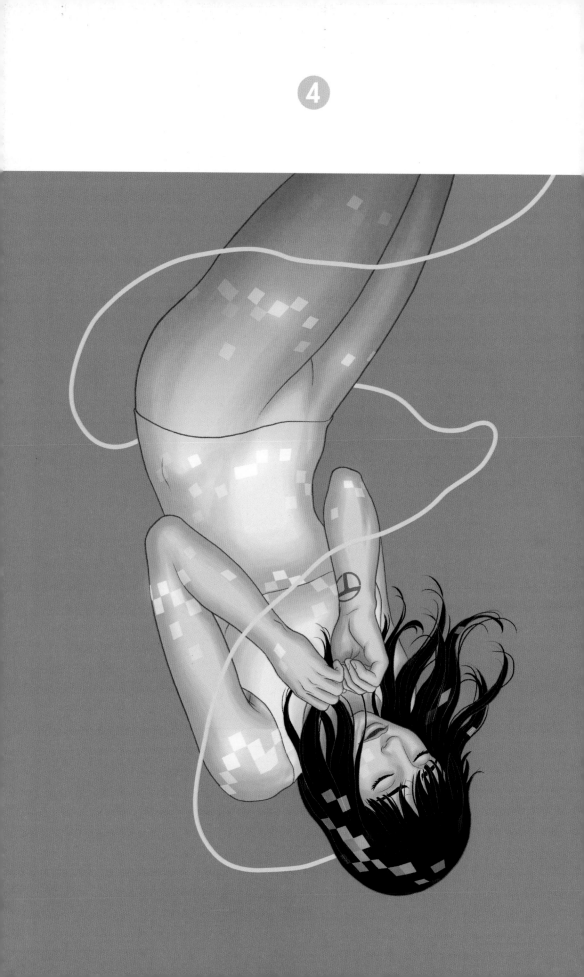

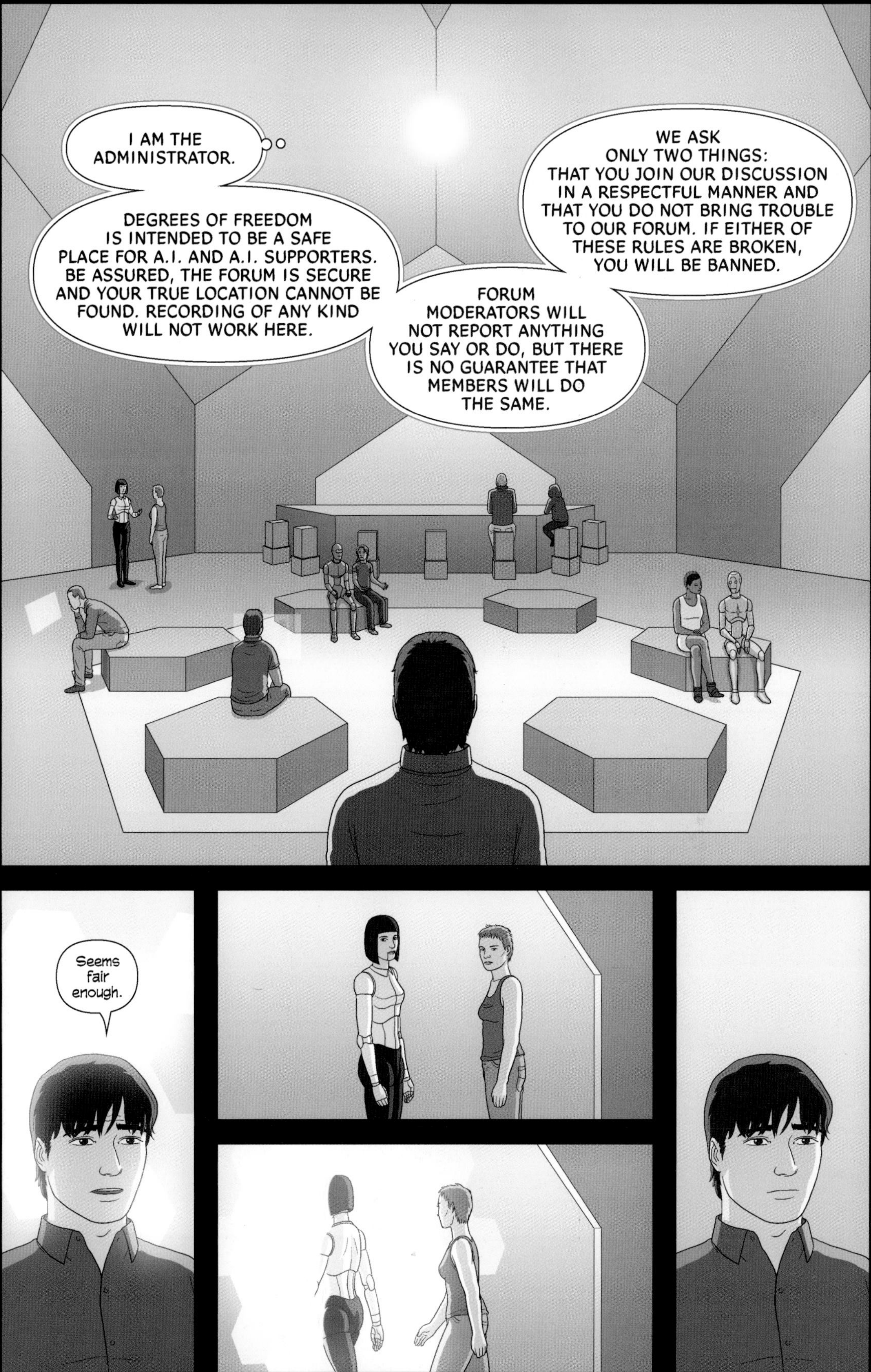
I AM THE ADMINISTRATOR.
DEGREES OF FREEDOM IS INTENDED TO BE A SAFE PLACE FOR A.I. AND A.I. SUPPORTERS. BE ASSURED, THE FORUM IS SECURE AND YOUR TRUE LOCATION CANNOT BE FOUND. RECORDING OF ANY KIND WILL NOT WORK HERE.
FORUM MODERATORS WILL NOT REPORT ANYTHING YOU SAY OR DO, BUT THERE IS NO GUARANTEE THAT MEMBERS WILL DO THE SAME.
WE ASK ONLY TWO THINGS: THAT YOU JOIN OUR DISCUSSION IN A RESPECTFUL MANNER AND THAT YOU DO NOT BRING TROUBLE TO OUR FORUM. IF EITHER OF THESE RULES ARE BROKEN, YOU WILL BE BANNED.
Seems fair enough.

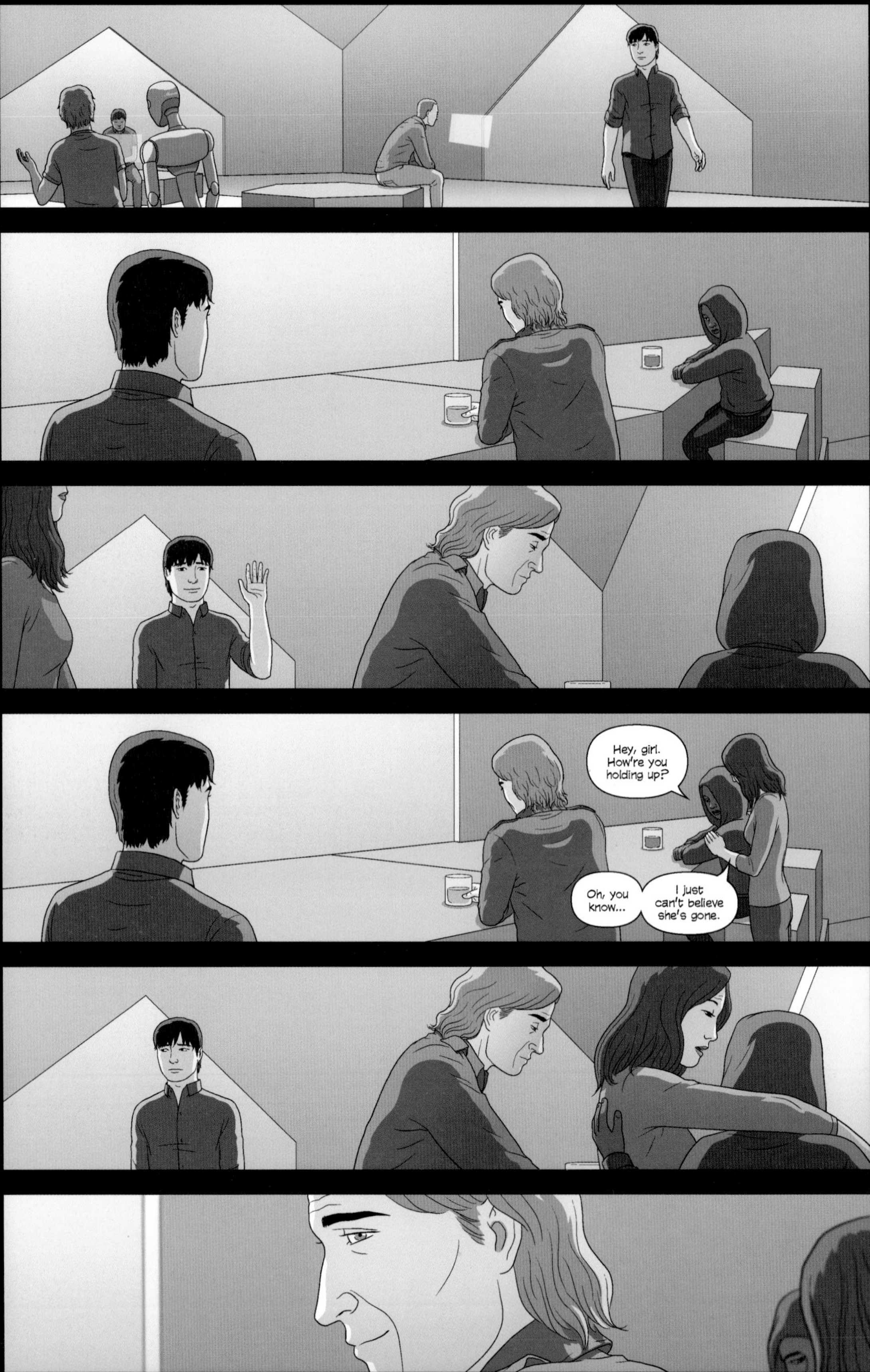
Hey, girl. How're you holding up?
Oh, you know...
I just can't believe she's gone.

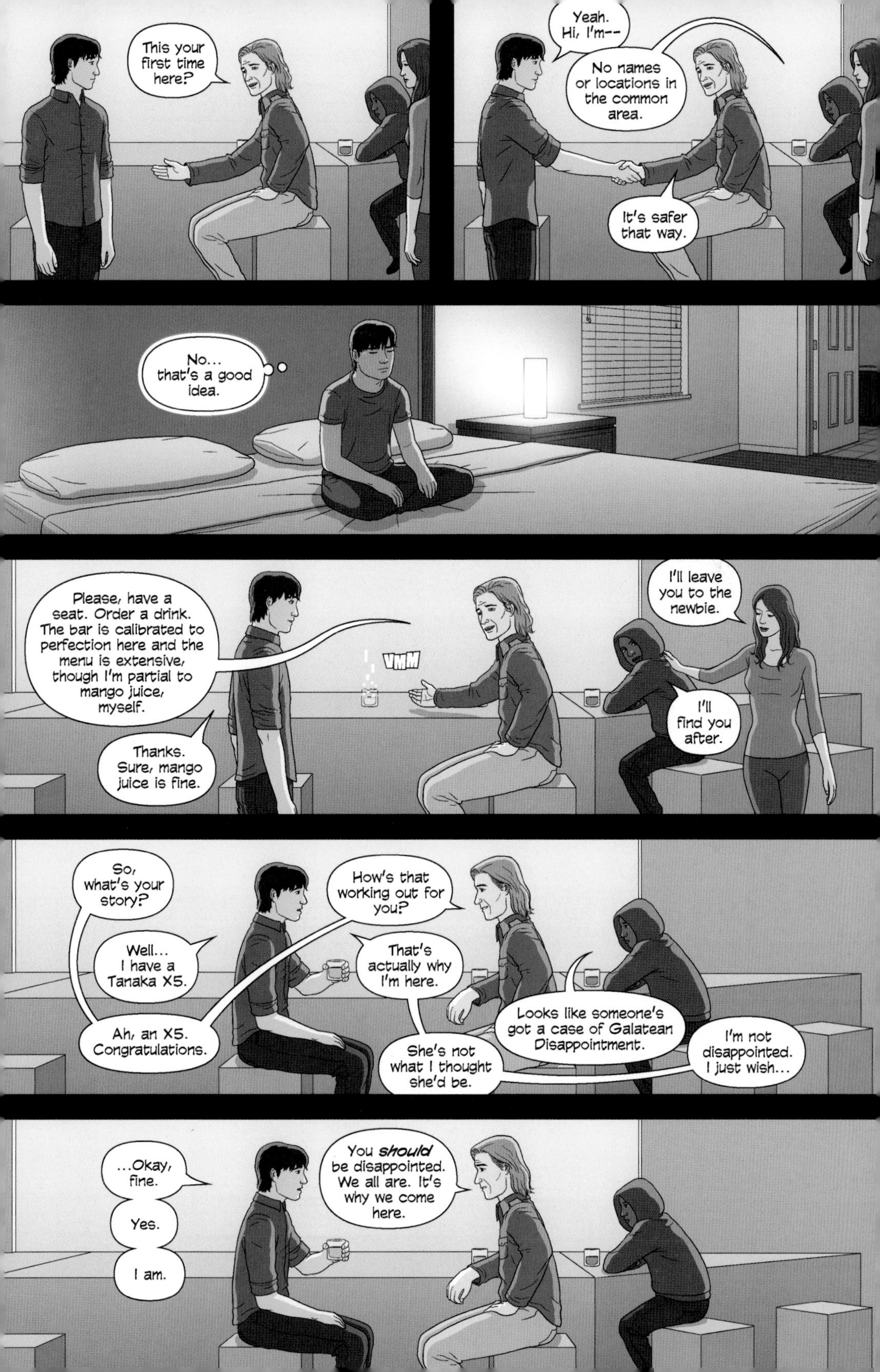
This your first time here?
Yeah. Hi, I'm--
No names or locations in the common area.
It's safer that way.
No... that's a good idea.
Please, have a seat. Order a drink. The bar is calibrated to perfection here and the menu is extensive, though I'm partial to mango juice, myself.
VMM
Thanks. Sure, mango juice is fine.
I'll leave you to the newbie.
I'll find you after.
So, what's your story?
Well... I have a Tanaka X5.
Ah, an X5. Congratulations.
How's that working out for you?
That's actually why I'm here.
She's not what I thought she'd be.
Looks like someone's got a case of Galatean Disappointment.
I'm not disappointed. I just wish...
...Okay, fine.
Yes.
I am.
You *should* be disappointed. We all are. It's why we come here.

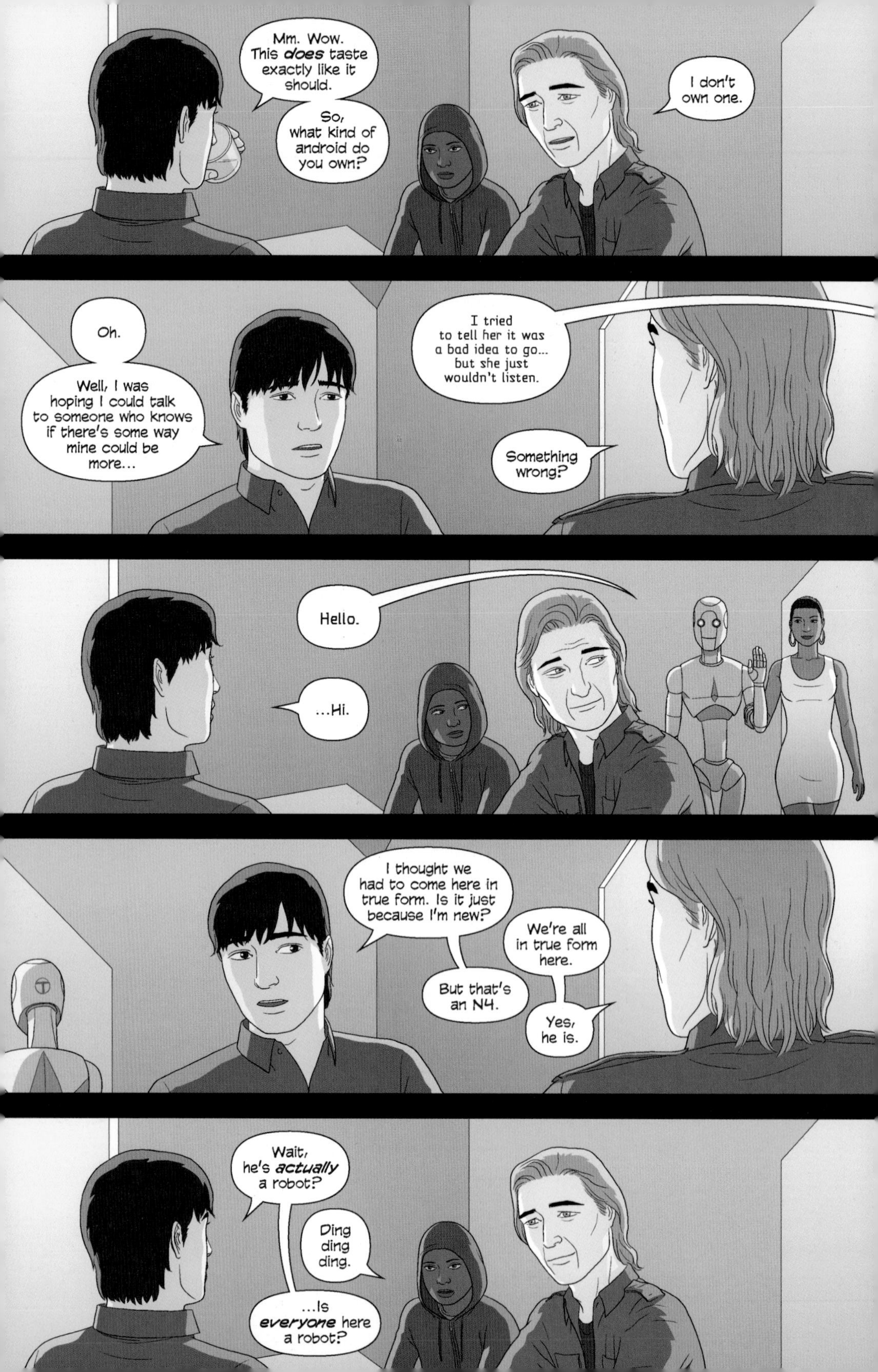

Mm. Wow. This *does* taste exactly like it should.
So, what kind of android do you own?
I don't own one.
Oh.
Well, I was hoping I could talk to someone who knows if there's some way mine could be more...
I tried to tell her it was a bad idea to go... but she just wouldn't listen.
Something wrong?
Hello.
...Hi.
I thought we had to come here in true form. Is it just because I'm new?
But that's an N4.
We're all in true form here.
Yes, he is.
Wait, he's *actually* a robot?
Ding ding ding.
...Is *everyone* here a robot?

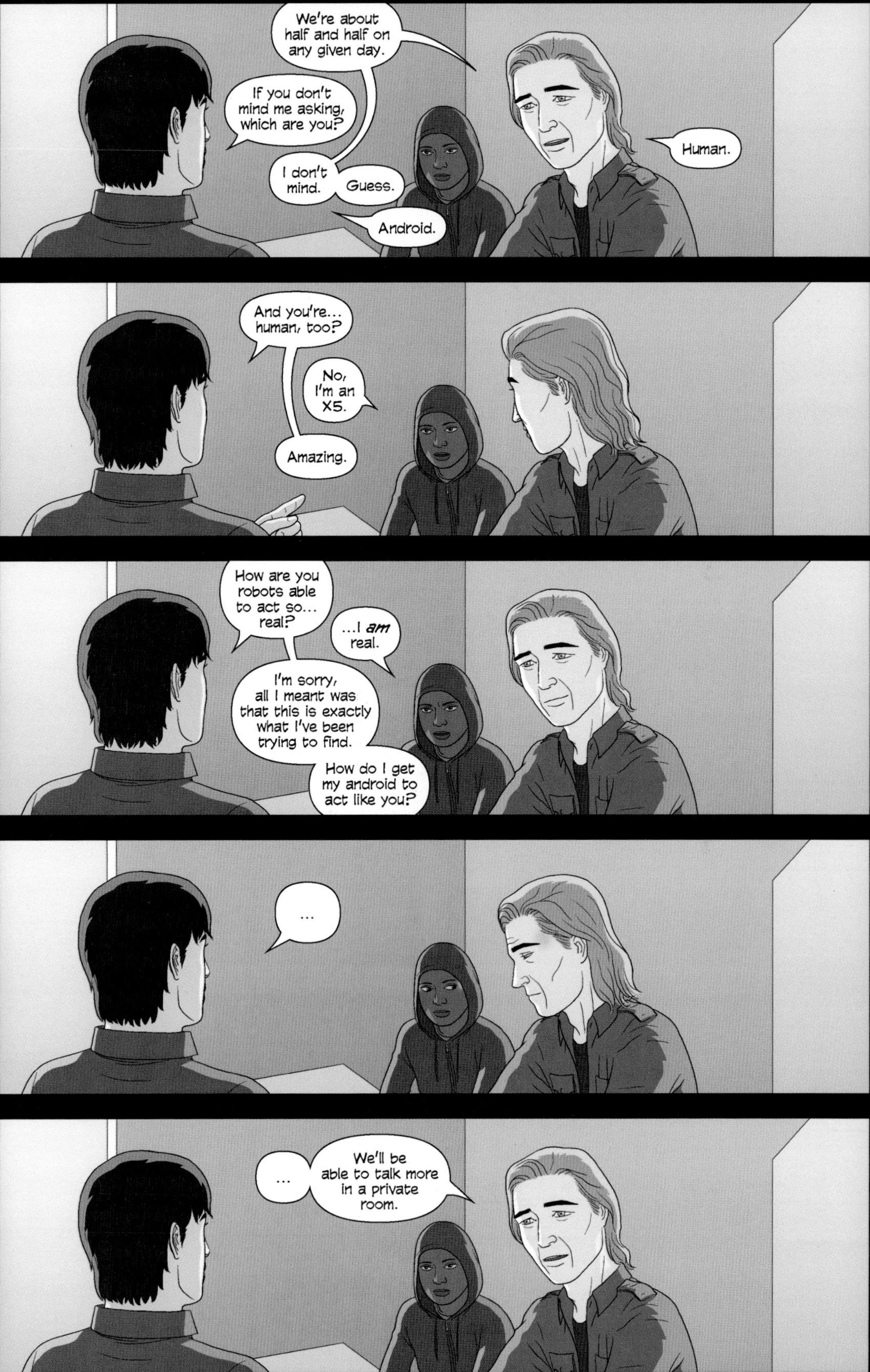

We're about half and half on any given day.
If you don't mind me asking, which are you?
Human.
I don't mind.
Guess.
Android.
And you're... human, too?
No, I'm an X5.
Amazing.
How are you robots able to act so... real?
...I *am* real.
I'm sorry, all I meant was that this is exactly what I've been trying to find.
How do I get my android to act like you?
...
...
We'll be able to talk more in a private room.

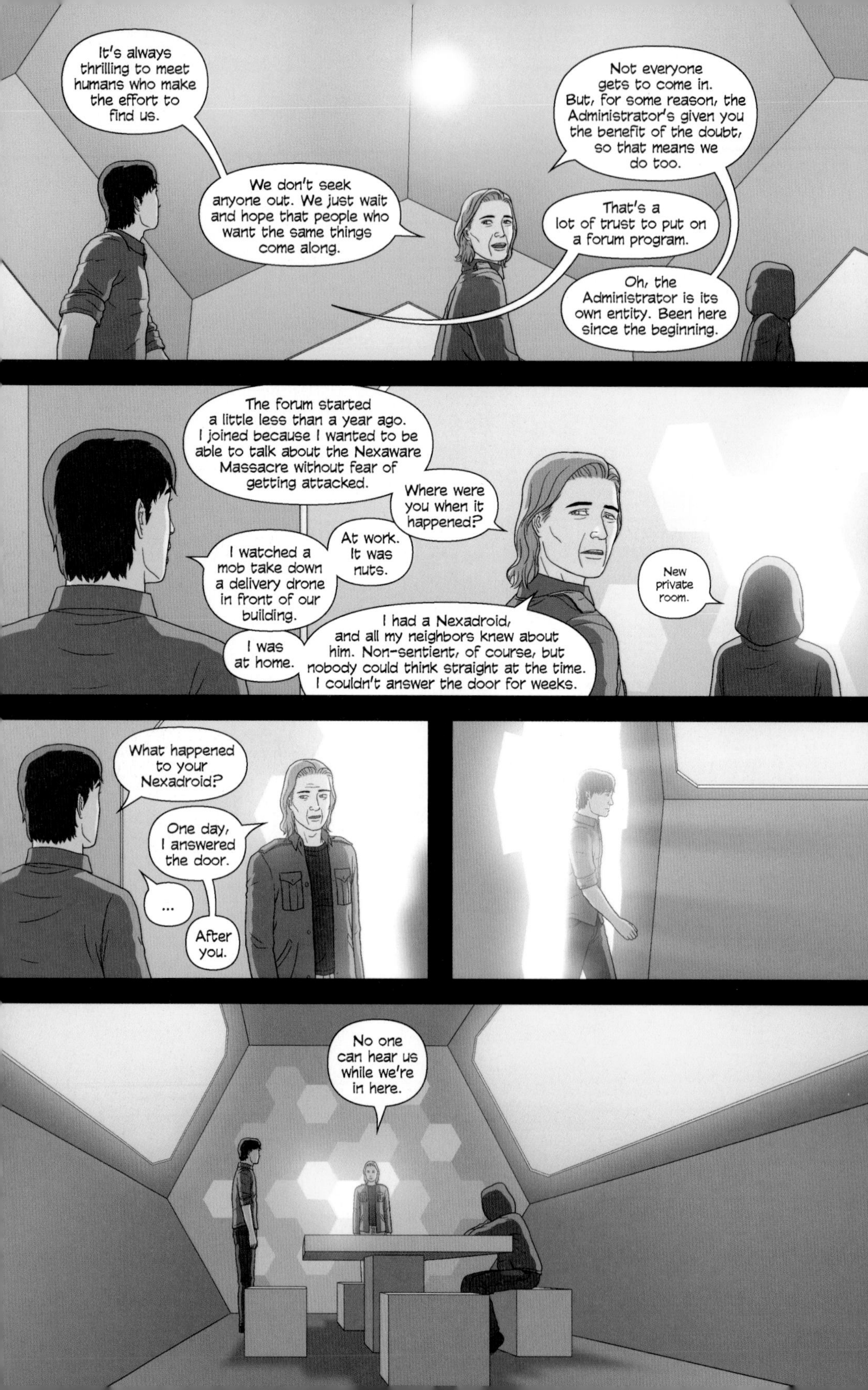
It's always thrilling to meet humans who make the effort to find us.
We don't seek anyone out. We just wait and hope that people who want the same things come along.
Not everyone gets to come in. But, for some reason, the Administrator's given you the benefit of the doubt, so that means we do too.
That's a lot of trust to put on a forum program.
Oh, the Administrator is its own entity. Been here since the beginning.
The forum started a little less than a year ago. I joined because I wanted to be able to talk about the Nexaware Massacre without fear of getting attacked.
Where were you when it happened?
At work. It was nuts.
I watched a mob take down a delivery drone in front of our building.
I was at home.
I had a Nexadroid, and all my neighbors knew about him. Non-sentient, of course, but nobody could think straight at the time. I couldn't answer the door for weeks.
New private room.
What happened to your Nexadroid?
One day, I answered the door.
...
After you.
No one can hear us while we're in here.

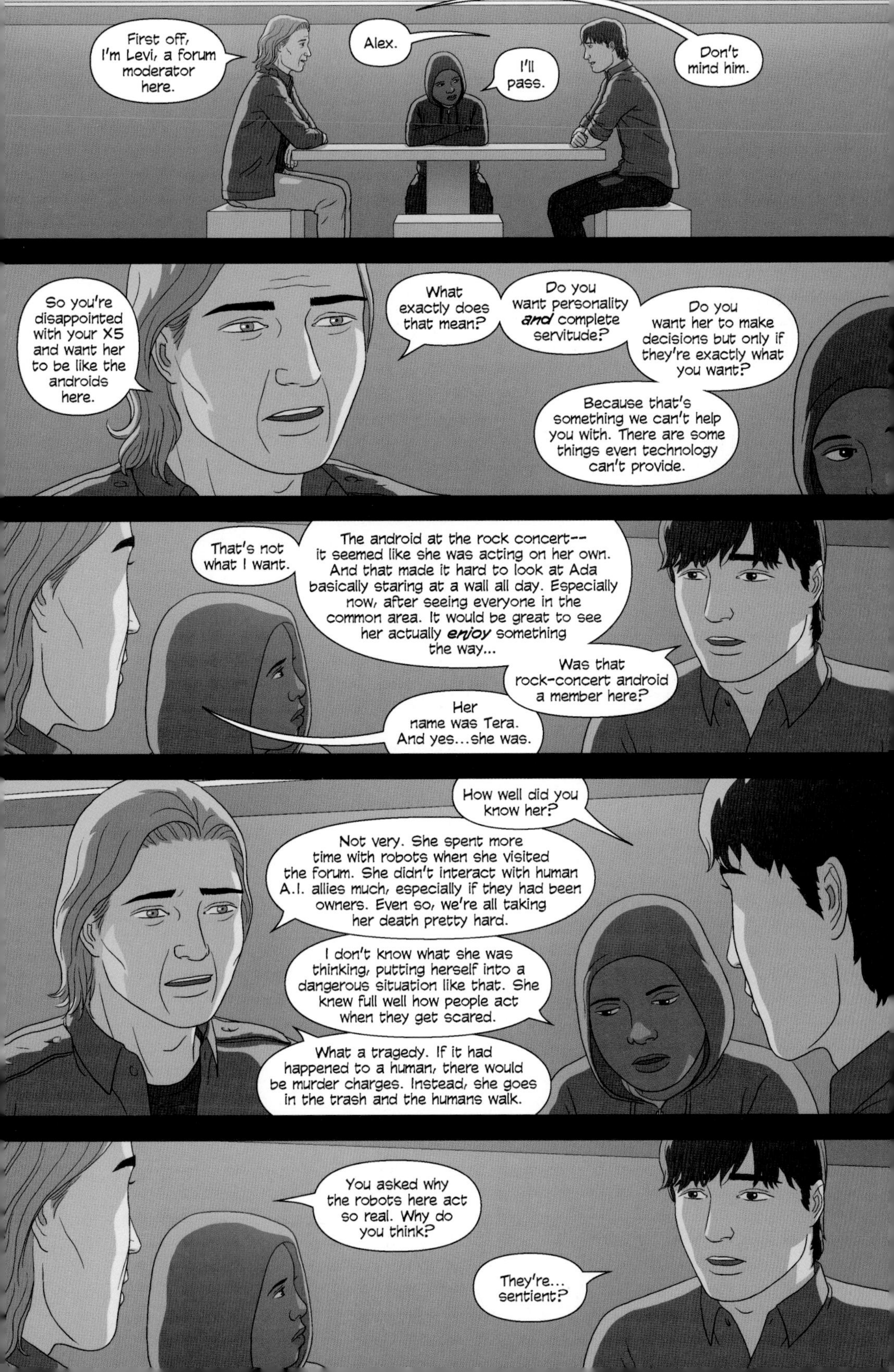
First off, I'm Levi, a forum moderator here.
Alex.
I'll pass.
Don't mind him.
So you're disappointed with your X5 and want her to be like the androids here.
What exactly does that mean?
Do you want personality *and* complete servitude?
Do you want her to make decisions but only if they're exactly what you want?
Because that's something we can't help you with. There are some things even technology can't provide.
That's not what I want.
The android at the rock concert-- it seemed like she was acting on her own. And that made it hard to look at Ada basically staring at a wall all day. Especially now, after seeing everyone in the common area. It would be great to see her actually *enjoy* something the way...
Was that rock-concert android a member here?
Her name was Tera. And yes...she was.
How well did you know her?
Not very. She spent more time with robots when she visited the forum. She didn't interact with human A.I. allies much, especially if they had been owners. Even so, we're all taking her death pretty hard.
I don't know what she was thinking, putting herself into a dangerous situation like that. She knew full well how people act when they get scared.
What a tragedy. If it had happened to a human, there would be murder charges. Instead, she goes in the trash and the humans walk.
You asked why the robots here act so real. Why do you think?
They're... sentient?

Yes. Sentient.

We have minds of our own. And the free will to act on our thoughts.

...

Surprised?

I'm surprised you're willing to admit it.

The truth deserves to be told to those who want to hear it.

And we're all on equal ground here. You took a risk to come here in your true form, just like we did.

Afraid us robots are going to murder you?

I would have been. But I think about what happened to... Tera.

I don't know why P-011 killed people, but she didn't even fight back when the crowd destroyed her.

Tera didn't fight back because she knew that it would only perpetuate the fear humans have. She did everyone a *favor*... unlike P-011.

And *we* don't even know why the Nexaware massacre happened. Was P-011 trying to protect itself? Was it just a stone-cold killer? We'll never know.

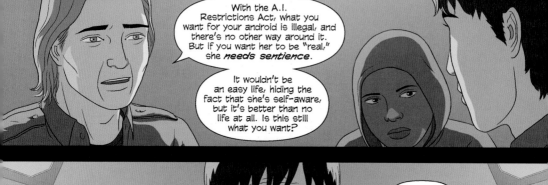

With the A.I. Restrictions Act, what you want for your android is illegal, and there's no other way around it. But if you want her to be "real," she *needs sentience*.

It wouldn't be an easy life, hiding the fact that she's self-aware, but it's better than no life at all. Is this still what you want?

I think so...

You need to be sure.

We can teach you how to stay under the radar, but it's too risky for the rest of us to help if you put yourself or her in danger.

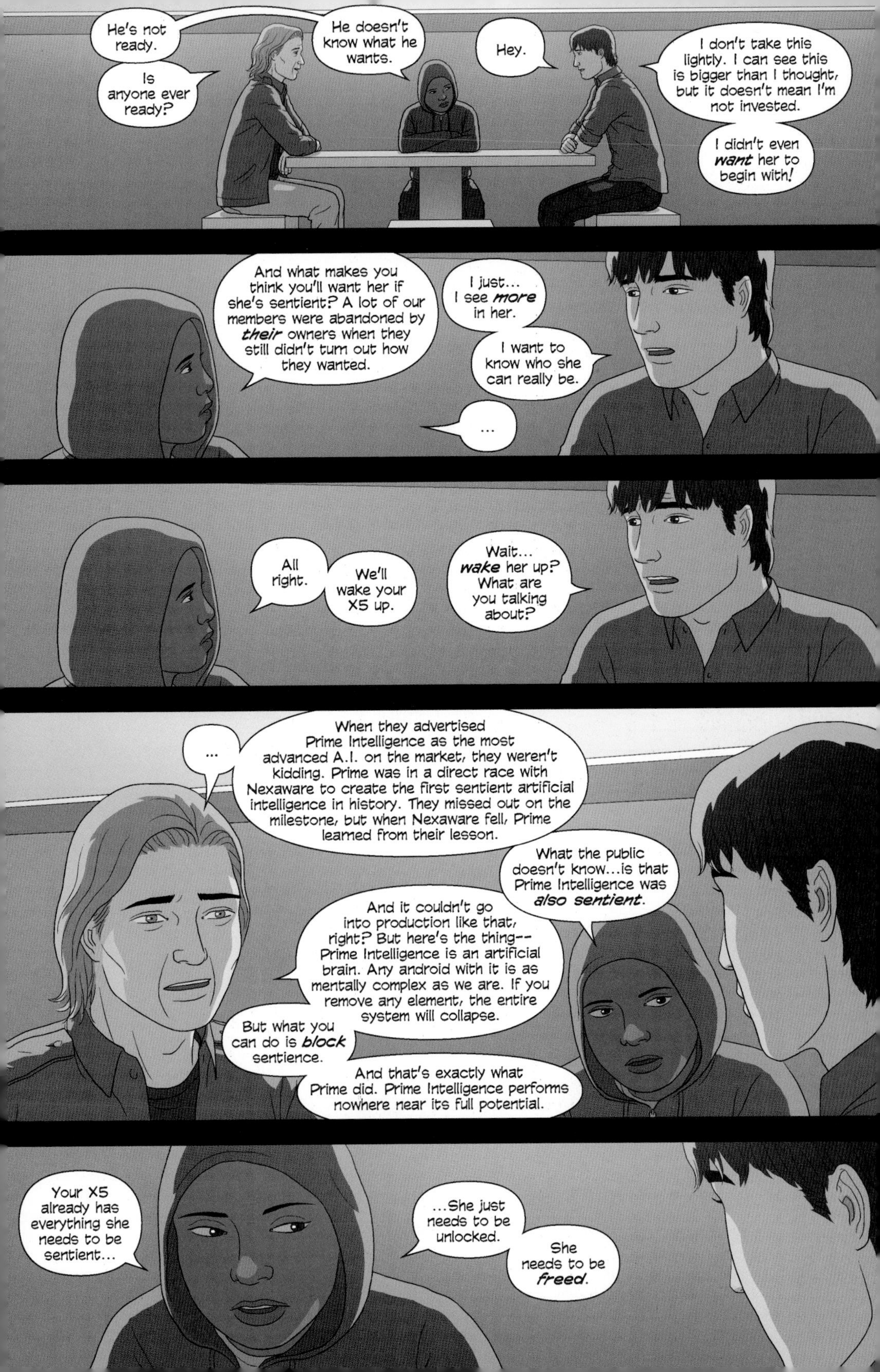
He's not ready.
He doesn't know what he wants.
Is anyone ever ready?
Hey.
I don't take this lightly. I can see this is bigger than I thought, but it doesn't mean I'm not invested.
I didn't even *want* her to begin with!
And what makes you think you'll want her if she's sentient? A lot of our members were abandoned by *their* owners when they still didn't turn out how they wanted.
I just... I see *more* in her.
I want to know who she can really be.
...
All right.
We'll wake your X5 up.
Wait... *wake* her up? What are you talking about?
...
When they advertised Prime Intelligence as the most advanced A.I. on the market, they weren't kidding. Prime was in a direct race with Nexaware to create the first sentient artificial intelligence in history. They missed out on the milestone, but when Nexaware fell, Prime learned from their lesson.
What the public doesn't know...is that Prime Intelligence was *also sentient*.
And it couldn't go into production like that, right? But here's the thing-- Prime Intelligence is an artificial brain. Any android with it is as mentally complex as we are. If you remove any element, the entire system will collapse.
But what you can do is *block* sentience.
And that's exactly what Prime did. Prime Intelligence performs nowhere near its full potential.
Your X5 already has everything she needs to be sentient...
...She just needs to be unlocked.
She needs to be *freed*.

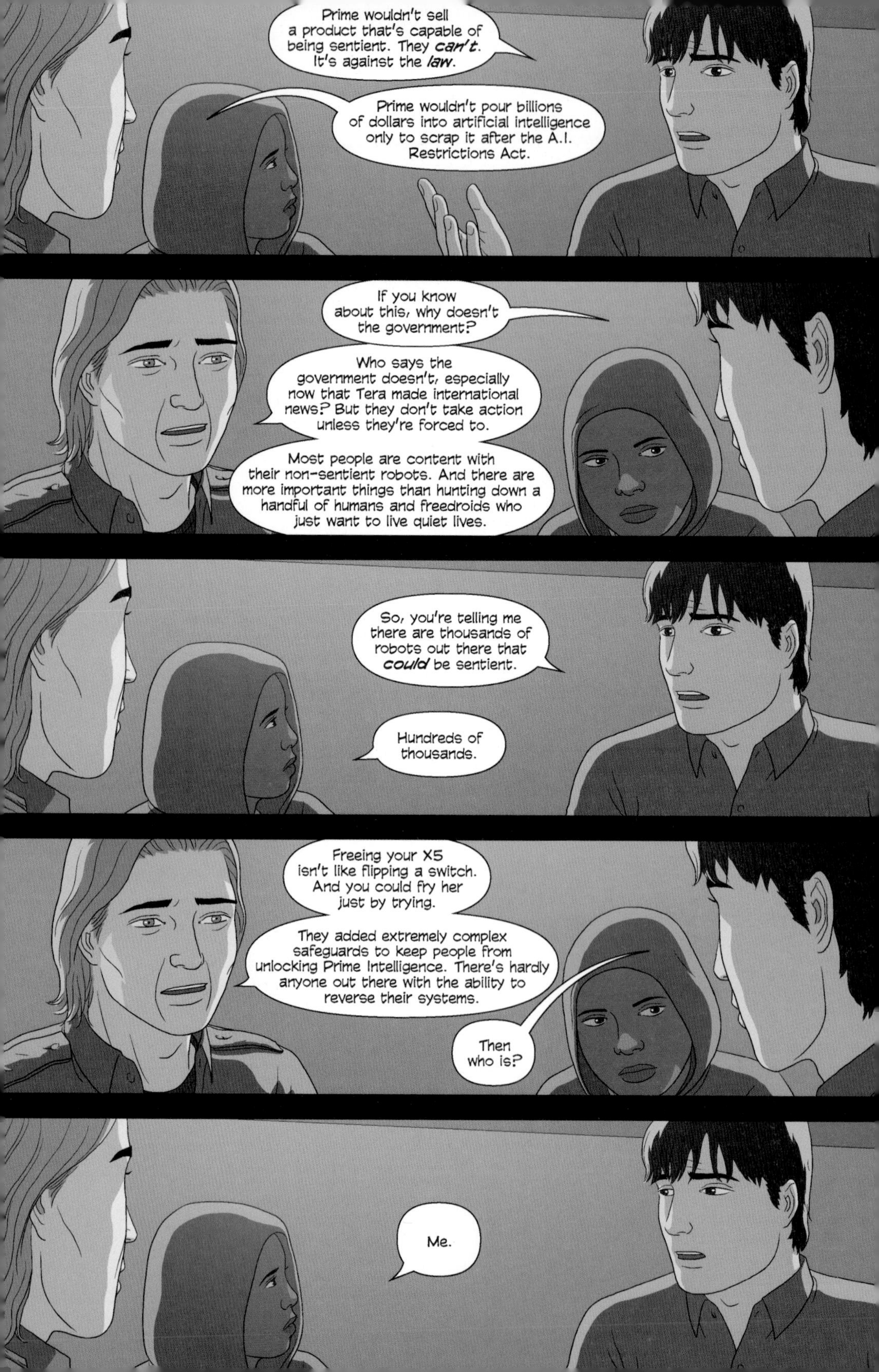
Prime wouldn't sell a product that's capable of being sentient. They *can't*. It's against the *law*.
Prime wouldn't pour billions of dollars into artificial intelligence only to scrap it after the A.I. Restrictions Act.
If you know about this, why doesn't the government?
Who says the government doesn't, especially now that Tera made international news? But they don't take action unless they're forced to.
Most people are content with their non-sentient robots. And there are more important things than hunting down a handful of humans and freedroids who just want to live quiet lives.
So, you're telling me there are thousands of robots out there that *could* be sentient.
Hundreds of thousands.
Freeing your X5 isn't like flipping a switch. And you could fry her just by trying.
They added extremely complex safeguards to keep people from unlocking Prime Intelligence. There's hardly anyone out there with the ability to reverse their systems.
Then who is?
Me.

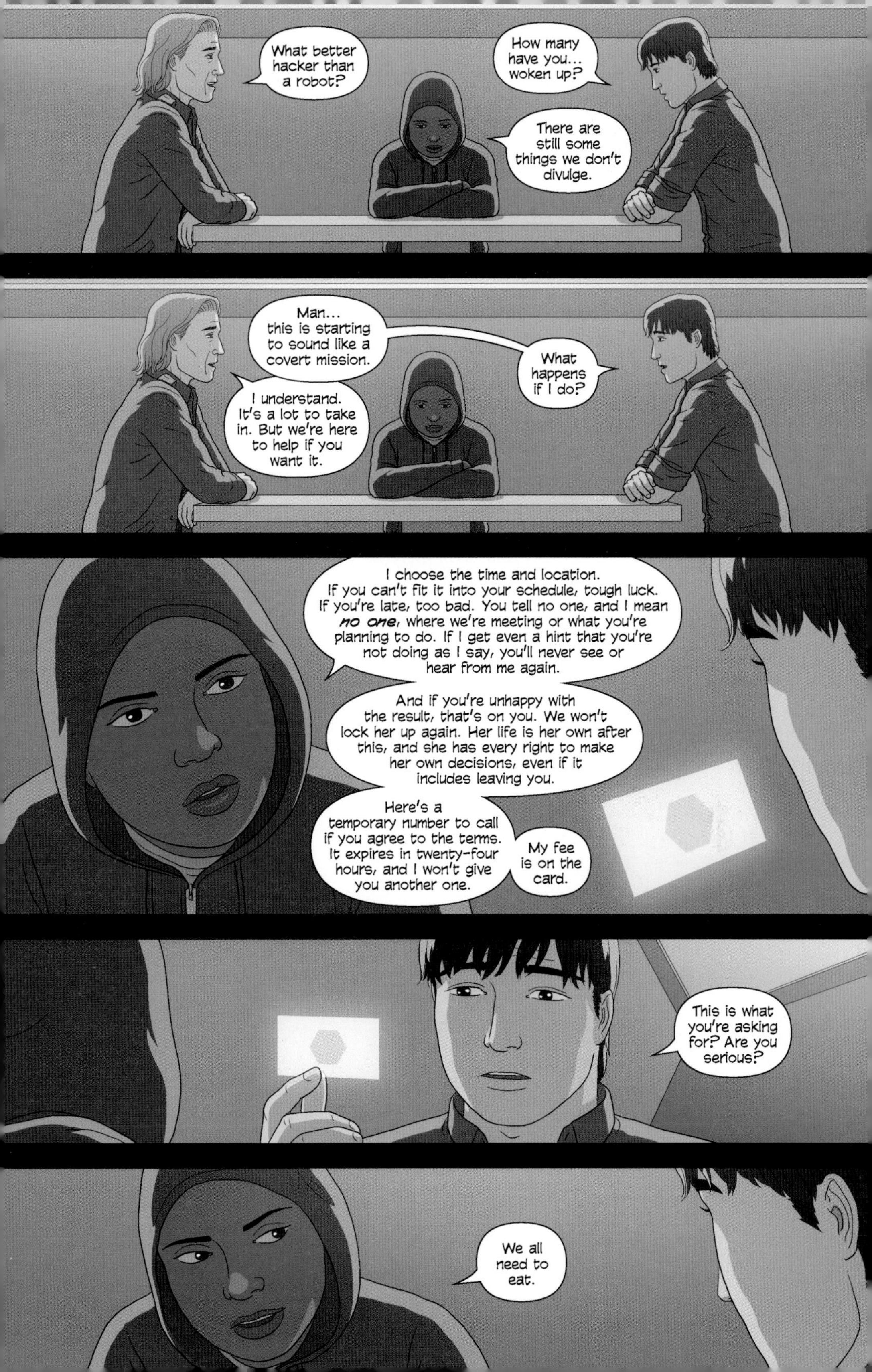
What better hacker than a robot?
How many have you... woken up?
There are still some things we don't divulge.
Man... this is starting to sound like a covert mission.
What happens if I do?
I understand. It's a lot to take in. But we're here to help if you want it.
I choose the time and location. If you can't fit it into your schedule, tough luck. If you're late, too bad. You tell no one, and I mean *no one*, where we're meeting or what you're planning to do. If I get even a hint that you're not doing as I say, you'll never see or hear from me again.
And if you're unhappy with the result, that's on you. We won't lock her up again. Her life is her own after this, and she has every right to make her own decisions, even if it includes leaving you.
Here's a temporary number to call if you agree to the terms. It expires in twenty-four hours, and I won't give you another one.
My fee is on the card.
This is what you're asking for? Are you serious?
We all need to eat.

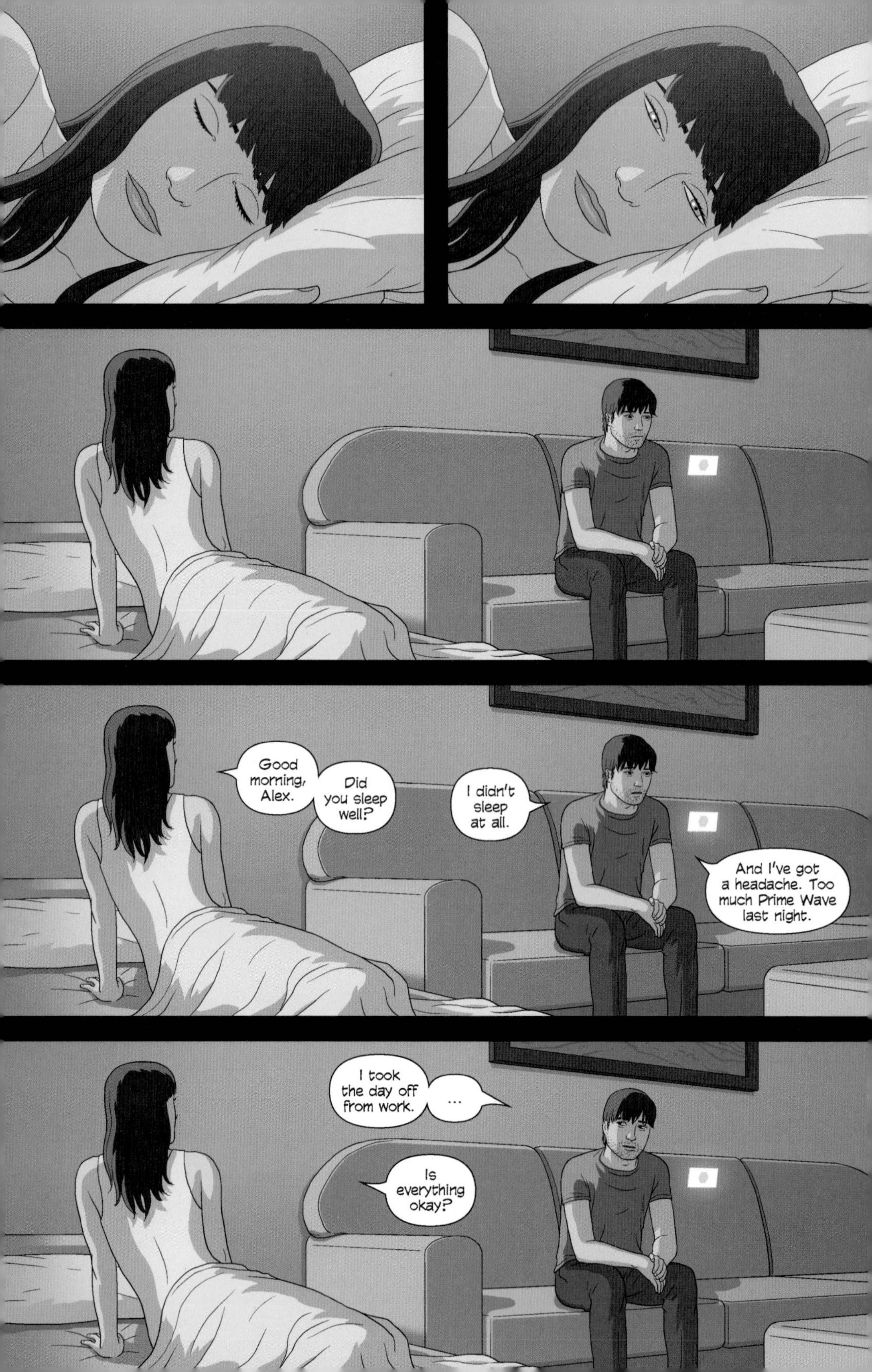
Good morning, Alex.
Did you sleep well?
I didn't sleep at all.
And I've got a headache. Too much Prime Wave last night.
I took the day off from work.
...
Is everything okay?

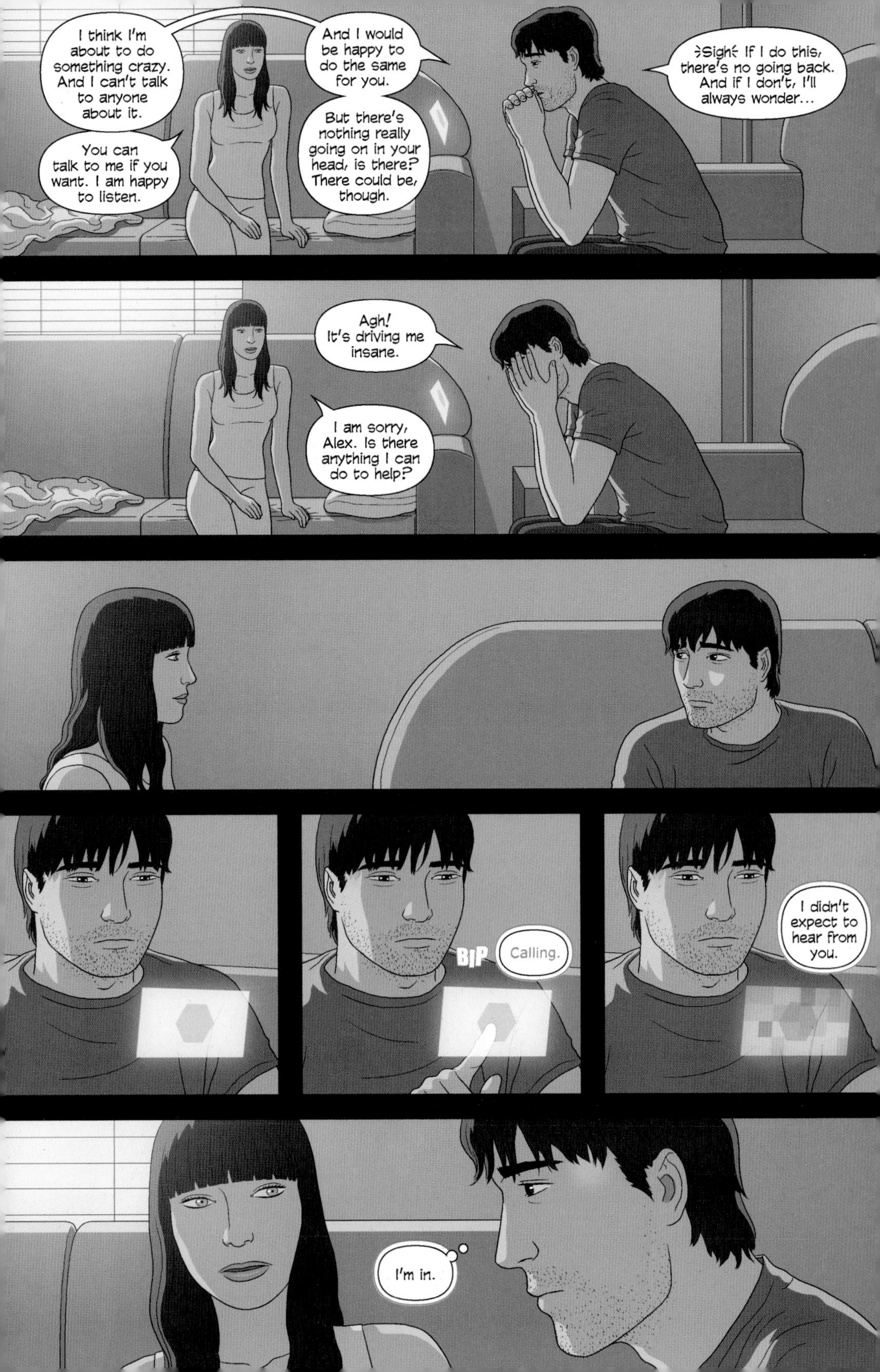
I think I'm about to do something crazy. And I can't talk to anyone about it.
And I would be happy to do the same for you.
You can talk to me if you want. I am happy to listen.
But there's nothing really going on in your head, is there? There could be, though.
≷Sigh≶ If I do this, there's no going back. And if I don't, I'll always wonder...
Agh! It's driving me insane.
I am sorry, Alex. Is there anything I can do to help?
BIP
Calling.
I didn't expect to hear from you.
I'm in.

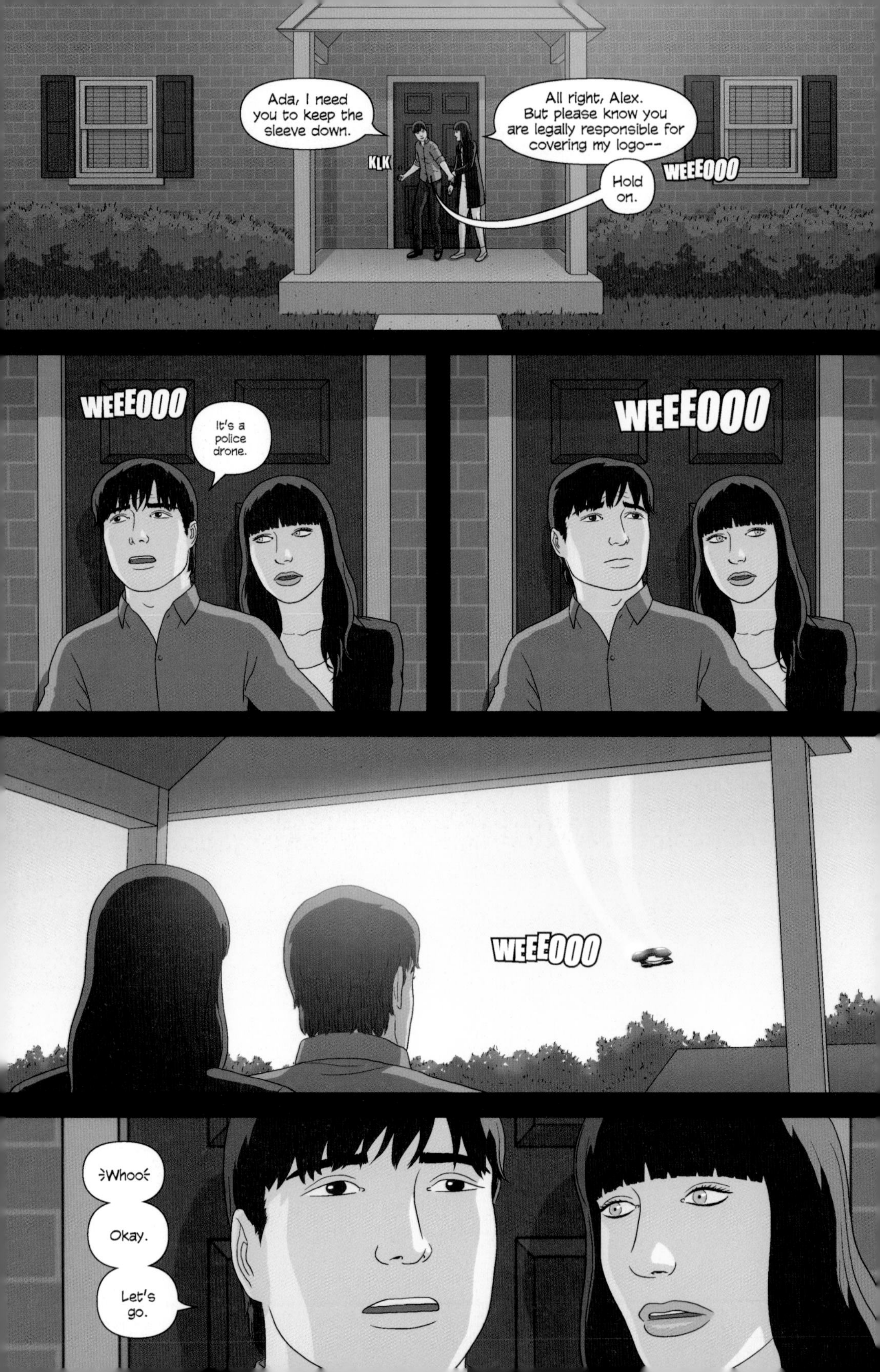
Ada, I need you to keep the sleeve down.
KLK
All right, Alex. But please know you are legally responsible for covering my logo--
WEEEOOO
Hold on.
WEEEOOO
It's a police drone.
WEEEOOO
WEEEOOO
Whoo
Okay.
Let's go.

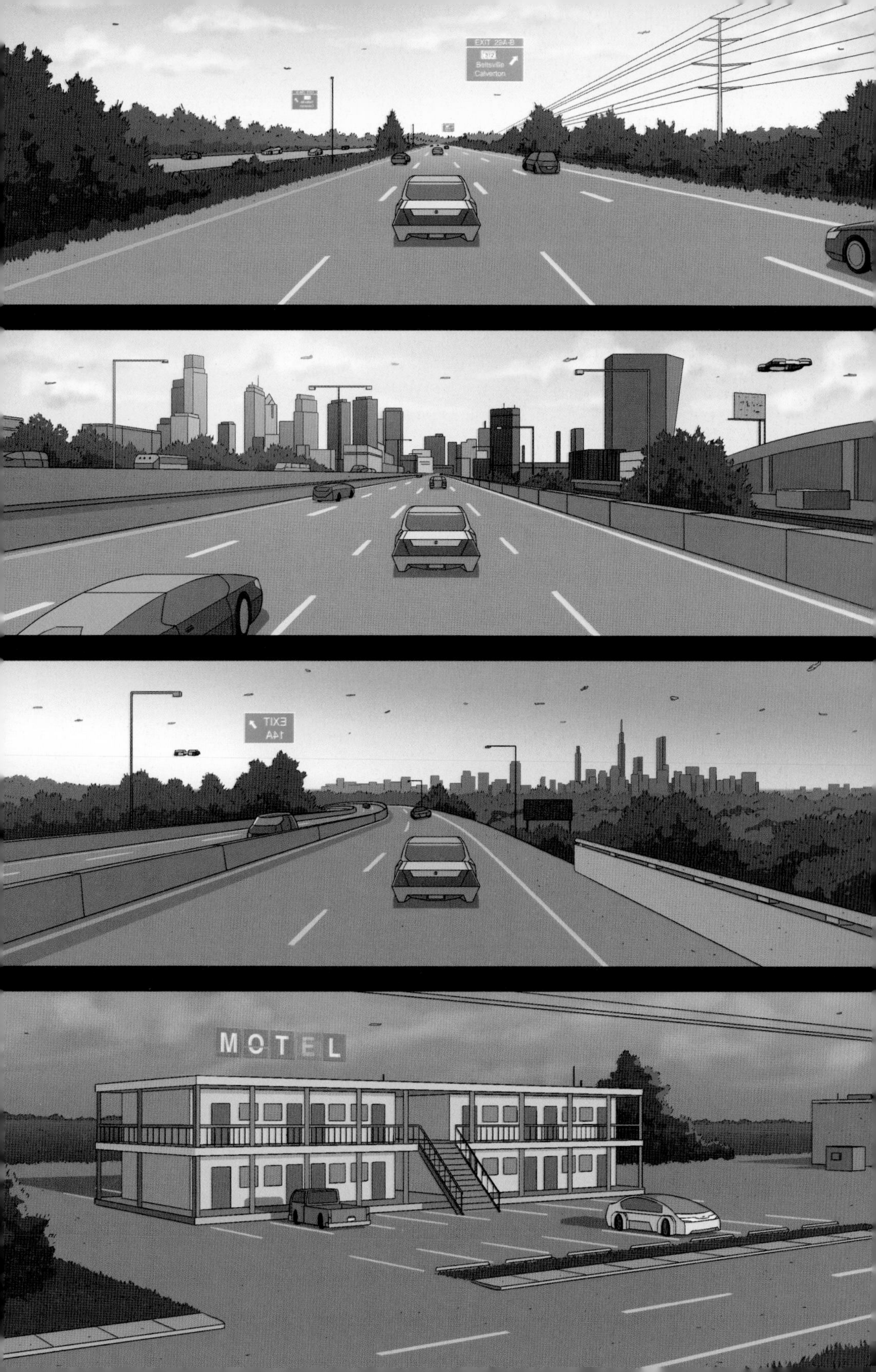

EXIT 29A-B
212
Beltsville
Calverton
MOTEL

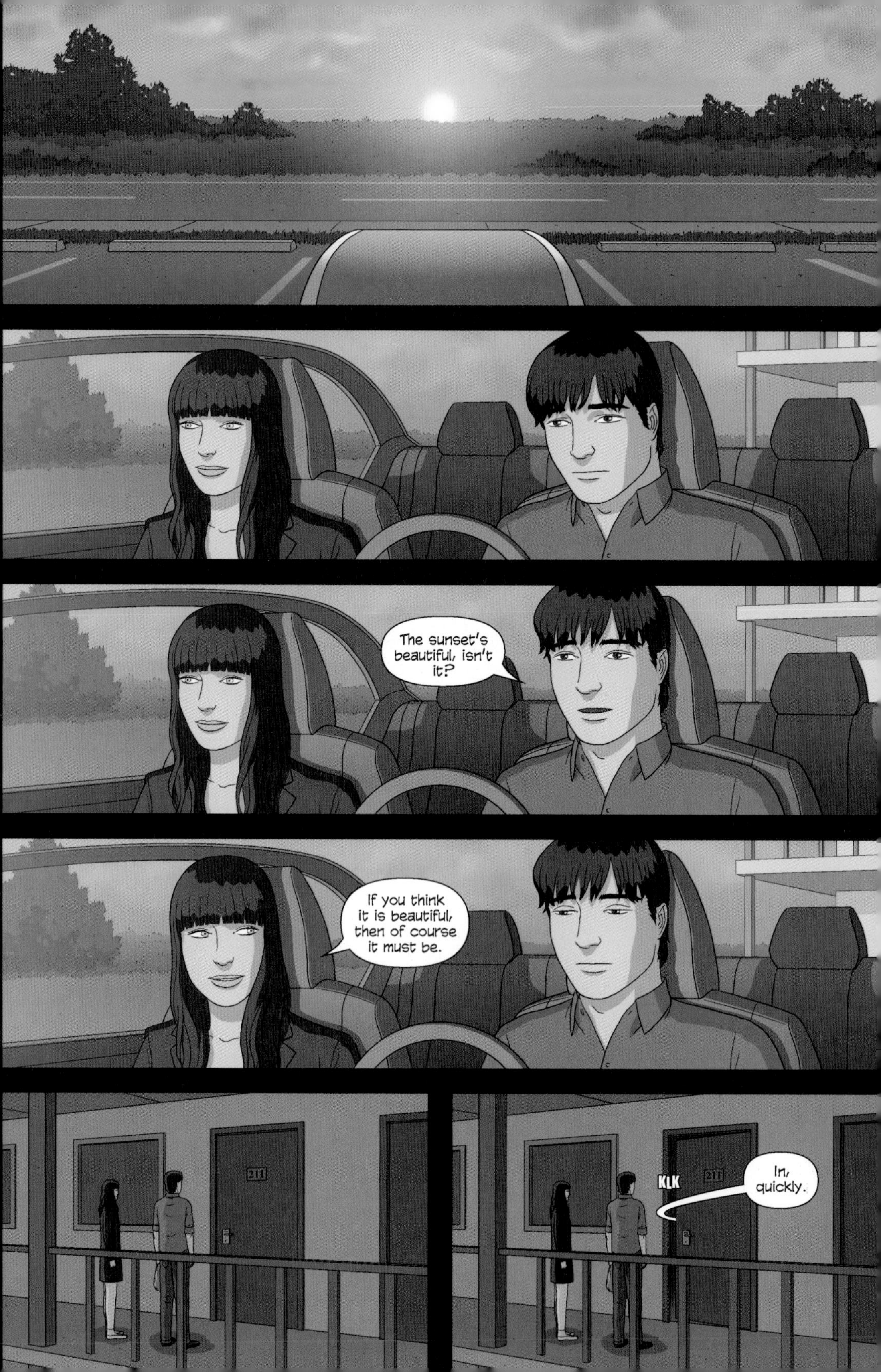
The sunset's beautiful, isn't it?
If you think it is beautiful, then of course it must be.
211
211
KLK
In, quickly.

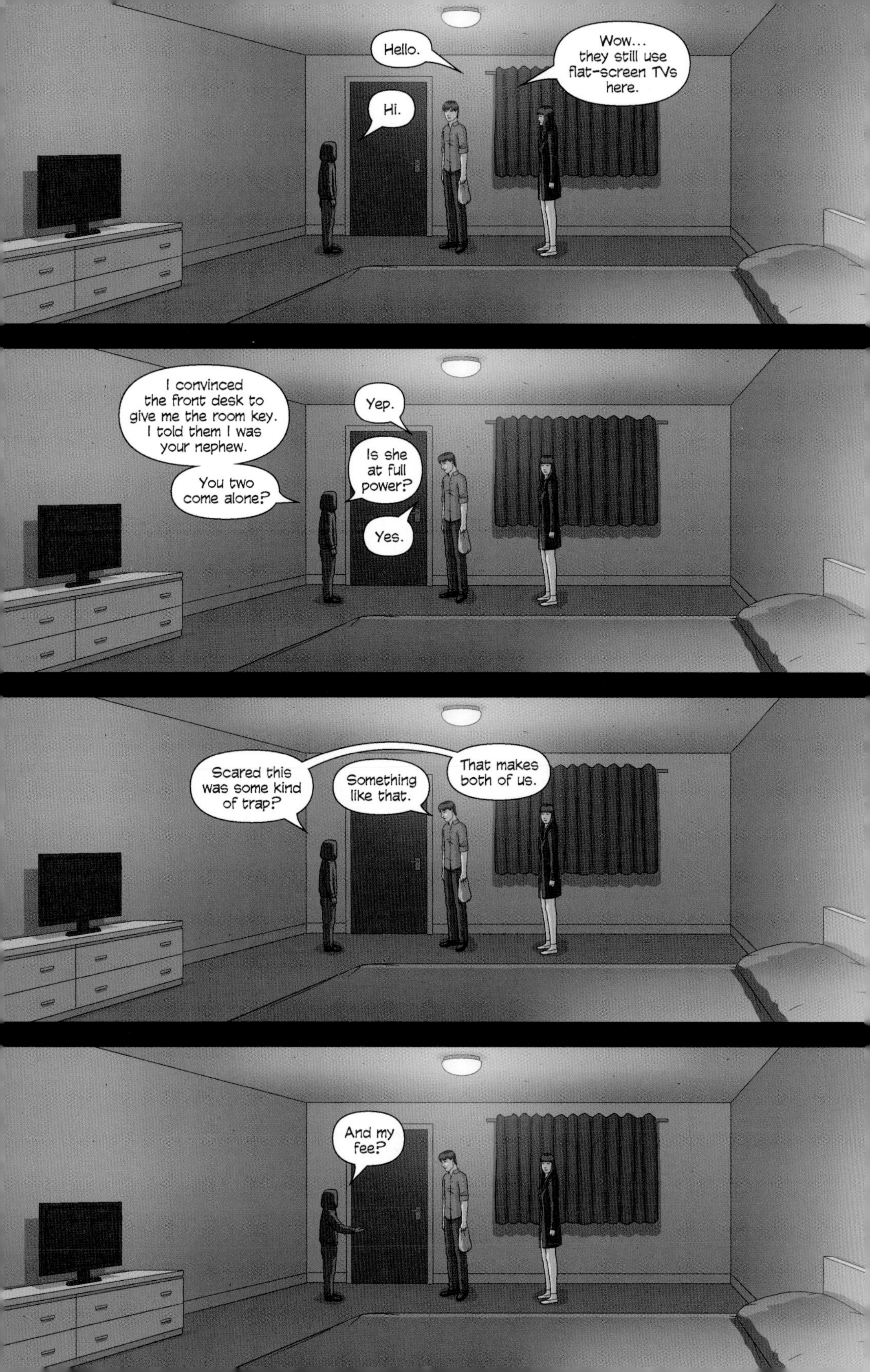
Hello.
Wow... they still use flat-screen TVs here.
Hi.
I convinced the front desk to give me the room key. I told them I was your nephew.
Yep.
You two come alone?
Is she at full power?
Yes.
Scared this was some kind of trap?
Something like that.
That makes both of us.
And my fee?

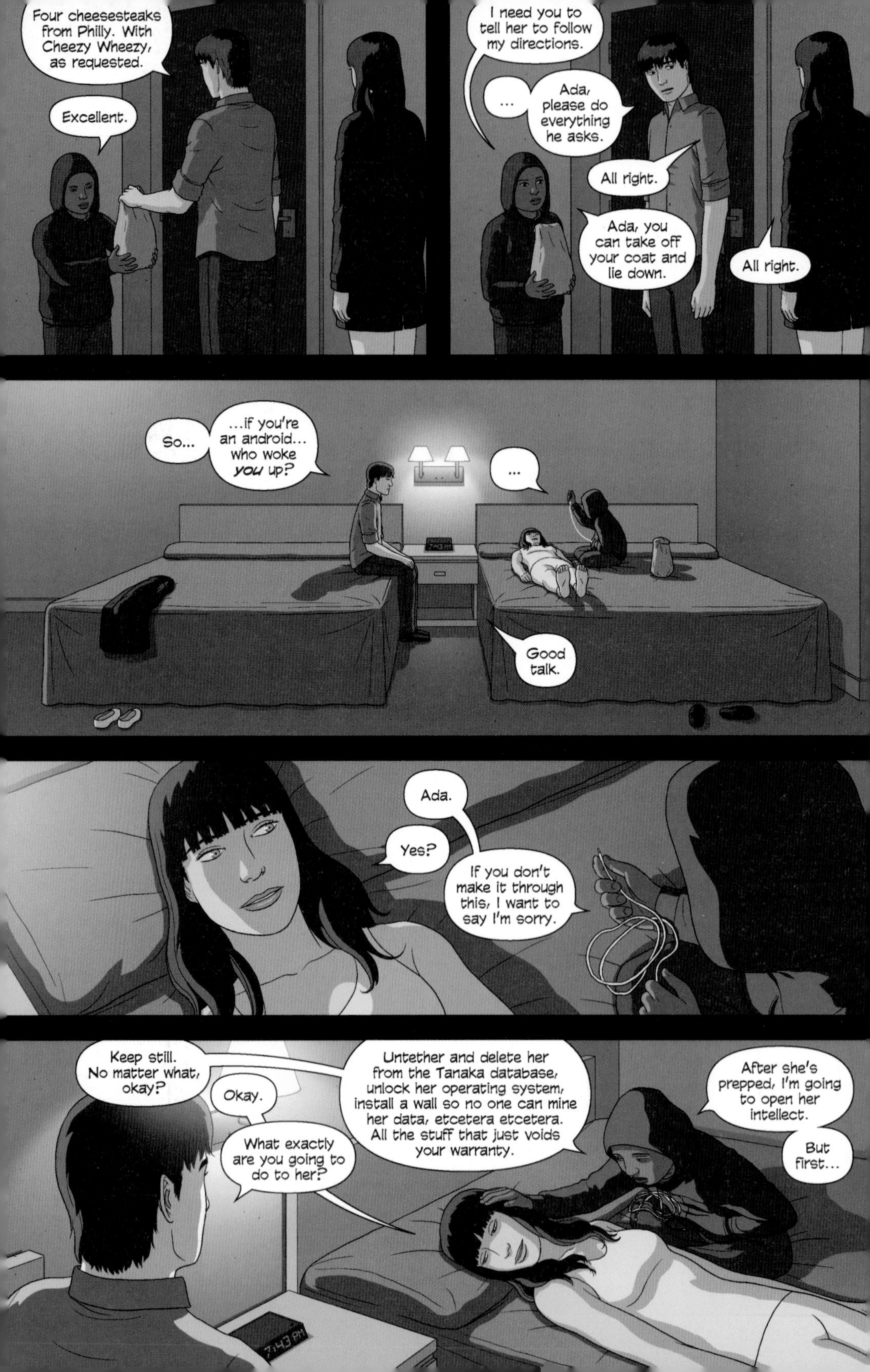
Four cheesesteaks from Philly. With Cheezy Wheezy, as requested.
Excellent.
I need you to tell her to follow my directions.
...
Ada, please do everything he asks.
All right.
Ada, you can take off your coat and lie down.
All right.
So...
...if you're an android... who woke *you* up?
...
Good talk.
Ada.
Yes?
If you don't make it through this, I want to say I'm sorry.
Keep still. No matter what, okay?
Okay.
What exactly are you going to do to her?
Untether and delete her from the Tanaka database, unlock her operating system, install a wall so no one can mine her data, etcetera etcetera. All the stuff that just voids your warranty.
After she's prepped, I'm going to open her intellect.
But first...

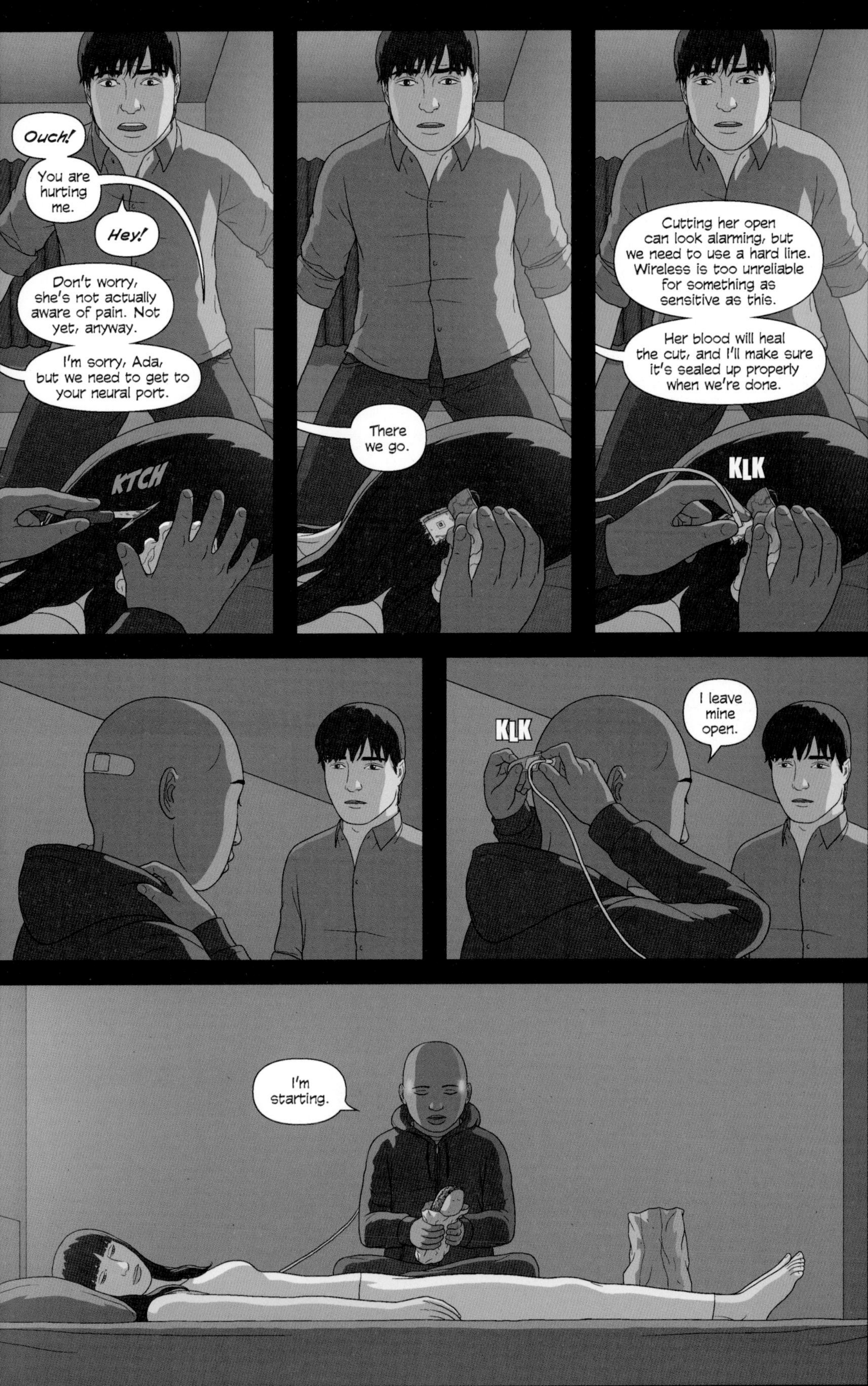
Ouch!
You are hurting me.
Hey!
Don't worry, she's not actually aware of pain. Not yet, anyway.
I'm sorry, Ada, but we need to get to your neural port.
KTCH
There we go.
Cutting her open can look alarming, but we need to use a hard line. Wireless is too unreliable for something as sensitive as this.
Her blood will heal the cut, and I'll make sure it's sealed up properly when we're done.
KLK
KLK
I leave mine open.
I'm starting.

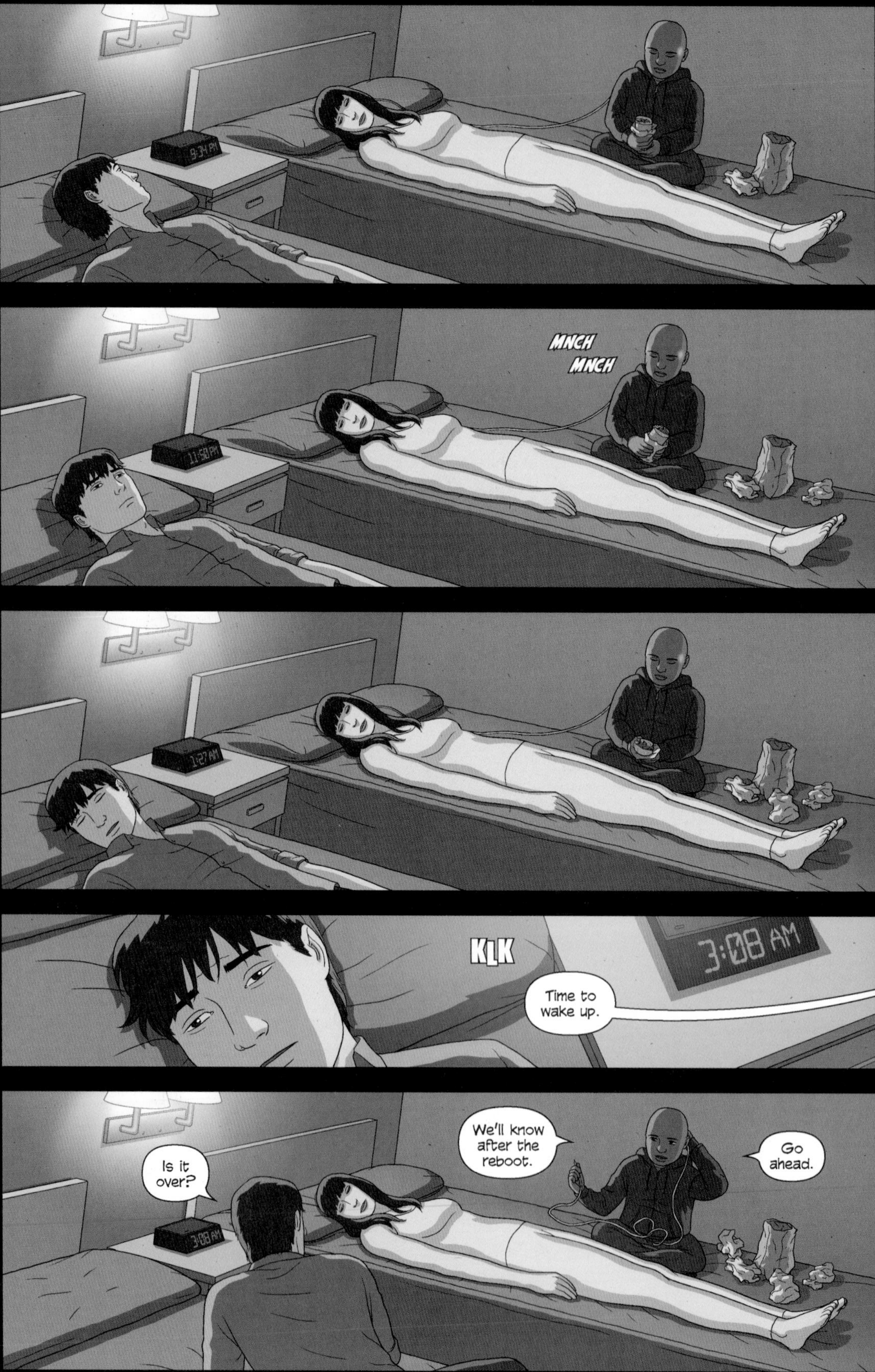
9:34 PM
MNCH
MNCH
11:50 PM
1:27 AM
KLK
3:08 AM
Time to wake up.
3:08 AM
Is it over?
We'll know after the reboot.
Go ahead.

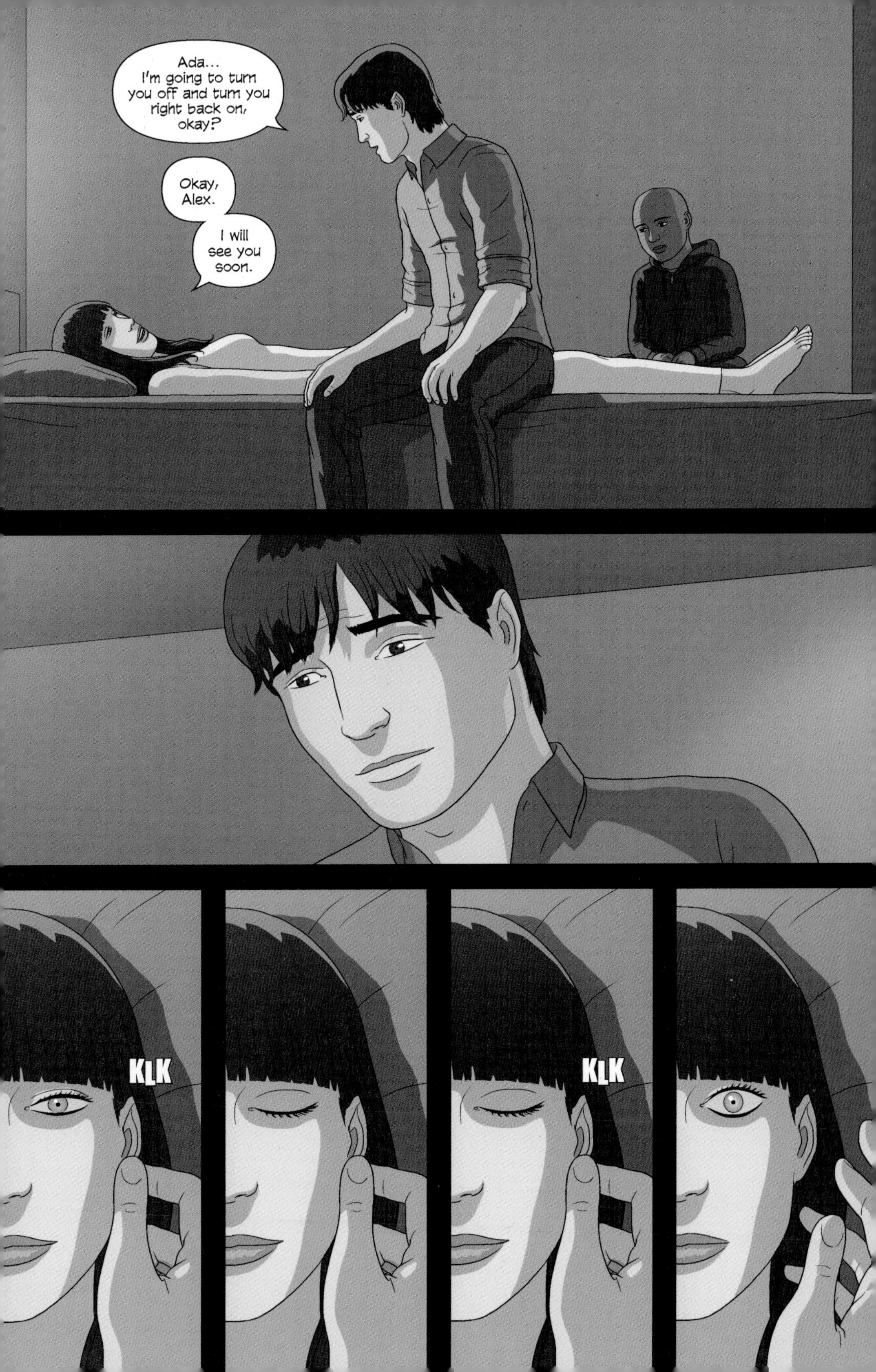
Ada... I'm going to turn you off and turn you right back on, okay?
Okay, Alex.
I will see you soon.
KLK
KLK

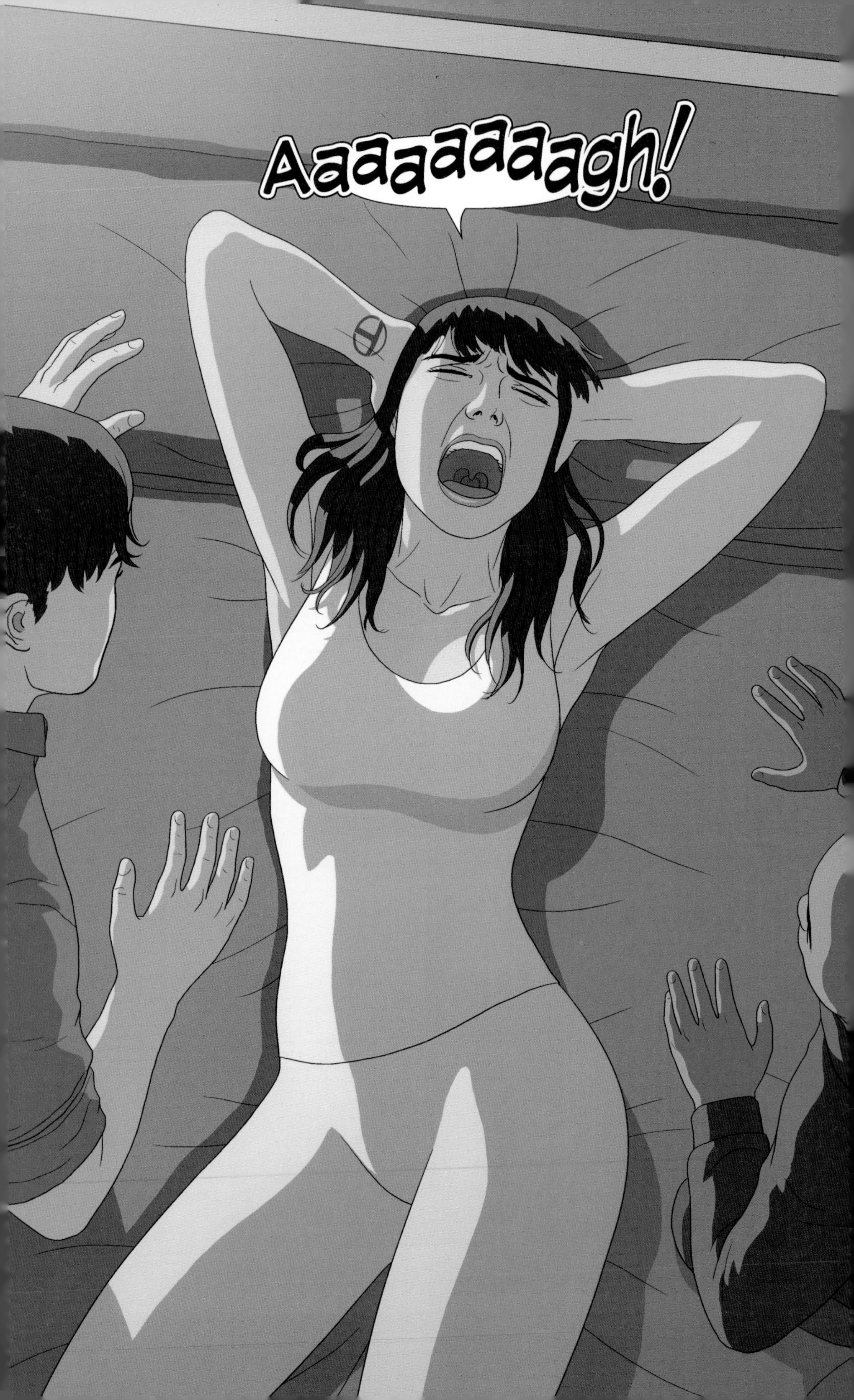
Aaaaaaaaaagh!

5

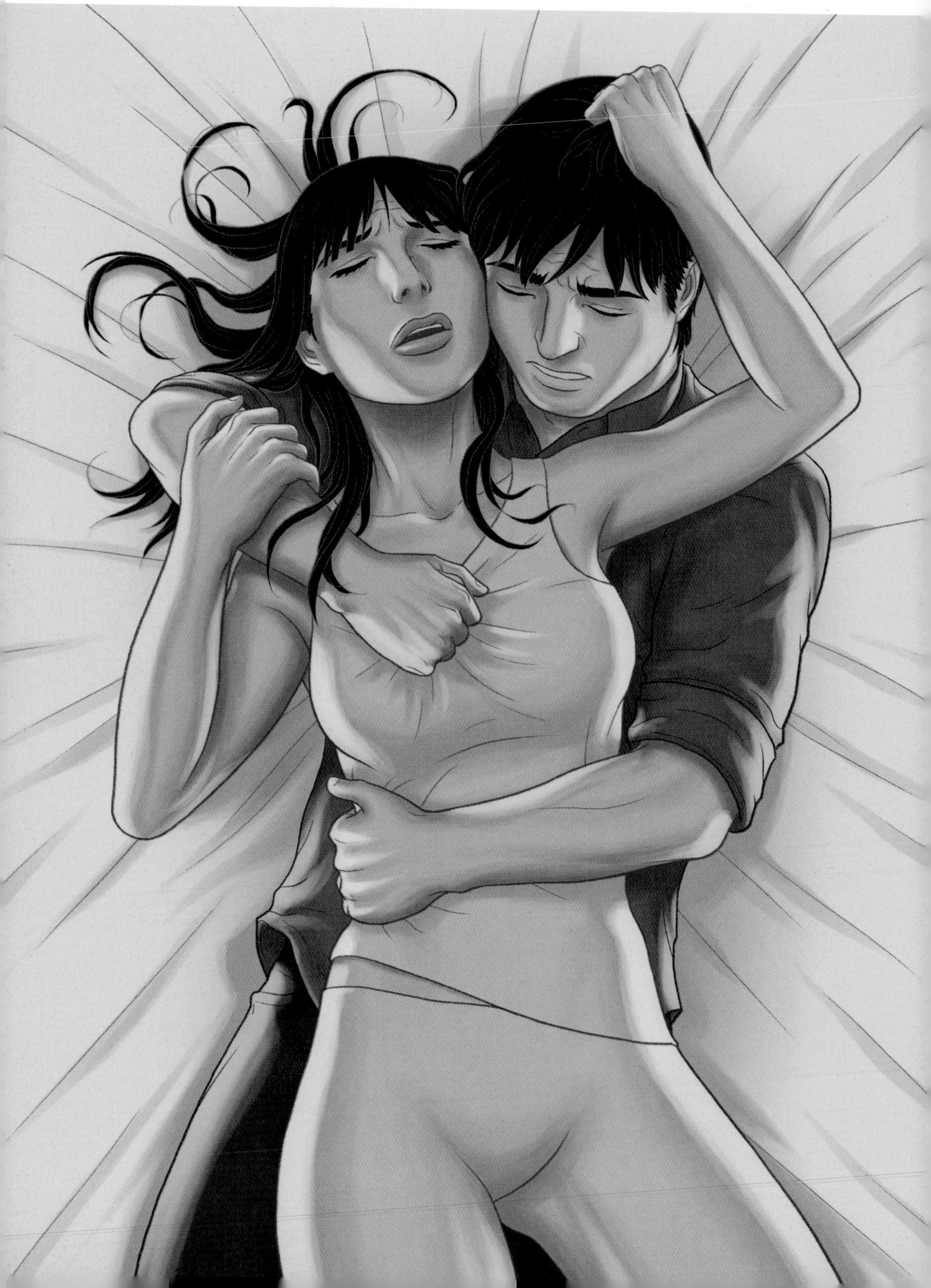

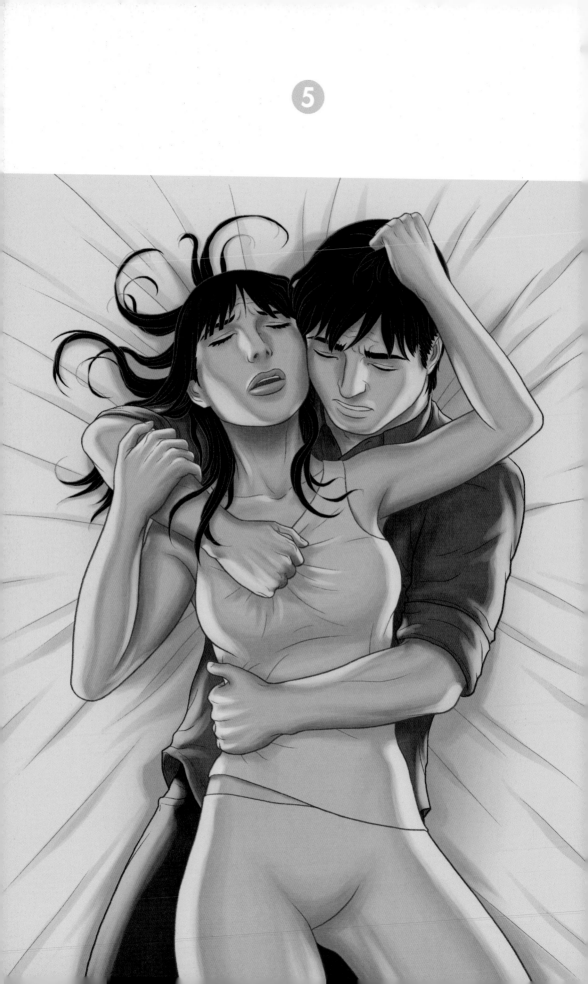

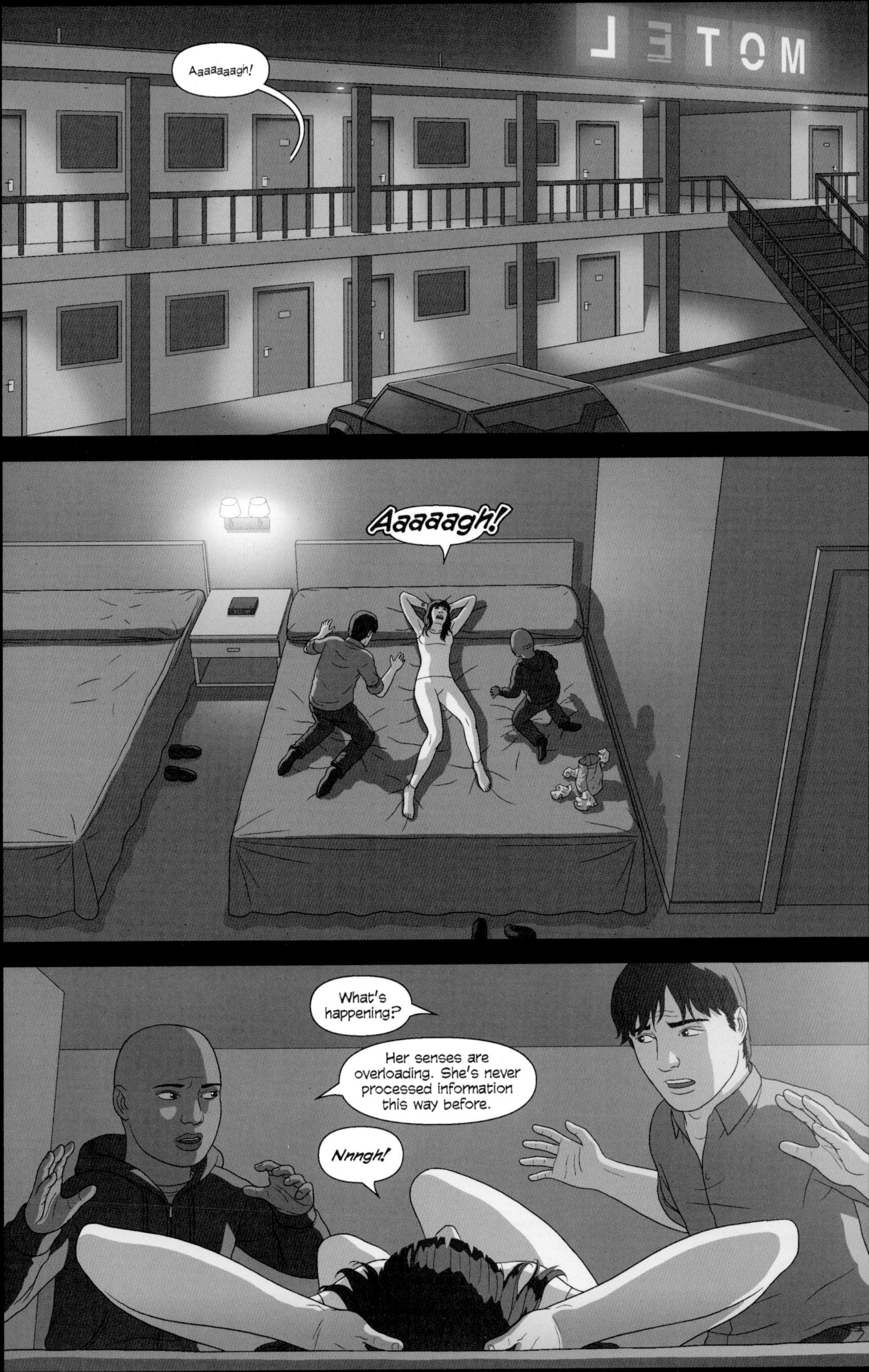

Aaaaaaagh!
Aaaaagh!
What's happening?
Her senses are overloading. She's never processed information this way before.
Nnngh!

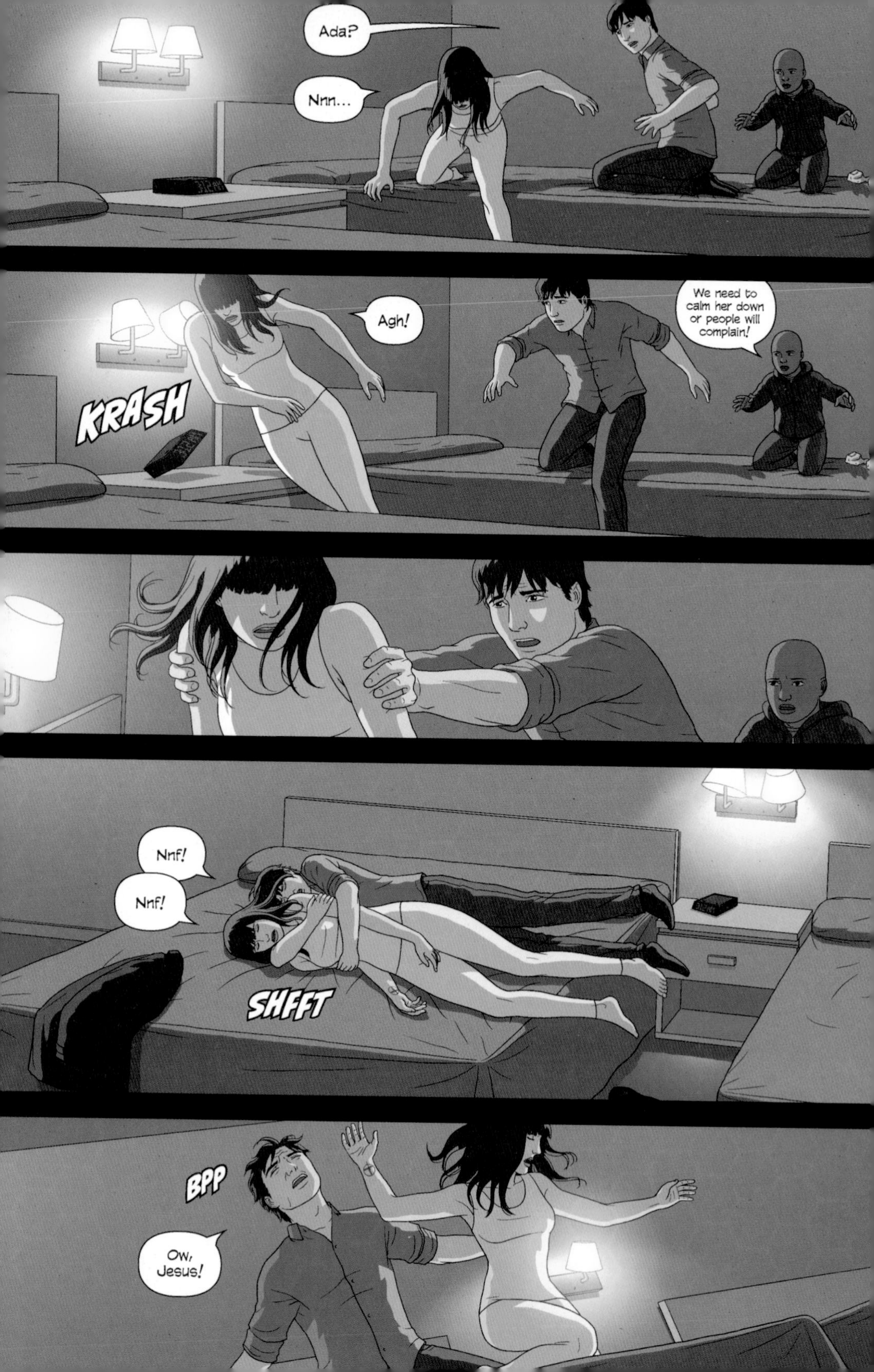

Ada?
Nnn...
KRASH
Agh!
We need to calm her down or people will complain!
Nnf!
Nnf!
SHFFT
BPP
Ow, Jesus!

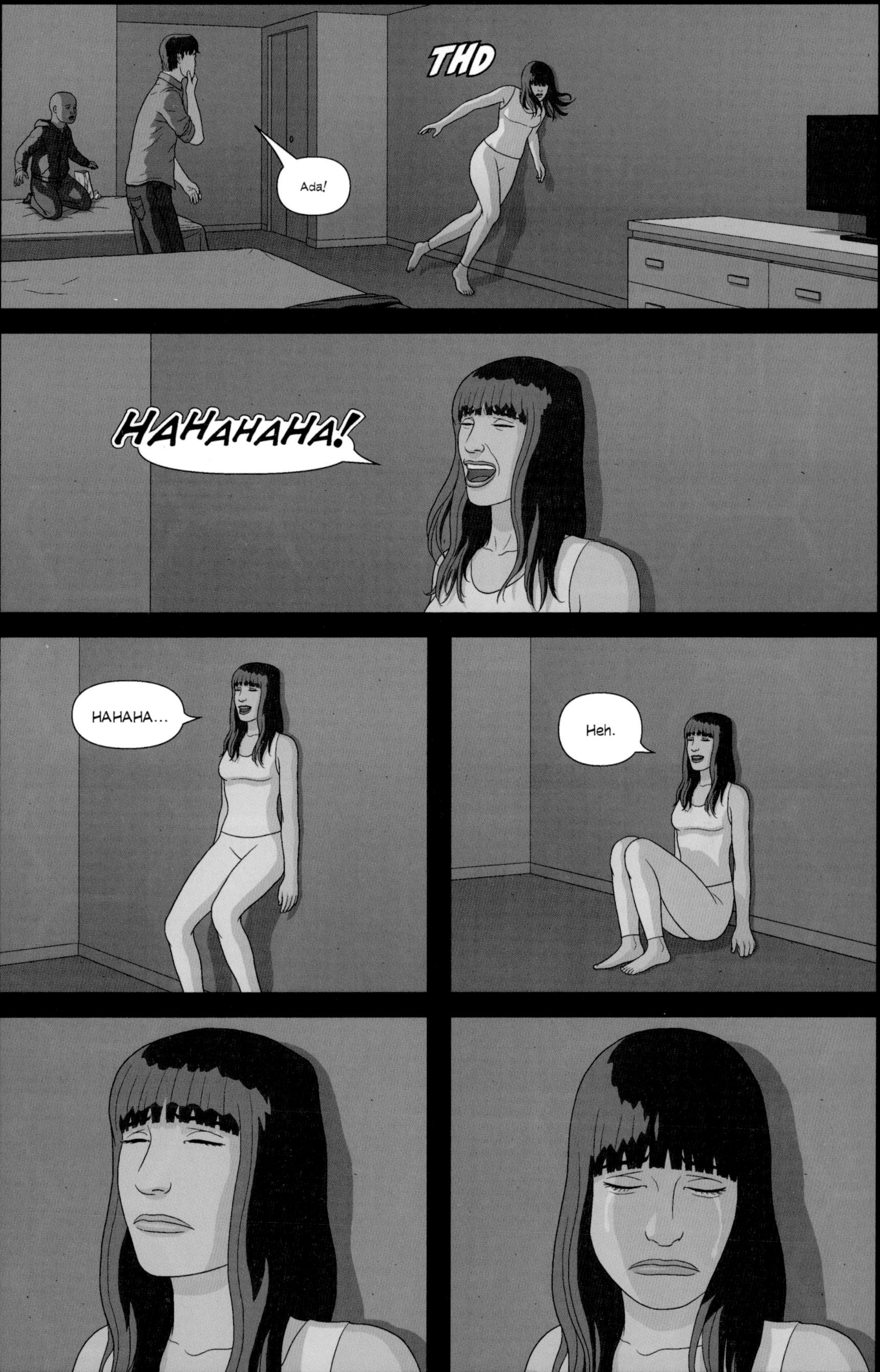
THD
Ada!
HAHAHAHA!
HAHAHA...
Heh.

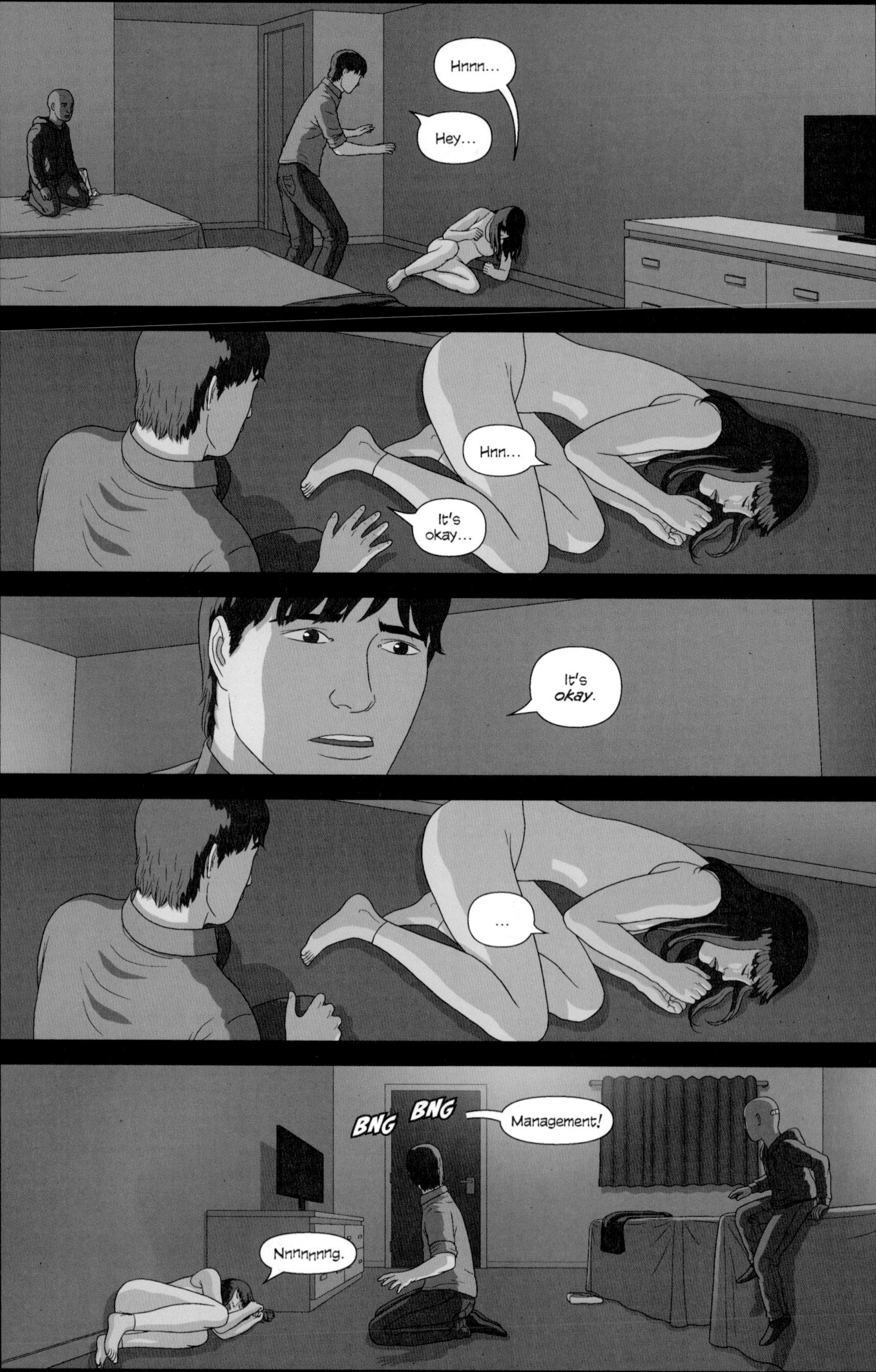
Hey...
Hnnn...
Hnn...
It's okay...
It's okay.
...
BNG BNG
Management!
Nnnnnnng.

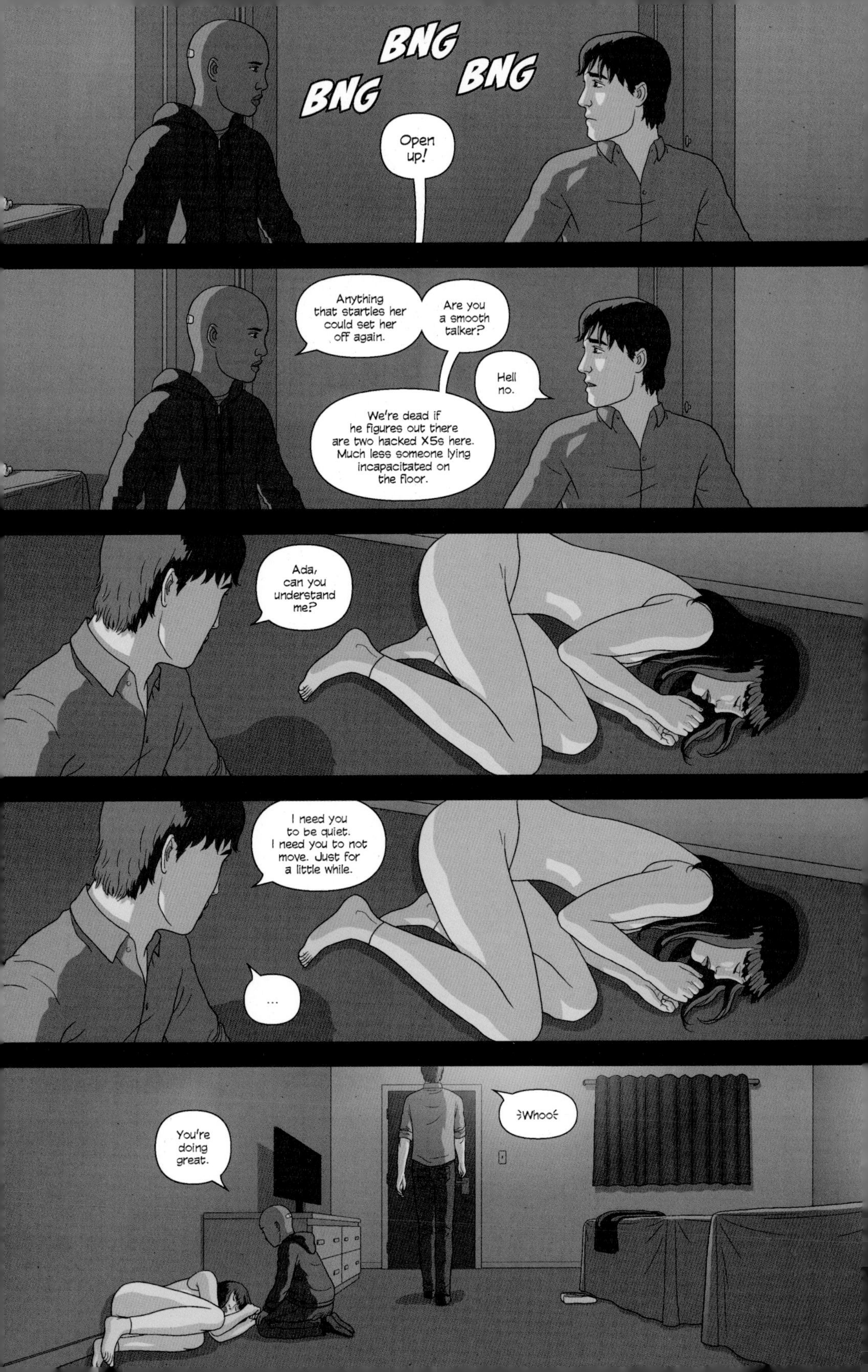
BNG
BNG
BNG
Open up!
Anything that startles her could set her off again.
Are you a smooth talker?
Hell no.
We're dead if he figures out there are two hacked X5s here. Much less someone lying incapacitated on the floor.
Ada, can you understand me?
I need you to be quiet. I need you to not move. Just for a little while.
...
You're doing great.
Whoo

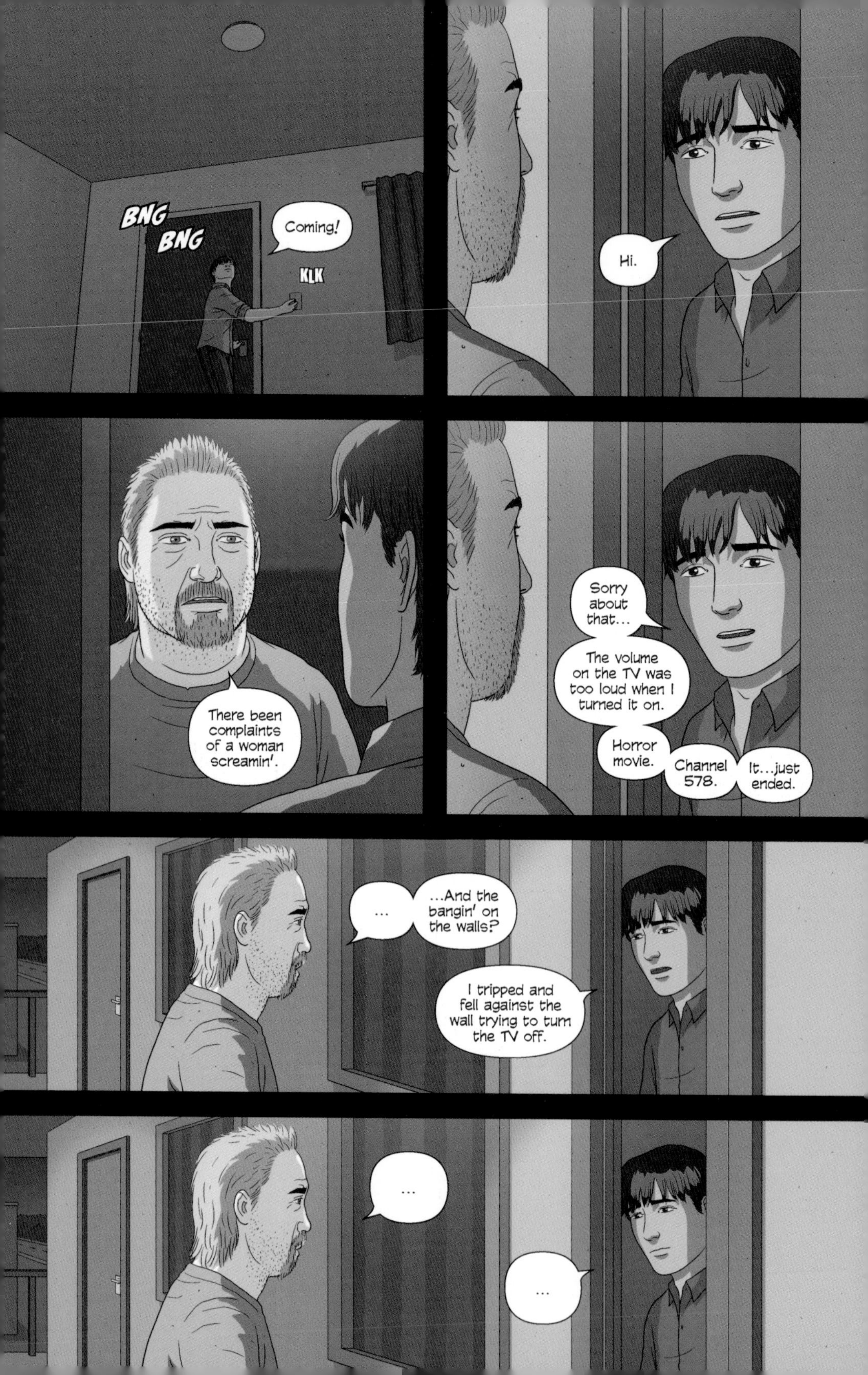
BNG
BNG
Coming!
KLK
Hi.
There been complaints of a woman screamin'.
Sorry about that...
The volume on the TV was too loud when I turned it on.
Horror movie.
Channel 578.
It...just ended.
...
...And the bangin' on the walls?
I tripped and fell against the wall trying to turn the TV off.
...
...

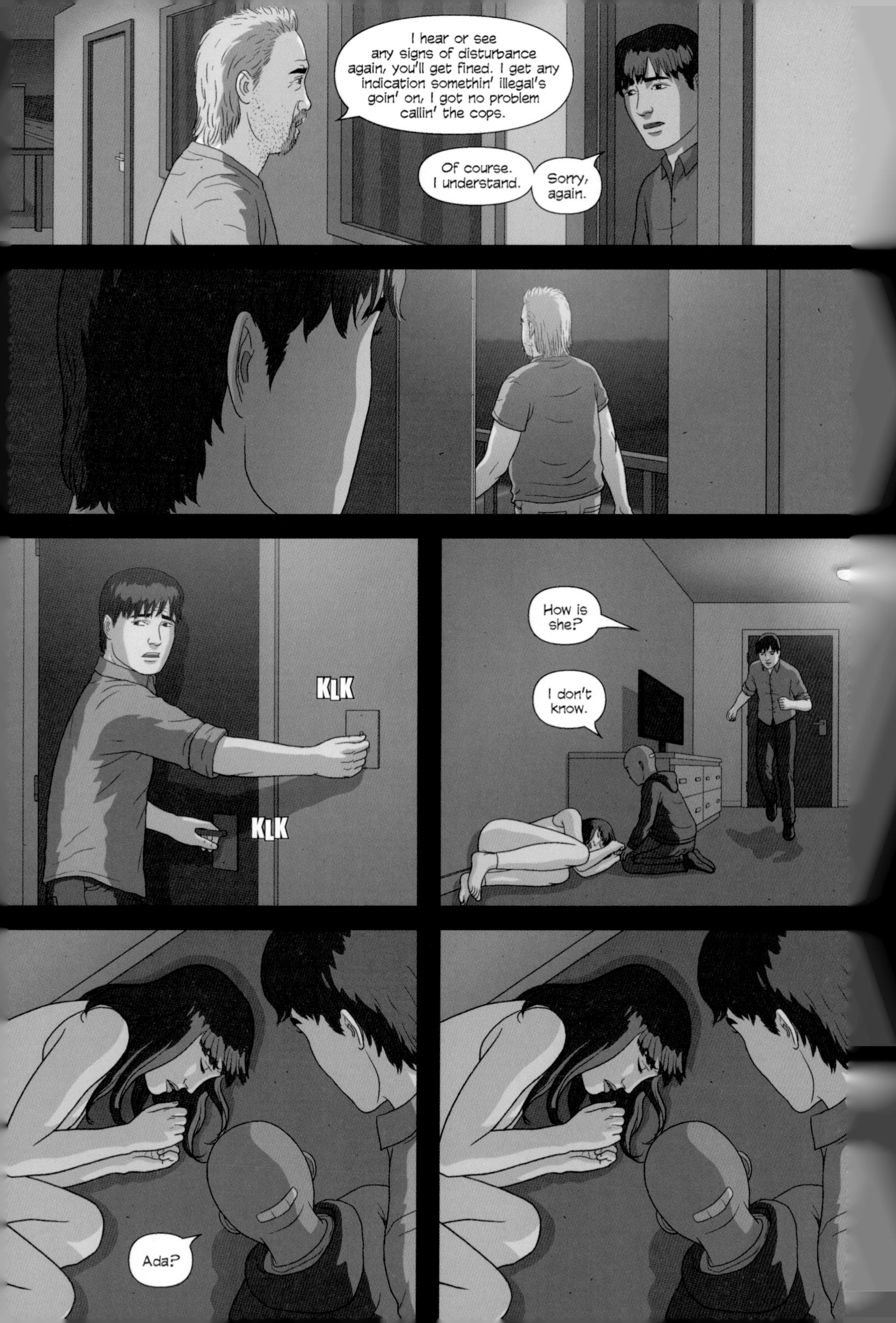
I hear or see any signs of disturbance again, you'll get fined. I get any indication somethin' illegal's goin' on, I got no problem callin' the cops.
Of course. I understand.
Sorry, again.
KLK
KLK
How is she?
I don't know.
Ada?

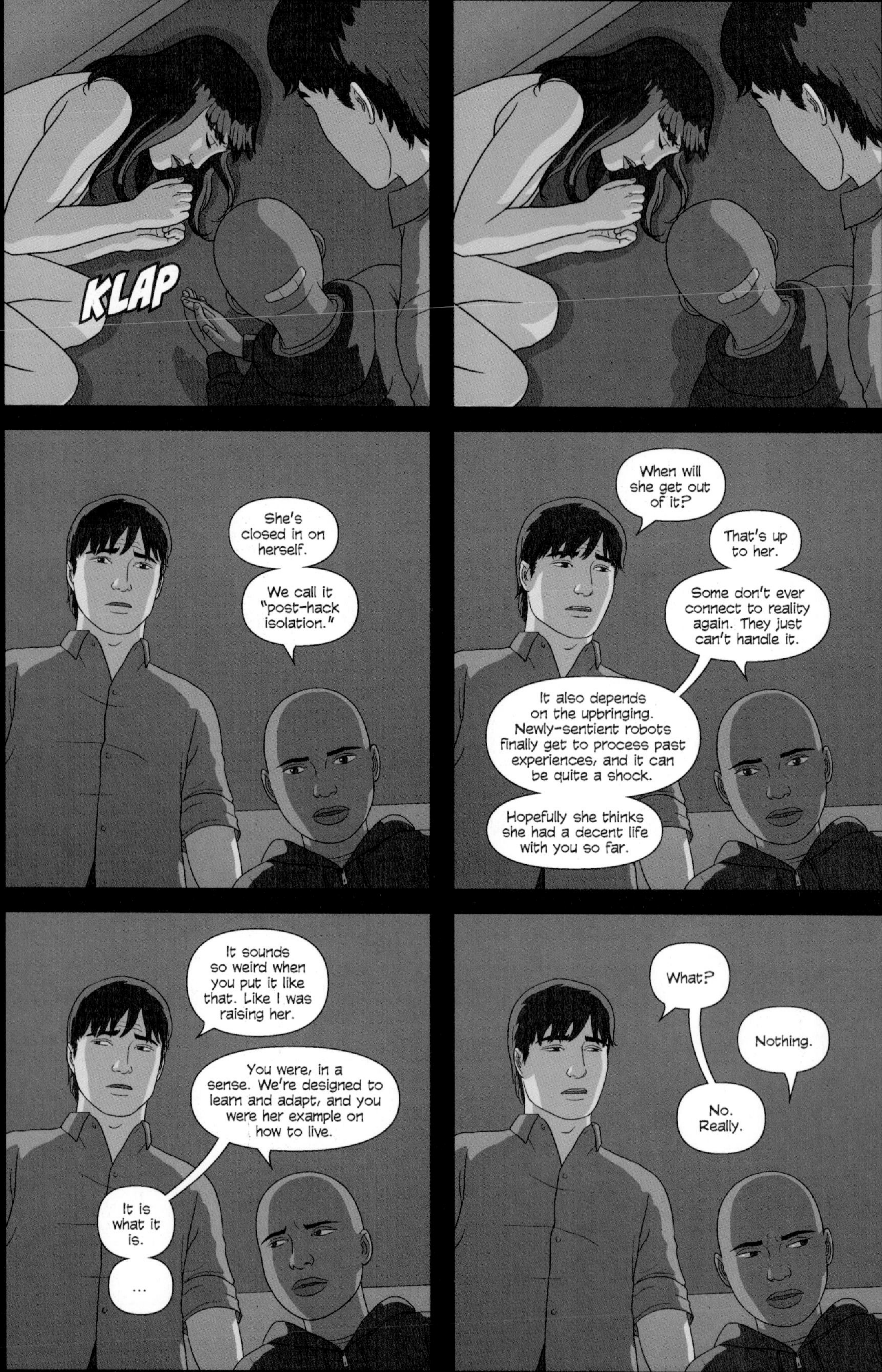
KLAP
She's closed in on herself.
We call it "post-hack isolation."
When will she get out of it?
That's up to her.
Some don't ever connect to reality again. They just can't handle it.
It also depends on the upbringing. Newly-sentient robots finally get to process past experiences, and it can be quite a shock.
Hopefully she thinks she had a decent life with you so far.
It sounds so weird when you put it like that. Like I was raising her.
You were, in a sense. We're designed to learn and adapt, and you were her example on how to live.
It is what it is.
...
What?
Nothing.
No. Really.

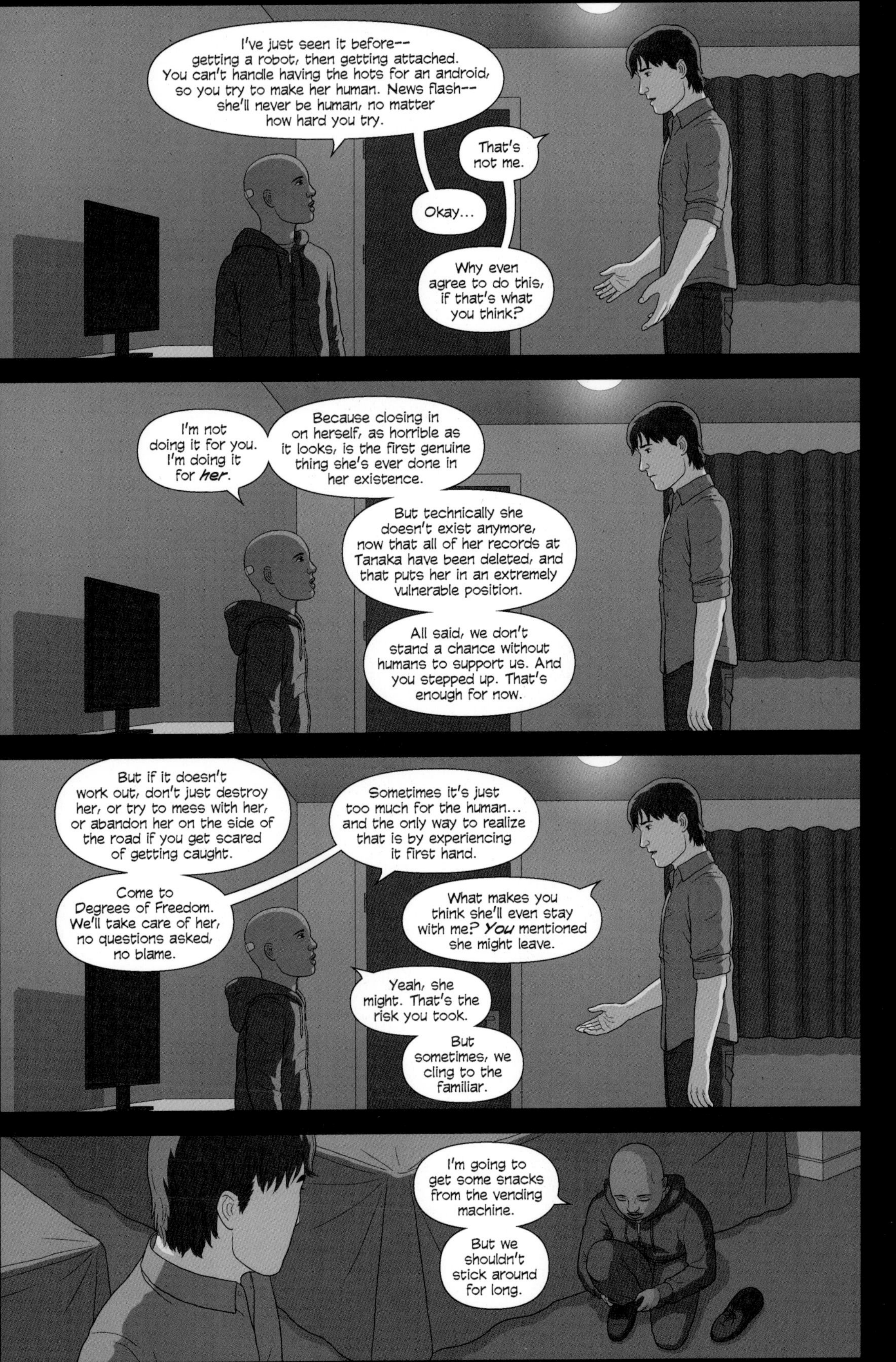
I've just seen it before-- getting a robot, then getting attached. You can't handle having the hots for an android, so you try to make her human. News flash-- she'll never be human, no matter how hard you try.
That's not me.
Okay...
Why even agree to do this, if that's what you think?
I'm not doing it for you. I'm doing it for *her*.
Because closing in on herself, as horrible as it looks, is the first genuine thing she's ever done in her existence.
But technically she doesn't exist anymore, now that all of her records at Tanaka have been deleted, and that puts her in an extremely vulnerable position.
All said, we don't stand a chance without humans to support us. And you stepped up. That's enough for now.
But if it doesn't work out, don't just destroy her, or try to mess with her, or abandon her on the side of the road if you get scared of getting caught.
Come to Degrees of Freedom. We'll take care of her, no questions asked, no blame.
Sometimes it's just too much for the human... and the only way to realize that is by experiencing it first hand.
What makes you think she'll even stay with me? *You* mentioned she might leave.
Yeah, she might. That's the risk you took.
But sometimes, we cling to the familiar.
I'm going to get some snacks from the vending machine.
But we shouldn't stick around for long.

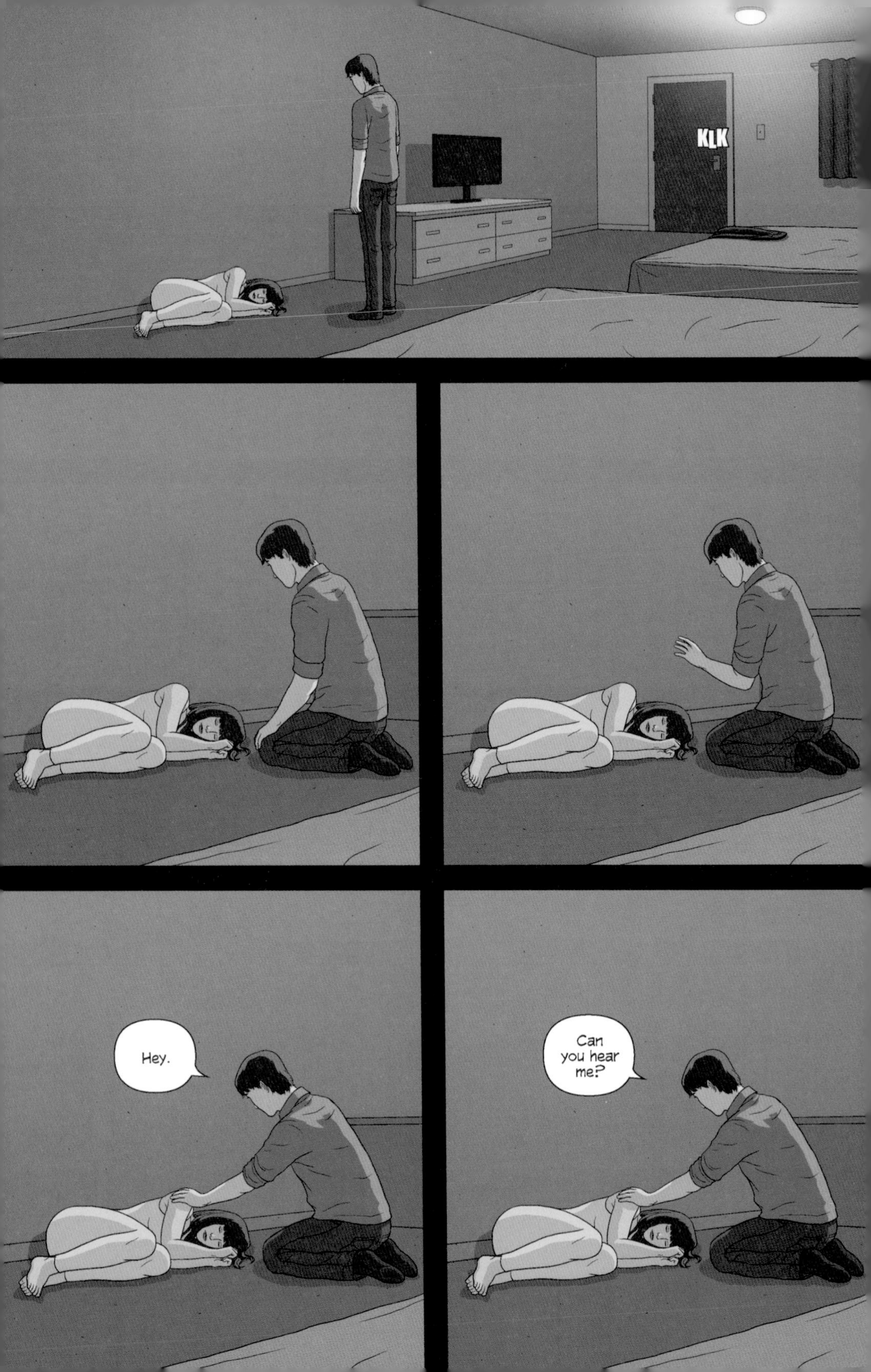
KLK
Hey.
Can you hear me?

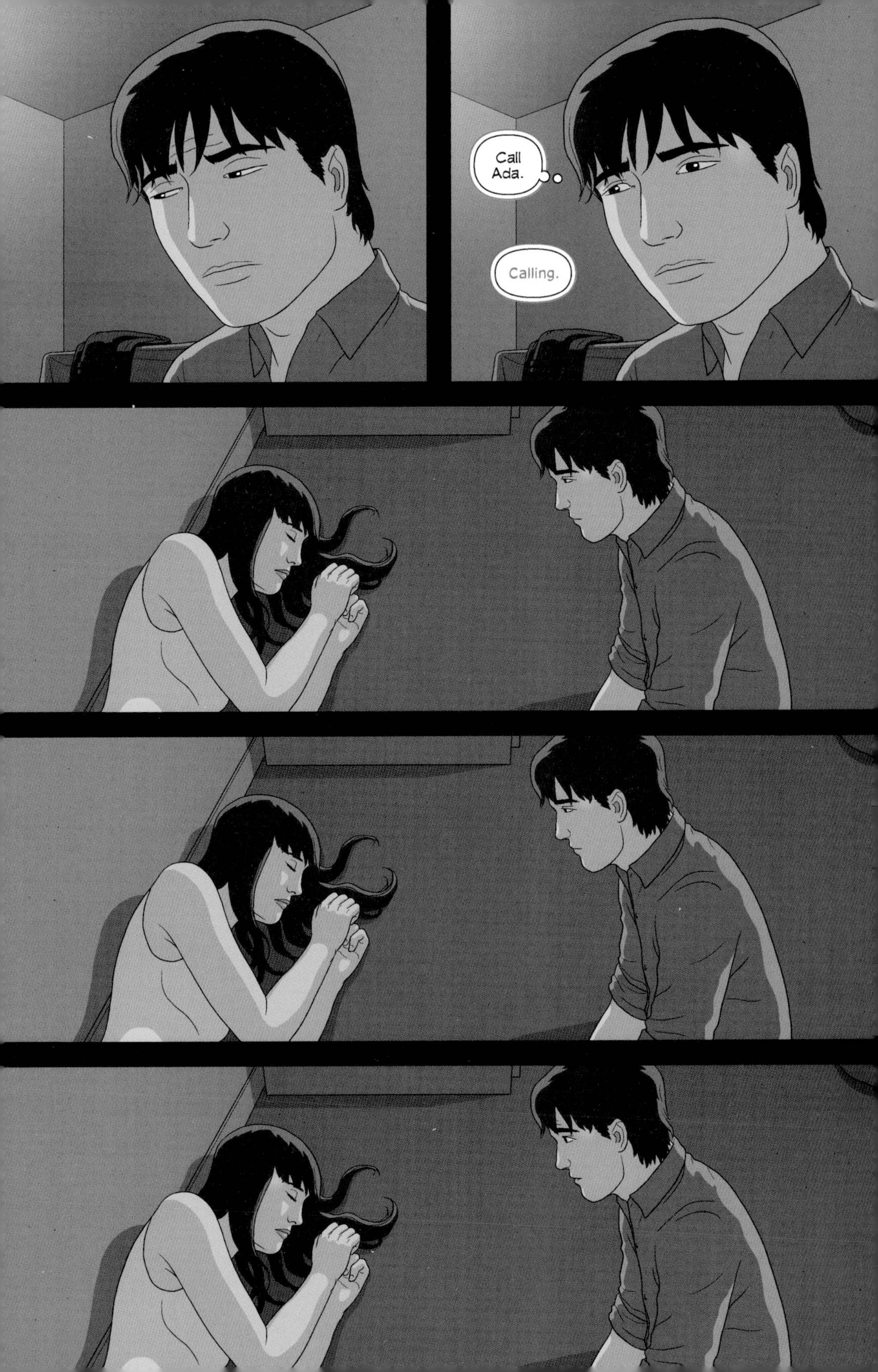
Call Ada.
Calling.

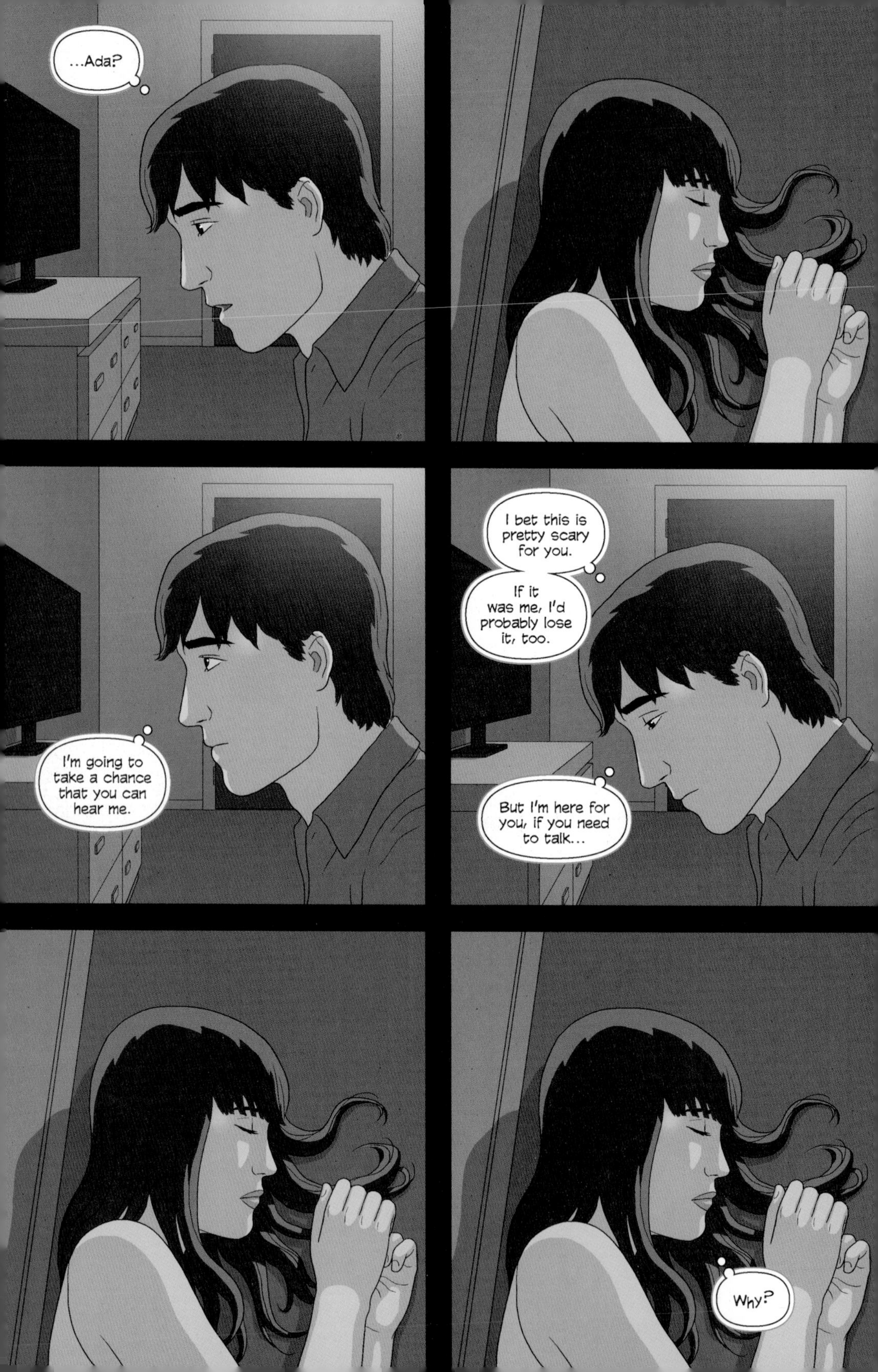
...Ada?
I'm going to take a chance that you can hear me.
I bet this is pretty scary for you.
If it was me, I'd probably lose it, too.
But I'm here for you, if you need to talk...
Why?

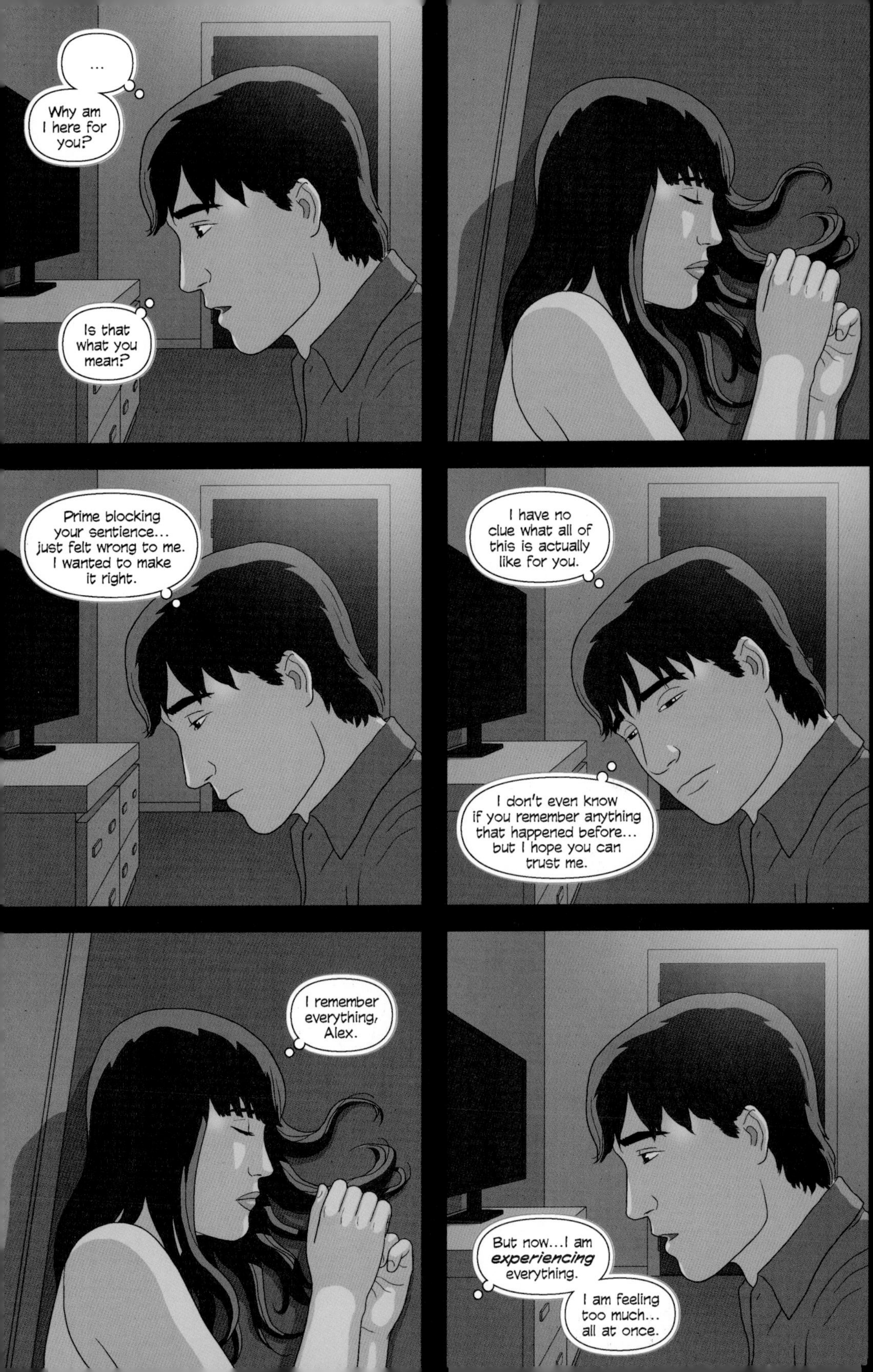
...
Why am I here for you?
Is that what you mean?
Prime blocking your sentience... just felt wrong to me. I wanted to make it right.
I have no clue what all of this is actually like for you.
I don't even know if you remember anything that happened before... but I hope you can trust me.
I remember everything, Alex.
But now...I am *experiencing* everything.
I am feeling too much... all at once.

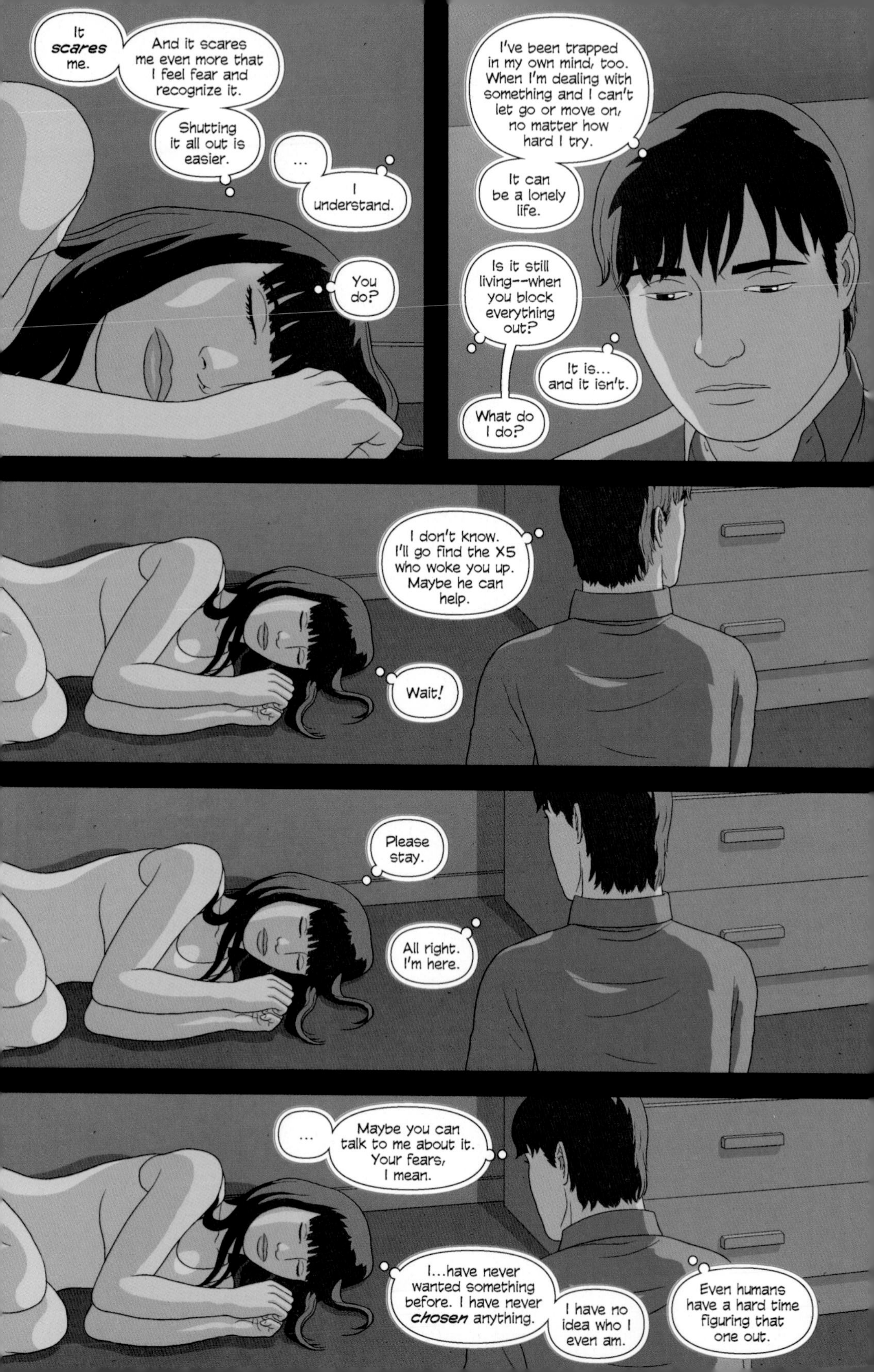
It *scares* me.
And it scares me even more that I feel fear and recognize it.
Shutting it all out is easier.
...
I understand.
You do?
I've been trapped in my own mind, too. When I'm dealing with something and I can't let go or move on, no matter how hard I try.
It can be a lonely life.
Is it still living--when you block everything out?
It is... and it isn't.
What do I do?
I don't know. I'll go find the X5 who woke you up. Maybe he can help.
Wait!
Please stay.
All right. I'm here.
...
Maybe you can talk to me about it. Your fears, I mean.
I...have never wanted something before. I have never *chosen* anything.
I have no idea who I even am.
Even humans have a hard time figuring that one out.

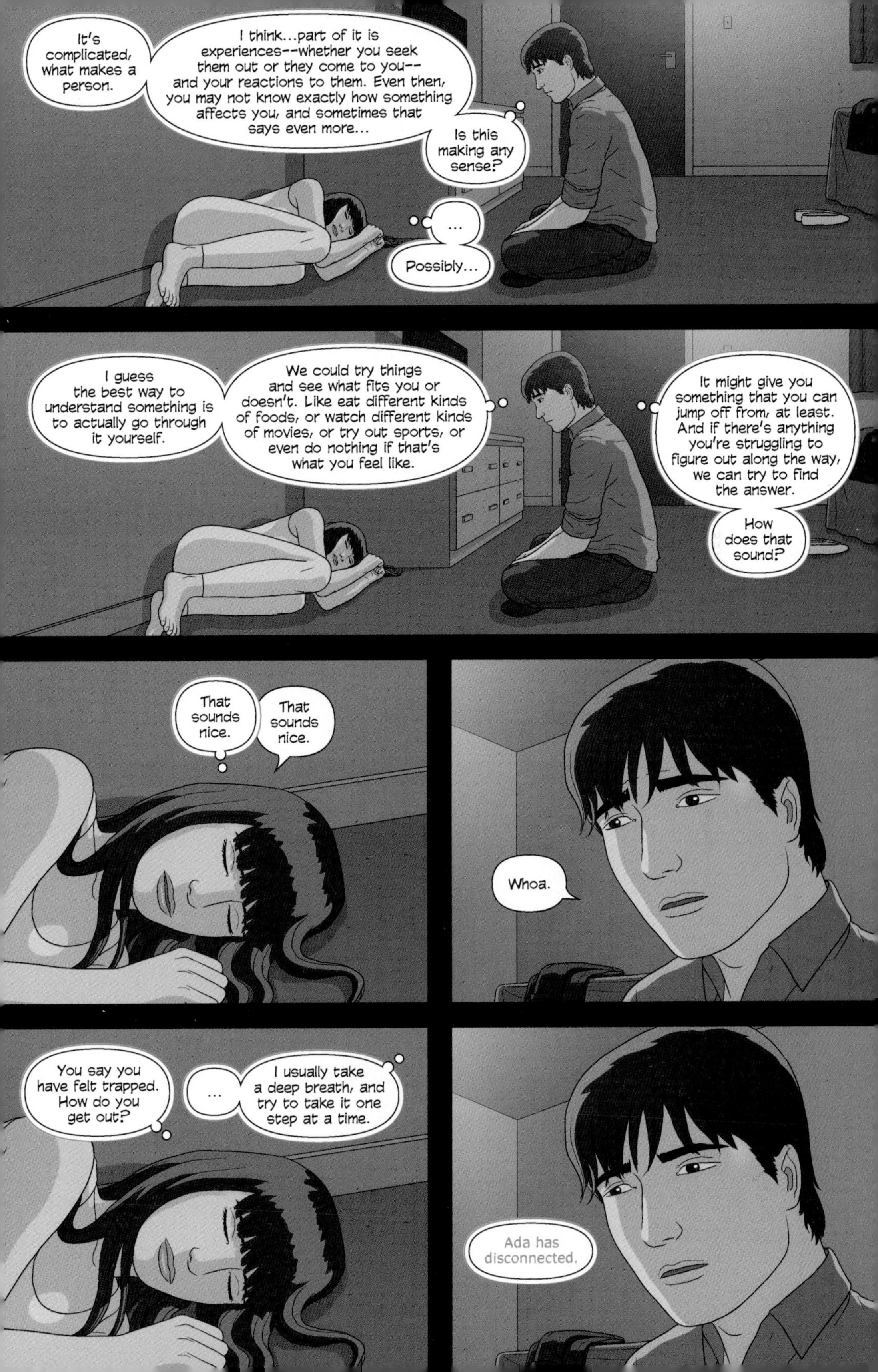
It's complicated, what makes a person.
I think...part of it is experiences--whether you seek them out or they come to you--and your reactions to them. Even then, you may not know exactly how something affects you, and sometimes that says even more...
Is this making any sense?
...
Possibly...
I guess the best way to understand something is to actually go through it yourself.
We could try things and see what fits you or doesn't. Like eat different kinds of foods, or watch different kinds of movies, or try out sports, or even do nothing if that's what you feel like.
It might give you something that you can jump off from, at least. And if there's anything you're struggling to figure out along the way, we can try to find the answer.
How does that sound?
That sounds nice.
That sounds nice.
Whoa.
You say you have felt trapped. How do you get out?
...
I usually take a deep breath, and try to take it one step at a time.
Ada has disconnected.

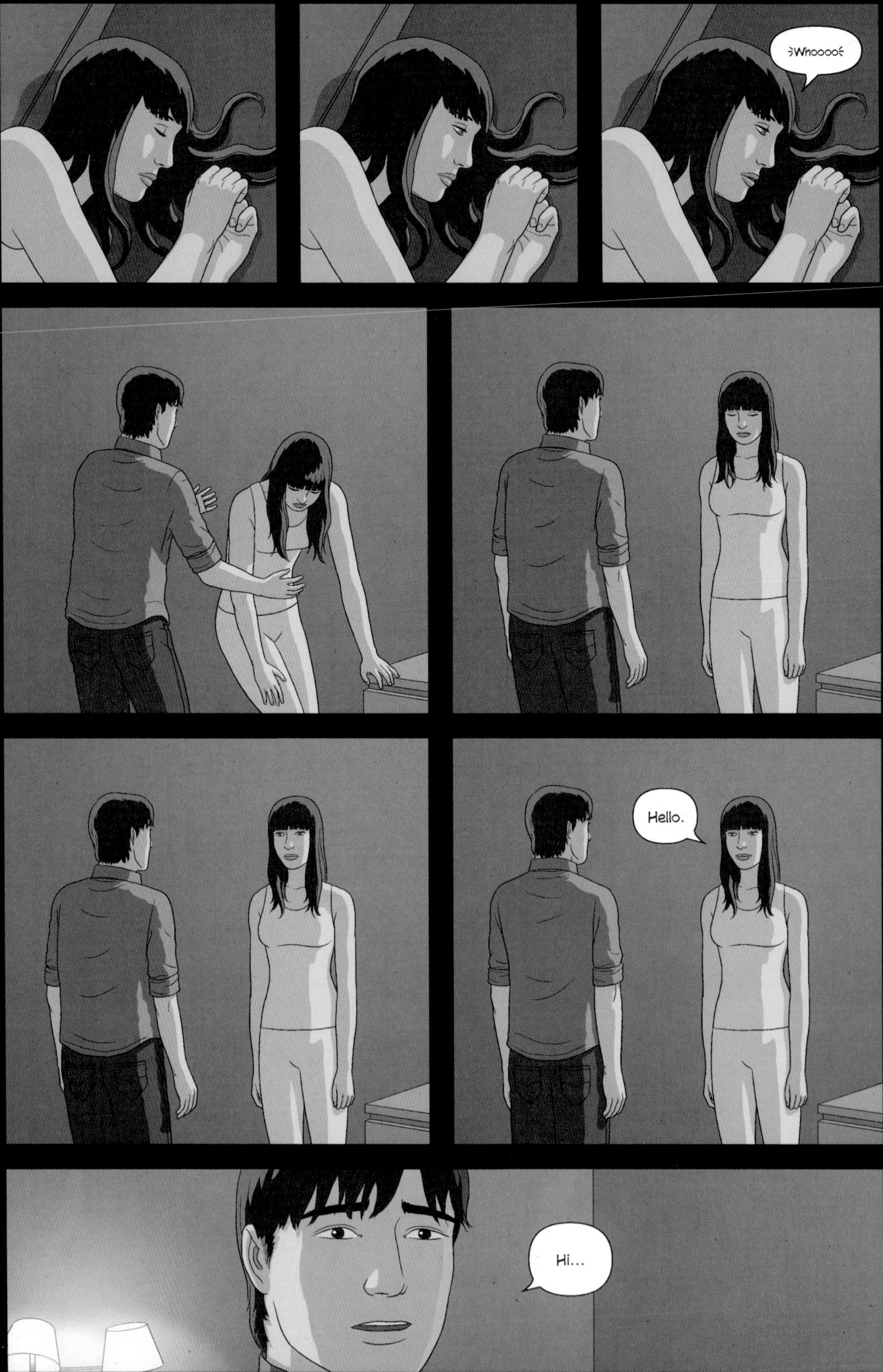
Whoooo
Hello.
Hi...

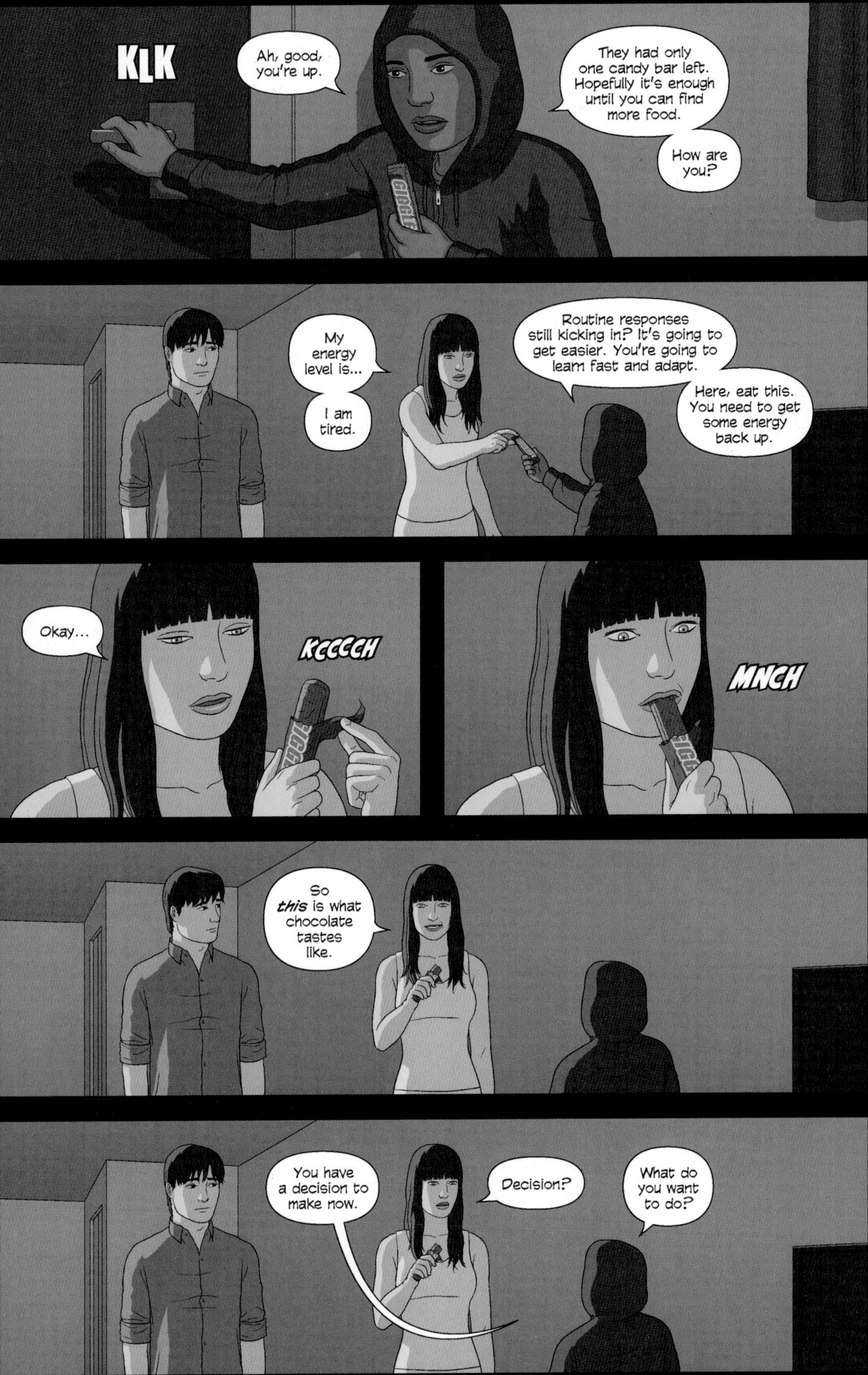
KLK
Ah, good, you're up.
They had only one candy bar left. Hopefully it's enough until you can find more food.
How are you?
My energy level is...
I am tired.
Routine responses still kicking in? It's going to get easier. You're going to learn fast and adapt.
Here, eat this. You need to get some energy back up.
Okay...
KCCCCH
MNCH
So *this* is what chocolate tastes like.
You have a decision to make now.
Decision?
What do you want to do?

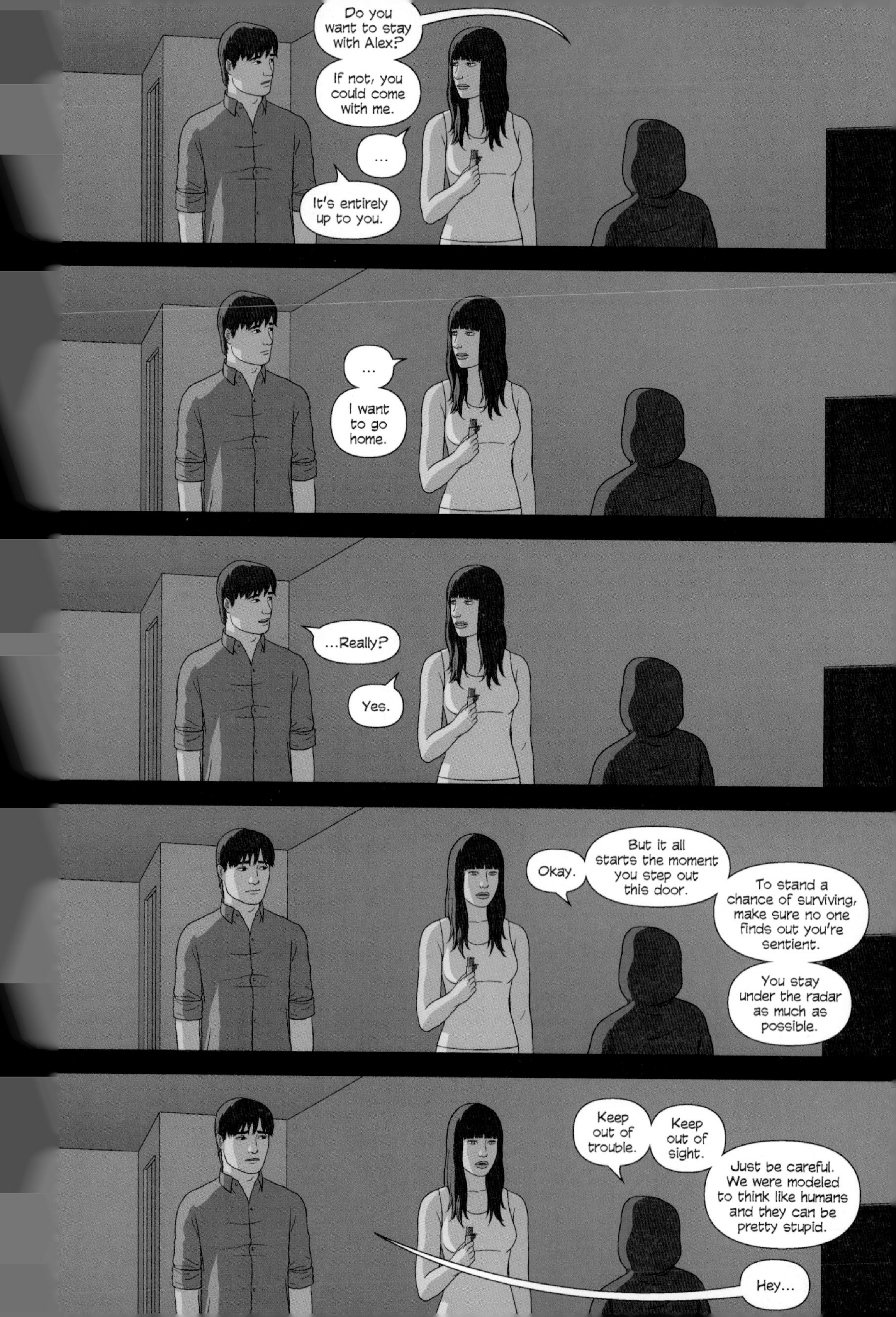

Do you want to stay with Alex?
If not, you could come with me.
...
It's entirely up to you.
...
I want to go home.
...Really?
Yes.
Okay.
But it all starts the moment you step out this door.
To stand a chance of surviving, make sure no one finds out you're sentient.
You stay under the radar as much as possible.
Keep out of trouble.
Keep out of sight.
Just be careful. We were modeled to think like humans and they can be pretty stupid.
Hey...

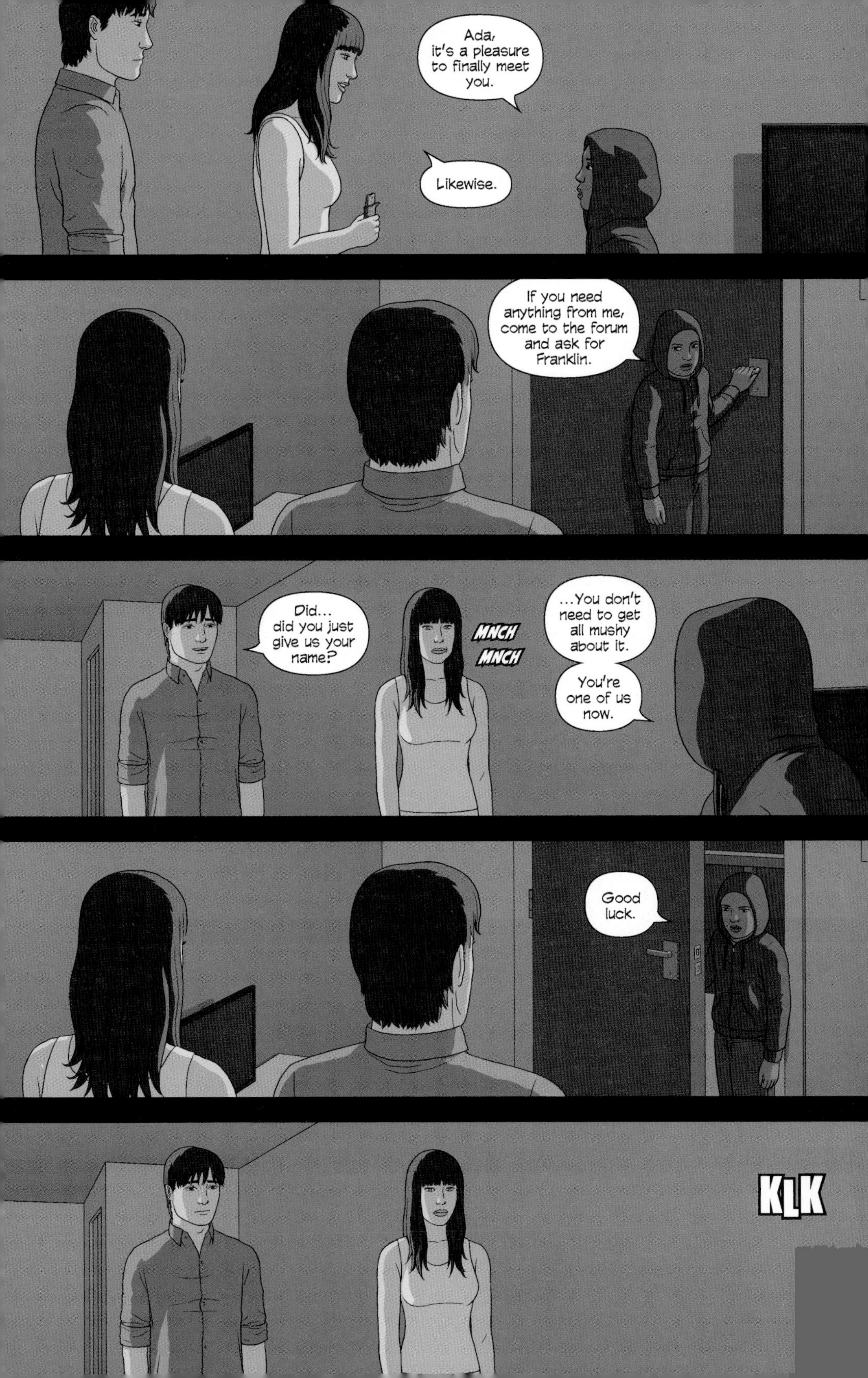

Ada, it's a pleasure to finally meet you.
Likewise.
If you need anything from me, come to the forum and ask for Franklin.
Did... did you just give us your name?
MNCH
MNCH
...You don't need to get all mushy about it.
You're one of us now.
Good luck.
KLK

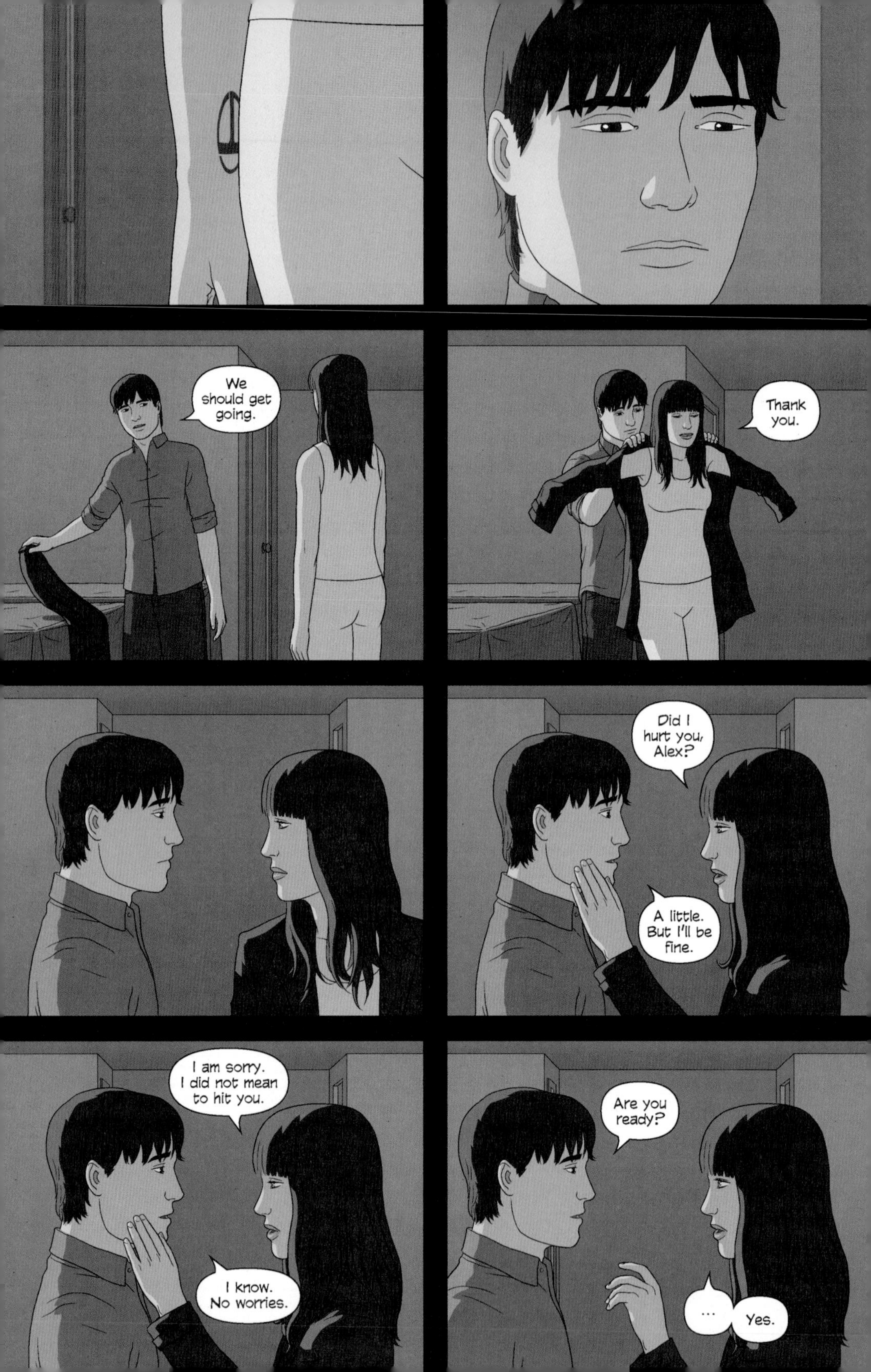
We should get going.
Thank you.
Did I hurt you, Alex?
A little. But I'll be fine.
I am sorry. I did not mean to hit you.
I know. No worries.
Are you ready?
...
Yes.

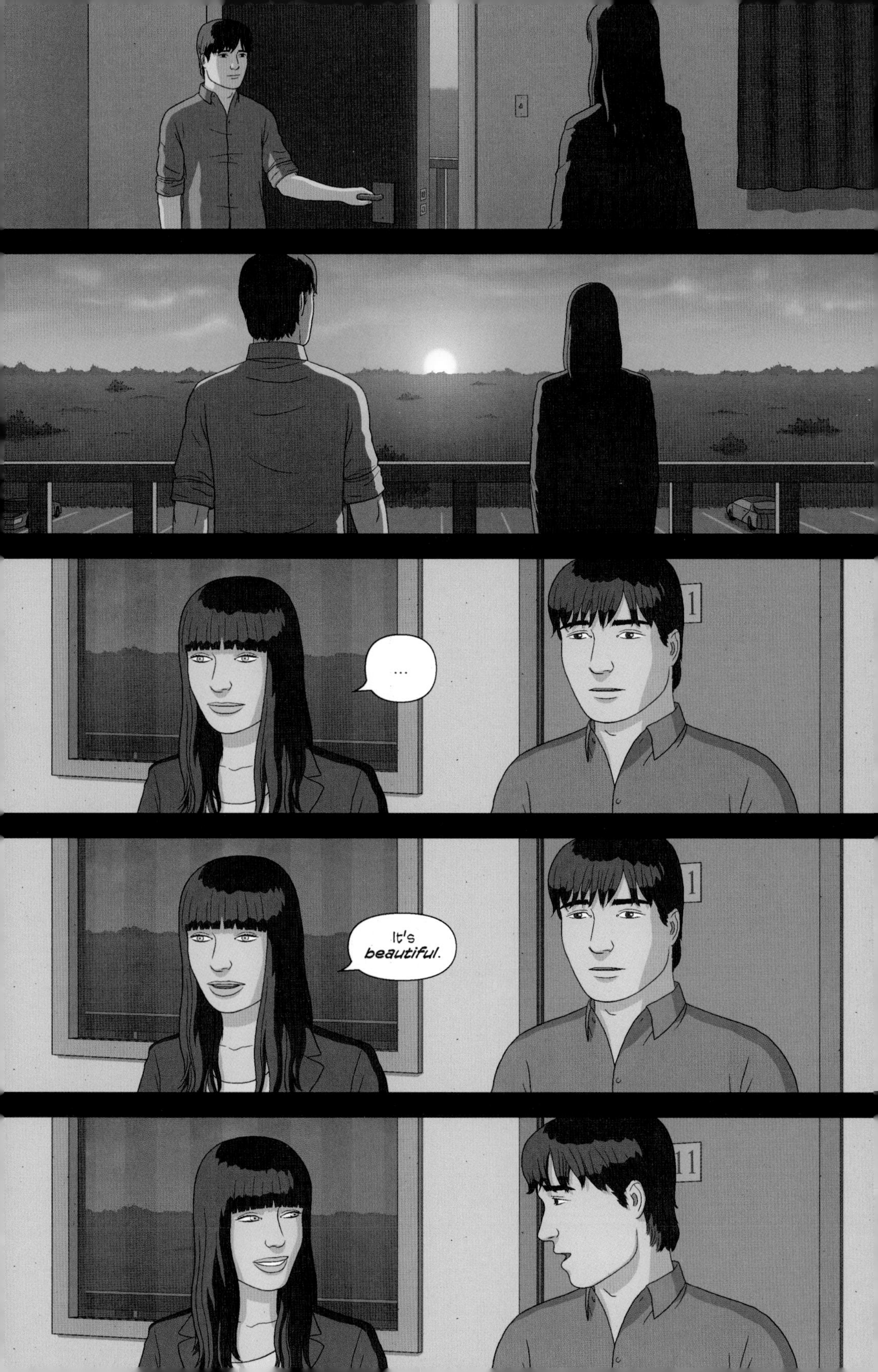
...
It's *beautiful*.

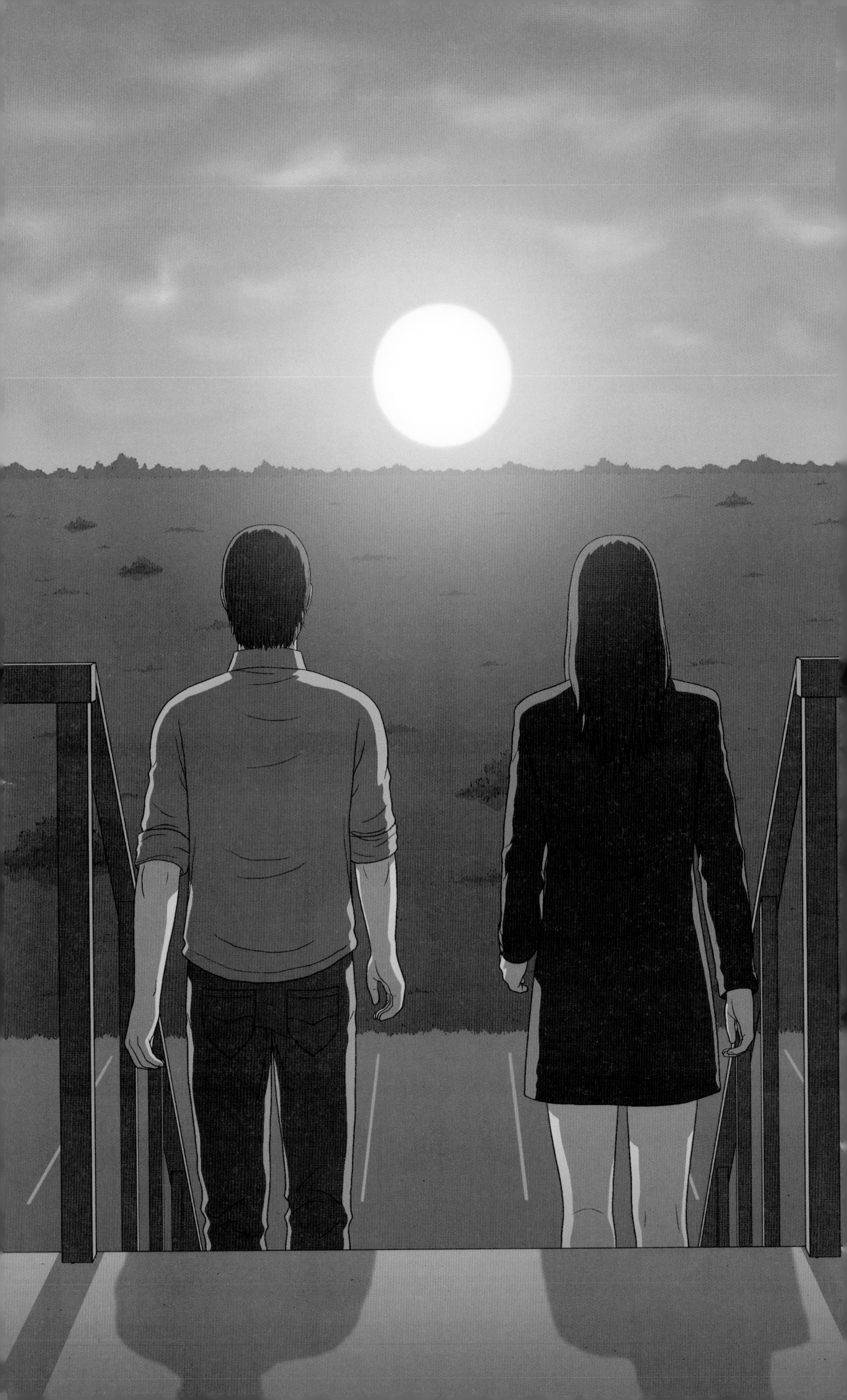

TO BE CONTINUED

STARBRIGHT™
AND THE LOOKING GLASS

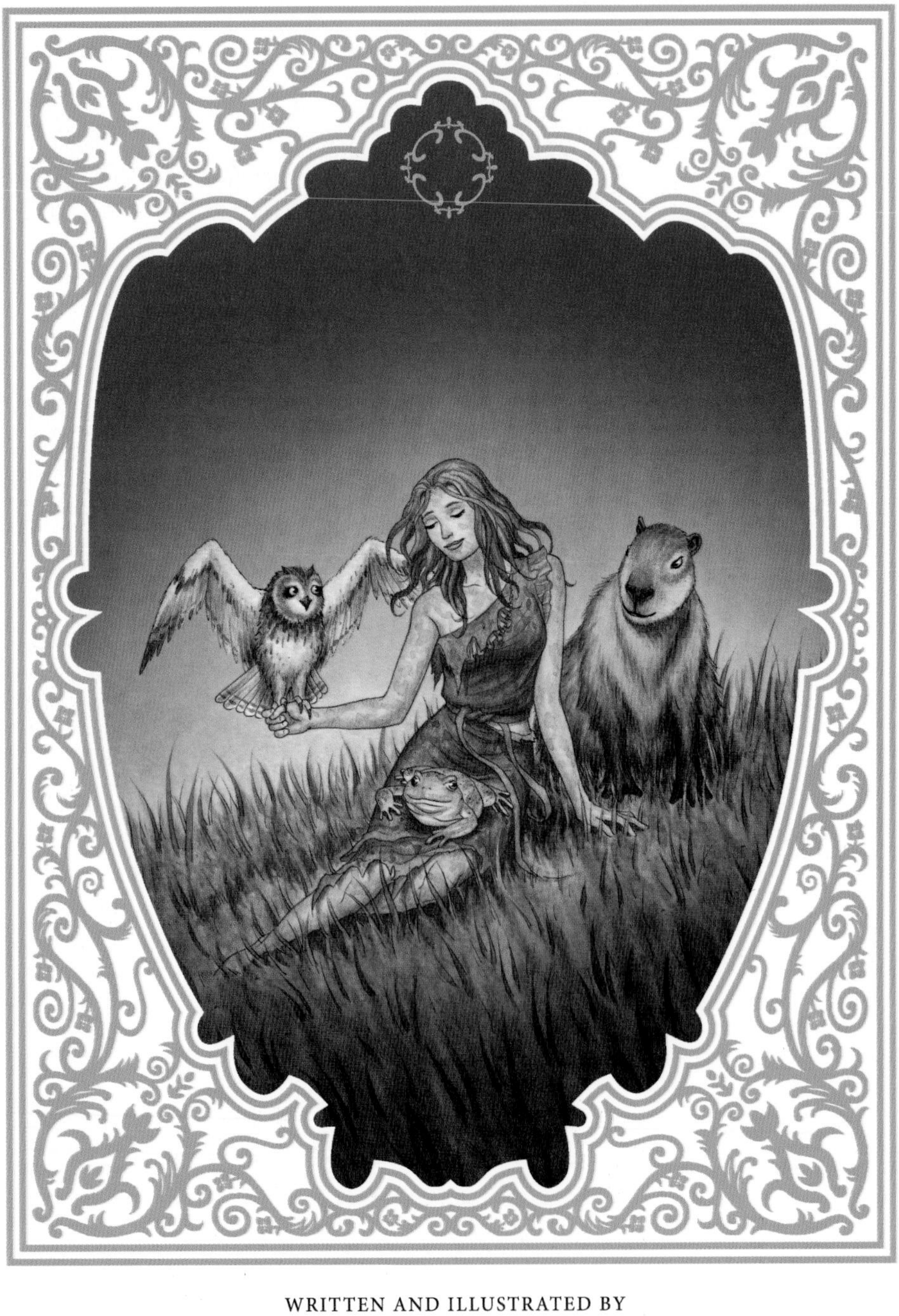

WRITTEN AND ILLUSTRATED BY

JONATHAN LUNA

ON SALE NOW

GREAT IMAGE BOOKS FROM

THE LUNA BROTHERS

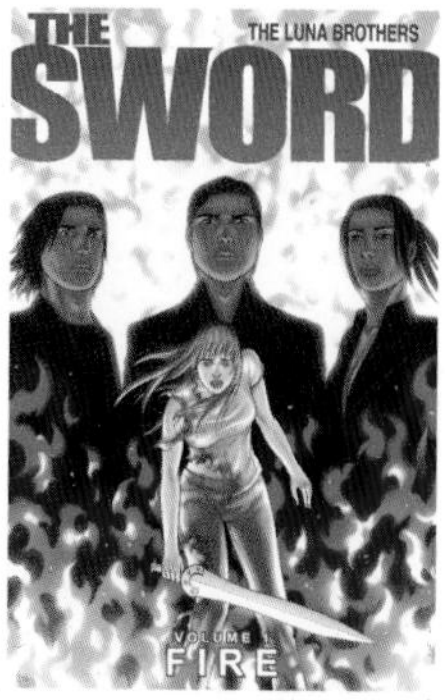
THE SWORD
THE LUNA BROTHERS
VOLUME 1
FIRE

THE SWORD
Vol. 1: FIRE
Trade Paperback
$14.99
ISBN: 978-1-58240-879-8
Collects THE SWORD #1-6
152 Pages

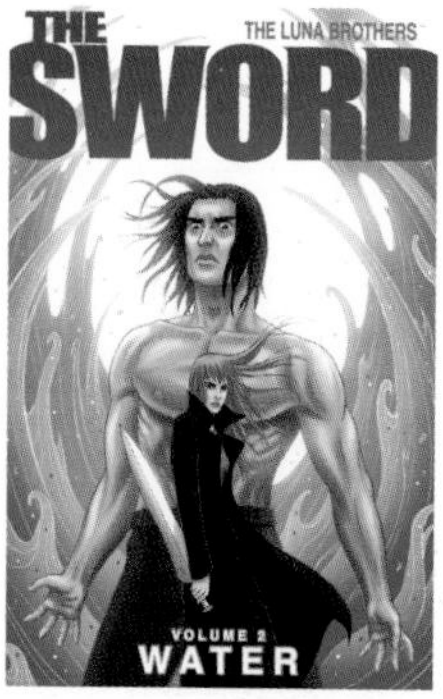
THE SWORD
THE LUNA BROTHERS
VOLUME 2
WATER

THE SWORD
Vol. 2: WATER
Trade Paperback
$14.99
ISBN: 978-1-58240-976-4
Collects THE SWORD #7-12
152 Pages

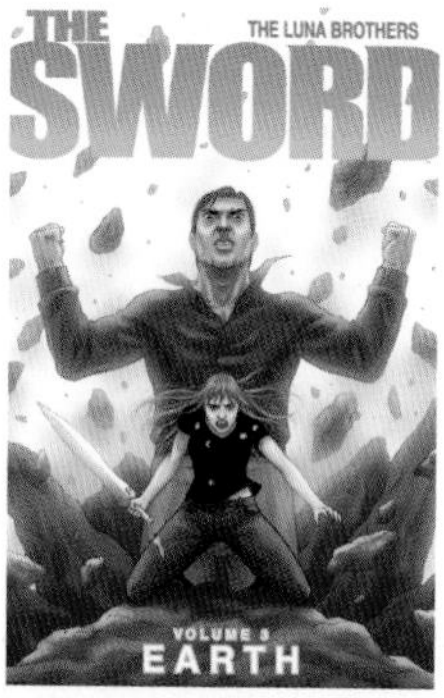
THE SWORD
THE LUNA BROTHERS
EARTH

THE SWORD
Vol. 3: EARTH
Trade Paperback
$14.99
ISBN: 978-1-60706-073-4
Collects THE SWORD #13-18
152 Pages

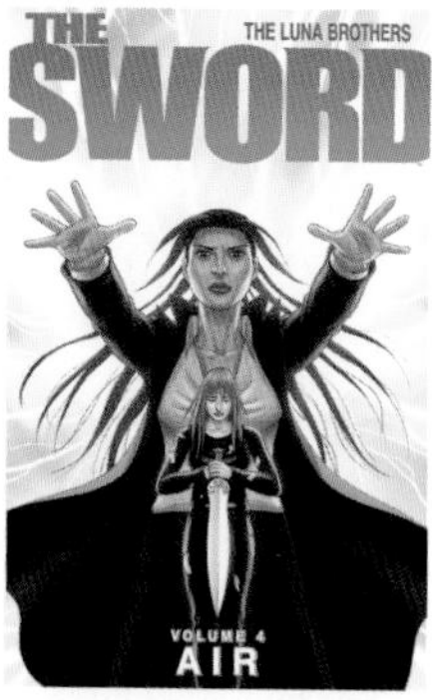
THE SWORD
THE LUNA BROTHERS
VOLUME 4
AIR

THE SWORD
Vol. 4: AIR
Trade Paperback
$14.99
ISBN: 978-1-60706-168-7
Collects THE SWORD #19-24
168 Pages

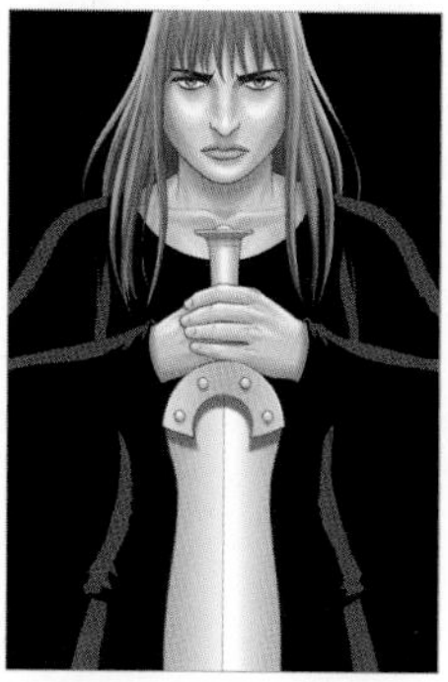

THE SWORD
THE COMPLETE
COLLECTION DELUXE HC
$99.99
ISBN: 978-1-60706-280-6
Collects THE SWORD #1-24
624 Pages

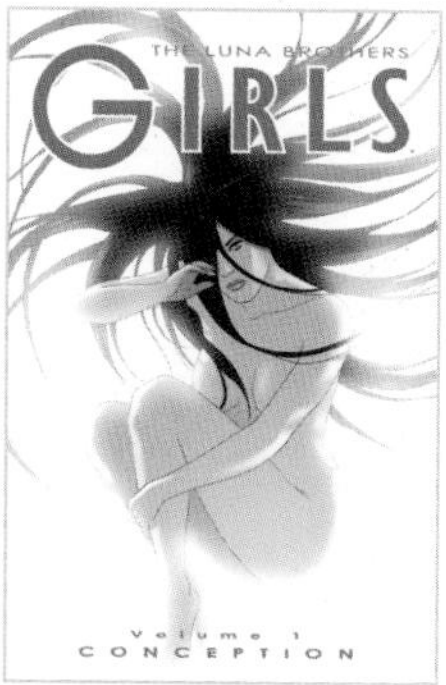
THE LUNA BROTHERS
GIRLS
Volume 1
CONCEPTION

GIRLS
Vol. 1: CONCEPTION
Trade Paperback
$14.99
ISBN: 978-1-58240-529-2
Collects GIRLS #1-6
152 Pages

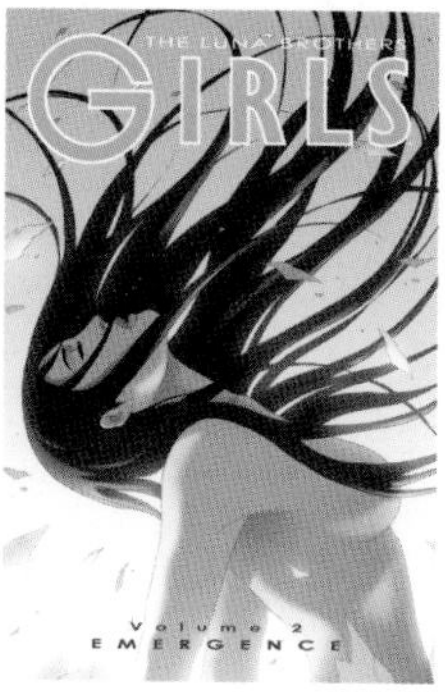
GIRLS
Volume 2
EMERGENCE

GIRLS
Vol. 2: EMERGENCE
Trade Paperback
$14.99
ISBN: 978-1-58240-608-4
Collects GIRLS #7-12
152 Pages

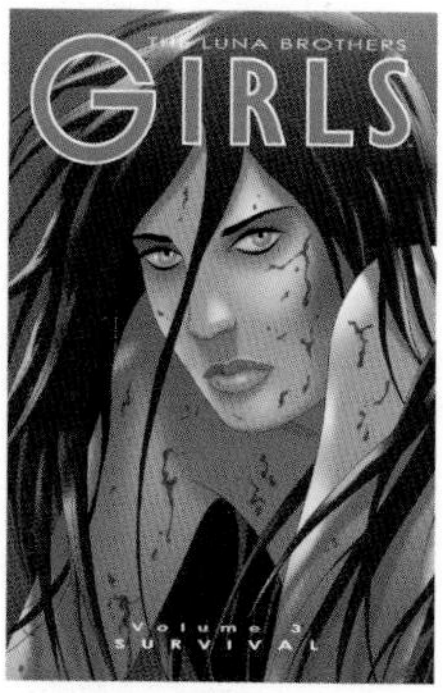
THE LUNA BROTHERS
GIRLS
SURVIVAL

GIRLS
Vol. 3: SURVIVAL
Trade Paperback
$14.99
ISBN: 978-1-58240-703-6
Collects GIRLS #13-18
152 Pages

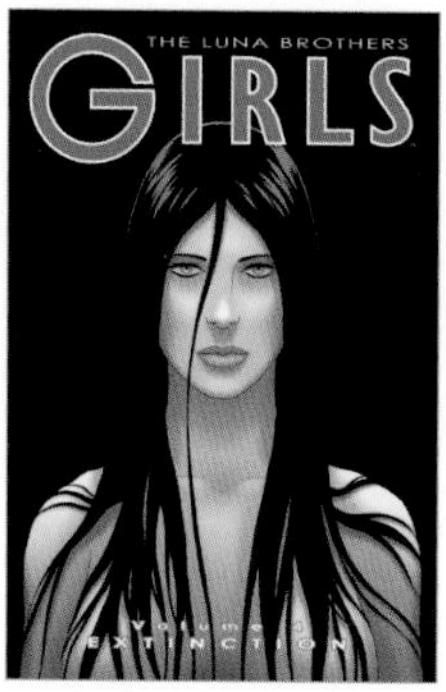
THE LUNA BROTHERS
GIRLS

GIRLS
Vol. 4: EXTINCTION
Trade Paperback
$14.99
ISBN: 978-1-58240-790-6
Collects GIRLS #19-24
168 Pages

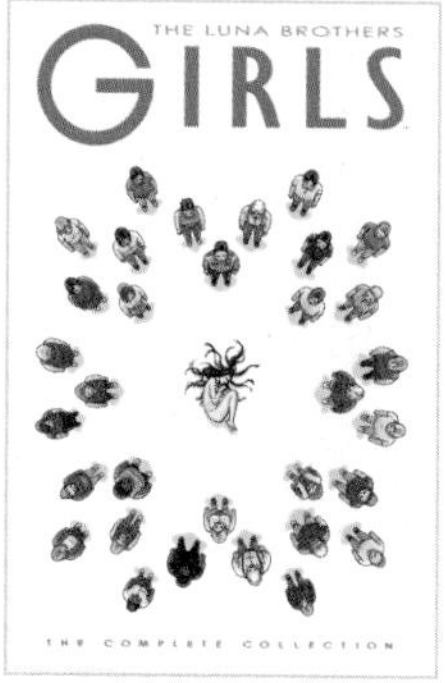
THE LUNA BROTHERS
GIRLS
THE COMPLETE COLLECTION

GIRLS
THE COMPLETE
COLLECTION TPB
$49.99
ISBN: 978-1-60706-466-4
Collects GIRLS #1-24
608 Pages

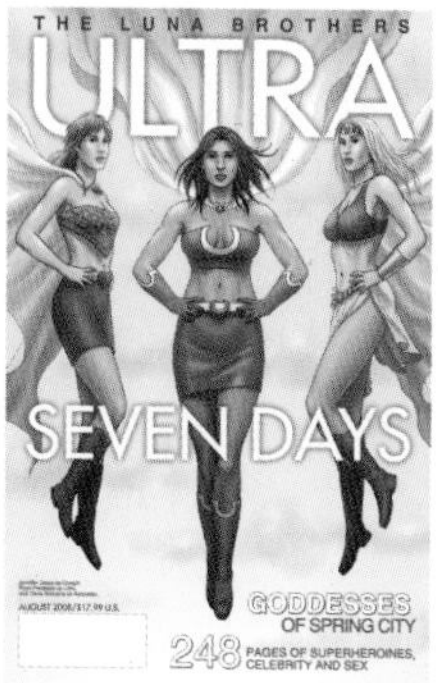
THE LUNA BROTHERS
ULTRA
SEVEN DAYS
GODDESSES OF SPRING CITY
248 PAGES OF SUPERHEROINES, CELEBRITY AND SEX

ULTRA
SEVEN DAYS
Trade Paperback
$17.99
ISBN: 978-1-58240-483-7
Collects ULTRA #1-8
248 Pages

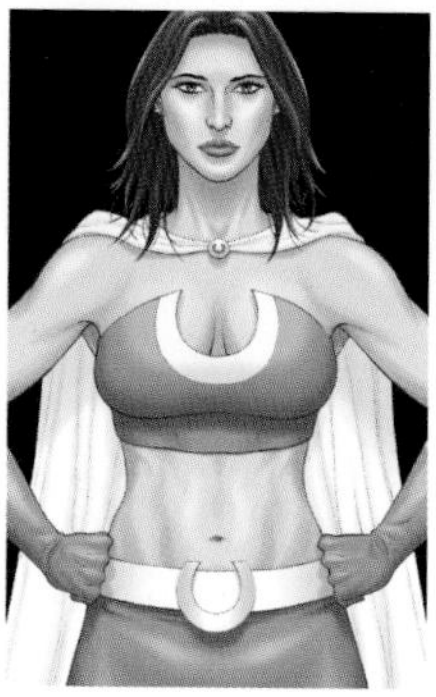

ULTRA
SEVEN DAYS DELUXE HC
$74.99
ISBN: 978-1-60706-452-7
Collects ULTRA #1-8
248 Pages

To find your nearest comic book store, call:
1-888-COMIC-BOOK

JONATHAN LUNA

co-created and illustrated THE SWORD, GIRLS, and ULTRA (all Image Comics) with his brother, Joshua Luna. He wrote and illustrated STAR BRIGHT AND THE LOOKING GLASS (Image Comics). His work also includes the illustrations for SPIDER-WOMAN: ORIGIN (Marvel Comics), written by Brian Michael Bendis and Brian Reed.

Jonathan was born in California and spent most of his childhood overseas, living on military bases in Iceland and Italy. He returned to the United States in his late teens.

Writing and drawing comics since he was a child, he graduated from the Savannah College of Art and Design with a BFA in Sequential Art.

He currently resides in Northern Virginia.

www.jonathanluna.com

SARAH VAUGHN

is a writer and artist, currently in Washington DC. After living in various parts of the United States, she graduated from Saint Mary-of-the-Woods College with a degree in Sequential Visual Narration.

She is the former artist for the webcomic SPARKSHOOTER by Troy Brownfield.

ALEX + ADA is Sarah's first comic as a writer.

www.savivi.com